PRAISE FOR

# THE END OF MEN

"Compelling and heartbreaking. A remarkable achievement."

—Abi Daré, author of *The Girl with the Louding Voice*

"Brilliant, prescient, and unputdownable."

—Jenny Colgan, author of *The Bookshop in the Corner*

"Moving, thought-provoking, and terrifyingly prescient."

—Tammy Cohen, author of *When She Was Bad*

"I ripped through this. It's pacey, devastating, prescient, compelling, and confronting, not only because it's the first thing I've read that even touches the sides of the very real pandemic we're living through, but also because a world without men? It was uncomfortable and fascinating to read about. This is a surefire hit, and rightly so."

—Laura Jane Williams, author of *Our Stop*

"A powerful, gripping book that has made me feel a little better about the world we are living in right now."

—Bryony Gordon, author of *No Such Thing as Normal*

# THE END OF MEN

# CHRISTINA SWEENEY-BAIRD

DOUBLEDAY CANADA

# THE END OF MEN

Doubleday Canada and colophon are registered trademarks of Penguin Random House Canada Limited

Library and Archives Canada Cataloguing in Publication

Title: The end of men / Christina Sweeney-Baird
Names: Sweeney-Baird, Christina, author.
Identifiers: Canadiana (print) 20210115432 | Canadiana (ebook) 20210115440 | ISBN 9780385696630 (softcover) | ISBN 9780385696647 (EPUB)
Classification: LCC PR6119.W44 E53 2021 | DDC 823/.92—dc23

This book is a work of fiction. Names, characters, places and incidents are products of the author's imagination or are used fictitiously. Any resemblance to actual events or locales or persons, living or dead, is entirely coincidental.

Book design by Laura K. Corless
Cover design by David Litman

Printed and bound in the USA

Published in Canada by Doubleday Canada,
a division of Penguin Random House Canada Limited

www.penguinrandomhouse.ca

1st Printing

Penguin
Random House
DOUBLEDAY CANADA

For my mum, Margarita.
I'm so very glad to be your daughter.

# THE END OF MEN

BEFORE

# CATHERINE

Do you need to dress up for Halloween if you're a parent? This has never been an issue before. Theodore turned three a few months ago so until now I've just dressed him up as something cute (a carrot, then a lion and then an adorable fireman with a fuzzy helmet) and taken photos of him in the house. I don't want to be a boring parent who everyone thinks is snooty and above the joy of dressing up. I also don't want to be embarrassingly keen. Do all the other parents make an effort? Do any of them? Why does no one ever explain this stuff to you in advance?

Beatrice, my only real friend at Theodore's nursery, said she would rather die than dress up in something flammable, but she works in investment banking and buys £2,000 handbags when she's "had a bad day" so I don't think she's necessarily a good indication of what the other mothers in this quiet part of South London will do.

I'm eyeing up the costumes uneasily. "Sexy witch." No. "Sexy Handmaid's Tale Handmaid." Will get me banned from the St. Joseph's Parent Teacher Association for life. "Sexy pumpkin." Nonsense. What would Phoebe do? She's the most sensible and pragmatic of my friends, with an uncanny ability to conjure up an easy answer to a problem as if it had been there, waiting for you all along. Phoebe would say to just wear black and throw on a witch hat, so that's what I decide to do. I suspect the results of Phoebe's daughters' trick-or-treating will be slightly more upmarket than the sweets we'll be collecting tonight. She lives in a terrifyingly expensive area of Battersea thanks to a huge inheritance from her father last year. He left her his five-bedroom house with a massive garden but, as she likes to joke, her Roman nose was a steep price to pay.

Looking down at my watch I realize I'm running late for pickup again. I take the hat and leg it to the nursery. I'm charged £20 per five minutes that I'm late, a rate so extortionate I'm tempted to set up my own nursery because it must be the highest legal interest rate in the country.

I do the rushed *Hi, hi, hello, yes, I know, late again, despite working from home a lot! Ha! Yes, I am disorganized, funny, hilarious, such humor* interaction with the other mothers as I throw myself through the door and pick up a forlorn Theodore.

"Mummy was late again." He sighs.

"Sorry darling, I was buying a witch hat for tomorrow."

His face lights up. The power of distraction. Halloween has suddenly flipped from being a thing he had a remote understanding of last year to being the most exciting event imaginable (until Christmas). This is what I always imagined being a parent would be like. My parents died when I was ten and I don't have any siblings so babyhood was an unpleasant series of surprises. I'm *how* tired? He's getting sick *how* often? I feel *this* lonely? Halloween, Christmas and birthdays are safe spaces in which my dreams of being a perfect, Pinterest mother can be briefly indulged.

We bundle in the door from the cold, and I dive straight into cooking. I've been trying to feed him before Anthony gets home and the chaos of seeing his father leaves vegetables and the appeal of eating forgotten on a sad-looking plate. The negotiations required to ensure a three-year-old eats a reasonably balanced diet know no bounds and tonight's are particularly excruciating. *One more pea, and then you can have two more pieces of pasta. Five peas and then you can watch a movie on Saturday.*

Anthony arrives home just as Theodore has trudged up the stairs, weary of the requirement to bathe before bed, yet again. He's still on the phone finishing up a work call as he walks in the door. He looks tired and worn. We need a holiday. Now that we're in our mid-thirties I seem to say that every fortnight, even when we've just had a holiday.

Anthony is finally off the call. Something to do with blockchains and other indecipherable words that mean nothing to me. After a decade of marriage, I've happily moved from feeling guilty about my lack of understanding about my husband's work to being merrily ignorant. If an in-depth understanding of your spouse's job was a requirement for a long-lasting and happy marriage, no one would stay married. Besides, Anthony could no more name one of my most recent published papers than I could write a script in Java, a word that never fails to make me think of body lotion before it leads my mind to programming.

I get a hello, a kiss on the cheek and a quick hug before Anthony makes his way upstairs. Bath and bedtime are his. School pickup and dinner are mine. It's a rare and wonderful night when they're shared. As I pour a glass of red wine—stacking the dishwasher can wait, although answering e-mails can't—the thought pops into my head that I couldn't do this if we had another baby. No quiet, tidy-ish kitchen with a glass of wine in hand. No evening stretching ahead of me for conversation with my husband, watching TV undisturbed and a long night of brain-enhancing, relationship-maintaining sleep.

"How was your day?" Anthony is back downstairs. No wine for him tonight, I notice, as he throws some of the pasta I left for him into a bowl.

"Editing, editing, editing. My favorite bit of writing a paper," I say, my sarcasm heavy. One of my tutors at Oxford once told me that becoming an academic meant a lifetime of homework, and I didn't believe her at the time, but God she was right. Three beta readers have all read my latest paper on the differences between parenting styles in Denmark and the UK and their impacts on educational attainment, and somehow they all want the paper to change in different, conflicting ways. By the end of an eight-hour day deciphering the comments, I was so exhausted I wanted to throw my laptop out the window. I suggested hopefully to my lovely boss, Margaret, that that probably meant I could ignore them but she just tutted sternly and told me to have an extra-large glass of wine tonight before picking them back up tomorrow.

I explain the witch costume situation and Anthony looks at me seriously. "That's a good plan," he says. "Plan A: Witch. Plan B: Normal lady in black." The gravity with which he approaches these issues when we discuss them is one of the many things I love about him. He would never say, "This is such a silly conversation, why are we having it?" Once, my friend Libby's ex-boyfriend told her she was being ridiculous raising something—I can't remember what now—when we were having a double date at a sushi place in Soho. Anthony said, without a trace of humor in his voice, "If she's bringing it up then it's not ridiculous. She's not ridiculous."

Libby says Anthony is one of the reasons she's single, because she can see what love should be like. I try to remind her of what we were like at university. We've been together half our lifetimes now. You don't become two halves of a whole overnight. I think I once might have said something about a relationship being a "journey" and Libby refused to talk to me until I'd bought her a double gin and tonic.

After Anthony has finished clearing the plates away, which I kind of, sort of, definitely left for him to do because he's tidier than I am, I sit back with a contented sigh. He's looking at me intensely. He either wants to have sex or he wants to have the big F conversation. To have IVF or not to have IVF? The question that couples have only had the luxury of pondering for forty years. I saw in Anthony's work diary a capital F in the corner of the page for Friday a few months ago. Immediately I assumed, despite no evidence whatsoever, that he was having an affair. Freya? Flora? Felicity? Who is she? For a few weeks I kept dropping women's names starting with F into conversation worrying that he'd go a bit pink and look guilty but he just thought I was trying to subtly suggest baby names.

I kept checking his diary, every few weeks after that, and kept seeing the F. I don't know why I didn't just ask him what the F was. He doesn't lie to me and it was probably some boring work thing but something about it stuck in my brain. I wanted to figure it out for myself. And then, a fortnight ago I realized. The F was always on a day that we ended up having a conversation about fertility, or my lack thereof. I went back through my journals and there it was. On the day he would mark F, we would somehow end up sliding into our recurring conversation. Anthony is a planner and cannot let things just take their course. It's wonderful for holidays as I don't have to do anything and before I know it, I'm in a beautiful hotel in Lisbon that he booked for a decent rate eight months ago. It's even better for date nights and school admissions. But for the Big Conversations that can ruin a Wednesday evening when you were hoping your husband was trying to seduce you, it's a bit of letdown.

In some ways I envy the women who were in my position before the torturous miracle of fertility treatment. Lots of women had one child, or no children, and that was that. There would be tears and prayers, maybe some self-pitying wondering "Why me?" But there would be no choice in the matter. It would be out of my hands. I dream of such a lack of control.

We've been having these conversations for nearly a year now. We

7

tried for a year before that, assuming it would happen. But then, nothing. Radio silence from my ovaries. I tried a drug called Clomid to "wake them up," but they pressed the snooze button and rudely ignored my pleas for cooperation.

"I was talking to my boss, at work today." I flinch at the mention of her; not again. She's always trying to persuade him to persuade me to start IVF. I've never met her but I loathe her. It's none of her business. But I promised in our wedding vows to always listen and never judge. I was twenty-four! I didn't know anything about how annoying it can be to have to listen when you just want to have a glass of wine. But I did promise, so I smile and ask, "What about?"

"She was saying how much better things are for Alfie now that he has a sibling. He's more sociable. Talks more. She thinks it's made him more empathetic."

I bristle at the implied criticism of my family setup from this awful woman. As though I'm raising a creepily silent future sociopath because I haven't produced multiple children. I make a noncommittal noise and drain my wineglass, an act of defiance in the face of alcohol's fertility-busting qualities.

"We should do it," he says with a burst of reckless energy. I've heard this before. "I've really thought about it. We need to stop going back and forth on it. Neither of us is getting any younger. You turn thirty-four in two months' time and the statistics for IVF only get worse as you get older." He's looking at me as though the answer is simple, I just need to get on board and everything will be fine!

"We've had this discussion before. We know about the statistics, but . . ." I don't really have anything to say that I haven't said a thousand times before. If I could guarantee that a round of IVF would give me a baby—that new member of the family we've wanted for so long— I would do it in a heartbeat. But that's not a promise anyone can make me. I know the odds of it working. They're not good and I've never liked gambling. It feels nauseatingly reckless to start IVF when we already have Theodore and I can devote all my time to him and I've learned to accept our family the way it is. What if I can't look after him when I'm sick from the hormones they'd pump me full of or emotionally drained from the disappointment? What if in pursuit of another child I stop being as good a mother to the child I already have? Still, the desire for another Theodore, and to see him playing with a sibling, sometimes punches me in the gut, and for a day I'll understand Anthony's steadfast certainty that we need another baby.

I go through phases. Sometimes I feel determined and ready. I can do this. Send me the needles, shoot me up, strap me down. I will do anything for a baby. Other weeks, the idea of all of those people and objects and wires and things being inside me makes me want to curl myself in a protective hunch. *No,* my body says. *This is not right.* Anthony's more prone to baby-induced broodiness than I am. A friend's snuffly newborn or his godchild doing something adorable will inevitably lead to an earnest declaration that we should just do it, let's do it, what have we got to lose? Like tonight.

What do we have to lose? *Everything, Anthony,* I want to cry each time. Occasionally I'll convince myself I can do this whole IVF thing but I can't do it flippantly. For a man so keen on planning, he can be remarkably gung ho about the impact of IVF and babies or, worse, IVF and no babies, on our lives. I need an acknowledgment of the potential worst-case scenario. I need him to understand how hard it's going to be for me. Because, as with all things involved in the growing of a human child, it will be the woman in this equation who experiences the negatives. And that assumes it would even work; what if it was for nothing?

"I need some more time to weigh it up, think about the pros and cons."

"Why do you always assume it will go wrong?"

"I don't."

"You do," he says, frustration moving right to the front of his voice and staying put. "You talk about the financial cost and the emotional cost and the physical cost as if it's guaranteed you're going to be having IVF for the next three years. What if it works the first time? What if it's a success? What if having a baby is completely within our grasp but we just don't take the chance?"

"Easy for you to say," I mutter.

"What was that?" he asks, even though he heard me. Of course he heard me.

"I said, it's easy for you to say. You're not the one who it's going to happen to."

"We're in this together, Cat. Please, I can't do this for you. I know it's unfair but I can't. Please. Just think about it."

We settle in to the sofa next to each other to watch something Anthony says is meant to be good and I realize that my heart rate isn't up. I'm calm. These conversations used to leave me tear stained and weepy, but now the sting has dissipated. What does that mean? That I've accepted that we're going to have just one child? Does it mean I'm happy about it? Can I make this decision for us when the question of children is something that affects him as much as it does me?

The thing is, Anthony is asking me to do something I cannot do. I cannot make a decision on this. A significant part of me hopes, secretly, that it will just happen. If we keep waiting and pushing it off for another month, and another, and another, maybe this month will be the one. I fell pregnant with Theodore after six months of entirely enjoyable regular attempts at baby-making, and just as I was starting to panic there it was. Morning sickness so bad it could have felled a horse. I know it's been two and a half years of trying with no success. I know that my egg reserve isn't great and my uterus is a weird shape that makes it less "hospitable" to an embryo (a word so cruel, in the context of fertility, that I wanted to strangle the haughty consultant insulting my anatomy with his tie). I know all of these things and I wish I didn't. I wish we could be ignorant and hopeful because it might happen. We just don't know yet.

That night, passing the photos of us on my way up the stairs, I marvel, as I often do after our fertility conversations, at this thing we've constructed. A family from the ground up. From the photo of us in our first year together, limbs easily entwined in the College bar, gazing at each other, to the photo of the three of us Phoebe took a few months ago in Battersea Park. My dark curls flying in the breeze contrasted with Theodore's perfect chestnut mop inherited from Anthony.

Later, I'm lying in bed reading. Anthony climbs in after me and I fall into our routine. My book to one side, I pass him his eye mask, light off, my head on his shoulder, my arm on his chest, his hand on my elbow, safe.

"Anthony," I whisper.

"Yes," he replies. I love this about him. He doesn't say "what" or even "hmm." He says yes to whatever I might want to say.

"I don't want to make a decision. I can't." A lump is in my throat. I rarely cry now about our years of infertility. I try to swallow it down because really, you cannot spend every night crying for two years. It's too depressing for words. "What if it happens naturally? I want it to—"

"Oh, Cat," Anthony says softly, and his voice undoes me. By revealing it, my secret has lost its power. It's a sad, small, silly hope. And yet, who knows?

"I understand," he says. "We'll give it one more month."

In that moment, I have never loved my husband more.

# OUTBREAK

# AMANDA

Novemer is always busy but this is ridiculous. The area around Gartnavel has never shown its divisions more apparently. The ice-induced falls and chesty coughs of Glasgow's polished, middle-class West End residents appear in A and E in a flurry of expensive highlights, knowledge of different kinds of antibiotics and clipped accents making clear they want their parents and grandparents to be seen *now*. The other side of this tale of two cities is liver cirrhosis, chronic poverty and the unglamorous side effects of a life of smoking.

"It's another SLS," Kirsty, an excellent young nurse, says gaily as she swings past me, unceremoniously plonking a chart into my arms. Shit Life Syndrome. Doctor speak for, "There's actually nothing wrong with you. You're just really sad because your life is really, really hard and there's nothing I can do about that." I used to try to help, little naïve waif that I was. *What if they have nobody else?* I would think desperately as I phoned social services seven times in one night until they stopped answering me. As a consultant, my approach is a bit different.

"Why am I seeing them then?" I ask. This is a waste of my time—a classic, shit junior doctor task if there ever was one.

"They've specifically asked to see a consultant and won't talk to anyone else." Ah. Unfair as it is, being loud, insistent and generally a pain in the ass will often get you better care in hospital. Not because we respect those kinds of antics. We just want to get you out the door.

I walk into the cubicle, the curtain providing a thin semblance of privacy. "What can I do for you?" I ask in my special chirpy but curt voice that I save for the healthy in my overcrowded, underfunded A and E Department.

"He's naw well," the pasty woman to my left growls, pointing at a child who, while bored, looks to be in good health.

"What appears to be the problem?" I ask, sitting in front of him. From his notes I can see his vitals are all normal. He doesn't even have a temperature. He's fine.

"He keeps sleepin' 'til late an' he's got a cough." The child has literally not made a sound.

A few harmless questions later and all is revealed. He's going through a growth spurt and tried a cheeky cigarette on the way home from school with a fellow wayward friend. Somebody call Sherlock, I have a gift.

As I'm waving the sheepish boy and his mother out the door, I hear the ring of the trauma phone. I take the call. A two-month-old child, suspected sepsis. On the way in.

There's an adrenaline rush when the phone rings for an incoming trauma that, even after twenty years as a doctor, I'm never immune to. After forty-five minutes of breathless work stabilizing the baby, he's being whisked upstairs to the ICU. There's barely a moment to turn around and think before another trauma comes in. This one's more routine. A road traffic collision has resulted in some nasty gashes and suspected internal bleeding. That one's off upstairs to a CT scan within twenty minutes. I'm washing my hands and trying to remember what time my son's parents' evening starts when one of my first-year junior doctors grabs me.

She's babbling about a patient crashing who had been fine and now he's not fine and help. She's a mess. I've seen it so many times before. She's only been on the ward for ten weeks and she has a patient deteriorating and she's panicking. I know I should be respectful and aware of the fact that she's only a junior doctor and we all have to learn but really, it's just annoying. I can understand a lack of knowledge and I can tolerate the mistakes made due to exhaustion. But sheer panic in an A and E Department is as useful as a papier mâché boat with a trapdoor. It sounds unkind even as I think it but my immediate thought is, she's never going to be an A and E doctor. If you can't keep your head screwed on when a patient's crashing then an area of medicine devoted to emergencies is not for you.

I run with her back to the cubicle. The patient's wife is standing next to the bed with him, crying. I practically hiss at Fiona to get him into a room and ask as quietly, and furiously, as possible why he isn't there already. Even a cursory look at this man and his vitals shows that he's seriously unwell. Jesus, you don't even need to look at him. Every machine is beeping in persistent, whining concern.

Fiona says he's had the flu, and he was fine when he arrived, just fine! She gave him fluids and Paracetamol and had clearly hoped that he'd go away after a while, having been convinced that it was, in fact, just the flu and nothing more.

By this point the patient is dying. His breathing is labored with the shallow pant of a body not coping with the basic requirements of taking in air. His skin has the gray pallor of someone whose bodily systems are shutting down, and his temperature is climbing higher and higher. There are now seven members of staff surrounding him. Matron is taking his temperature at two-minute intervals and announcing with barely disguised disbelief that it's climbing this quickly. We strip him and surround him with ice and cold towels. I examine his entire body, looking for a wound, an insect bite, a shaving cut, a scratch. Anything that could be causing sepsis. There's nothing. No rash, so meningitis is unlikely. By this point I'm starting to think he's past the point of no return. There's not a huge amount you can do once the organs start shutting down. We catheterize him, give him fluids and oxygen. We pump him full of massive amounts of antibiotics and antivirals to start fighting whatever it is that's burning him up, we give him steroids for his breathing, we do everything we can. We take bloods to screen for infection, and if he can at least survive until we get those back, we can tailor the antibiotics or antivirals we're giving him, but now his kidneys are shutting down. There's zero urine output—the bag under the bed from the catheter is flapping in the air, depressingly empty. I often tell my friends when they half-jokingly ask me if they're dying, if you still need to pee, you're fine.

As I stand back and watch the scene unfolding in front of me, I keep my face arranged in an expression of grave calm. He's a handsome lad. Dark hair, stubble across his chin, he looks kind. His wife keeps getting in the way, crying and crying, inconsolable. She can see the writing on the wall. We all can. She occasionally shouts at us to do more, but there's nothing more we can do but wait and hope that by some miracle his body will turn itself around. Three hours after he arrived in A and E, the machine we've all been waiting for begins its long shriek. His heart has stopped. In an odd way it's a relief. The tension in the room has dissipated. Finally, we can all do something. Matron starts with compressions. I order for the epinephrine to be given. We shock him once, twice, three times. A nurse has his wife, mute now with shock, in the corner of the room, keeping her upright and away from the bed. The violence of an electric shock is not something a loved one should see if it can be helped. In the effort to bring someone back from death we pulverize them, shock them, try to fight their hearts back into a grudging rhythm.

It's not working, but we all knew this would be the outcome. This is a man whose body has been ravaged by something, but we don't know what yet. Our arms tire. Matron looks at me questioningly with the paddles in her hands. I shake my head. We have done everything we can and should. To keep going now would be to inflict unnecessary torture on the body of a dead man. After fifty-two minutes I make the order. "Everybody stop. Enough."

"Time of death, 12:34 p.m., November 3, 2025." I leave one of my senior registrars to complete the admin that comes with death and comfort this poor man's grieving widow. Only a matter of minutes ago she was a wife.

Fiona, my panicking junior doctor, is distraught. It's the first young patient she's lost in the department and it's different when they're young. It's never easy to lose a patient but when someone's eighty-five and they've had a long life and suffered a stroke or a massive heart attack; you're sad but there's a sense that this is part of life. Death comes for us all and you've had a good innings. Godspeed and see you on the other side.

But when someone young dies it's because something has gone seriously wrong and we have been unable to fix it. The patient was called Fraser McAlpine. His wife is sobbing over and over again that it was just the flu.

I take Fraser's chart and lead Fiona to the Staff Room. I sit her down so she can recover from the stress and go over what happened and why. It's a technique I learned from a consultant when I was training in Edinburgh. When you've lost a patient, you go through the chart right away from start to finish, step by step. What did you do, when did you do it, why did you do it, how did you do it? Normally it makes the junior doctor realize that they did everything right and it was completely beyond their control. And if they did something wrong, it provides a learning experience. It's a win-win.

We go through the chart with a fine-tooth comb. Fraser arrived at A and E at 8:39 a.m., so far so normal. He was seen by a triage nurse at 9:02 a.m. who deemed him to be low-urgency based on him appearing to have the flu. He only had a slightly elevated temperature and was breathing normally. He complained of feeling lethargic and having a headache. He saw Fiona at 10:15 a.m., who put him on fluids and gave him Paracetamol. She offered to run a blood test to see if he had a bacterial infection or a virus, and to treat him accordingly. He was put on the list for the nurse to take blood. His temperature at 10:15 a.m. was 100.4 degrees. That's barely elevated. Even a new parent with a six-week-old baby wouldn't lose sleep over that.

Thirty minutes later, at 10:45 a.m., three-quarters of an hour before his heart stopped, his temperature was 107.6 degrees. At that point you're basically dead. That's when Fiona came to get me. My blood runs cold. His body went from being normal to near dead in under an hour.

I can see Fiona relaxing as we review his notes. I haven't mentioned a mistake she made and I'm clearly unnerved. This is not a simple case of junior doctor error. This is horrifying. This wasn't flu and it doesn't appear to be sepsis. He was a healthy young man. People drop dead sometimes, even young healthy people. But normally it's clear what has gone wrong.

Then I see something that causes a wave of nausea to roll through my stomach. He was in the hospital two days ago. My immediate thought is that we must have missed something. One of my team, my doctors or nurses, must have missed something that caused this man to lose his life. I read the notes—he was in with a sprained ankle after a rugby match.

Death is not a side effect of x-raying and icing a sprained ankle.

Then the thought of MRSA pings itself into my brain. It's one of the deep fears of any doctor. But this . . . I don't know. I haven't seen a MRSA case before, thank God. But this doesn't match up.

I'm poring over the notes, trying to find something, anything that would explain what happened. There's a jagged edge to a memory. Something is nagging at me but I can't quite bring it to the front of my mind. What is it? It's not from yesterday. Maybe the day before? It dawns on me. A patient I treated two days ago. An older man, sixty-two, who was flown down from the Isle of Bute. He was gravely ill when he arrived. They'd intubated him on the helicopter. Kidneys had packed up. I wasn't entirely sure why they had bothered moving him but the paramedic seemed pretty flustered and said, "He wasn't this bad when we picked him up. His temperature has shot up." I didn't think much of it at the time. Sick person's temperature goes up. It's not a huge surprise.

He had died about a quarter of an hour after arriving. We had done the same thing as we did with Fraser McAlpine—we took bloods to identify what bacteria or virus was attacking the patient. We never followed up on the results, though, because he died. That was something for the morgue to look at. I check the bed numbers. They weren't even close. Patients with sprained ankles don't go into Recuss. Then I check the staff who treated the man from Bute. I was the consultant who treated him along with a junior, Ross. One of the nurses, though, was the same. Kirsty treated the man from Bute and Fraser McAlpine.

Please, God, let Kirsty be a murderer, because that would be so much less stressful than this being a contagious infection or a hygiene problem. No, what am I thinking? Murders involve a lot of paperwork.

I can feel the anxiety rising. It's not the deaths—I'm used to those. It's the uncertainty. The thing I like most about medicine is the certainty. There are plans and systems, lists and protocols. There are autopsies and inquests. No question is left unanswered. I try to remember how bad things were in my third year at university after Mum died. It's like exposure therapy I do in my brain. I survived that so I can survive this. I survived panic attacks so if I have one now, I will survive it. I thought I was going to die then but I didn't. Just because I think I might die now doesn't mean I will. I didn't know if I could be a doctor then but I am a doctor now. Be wary of that little voice that tries to twist one scary thing into a spiral of despair.

Do not panic, Amanda. This is just my anxiety talking. Two patients are not an outbreak of an antibiotic-resistant infection. Two patients are not a pandemic. Two patients don't even comprise a pattern.

Fiona says she has to go. I stare at her blankly, unsure how long we've been sitting here. It's okay, you can take a few minutes, I reassure her. Losing a patient is a lot to deal with. She says that she can't, because someone's called in sick. "Ross isn't feeling well so we're down a doctor."

In a split second I do something that's completely insane. If my husband was there, he would say that I need to book in to see my psychotherapist and that my anxiety has gotten completely out of control. But he's not and I don't because what if? My mum always told me to trust my gut and my gut is telling me this is a fucking disaster. I can feel the weight of the knowledge on my chest. I need to tell other people. I need to do things and not just worry in silence.

I go back out to the ward. I tell Matron to ask all the patients in the department if they were in A and E two days previously. She just looks at me disapprovingly and I don't have the time to have a discussion with her so I move on to the waiting room. I ask who was here two days ago and two men stand up. One man just raises his arm. He's paler than the other two. I get him on a stretcher. My heart is starting to do the clenching thing it does when I'm getting a panic attack but there's actually a reason for the panic. This has never happened before.

It's always been a panic attack because I was panicking about nothing, it's not meant to be *legitimate* panic. I want to cry, slump down in one of the staff room chairs and leave someone else to deal with whatever this is.

They all have flu-like symptoms. Either they or their wives are concerned it's something sinister like sepsis—there was a sepsis campaign put out by the government in October. It's saved around twenty lives in this hospital alone and has also single-handedly increased waiting times. Everyone and their mother are convinced they have sepsis.

I want to tell these men that actually I think this might be a lot worse than sepsis, ten times more terrifying than one of the nation's biggest killers, but I don't. I stay quiet and determined and outwardly calm. No one dares to question what I'm doing until I chuck everyone out of the Minor Injuries Unit and place the suspected infection patients in there. One of the nurses starts spluttering at me but I just tell her to go to triage. I can't explain things right now, there's no time. Matron has done as I asked and found two patients who were in A and E two days ago and are now back. I have three from the waiting room. That makes five. Fraser McAlpine makes six. The man from the Isle of Bute makes seven. This isn't a coincidence.

Fiona bursts through the doors of the Unit. "Ross has been brought in by ambulance."

Eight.

It's not my anxiety, I know that now. With freezing fingers, I phone my husband.

"There's an infection. It's really bad."

"Wait, what? What kind? MRSA?"

"No, something I've not seen before. It's spreading too fast. You have to go home. Now."

"Are you sure it's not your anxiety talk—"

"Fuck. Off. I have eight patients dying in a row lined up like we're in World War Fucking Two. They're all men. I don't know if that means anything yet but it's not a good sign. Go home. I swear to God, if you don't claim you've just thrown up and go home I will divorce you." I'm hysterical. I have never threatened to leave my lovely, supportive, oncologist husband before. I never imagined anything could drive me to such a threat. But I never imagined this.

"Go home. Touch no one, speak to no one, just go. Pick up the boys on your way home. Get them to come out to you. Don't go into the school. Please go get them." I'm begging now. Will agrees. I don't know if he's terrified of me or for me. I don't care. He just has to be home safe with our sons. I punch out a text to my boys telling them their dad is on his way to pick them up and they're to go outside and wait for him. I'll write whatever note they need. I'll say anything.

I vaguely know someone who works at Health Protection Scotland. We were at university together and now she's a deputy director there. She's always been a bit snippy but I don't care. I need her to listen to me. I call her and try to sound calm as I speak to the switchboard. When I tell her everything in a rush she keeps making small noises as though she wants to get off the phone. She doesn't sound worried but also, it seems like she thinks she's seen this all before. She hasn't been a doctor for more than ten years but somehow it sounds like she just doesn't trust me. Maybe the urgency isn't translating when I explain. It's so clear to me but it sounds so minor—eight people are sick, okay, we'll see what happens and we'll look into it. I put everything down in an e-mail as well and say, at the very least, that they need to send someone to look into it, just in case. I sit down by one of the patients and check his pulse. It is 45 bpm. He will die soon. They all will. Breathe, Amanda. The cavalry will charge in soon. I won't have to deal with all of this on my own. There will be someone I can hand the reins over to. Someone qualified who wears a hazmat suit for a living will come and make everything better and let me go home and forget that this ever happened.

The doors of the Minor Injury Unit swing open. It's Matron. "There's four more just arrived in ambulances. Two were here two days ago, and the other two were here yesterday. I don't know what to do."

My worst nightmare is coming true.

E-mail from Amanda Maclean (amanda.maclean@nhs.net)
to Leah Spicer (l.spicer@healthprotectionscotland.org)
6:42 p.m. on November 3, 2025

Leah,

Found your e-mail online. Realized that you forgot to give it to me on the phone after you said to e-mail you. I've just arrived home from my shift. When I left there were nineteen live patients in A and E all showing symptoms of what I think is a virus (antibiotics made no difference although obviously need pathology to confirm what's going on. Is that easier for your lab to do over at HPS or is it quicker for us to just crack on here at Gartnavel?). Of the twenty-six I think we've seen so far, five died before I left the hospital. One man, the first I saw, from the Isle of Bute two days ago. Fraser McAlpine this afternoon. Three other men died quickly after coming in, including one of my junior doctors, Ross.

They're all men. Too small a sample size so far obviously but I've never seen that before. Maybe men are more vulnerable to it? Can we have a call to discuss all of this please, also maybe loop someone more senior in? This is very bad, Leah. You need to understand how quickly the disease affects them. They go from having normal flu symptoms and feeling quite unwell to being dead with a temperature of over 109 degrees in a few hours.

Please get back to me as soon as you can.

Amanda

E-mail from Amanda Maclean (amanda.maclean@nhs.net)
to Leah Spicer (l.spicer@healthprotectionscotland.org)
6:48 p.m. on November 3, 2025

Leah, there was a baby as well, I just realized. We thought it was
sepsis. He was in before Fraser McAlpine. He was only two months
old. I thought he was stable when we sent him up to the Pediatric
ICU but I just called them and he died a few minutes after they
wheeled him out of the lift. He was here a few days ago, being
treated in A and E.

That makes twenty-seven I saw today. Six deaths. Oldest aged
sixty-two. Youngest aged two months.

Amanda

FW: E-mail from Amanda Maclean (amanda.maclean@nhs.net)
to Leah Spicer (l.spicer@healthprotectionscotland.org)
6:48 p.m. on November 3, 2025. FW to Raymond McNab
(r.mcnab@healthprotectionscotland.org)
10:30 a.m. on November 4, 2025

Ray,

See below two e-mails from a woman I went to uni with. She's a
consultant at Gartnavel. I think she's mistaking a bad case of the flu
(it's November after all . . .) with ensuing sepsis/likely death from
other, complicating factors for something more serious. There's
been no other reports of anything on the Category 1 list so I think
we're safe on the SARS/MRSA/Ebola front.

Between you and me, she had a breakdown at university.
Completely cracked up and had to take a year off. I think one of her
parents died or something? Anyway, she's quite fragile. I intend to

send a holding e-mail advising good infection control practice and to get in touch if anything further. Flag if you disagree.

Thanks,
Leah

E-mail from Raymond McNab
(r.mcnab@healthprotectionscotland) to Leah Spicer
(l.spicer@healthprotectionscotland.org)
10:42 a.m. on November 4, 2025

Thanks Leah.

By the sounds of it, a stark raving lunatic who's trying to waste the limited resources and time of this institution. Not to mention my patience. Ignore please.

Ray

# CATHERINE

've never been good at the school pickup. I don't like talking to groups of people I vaguely know. Strangers are fine, as are, obviously, friends. I just cannot form a clique to save my life. The nursery gates are rife with stressful opportunities for me to put my foot in my mouth or misinterpret a friendly hello as a "Come and talk to us!" wave when actually it was a "I'm busy talking to someone, nice to see you from a distance!" wave. I have a PhD in Social Anthropology and yet the difference between these two waves can easily be lost on me. The irony, by contrast, is most certainly not.

For the last few days pickup has been stressful in a different way. Everyone wants to talk, not because they think I'm a brilliant conversationalist (although I live in hope). No, they seem to want a verbal sounding board for their mounting anxieties. The Plague is all anybody can talk about even though we're all assuring each other that it's very far away, what is it up to Glasgow? Four hundred, five hundred miles? Perfectly safe. The authorities will have it all in hand soon. One of the other mums, a lawyer, has told me three days in a row, in the resolute, inarguable tone I'm sure she uses in court, that there is absolutely nothing to worry about. Absolutely. Nothing. If she's trying to convince herself I hope she's more successful than she's been in convincing me because all she's done is stoke the panic I've kept simmering away.

It feels like yesterday we were celebrating Guy Fawkes Night at the St. Josephs fireworks night. It was an evening of hot dogs, mittens, adorable pictures of Anthony holding a pink-cheeked excited Theodore. It was the last time I remember feeling truly relaxed and happy in a crowd of people and it was only five days ago. The news is still using the subdued tones of journalists who deal in *facts* not *opinions*. But the facts are becoming increasingly nauseating on their own. A virus affecting only men. "This has not been confirmed by officials but has been widely observed in the outbreaks in Glasgow, Edinburgh and along the West Coast of Scotland," they intone on the news.

I've been racking my brain and I can't think of a single infectious disease that affects only men. I mean, it's not like I have a particularly good knowledge of infectious diseases, but still. Isn't it weird? Why is no one from a hospital or the government confirming how weird that is? It would make me feel better in a strange way if someone from an official body came out and said, "This is unheard of. We have no idea what is going on."

Beatrice, normally my social savior—my "nursery" friend—grabs me by the hand, frightening me.

"Beatrice!" She sent her nanny to do pickup the last few days. It's a relief to see a friendly face but the relief quickly dissolves. She is drawn and haggard.

"I'm moving to Norfolk. Tomorrow."

"What? You're what?" I splutter. Beatrice has a country house in Norfolk where she spends, at best, four weekends a year, letting it out on Airbnb the rest of the time.

"The virus. I don't like the sound of this, Catherine. There's been an outbreak in Streatham. I'm getting out of the city before it's too late."

"Before it's too late for what?"

"There's no point in leaving if the worst has already happened."

Beatrice is terrifying me. She is the calmest person I know and she looks and sounds unhinged.

"I have three sons, Catherine. Two brothers. My mum died last year. My dad is my only parent left. We're not staying in London to find out how bad this is going to get."

I don't know what to say. I have no arguments against what she's saying, only platitudes to recite from the other mothers and the feeling of vomit rising in my throat as I think of my own statistics. One son. One husband. No mother. No daughter. This would not end well for me.

"How are you affording it?" I finally find the words to ask a sensible question.

Beatrice looks at me with an expression fast approaching pity. "Why do you think Jeremy and I have always worked so hard, darling? Why do you think we live here? Between the two of us we don't need to work for a few years."

She dashes off, Dior bag still slung over one shoulder, to scoop up Dylan from the playroom of this quiet, kind Montessori school in a part of South London I've just realized Beatrice considers to be deeply beneath her. Unlike her, I don't have anywhere to go. I have to stay here and wait.

# AMANDA

Is the beginning of a plague a good time to get a divorce? Or maybe I should just kill him and avoid the paperwork? Will, the fucking idiot, went to work. He *knew* not to. I have been so careful.

When I left the hospital on November 3 at the end of my shift I changed out of my scrubs and walked, in my underwear, to the fire exit in the changing room and put fresh scrubs from the plastic on just before I left through the door emblazoned with FIRE EXIT ONLY. I did not give one single solitary fuck about fire exits.

After getting out of the car once I got home, I ignored the front door, stripped in the garage and burned the clothes. I walked naked through the house and showered with the water as hot as I could bear and a new bottle of sterilizing scrub wash I took from the hospital storeroom. I didn't go near the boys and screamed at them when they started jokingly coming toward me in pigeon steps. Will was incredulous for the first night as I slept in a camp bed in the garage. He went to work the next day despite my telling him on pain of death not to—he left before I woke up—and when he came home, he was white with shock.

"I believe you," he said. Fat lot of good that will do us now, I wanted to scream. He had been exposed unnecessarily. He had gone back to the hospital. The one place in the country with a higher number of infected bodies than anywhere else.

He hadn't gone to work again. Until yesterday. It had been eight days since the day in A and E when this miserable thing started and he was still fine. The incubation period can't be more than a few days based on the speed with which men were returning to A and E. We were safe, out of the danger zone just enough for me to sit in the same room as Will and the boys and laugh along to something on Netflix without having a heart attack every time one of them sneezed. My moron of a husband went in to work on November 4 and somehow escaped death and then, a week later, must have decided that life here in this quiet suburb on the north side of Glasgow just isn't thrilling enough for him.

"It's a baby," he shouts at me when I finally run out of steam after his return. He was only gone a few hours. "She's going to die if I don't help. I'm the only pediatric oncologist in the hospital at the moment." He doesn't say why he's the only pediatric oncologist because he knows it answers my questions for me and makes his arguments absurd. He's the only pediatric oncologist in the hospital at the moment because the other two fucking died.

"You have two children here in this house," I scream with fury. "You might be a better doctor than me but I'm a better parent. I care more about Charlie and Josh than some toddler."

Will is weeping now. I've never made him cry before. It makes the words I want to shout die in my throat. "Her mother called me on my mobile. She begged me, she was going to die. No one had given her the chemo in over forty-eight hours. She's, she's, I. I just . . ." He breaks down into sobs. I so desperately, even through my anger, want to reassure him, hold him and rock him and say it's okay, no mistake is irreversible, I forgive you.

But this mistake is not reversible. I cannot touch my husband because if he is carrying the virus I might catch it and then our boys will be more likely to get sick. I cannot forgive him if the boys die because of this. A nameless, faceless child in a hospital ward four miles away is not my concern. My boys—Charlie and Josh, with the beginnings of stubble growing across their jaws and hazel eyes and freckles and creased foreheads when they're concentrating on homework—are my concern. I cannot forgive Will for not putting them first. They are all that matters.

"Sleep in the garage. Don't touch anything. Don't do anything and don't go anywhere near the boys. If they try to come into the garage, scream at them like they're about to touch a burning flame."

Will just sobs and nods in response.

"I love you," I say. I remember seeing a woman in A and E a few years ago. She had found her husband hanging from a curtain pole in their bedroom after a vicious fight. She was going into the bedroom to apologize and make up. I never told Will about it but since then, no matter how awful the argument, I've always told him I love him before I leave the room. The Plague is making fast work of men. We don't need to do its job for it.

"I love you too. I'm sorry."

I know, darling. But I will never forgive you.

# LISA

### Toronto, Canada
### Day 13

**H**ey babe, have you seen this?"

My wife is brandishing an article in the *New York Times* Science section at me. I'm used to her imploring me to read things but this must be the first time in fifteen years that she's led me to the Science section of anything.

"An outbreak of an aggressive strain of flu has affected tens of thousands across Scotland after originating in Glasgow in early November. There are also reports of outbreaks in London, Manchester, Leeds, Liverpool, Birmingham and Bristol. Anecdotal reports suggest the flu strain only affects men. No women have so far reported suffering the disease. The mortality rate appears to be far higher than for the flu with over five thousand deaths so far reported."

Over five thousand dead? That's a lot for the flu. And in only a couple of weeks.

"Wait," I say, my brain rewinding. "Did you say it only affects men?"

Margot nods decisively. "Yep."

I sit down next of her, my brain turning. "Only men? A flu? How bizarre. I've never heard of anything like that before."

"Neither have I," Margot agrees, the difference being that Margot is a professor of Renaissance history who writes romance novels on the side, neither of which are careers in which flu strains are discussed in any great detail unless it's to almost-but-not-quite fell a romantic hero. In my line of work, by contrast, flu is of utmost importance. If I've never heard of a flu disease, or in fact any infectious disease, affecting only men, then it probably doesn't exist, or at least hasn't been studied before. This could be interesting. I type out an e-mail to my assistant, Ashley, for tomorrow morning.

Ashley,

Seen report tonight in *NYT* Science section about flu in Scotland affecting only men. Can you dig up all research on this asap tomorrow am and bring to me in a binder by 11?

Thx
Lisa

---

Dr. Lisa Michael
Professor of Virology, Head of Virology Department,
University of Toronto
"Nolite Te Bastardes Carborundorum"

# AMANDA

No one is listening to me. I'm starting to think I'm going mad. I'll send an e-mail and wonder afterward, as it goes unanswered, if I actually sent it. I'm being gaslit by the entire Scottish medical establishment. Gartnavel fired me today, which makes sense. I haven't been to work in fifteen days. There is absolutely no way I'm prioritizing the health service over my own children. The woman on the phone, some numpty called Karen (of course she was called Karen) said, "You should be ashamed of yourself, abandoning your patients in their time of need." I asked Karen what she did for a living: she's an administrator. "What exactly would you know about my patients' needs?" I hissed, feeling the curious eyes of my children on my back as I moved into a different room and closed the door behind me. "This virus doesn't respond to treatment, doesn't respond to antivirals. Nothing makes a difference. I could be the Virgin Mary herself and I wouldn't be able to save anyone." Then she hung up.

Well, technically I told her to go fuck herself and then she hung up. Probably to phone some other doctor desperately trying to save his or her family and bully them into coming to work. Will's just been ignoring the phone calls, which is for the best. He's a terrible people pleaser.

I still sometimes wonder if we're only married because after three years he was getting a bit nervy about upsetting me if he didn't propose, rather than because he loved me so much he had to marry me.

I've now written to fourteen newspapers around the world. I have sent Health Protection Scotland eight e-mails and called twelve times, not a single one of which has been answered. I've e-mailed the WHO in London and Geneva nine times. I. Am. Screaming. Into. The. Void.

The news is showing the descent of Glasgow and Edinburgh into the nightmare of a pandemic. The army has been brought in to drive ambulances, fire engines and trucks carrying food to and from farms and factories and supermarkets. Makes sense when you think about it. Have you ever seen a female truck driver? Dundee and Aberdeen have just announced the closure of schools on Friday, which might be the most laughable public health policy I've ever heard of. Yes, that's a good idea, let's slow down the spread of this almost-always fatal virus just a wee bit. Give it a long weekend, see if that cheers it up so it won't kill the Primary One class on Monday.

The people in charge need to listen to me. They are wasting precious time. I'm cooped up in my house with sons whose fear grows by the day as they follow the mushrooming panic of the Plague on Twitter, Facebook, Snapchat, their phones always glowing in their faces. Charlie said yesterday, his thirteen-year-old voice sounding far higher and more like a child's than it has in years, "Mum, Taylor died." My first thought was *Who's Taylor?* But that wouldn't have been a helpful response. "He actually died," Charlie said in wonder before going up to his room, playing unbearably loud music and shouting at me as I came in every ten minutes to "check if you wanted anything to drink" (check if he was trying to kill himself).

Sometimes being a doctor makes me a worse parent emotionally but a better parent practically, and this is one of those times. I never think, "Oh, he'll be fine." In the course of my career I've seen over a hundred girls, boys, men, women who've killed themselves in minutes, brought to hospital still warm by parents and spouses who never imagined they would kill themselves. The ones who everyone was worried about go straight to the morgue. They tend to plan it better. My sons are alive because I have somehow kept this awful disease out of this house and away from them. But they are starving for my care and affection and I cannot give it to them. I don't hug them. I don't cook their food. I don't go near them if I can possibly help it. I cannot be too careful when their lives are at stake.

Every minute that my e-mails go unanswered is another minute away from a vaccine. This Plague is not just going to flit away into thin air. It's only going to get worse, and everybody is wasting time. I'm a doctor, not a pathologist. I can't fix this, but if no one listens to me, then how are we ever going to fix it?

Will thinks I'm being silly. He thinks that the authorities are working on this "behind the scenes" and actually, they just haven't announced it. I say bollocks. Everyone I've ever met involved in public health policy or politics would drown their own granny to get some good press. They would all be crowing about "having this all in hand" and "the finest minds in the country working on a solution." There'd be a task force. There's always a task force. If anybody was listening to me, I'd know it, but instead there is only bleak, awful silence and time being wasted.

E-mail from Leah Spicer (l.spicer@healthprotectionscotland.org) to Richard Murray (r.murray@healthprotectionscotland.org), Kitty McNaught (k.mcnaught@healthprotectionscotland.org) and Aaron Pike (a.pike@healthprotectionscotland.org) at 9:20 a.m. on November 19, 2025

Richard, Kitty, Aaron,

Please can one of you call me urgently. No response from Daniel in Edinburgh. I'm swamped here. Louise hasn't come to work all week. I'm trying to finalize infection protocol but unsure of best way forward as it is gender neutral but we need different policies for men and women now? All hospitals in Greater Glasgow have declared an emergency and Queen Elizabeth's has started turning away men from A and E. Mobile is 07884647584. Please call as soon as you can. Very, very urgent.

E-mail from Richard Murray
(r.murray@healthprotectionscotland.org) at 9:20 a.m.
on November 19, 2025

Thank you for your e-mail. I am currently out of the office with an illness. If you require urgent assistance, please contact another member of my team.

E-mail from Kitty McNaught
(k.mcnaught@healthprotectionscotland.org) at 9:20 a.m.
on November 19, 2025

I am out of the office on compassionate leave. I will reply to your e-mail on my return.

E-mail from Aaron Pike (a.pike@healthprotectionscotland.org) at 9:20 a.m. on November 19, 2025

I am currently out of the office due to ill health. Please try contacting another member of your case team if your query is urgent.

# ARTICLE IN *THE TIMES* OF LONDON ON NOVEMBER 20, 2025

**"Exclusive: Scottish doctor who treated first patient says 'This is the new plague and it's only getting worse'"**

**by Eleanor Meldrum**

I wish I could tell you what Dr. Amanda Maclean is like in person but I can't. She wouldn't meet with me out of fear that I would be a host of the "Plague," as she calls it, a mysterious virus with a high mortality rate that has quickly caused havoc in Scotland. There are also a number of reported cases in Manchester, Newcastle, Leeds and London. When I assured Amanda over e-mail that I was not infected, she responded, "You have no way of knowing that. Women are asymptomatic hosts. When I treated two of the first cases I quickly realized that the only link between them was a female nurse."

If Amanda's intention is to worry me, she succeeds. Hearing this, I start to look back over my interactions with the men I care about with a different perspective: my boyfriend (kissed on the lips this morning), my dad (saw him for coffee at lunchtime, hugged him good-bye), my brother (seeing him for dinner in two days' time).

"Part of the reason this has spread so fast is that women and men are both carrying it. Women never know and men don't show symptoms for two days. There's hundreds of thousands of people walking around spreading the virus and they don't even know it." I respond by asking why there aren't more reported cases then? Surely if, as Amanda says, there are hundreds of thousands of people walking around spreading this disease, then there would be hundreds of thousands, millions of cases?

She is resolute. "There will be, but there's also already far more cases than currently reported. The Plague can easily appear to be a case of sepsis or other fast-acting illness." She points me in the direction of a news report from November 18, 2025, in *The Dubai Daily*, a British expat newspaper. It reports the "unusual death of three men who all recently returned from a golfing trip in Scotland at the Gleneagles Resort." They flew from Glasgow Airport to Dubai. Amanda is incredulous that this has not been defined as an outbreak already. "The WHO are asleep at the wheel. Health Protection Scotland is no better. The way they have failed to deal with this is an absolute outrage."

Doesn't she mean *are* failing to deal with it?

"They *have* failed. There is very little we can do now that the Plague has escaped Glasgow. It's too late to track who went where. The ease with which it spread from the first patient I treated, a man from the Isle of Bute, to a nurse in the hospital who then passed it on to patients is remarkable. I was in touch with Health Protection Scotland by phone and e-mail on November 3. I have sent tens of e-mails to HPS and the WHO and been ignored at every turn. If I had been listened to back then we might have been able to set up effective quarantines and bring it under control."

I tell Amanda that she sounds like a paranoid conspiracy theorist. She assures me that she knows, but that she'll soon be proved right. Amanda thinks that the disease is "genuinely destined to ravage the male population if we don't create a vaccine soon. We needed a treatment yesterday."

So, what can we do to reduce infection risk? "Do what I'm doing. Stay home, whether you're a man or a woman, stay home. Avoid crowds, avoid public transport, for the love of God don't get on a plane. Anyone can be infected, so you need to interact with as few people as possible. Neither my sons nor I have left our house since November 4."

I can't help but ask at this point how this can be the case when Amanda is a consultant in the A and E Department at Gartnavel Hospital in Glasgow's West End. Don't her patients need her now, more than ever?

Amanda sighs heavily before she answers. "There is absolutely nothing any doctor can do to prevent this virus from killing a boy or man. Nothing. When we treated one of the first patients who died, a young, fit, healthy man in his twenties, we gave him everything: antivirals, antibiotics, fluids, steroids. Nothing worked, it didn't matter. I'm not going to put my family at risk for the lost cause of saving men who can't be saved. I won't apologize for keeping my sons alive. Why do you think none of the advice from official agencies has told people to go to hospital to seek treatment?"

I finish my conversation with Amanda thoroughly unnerved. After we've spoken, I go through the official statements made by Health Protection Scotland and Public Health England. She's right. Nowhere does it say, "Go to hospital and seek treatment" or even "Seek medical advice." The only advice is to stay home, the obvious implication being that men should stay home and die.

Before speaking to Amanda I had hoped to answer many of my questions about the Plague and its possible impact on hospitals, schools, maybe even how the science behind it works. After speaking to her, I have more questions than I could have imagined, but she can't answer any of them. I don't know if anyone can. How bad will the Plague become? How many men will die? Could the authorities be doing more? What, if anything, can they now do? Will my family be safe? Will this be the end of us?

---

# CATHERINE

London, United Kingdom
Day 35

I t's the first year of my life I'm not looking forward to Christmas. How can I when the apocalypse seems to be dawning? The shops are continuing on as if nothing is happening, determined to avoid the financial ruin of closure in December, a month of gold. How can people go into the Liberty Christmas Department and spend £30 on a sequined robin decoration when our husbands, our sons, our fathers, our friends, might all be dying?

Theodore is blissfully unaware. I used to worry about having such an unobservant child—he would tell me he couldn't find something when it was literally right in front of him—but now it seems like a blessing. If he senses my unease, he isn't showing it but our house is full of fear. You can practically see it seeping through the letterbox. The first case was only five weeks ago in Glasgow but it's already everywhere. There are reports of cases in every city: Manchester, Newcastle, Bristol. London is erupting with it. St. Thomas's Hospital announced an emergency yesterday, so terrifyingly close it might as well be next door. Our small, lovely house in Crystal Palace used to feel like a haven from the stresses of daily life. Now it is a puny, insignificant life raft. It cannot do what I need it to. It cannot assure me that my husband and son will be safe.

Last week we put up the Christmas tree. I was insistent it would happen on the first day of the month, as it always has done. It's the one tradition I gleaned from my short time with my mother. Christmas starts when the tree goes up on December 1. Anthony and I heaved boxes of plastic fir branches and dusty ornaments down from the attic. Phoebe was always horrified by our fake tree, but when you're an orphan, you become sensitive to news stories of other orphans. Christmas trees going up in flames and turning family homes into charred skeletons of smoke and ash, killing almost everyone and leaving a few unfortunate children behind, are uncomfortably common.

Usually Anthony assembles the tree and then leaves me to the decoration. He'll grab a beer or a glass of red wine and sit comfortably on the sofa as I potter around considering red tinsel or silver. Is a gold theme what I want? Not this year. This year, he stood by my side and methodically placed ornaments and tinsel and Christmas lights over branches, transforming this squat, dense piece of plastic into a glowing, sparkling thing of festive wonder. He smiled as I hung the ornament Libby had made for us with a photo from our wedding on a beautiful white bauble. In the photo I'm looking up at Anthony, bliss personified. He's tucking one of my dark, bridal curls behind my ear, and I remembered the moment as clearly as if it were yesterday. My heart plummeted in my chest with fear and longing. Anthony carefully placed the angel Theodore made at nursery last year at the top of the tree, forehead creased in concentration to avoid it being wonky. He looked up at the tree and then down at me, a soft smile on his face. We were both thinking the same thing and he knew it and I knew it but we didn't say it because what's the point in breaking someone's heart when it won't change anything? The words hung in the air, illuminated with worry. *Will this be our last Christmas together?*

Theodore was entranced by the tree for a grand total of four minutes before returning to the much more exciting task of "building a boat," which seemed to involve sitting in the empty ornament box and yelling, "Boat, boat, boat." It's as fine a way as any to build a boat.

Anthony hasn't gone to work all week. I wouldn't let him. I told him in all seriousness that I would rather we lived on my income and he never worked another day in his life than have him leave the house one more time. Most of the time I work remotely, and I'm not teaching classes this term, so it's not a problem for me. I work. Anthony cares for Theodore. I go out to get food, briefly and carefully as late as possible in the quiet of nighttime, touching no one, standing near no one. I watch my two loves with beady eyes, interpreting the smallest cough as a sign that it is here. My tall, strong husband and small son, now equally vulnerable.

The news started off so casually. There had been an outbreak of a form of flu in Glasgow. Thirty dead, many more infected. It sounded so quotidian; the flu. Glasgow seemed so far away. I assumed the powers that be would find a solution. It would be yet another scary news story and nothing more. We're used to scary diseases starting in faraway places and being brought here. Maybe that's why we underestimated it. *Scotland?* we all thought. *Surely a dangerous disease can't start there.*

But it's only gotten worse. Every day the newscasters' tones have become graver and graver. First it was thirty cases, then fifty, then one hundred, then it jumped suddenly to thousands and tens of thousands and what's next? Millions? Billions? Everyone dead? Tonight, I realized the man who usually does the *News at 10* wasn't on. It was a woman. I burst into tears and Anthony asked me what was wrong, the news hadn't even started yet, what could be wrong?

I didn't say anything, just bawled. *What if the newsreader is sick? They film it in London, don't they? What if he has it? What if you have it but you're just not showing symptoms yet,* I wanted to cry. I haven't talked about any of this with my friends, not properly. I don't know how. Most of us have kids so it's not like we're popping around to each other's houses on a moment's notice anyway, but I don't know what to say even to my best friends. Libby lives in Madrid and is desperately trying to figure out how to get to London and what to do for work once she gets here. I don't want to burden her and I don't know what I'd say. Phoebe has two daughters so it's different for her. I can't quite bring myself to talk to her and hear her comfort me about the risk of my son dying when the reality is, I'm nauseous with jealousy that she has two girls. Her husband is at stake but her children aren't. It's not the same. No, I'm staying quiet for now. I stopped taking Theodore to nursery weeks ago. The idea of it made me shiver; putting him in a big room with thirty other children and adults who could have been anywhere, touched anything, be carrying it but not know. Anyone could have it.

So, we stay here in the house, hibernating, hoping to outlast the Plague as if it will recognize our fortitude and strength of will, see our house and go, "No, let's leave them alone. They don't deserve this." I don't want to voice my fears any more than I have to and ruin precious time with Anthony but we have no one else to talk to. At night we whisper to each other the frantic fears of two people with death peeking in the window, waiting. Last week was the first week in a year that we didn't have our fertility conversation. Of course, now there is nothing I want more than to be pregnant. I need the safety of numbers. My happiness, my soul, is wrapped up in Theodore and it's too much. It's so fragile I can't bear it. All I want is to know that I'm pregnant with a new life, a safe new life. A girl. I need to be pregnant with a girl. I would inject myself every minute of the day with a thick, stinging serum if I could have a girl now.

I was so disappointed when Theodore was a boy. You're not supposed to say that, but I was. I cried when the sonographer told us. Anthony didn't know what to say as I wept on the table, the jelly cold and wet on my stomach. I was weeping for boring blue dungarees and diggers and running around parks that I didn't have the energy for. I wanted to replace the relationship I had with my mother before she died. If only I could go back and tell myself what I know now. I would also weep for the safety lost.

No one from the scientific community has made a statement about why it affects only men. We all know that it does; it's obvious. But no one has said why. Maybe they don't know? Surely they know. We can separate conjoined twins and treat cancer and prevent AIDS with drugs. Surely they know why men, and only men, are dying. And nearly all of them die. The death rate is staggering. A 3.4 percent recovery rate, which seems to be completely random. There is no rhyme or reason. An elderly man was on the television last night telling his tale of coming close to the brink and somehow staving off death despite the Plague's best efforts. In the next clip a mother cried about her twenty-four-year-old son, a promising footballer who looked almost embarrassingly strong and healthy. He contracted it on the bus, she thinks, or maybe from one of the other players on his team. Nine of the other players have died. The team is disbanding.

Anthony sits on the sofa next to me, grasping my left hand as I journal. We haven't discussed it but we spend as much time as possible together. We sit next to each other at dinner, as close as we can physically be. We curl into each other on the sofa. We sleep entwined like otters.

He hasn't commented on my incessant writing, but he's used to it now. I've always journaled, on and off. More so when there are things to write about. Now there is everything to write about. The small part of my brain that is still engaged in my work can't help but pick up on the changes we're seeing through the television. I will record this. I know I will. I'm not sure how, but I will. I don't understand how everyone isn't already recording everything. I'm taking tens of photos and videos of Theodore and Anthony a day. I flick through them before I have a bath as I get all of the weeping I want to do all day out of my system in the quiet calm of the early morning.

I can't bear the possibilities. The questions flap around me. Will Theodore catch it? Will Anthony catch it? Will my gorgeous baby boy die? Will my husband die? Will everyone catch it? Will there be a cure? When will there be a cure? What if there is never a cure? What if this never ends? Is this the end of the world as we know it?

They started calling it "The Great Male Plague" last week. The tabloids had a field day after the doctor who treated the first patients, Amanda Maclean, did an interview. She said it was the worst virus she had ever seen. She called it the new Plague and it stuck. She says she wasn't listened to and if Health Protection Scotland had taken her seriously we could have gotten control of it. I don't know what to think about that.

You always assume that the people in power will know what to do. Surely they've all got it figured out, but I don't think anyone knows what to do. Nothing like this has ever happened. We're all blindly stumbling around in the dark and none of us knows a thing.

They're showing a clip on the TV of one of the trains leaving Glasgow. It looks like a scene from a film. There are people pushing ticket inspectors to one side and shoving themselves onto trains. They've all gone mad. The whole world is going mad.

Anthony switches off the TV with a decisive click.

"That's enough news for tonight," he says quietly before pulling me into his arms.

# ELIZABETH

**London, United Kingdom**
**Day 37**

As I get off the plane, I'm asked to step to one side. Immediately I panic that I've made an egregious mistake at work and the US government has decided I need to be dealt with while I've been on the flight to London. I'm never sure how to marry up the objective ability of my brain as a scientist with the feeling I so often have that I've done something wrong.

"Ms. Cooper, I have a car here to take you to see Dr. Kitchen." The man is subtly well dressed and serious.

A sleek business car is waiting for me. I gulp but try to eke out a friendly smile even though I'm unnerved. Government science departments don't tend to be Mercedes S-Class kinds of places. At least not for small-time visitors like me.

We make our way swiftly through the gray streets of West London snaking away from Heathrow. Everything looks so normal. Nobody is freaking out, yelling in the streets. There are Christmas lights up as the city prepares for the holidays. There's traffic and a garbage truck making its way slowly down the road and a woman with her daughter on the way to school, unicorn-covered backpack bouncing up and down as they walk down the street.

Maybe this was all a mistake. I cringe at the memory of the conversation with my boss that led me here. It took every ounce of strength, and a lot of the techniques I learned at an "Assertiveness for Women in the Workplace" workshop, not to apologize, back out of his office slowly and leave as if nothing had happened. I didn't though. For the first time in my life since I was eighteen, I was bold and brave and maybe even a little reckless. I use the example of Stanford versus Ole Miss whenever I need to feel like I'm making the right choices; it never fails me. My parents were so sure they were right and I was wrong. Who did I think I was acting like I was too good for the University of Mississippi? They were convinced Stanford would be an expensive waste of time. They were wrong. I was right. I need to remember that more often.

My boss is expecting me back in three weeks, in time to start work again by January. "The European Plague is going to die out, Elizabeth. It's clearly got some kind of genetic component." His arrogance is breathtaking. He's not a geneticist and neither am I. I aspire to think so much of my own opinion that, having never even seen it under a microscope, I can blithely reassure someone that a virus has a genetic element, using the justification of an area of science *I don't even have a master's in.* I know for certain that this is where I need to be. What's the point in having spent nine years getting my undergrad degree, master's and PhD specializing in vaccine development if not to help find a cure for a disease? This is what I did all of that work for. It's not just to have certificates on the wall.

It's lucky that I even saw the e-mail from Dr. Kitchen. I had been covering for Jim—who's such a moron I still can't believe that he a) got into Yale; b) works at the Centers for Disease Control and c) has the same job as me. In his e-mail, Dr. Kitchen sounded desperate and sensible and reasonable and terrified.

Two incredibly awkward conversations involving my dubious bosses, a long-haul flight and a car ride later and here I am. In the week since I responded to Dr. Kitchen and arranged this trip the crisis here has worsened. Back home the racist rhetoric is predictably ramping up. *It's not our Plague, it's not our problem. This is happening to the UK because of all those African and Middle Eastern immigrants. It's not going to happen to us. We're going to keep them out. I'm banning flights from London as soon as I can.* It hasn't happened yet but a growing part of me is worried that my return ticket for a flight home will lose any power to get me there. As I stare up at the imposing white stone of Whitehall I'm overcome by a wave of homesickness. What am I doing here? I could be in my lovely garden back home, picking tomatoes and spinach and scallions from the soil for my dinner. Instead I shiver as I'm led through the door into a vast hallway and through a never-ending warren of corridors.

I'm still wondering why Dr. Kitchen's office is in this massive building when the door to a conference room opens and I'm being introduced by an English man who's saying something about a delegation from the CDC. Oh, excellent, there must be someone else more senior here.

Sixteen sets of eyes look at me expectantly. I look around the room eagerly waiting for my fellow American to stand up and introduce themselves to me. Dr. Kitchen—I assume that's him anyway—says, "Elizabeth? Elizabeth Cooper? It is you, isn't it?"

Shit. They think, wait, no. What? They think I'm the CDC delegation.

"Yes, it's me," I say dumbly and, as I always do when I'm nervous, smile as though friendliness can solve even the most challenging of professional debacles. *Get it together Elizabeth, Jesus Christ.* "Apologies, I'm a little jet-lagged. Let me just grab a cup of coffee and . . ."

A cup of coffee appears in front of me and I'm sitting at the table and Dr. Kitchen is looking at me as though I'm meant to be saying something but I have absolutely no idea what. This is literally a stress dream I've had before, coming true. Dr. George Kitchen, according to his biography on the UCL website where he is a professor, has two PhDs, in the genetic abnormalities leading to susceptibility to infection and vaccine development. Why is he looking at me like *I* have the answers?

"Ms. Cooper, what is your background?" asks a small, curly-haired lady who looks thoroughly unimpressed with me. I try to read the card on the table in front of her with her name and job title on it as subtly as possible. *Mary Denholm, Health Secretary.* Great. I'm looking like an idiot in front of one of the most powerful politicians in the UK.

"I'm a pathologist at the CDC, specializing in virus identification and vaccine development," I say, omitting the word "junior" from my job title. "I have a PhD from Stanford in vaccine development, and I'm here to do whatever I can to help."

"Perfect," Mary says. "You're exactly the kind of person we need. What other resources are the CDC providing?"

Absolutely nothing besides me? "I think that's still not been decided. For now, it's just me." I'm not normally the kind of person who implies that the national organization she works for might be providing help that it absolutely doesn't intend to, but it seems to placate her.

Dr. Kitchen shoots me a grateful smile and then I get it. Understanding dawns; I'm not here to help, not really. He doesn't need me. He needs the impression that the CDC is helping. Part of me is completely baffled that, in a time of crisis, the political showmanship that's endemic in public institutions is still happening. Part of me is impressed he's so quickly managed to manipulate me without even saying a word.

I remember that his biography also mentioned he used to be a psychiatrist before switching to infectious diseases. Go figure.

I quickly gather that the task force that has been set up between Public Health England and the Hospital for Infectious Disease has nothing. A series of old white men in suits, professors at the best universities in England, give presentations in impenetrable language. The messages could be summarized as: we don't know why it only affects men, we don't have a cure yet, we haven't even figured out the beginning of a vaccine because this virus multiplies 1.8 times faster than HIV and we've only just started to identify enough men who are suspected to be immune to test their blood and DNA to see if the key to a vaccine or treatment is in immunity, if it even exists.

Mary is growing gradually paler and paler while I'm becoming more and more panicked. This is a proper, all-out disaster. This has the potential for Armageddon. The life cycle of the virus is chilling in its efficiency. For two days the infected male walks around asymptomatic, passing the virus on every time he coughs, wipes his nose and places his hand on a surface, kisses someone's cheek. The symptoms begin on day three. Death occurs on or by day five. You would struggle to design a virus better suited to quickly spreading through and ravaging the human population.

Thankfully, the health secretary is a woman so she'll be able to provide consistency throughout this crisis, but based on her questions, it quickly becomes clear that she has no concept of how long it will take to develop a working vaccine. I would be surprised if she has a grasp of eighth-grade biology. She was probably a lawyer or something before going into politics.

"Wait, so you're telling me, hang on," Mary interrupts the man making the speech about immunity—a professor of epigenetics at Imperial College London—and stands up. It looks like she's going to walk out of the meeting, she's so upset. The room collectively holds its breath. "You're telling me that you, the people with the answers, the greatest minds in this country and beyond, have nothing. That I have to go back to the House of Commons and just say 'Oh well, boys will keep dying, hug your sons, it might not be long!'"

I stand up too because it feels weird that she's the only person standing around the table and everyone has gone silent. I suppose, even in the midst of the worst public health emergency the country has seen since the bubonic plague, she's still their boss. I explain that the virus is incredibly powerful and mutates with a regularity that makes it far more like the HIV virus than the flu. There are three different ways that a vaccine against a virus can be created. Firstly, you can change the genes of the virus so that it replicates poorly. Secondly, you can destroy the genes of the virus so that it doesn't replicate at all. Thirdly, you can use a part of the virus but not all of it, which means that it can't replicate.

This virus replicates so quickly that the first two options are basically out of the question. That leaves the third option but that takes time. You have to identify the blueprint of the virus, all while it's still mutating.

"Well, what about the men who are immune?" she asks. I try to ignore the break in her voice. "Surely they hold the solution. He's just said he thinks around one in ten men are immune. There's lots of men you can surely . . ." She trails off because she doesn't understand the science and she's essentially begging me to tell her that everything is going to be okay.

"They could be part of the solution," I reply, trying to be as diplomatic as I can. "But there's a lot of work still to be done. It's no one's fault. It's the virus." And that's the end of her questions. She just sits through the rest of the presentations as if she's a statue.

The meeting comes to an end with a whimper. Mary's whisked away. Dr. Kitchen comes up to me, muttering apologies before stopping several feet away from me: social distancing 101.

"I am so, so, so sorry. She'd been talking for about fifteen minutes at the start of the meeting about how important international cooperation is and she interpreted my saying you would be here as more than it is." He smiles a crinkly, tired smile. Despite myself, and still smarting from my panic earlier, I can't help but like him. He has a kind face.

"Forgive me?"

"Forgiven, but only if you take me to lunch. Dr. Kitchen, I'm starving, and I have a lot of questions."

"Done, and please, call me George."

We leave the oppressive stillness of Whitehall and grab a table outside a pizza restaurant despite the freezing December weather. No man should be in a public enclosed space right now. George cleans the table with a wipe before sitting. I push my chair so we're two meters apart. "I'm not going to eat if that's all right by you," George says as I head inside to collect my pizza.

A few minutes later I'm back. "So, how bad is it?" I ask.

"The risk of infection is high and this virus has an extraordinary staying power. It can stay alive on a surface for up to thirty-eight hours."

I swallow a lump of pizza and try not to gawp at him. "Thirty-eight hours?"

"Indeed."

"Did you think she would be so hopeful? Mary, that is."

George is silent for a few moments and then shakes his head. "It's not the first time I've dealt with a response like that. I'd hoped she would be a bit more practical and engaged but it's shock. People, even those high up in government, will pin their hopes on the 'magical task force' as if scientists can whip up a solution out of thin air. But she just doesn't have a clue about how difficult this all is."

I manage a thin smile. "They never do."

George tips his head in acknowledgment. "When us scientists and virologists and doctors and the people who really *know* this stuff explain that actually it's far worse than they had even dared to fear, they freeze."

"You're a very tolerant man."

He barks out a laugh. "I'm not, but I used to be a shrink so I'm used to unreasonable behavior. Compared to what I've seen, Mary's little outburst was nothing."

"I'll stay as long as you need me," I offer, on impulse, but I mean it. This is the place where we're possibly going to save the world. They need all the hands, and brains, they can get.

"Thank you, Elizabeth," George says, and I get the bill and jump in a taxi. I've been booked into a horrible hotel on Euston Road. It's called a Premier Inn. Based on the photos online, there's a lot of purple in their interior decoration and I'm going to leave it at that because it's too depressing for words.

I start work tomorrow in one of the labs at the Hospital for Infectious Disease. George has assigned me to the team trying to identify exactly which part of the virus allows it to impact men but not women, even though women are hosts. That's the key thing that's allowing it to spread so fast. When half of the population is walking around, symptomless, carrying and spreading the virus, you're in trouble. And we are.

I e-mail my boss at the CDC and tell him I won't be coming back in three weeks' time. I don't care what his response will be; some things are more important. I include in my e-mail a long description of today's meeting. I'm trying to convey how unbelievably bad this is going to get and as I'm typing, I catch my breath.

My dad. My dad is in Jackson. It's not close to Europe, sure, but this virus is going to make its way to the US soon if it hasn't already. There have already been a few reports of the occasional case and surely it'll mushroom in the next few days.

Indecision immediately strikes. I should go home. No, I should stay here. I need to see my dad. I need to be here to help. He's my *family*. This is more important.

I send my dad a long e-mail setting out basic infection risk protocols. He's not to use public transportation or cabs. He's not to eat at restaurants or order takeout food. He's to stay in the house as much as he can and not meet up with anyone else. *Just stay inside with Mom*, I instruct. My dad has always responded better to shows of strength than what he sees as feminine pleading.

My boss replies. I already know what the e-mail is going to say before I open it but it's still a blow.

From: Garry Anderson (G.Anderson@cdc.gov) to
Elizabeth Cooper (E.Cooper@cdc.gov)
9:36 p.m. on December 10, 2025

Hi Liz,

Glad you arrived safe. I hear what you're saying but there's no way we can spare anyone right now. Let's see how things progress in London and then, if more resources are required in a month, we can consider sending three CDCers over to provide some assistance.

The focus here is more on helping the administration to shut down travel and identify cases quickly. The president's keen to minimize movement across the Atlantic and we think that's the right path.

Stay safe,
Garry

*It's not me who's in danger here, Garry!* Part of me is pathetically grateful for the offer of help but it's not enough. It's a dismissal, really.

At least they don't seem to think I'm exaggerating the problem. They're just going after one small part of the solution. It's too simplistic. Pandemics can't be kept out. It doesn't work like that, not anymore.

Before I turn off the light to sleep, I do something I've been meaning to all day. I read all the headlines from the big English news sites. The *Guardian*: "Department of Health assures public it is working on a vaccine." The *Telegraph*: "Marty Denhold says to stay calm; death toll reaches 100,000." The *Sun*: "You Try and Stay Calm, Mary, Men Are Dying." *The Times*: "Amanda Maclean follow-up: The doctor who raised the alarm accuses the WHO of negligence."

I try to sleep but despite the heaviness of jet lag there's a fog of panic. My thoughts are circling. Dad. Vaccine. George. Mary. No vaccine. Just starting. Dad. Dad. What will happen to my dad?

PANIC

# ARTICLE IN THE *WASHINGTON POST* ON DECEMBER 15, 2025

## "The Plague is here and someone should have warned you"

### by Maria Ferreira

This article is not going to be like any other article you've ever read in this paper or, most likely, in any other. I might as well get that straight here at the beginning. It is going to be told in the first person even though this is not the Comments section. It has not been edited by the editor or deputy editor because I went above their heads to seek permission from the owner of this paper to publish it. Now that's out of the way, I'm going to set out my credentials so you know the kind of journalist you're dealing with here. I've been nominated for the Pulitzer Prize twice (a prize that, I guarantee you, is not going to go ahead this year or next year or the year after that for reasons you're about to read), I have a master's degree in journalism from Columbia University, I am a former science editor for this paper and I have carried out more than twenty investigations into thorny, difficult issues with corruption and secrecy at the heart of them.

After seventeen years as a journalist, this is the most terrifying article I have ever had to write. The basic message is that your dad is going to die, your brother is going to die, your son is going to die, your husband is going to die, every man you've ever loved and/or slept with is going to die. Let me take you back to the beginning. This all started in early November 2025, not that most of you, our US-based readers, will know this. I knew there was something big going on because Twitter and Facebook over in the UK were hives of anxiety and panic. If you take one thing from this article, let it be that we should all have been talking about this a lot earlier. A doctor in Scotland named Amanda Maclean wrote in to newspapers, posted online, generally screamed into the void that there was a pandemic starting. She originally identified the virus and treated the person who is informally referred to as Patient Zero.

Amanda had a letter published in *The Times* on November 12. Now, immediately I thought that was weird. What kind of respected, senior ER doctor has to write in to a newspaper to tell the population about a pandemic? It shows that there's something being covered up. The letter was published on the newspaper's website and went viral on certain, often paranoid, parts of Twitter and Reddit.

I asked the CDC to make a statement on November 16 and received a "No comment" response. That was the second oddity about the whole situation. If someone's got their facts mixed up, you can just release a statement saying that they're wrong. But they didn't do that or say any of their usual comforting lines about "Confirming in due course once we have more information," or even "There is no reason to panic." Not being told not to panic made me panic.

Then, on November 20, Amanda Maclean was interviewed in *The Times*. She used the term "the Plague" to describe the virus affecting, by that point, much of Scotland (only the Highlands were so far largely unaffected); a virus, she claimed, with an almost guaranteed mortality rate, only affecting men but carried by women, easily transmitted and beginning with two days in which men were asymptomatic. The UK press went into meltdown at the news.

You might be wondering why I didn't report on this before now, and the answer is that my boss, the editor of the *Washington Post*, didn't want me to, which is ironic when you consider the fact that he is the one at risk of dying from this disease, not me. He didn't want to risk panicking people unnecessarily, especially as national and international institutions haven't made statements. And there's a lot of domestic political drama going on at the moment and he wants me to dig out a past indiscretion for every congressman from Texas to Ohio. Normally, I love that stuff. Hold powerful men accountable for their past transgressions? No problem. Burn down the patriarchy one corrupt politician at a time? Sign me up!

But this story is life or death. This story is the story, quite possibly, of the end of the world. It cannot wait any longer. I think my editor, and lots of other men who are gatekeepers to information around the world, are terrified. They are so frozen by panic that they can't bear to look reality in the face. So I'm here to do their job for them.

In the three and a half weeks since Amanda's interview was published, over one hundred thousand British men have died. Hundreds of thousands more are likely infected, or will come into contact with an infected man or woman, in the next few days.

The US has so far remained largely unaffected thanks to the government's restriction of flights to and from Europe regardless of whether you're an American citizen, a move as unpopular as it is wise. But this Plague is here. There are reports across the country—in Tampa, Nashville, LA, Little Rock, Newport—of men dying of "sepsis" and "sudden adult death syndrome" and "short, unexpected illnesses." Wake up, people. It is the Plague. Social media in Scotland is a screaming vortex of fear, sickness and people declaring that they are leaving the country despite ever fewer means to do so. Singapore is making changes to its capital control policies, banning the removal of capital by citizens *and* foreigners. The Singaporean government basically offers safety and economic stability in exchange for a very limited say in its governance. This is not just a red flag, it is a massive red cape we should all be watching carefully for the bull just behind it.

I've spoken to Amanda Maclean; she kindly gave me ten minutes of her time yesterday from her home in Glasgow, where she is holed up with her husband and sons. She is an extraordinary woman. She has shown me the e-mails in which she contacted Health Protection Scotland, Public Health England, the WHO, politicians, all of which were ignored. She says there has been incompetence at the highest levels of government in Scotland and England. I don't have the information to prove it one way or another. I have also received—from an anonymous and therefore unverified source—a report written on November 10 by a member of the British Intelligence Services. It sets out in detail the direction the Plague will take—the countries it will spread to, the number of men it will kill and where, and the difficulties of fighting it. According to my sources, the report was ignored by their superiors at MI5, who missed a vital opportunity to control the Plague at an early stage. They are now working in a different job outside of the Intelligence Services. An extract of the report is below:

*The virus appears only to affect men but is carried by women (who do not appear vulnerable to it). This analysis is based on seven days of information about the virus. We understand from social media posts made by Dr. Amanda Maclean—who claims to have treated Patient Zero—that it is not responsive to drugs or medical treatment. She claims it has a high mortality rate, with tons of men dying within twenty-four hours. If this information is correct, it seems inevitable the virus will quickly spread (if it hasn't already) to other major cities in England, Scotland and Wales. The number of international flights leaving Glasgow, Prestwick and Edinburgh airports on a daily basis make the chances of an international spread of the virus very high.*

*Key risks include: civil unrest (police, fire services, paramedics, armed forces, intelligence services all disproportionately male), major economic disruption, high death toll, vulnerability to terrorist attack (due to weakened security services), food shortages.*

*Risk rating: Urgent—requires immediate attention and escalation.*

I'm not a doctor and I don't work for MI5. I don't have any way of verifying this information. What I do know, from years of reporting, is that ignorance, incompetence and fear so often go hand in hand with government that none of us should be surprised if the institutions we thought would keep us safe would in fact be woefully inadequate in the face of a pandemic.

Journalism is an odd mix of the pursuit of truth and knowledge, and going on a hunch. Amanda Maclean is in a similar position.

When you read this story, it will be on the front page of the print edition and our website. I hope that, by the time you finish this article, the story of the Plague finally, *finally,* becomes the only thing that anyone in the US can talk about.

Another way of looking at it is that I am personally trying to succeed in sparking widespread panic and pandemonium.

You're welcome.

------------------------

# DAWN

### London, United Kingdom
### Day 43

"Have you seen the article?" Zara, my boss, looks so angry she's practically swivel-eyed. Yes, I have seen the article. No, I don't want to talk about it. Best to play dumb until I can decide what to do.

"The fucking *Washington Post* article. How is it, Dawn,"—give me strength, you don't need to repeat my name, Zara—"that a reporter in the United States of fucking America has managed to simultaneously make us look incompetent and corrupt, as though we knew there was a problem that we refused to fix and couldn't have fixed it even if we tried?"

"The mind reels," I murmur. What else is there to say? The British Intelligence Services have been cut off at the knees by the Plague but the article is painful to read because it's partly true.

We've been playing catch-up for weeks as the country descends into chaos around us. If only I could go back and shake myself when we first started hearing reports of an infectious disease in Scotland. WAKE UP, DAWN, I want to scream. THIS WILL BE WORSE THAN YOU CAN POSSIBLY IMAGINE.

Alas, hindsight is twenty-twenty. Balls, Zara is still looking murderous. I need to be careful. I've been working here for over thirty-five years and yet, still, I'm careful. Always. I was the only black woman recruited into the program in my year. I'm almost always the only person of color, and often the only woman—what a double whammy!—in a meeting. I suppress a frustrated sigh. Maybe I'm too old for this nonsense. I'm retiring in six weeks, the day I turn sixty, not that she knows that. I'm going to tell her in a fortnight and if she's not on board with it I'll quit regardless, if we don't have martial law by then. I've got a cottage by the sea, enough cans stocked up to last me six months and very few shits left to give.

Nonetheless, while I'm still here, I need to be kind. Zara is scared and grieving, so Zara's not really herself. I've worked with her for over a decade. She's changed completely. Can I blame her? Her husband died last week, followed by her son a few days later. Her daughter is only fifteen, reeling from the loss of a father and brother, but we are public servants. There is no such thing as time off in a public crisis. So, not only is Zara grieving but she's also feeling the mammalian urge to be with her child in the face of danger.

"I'll draft up a response," I say with a polite calm I don't feel and trudge to my desk (small office on the second floor, no natural light—depressing to say the least). The defenses start rolling through my head like a ticker tape. It just didn't seem to be in our authority. *Not in your authority? How could a global pandemic not be the responsibility of the security services?* Well, funny you should ask that, journalist lady whom I really dislike right now, but pretty bloody easily actually. We're not doctors, we're intelligence analysts. My job within this organization is to convince my superiors—who used to be two men called Hugh and Jeremy, RIP—that there is in fact a credible threat that only we can address. *Well surely you should be safe rather than sorry?* Again! Maria, you'd think so, wouldn't you? But we're not made of money and we can't throw our weight around like bulls in Pamplona. And, might I add, there's a not-so-little organization called the WHO, which has basically done sweet fuck all for the past two months. Shouldn't they have been sounding the alarm, not us?

*So why didn't you spring into action when it did become obvious that this was a disaster?* Because by that point, *Maria,* it was too late. The critical mass of infection occurred so quickly we didn't know what had hit us until we were reduced to glorified damage limitation. I will grant you that we should have clocked sooner that the low recovery rate and the fact it only affects men means it creates unique security concerns. Police, army, navy, fire services, paramedics, security services; primarily male professions each and every one.

*And what about the MI5 report? The one that I've so damningly excerpted in my article that shows that a female intelligence analyst brought the Plague to her superior's attention back on November 10 only for her to be ignored and dismissed so thoroughly that she quit and, according to my source, is now working as a policeman in rural England.* First of all, I would ask how you got your hands on that report and remind your source there is such a thing as the Official Secrets Act. And beyond that, Maria, I've got nothing. That analyst—and yes, of course I know who she is—was right. Her report predicts the consequences of the Plague with eerie precision, but I can't change the past.

Her supervisor was a sexist asshole called David Bird, and if it makes you feel any better he's dead now, so. There's that. We discovered her report last week, right around the same time as you did, I imagine, and I'm sure it's very vindicating for her, but it's not going to change anything now.

As satisfying as it is fighting with Maria Ferreira in my head, I have actual work to do. While I'm still here, I might as well make myself useful. A briefing paper the size of a waffly PhD thesis is sitting in my inbox. It starts with the death reports. Two more assistants dead, one senior director, six analysts. Of course, we're assuming they're dead.

They might just have slunk home to await their fate, and I can't say I blame them. It's more efficient to assume they're dead, as statistically they soon will be. The next section is what I like to think of as whack-a-mole. Every day I fight ten fires, and then the next day ten more appear.

Every other country is the same. The international section of the report provides some chilling news about the speed of transmission in France and some typically organized German responses that I'll keep an eye on to see if they actually help. All of our key allies are fighting to keep their heads above water—to keep unrest at bay, ensure domestic terror threats are managed and ensure that, as far as possible, intelligence and security services keep functioning. On the plus side, it turns out that male terrorists are as petrified as the rest of the population. And happily, terrorists are men most of the time. The surveillance that we're maintaining at a minimal level is finding that terror cells are breaking up and fleeing. We think a few hundred have left London, and about 110 have disappeared from Birmingham. I can only imagine they're unlikely to still be alive, which brings me absolutely no sadness whatsoever.

The media reports section is a painful read. The newspapers have had a field day. "The authorities ignored the problem," they're saying. But I'm still unsure as to what exactly it is that we could have done. Pushed for research earlier into a vaccine? We're not scientists. Warned people? Our role is to minimize unrest and panic, not create it. Perhaps we could have quarantined the sick, but women were hosts. I don't see how we could have kept enough people away from each other in a country with seventy-plus million people, and thousands of people flying in and out every day, to make much of a difference unless it was done in the first, critical few days.

But that's not a very PR-friendly answer. I'm meant to apologize profusely as though I personally concocted the disease and spread it to the British population myself at night like the BFG. So instead I write a brief press statement that's as vague as it is unhelpful.

*The security services are working tirelessly to minimize unrest and keep the British people safe. We will continue to provide updates as and when we know more.*

I've always been good at drafting press statements. The carefully constructed neutrality I convey lends itself to press statements that are unobjectionable. Whenever my daughter asks me what my job is like, I say that my job isn't just boring, my job is to *be* boring. Or at least it was, until the world imploded. We're doing what we can, and it's not enough, of course it's not, but I can say without any blight on my conscience that we're doing what could be expected in extraordinary circumstances. This is like a biblical flood or an extinction. This is not normal. Everyone's going to blame the authorities and we're going to take it because that's our jobs. But we are just about managing to survive as a nation, and at the moment, that's as good as it's going to get.

# CLARE

**San Francisco**
**Day 48**

Everyone in San Francisco has had the same three ideas. To go home to wherever they're from, to go north to Canada or to go east to the desert. But it's too late.

I walk through the airport, being jostled and thrown about by people rushing, rushing, rushing. It doesn't matter that I'm in a police uniform. What am I going to do, yell at them? Everyone is running away from death. They're not scared of me.

There's a huge crowd of people beneath every flight board. The red words, "Canceled, Canceled, Canceled," are bleeding down the screens. Every few minutes another flight goes from "Delayed" to "Canceled" and a group of people groan and yell. Not enough pilots are here to fly the planes and half the countries in the world have closed their borders so the flights can't land. The world is closing down.

I keep walking around the airport, ostensibly to "keep the peace" and "calm down any disagreements." But the place has the feeling of a lit match edging itself toward a pool of gasoline. The city's ready to burst. The tech bubble has officially popped. When the world's financial markets are in free fall, the stock value of a tech company that relies on widespread internet connection and an ever-growing middle class and has never actually turned a profit goes down, fast. Billionaires have become millionaires, the value of money has evaporated and this city built on sexism and man's ability to play God through technology is falling apart at the seams.

I need to stay calm, stay strong. I'm a woman. I'm not going to die. I'm always going to have a job as a cop. I cannot be fazed. There are plenty of cops here. The police are focused on the airport as the army deals with inner-city disturbances.

It would be easier though if every single flight was canceled and I could tell people to go home, but there's still a tiny number of flights leaving. A flight switches, accompanied by the chime of an announcement, from "Delayed" to "Boarding," and a horde of people start running toward the gate. The atmosphere shifts, becoming even darker. Everyone is seconds from crying or screaming or both and now they're jealous too. Why does that guy get to fly out of here? Why is that flight leaving? Why not me?

A lot of gun owners are carrying their guns, which makes me antsy at the best of times but now it's terrifying. They have nothing to lose and it makes them feel safer. They're dead men walking and they know it.

I'm walking around a corner when I hear it. The crack of a gunshot. I run toward the sound as everyone else screams and scatters. I hear a splintering sound and look up. Fuck. The man is sitting on the floor, the gun still pointed upward. The glass roof is above him. Fuck. Fuck. Fuck.

Another shot. I hit the floor. The shots keep coming. I look up. Is it the first shooter? No, there's a second man shooting and shooting. Oh God, please stop.

I can hear screams from all over the airport. There's not enough space, there'll be a stampede. My colleague Andrew arrives and shoots the second shooter in the arm. I get ahold of myself, get off the floor and shoot the first shooter in the shoulder. At the same time, Andrew shoots him in the head. More armed men are arriving, guns up and loaded. No, this can't be happening. This can't be happening.

Andrew goes down. The second shooter is shooting at him. No, no, no. I shoot, aiming for his head, praying I get him before he turns on me. Please God, don't turn around. Please let me survive this.

# AMANDA

My boys are dying. I sit by their bedside, the two of them side by side in what used to be Will's and my bed, watching them in disbelief. I should be amazed that they lasted this long. I've been exposed to the virus since November 1, the day I came home having treated Patient Zero, although I managed to keep away from them mostly, or so I thought. They've lasted eight weeks. They haven't been to school or left the house, but I had to. We were running out of food so I had to leave. I was as careful as I could be, sterilizing cans in the garage before bringing them in the house, touching no one for days afterward, but the Plague spreads easily and fast. I don't know exactly how it works, how long it survives on a surface. I can't see it or smell it or taste it. It could be anywhere. It could have been me all along.

When Charlie first came down with a fever, he knew what was happening. He said to me, "Mum, I don't understand, we haven't gone anywhere," and I didn't know how to respond. *I don't know, my darling boys. I don't know how this happened. I must have caught it when I went outside. I must be a host. I must have gotten too close to you. I'm so sorry.*

Will is downstairs now, drinking tea. He cannot bear to be in this room and watch the consequences of what he thinks he has done. He's convinced he's responsible for the boys being sick even though I've told him, again and again, that we don't know. We'll never know. It might not have been him, but nothing I say makes a difference. He is overwhelmed by guilt. He's not even the Catholic one of the two of us but then again, what do I have to feel guilty for? I did everything I could. Will went into the vipers' nest of the hospital and who knows what he brought back?

No matter what I tell him, the times he left this house and went to the hospital he put our boys in danger. But it might also be me, and that uncertainty kills me a tiny bit more every day. I can see the beginnings of insanity from here. In the delirium of old age, I will forget lots of things, maybe my children's names and Will's face and that I used to be a doctor, but I won't forget this. Was it me? Was it him? Who is to blame? You? Me? No one.

Charlie and Josh are dying in front of me and there's nothing anyone can do about it. They look like twins. They practically are twins, only thirteen months apart. My lovely, clever, kind boys. They're both now weaving in and out of consciousness. If I had morphine I would give it to them. It would speed things up but it would reduce the discomfort. They're having occasional hallucinations from the fever, panting words about footballs and rabbits and the other nonsense the delirious come out with. I phoned my friend Ann and asked her, a few days ago when the symptoms began, what I could do treatment wise. "Oh, Amanda, I'm so—"

I cut her off.

"Ann, we can't do this. I don't need that. I just need to know what you did for Ian to make it easier."

Ann is the finest palliative care doctor I know. She works in a hospice an hour away in Dumbarton. Her work is calm, contemplative and caring, everything mine is not. I'm used to high drama, urgency and the willingness to cause pain in the moment to prevent a problem down the road. I am not equipped for this. And yet, her advice was more for me than them. There is nothing for them; without morphine, it's just cold washcloths to ease the fevers and spoonfuls of water to quench the raging thirst. Ann's advice was for me to stay calm and in the present. She said being there for them is more important than anything. Don't think about the future without them. Don't reflect on what you could have done differently in the past. Treasure this time and be a soothing balm for their panicked, fractured minds riddled with pain.

I heard her and I listened but it is impossible for my mind to stay in this room. It's too painful. I keep thinking back to their childhoods for some relief, taking myself back in a haze to the times when they were happy and safe and had so many more years ahead of them than behind them. Doubts creep in inevitably to ruin the daydream. Is there anything I would do differently? Should I have given up work? Was it worth it, all those hours away from them? I could have been with them every day, every night, I should have been. But how was I to know? I could never have known.

I want to go back and do it all over again. Seeing the lines on the pregnancy tests and screaming with joy. Feeling their kicks and movements as they stretched in my tummy at the beginning of the day. Waddling around Mothercare the first time, bewildered and panic-buying things that promised sleep. The second time, exhausted, carrying a toddler and panic-buying toys that promised peace. I want to go back and tell myself every day for all those years to enjoy every second. I thought it would be endless. I assumed the good fortune of seeing my children grow up.

I dropped them off at nursery every morning and some days I would be so relieved to have peace I would beam as I walked down the street. I'm off to work! I'd be so thrilled to be absolving myself of the responsibility of looking after tiny humans. I left them to look after other people, to care for other parents' sick children. They've spent years at school, I've been calculating. Not just school years but actual years. They've spent thousands of hours away from me. All that time is gone. I want to do it again. I want it all back. Please God, let them come back from the brink. Give them back to me. Please.

# CATHERINE

**C**atherine."

Anthony never calls me by my full name. I immediately get up from the floor, where I'm trying to play with Theodore without touching him or being less than three feet away from him, and go to the hallway where Anthony is hovering. He doesn't come near Theodore at all anymore. Hasn't for days. The Christmas lights from Christmas are still up behind him, twinkling incongruously, almost insulting in their cheerfulness.

"I have a temperature."

On instinct I put my hand to his forehead. It is burning with the kind of heat that in a different life would have inspired a swift call to a GP and, if not better within a few hours, a frantic trip to A and E.

"I'm so sorry," he says to me and my heart cracks a little more in the slow process of its breaking that began last week when we agreed that if Anthony had a fever, that telltale sign It Was Here, we would not see each other again. Not in this life, at least. It is the only way to keep Theodore safe and prevent the spread of this vicious disease. We discussed it calmly last week before bursting into tears and holding each other, despite the danger, the mere thought of what it would involve too horrifying for words. A slow, painful death alone for him.

The torture of my husband being close, and yet unreachable, in this house as his body fails him. No more kisses, no more hugs, never again feeling the touch of his warm, broad shoulders under my fingers, or seeing his frame walking into the kitchen, before he looks up at me with a smile. It will be a bereavement in slow motion, knowing he is dying just feet above my head in the bedroom upstairs.

The moment is here but I'm not ready. Give me another week, another day, another hour. We haven't had long enough. We were meant to have a life together, grow old together, have more children together. It can't be ending yet. Please.

"You have to stay away from me, keep Theodore safe," Anthony says, his voice cracking within three words. His forehead already has a sheen of sweat. I have been strong for so many weeks, smiled through Christmas, but now, on the darkest day of my life, I have to say goodbye to my husband and I'm not ready. I'm never going to be ready to live without him.

"I'm not ready." I burst into shaking sobs, the awfulness of this washing over me. We are living a nightmare so painful it never even would have occurred to me to fear it. I'm meant to be with him in sickness and in health, not saying good-bye, abandoning him. Anthony reaches out to me instinctively and then drops his arms. The pain of proximity without being able to touch each other.

"Why is this happening?" I ask him, such an unfair question. He doesn't know any more than I do.

"I don't know, darling. I don't know. Just know I love you. I have always loved you."

I don't know what to say, wanting the last moment together to last forever. We stand, looking at each other in the hallway. So many memories of us in this place. Anthony opening the door carefully as we brought Theodore home from the hospital. Hundreds of blissful, ordinary days of putting wellies on our rosy-cheeked toddler, shrieking instructions at each other as we try to leave for a flight, rushing out the door with a quick kiss, waving good-bye to the babysitter as we leave for an anniversary dinner with the excitement of teenagers. How can it all come to this? It can't end like this, with a good-bye, at the bottom of the stairs, with tears and not even a kiss.

And yet it is. Theodore is calling me from the living room.

"Mummy, I want the blocks." The blocks are on the third shelf in the living room. He can't reach them on his own. If I don't go in, he'll come out here and the danger is too great.

"I love you," I say and he nods, smiling sadly.

"I know."

"Do you feel loved?" I ask, desperately elongating this good-bye, reminding us both of a back-and-forth we would whisper at night under sheets or on buses or walking around Oxford, wrapped up together when we first fell in love.

"So loved," he says. "Do you feel loved?"

"More than you can imagine."

"I have to go now," he says softly. He turns and starts walking slowly up the stairs, before looking back down at me and blowing a kiss from the safety of the eighth step. His handsome, tired, perfect face is all I can see as he moves away from me.

"I love you," I call again, one final time.

"I love you too." Our bedroom door closes with a thud.

I sink down to the floor and let out a wail of grief, unable to contain it. This can't be happening. It was inevitable and yet I hoped. Maybe, maybe we would be spared. Someone has to be immune. Why not us? Why couldn't it have been us?

"Mummy, Mummy, what's wrong with Mummy?"

Theodore is in the hallway with me, patting my hair the way I soothe him when he is upset. Tears are streaming down my face and dripping off my nose as I look my gorgeous boy in the eyes. His face is a picture of a concern. I wipe my nose. I need to keep him safe and that means keeping him away from me. In my life now, it seems, my love must express itself at a distance. I sigh and shoo Theodore into the living room. Now, all I can do is wait.

# MORVEN

A small farm next to the Cairngorms National Park,
the Independent Republic of Scotland
Day 63

Jamie pants as he runs up next to me, having dashed across the garden from the house. "Mum, it's the phone for you."

"Who is it, love?" He shrugs and I resist the urge to nag him about taking a message, or at least asking who's calling. He runs off, skinny as a string bean, to go find his dad, who's somewhere in the fields. I trudge back to the house, delighting in the quiet. After years of running a hostel, I had thought I was used to the low-level chaos that came with guests, bags and travel, but I wasn't. The silence and safety of my blissfully empty house is an ongoing source of joy. We have battened down the hatches, we have crops, water and medicine. I have my husband and my son, safe and sound. All will be well.

"Morven Macnaughton?"

"Yes, speaking."

"My name is Oscar. I work in the civil service. I'm phoning regarding the Highland Evacuation Program."

"The what?"

Oscar's voice is impatient. He sounds exhausted and explains in a rush, "The Highland Evacuation Program. We're evacuating teenage boys from urban areas to remote areas of the Highlands with good food and water supplies." Oh God, they're going to take Jamie. They're going to take my boy away. "Your family has been assigned as a host family in the program and due to the space in your hostel, you have been assigned a more significant number of boys than most families. Can you please confirm you are no longer taking hostel guests?"

I'm spluttering, making odd guttural noises and the concept of turning a sound into a word feels impossible. This can't be happening. We're safe here.

"No," I finally get out. "No guests and no. No, we won't take them. I won't do that. My son is safe here. No."

"That's not an option, Mrs. Macnaughton. It's a criminal offense to fail to abide by the requirements of the program."

"Since when?"

"Since yesterday, when the legislation was passed in Holyrood. The boys should arrive in one to two hours' time. More information will be provided to you when they arrive." He hangs up and I scream in frustration. No, no, no, no, no, no. I want to put my head in my hands and weep at the unfairness of it all. We have it all planned, we would escape relatively unscathed, or so we thought. We would wait it out, eat the vegetables we grow in the patch, eat the chickens' eggs, drink the milk from four cows, eat meat as it became available. We have a stash of antibiotics and plenty of first aid equipment. Everything was going to be fine.

The government of the Independent Republic of Scotland has other ideas.

I don't have long. Jamie. I need to keep Jamie safe. I run out to the fields screaming Jamie's and Cameron's names until I'm hoarse. Within minutes they're running toward me, terrified, chorusing *What's wrong? What is it?*

"The government is evacuating teenage boys. They're sending them here, to us." Cameron's face falls like a stone through water while Jamie's twists into a frown.

"They can't do that, we're safe here," he says, outrage tinging every syllable with scorn.

"But they are. We have to keep you safe."

"The hut," Cameron says. "It's right by the stream, it's far away enough." Yes, it's perfect. It's secure enough to survive however many months that Jamie must be away from us. We can deliver food a hundred meters away and never touch him. My heart lurches. Never touch Jamie, no hug, no ruffling his hair. No, I don't have time for this. The grief can be felt later.

We race around the house packing together everything we can think of. Sleeping bag, blankets, cooking equipment, books, magazines, walkie-talkie, medicine. Everything someone could need to survive alone.

An hour and a half later we hear the rumble of a coach on the gravel in the driveway. "You have to go now, son," Cameron says. Jamie has a huge pack on his back; it must weigh almost as much as he does. One of us has to stay here to deal with the arrivals.

"You go," I say to Cameron. "Go, get him settled." I grab Jamie and hug him so hard Cameron has to wrench me away again. "I love you."

"I love you too, Mum." He waves as he heads off to be alone and wait this awful disease out. His shoulders are set with determination and this attempt to be adult in the midst of fear cracks my heart open.

I walk up to the side of the house, swiping away treacherous tears. Teenage boys are starting to make their way off a coach. They all look terrified, cold and very young.

"Hello, I'm Morven," I call out. It's not these boys' fault that they've been sent here, away from their homes and families.

One of the boys hands me an envelope in shaking, cold hands.

*Dear Mr. and Mrs. Macnaughton,*

*Thank you for your cooperation in the Highland Evacuation Program. This is a government-mandated program requiring remote, safe locations to house uninfected boys aged between fourteen and eighteen for the duration of the Plague. You have been tasked with caring for seventy-eight boys aged fifteen and sixteen until a vaccine or cure is found and the boys can be safely reintroduced to their homes. Please see their names and addresses in Appendix 1, enclosed.*

*It is essential that you do not leave your property. A food delivery will be provided to you in a number of days, followed by additional monthly deliveries, and we understand that you have good food supplies on your property. Until a vaccine is discovered, these boys must be kept isolated to eliminate the risk of infection. Each of the boys you are caring for has been monitored for symptoms of the Plague virus.*

*Each boy has been provided with a package of supplies. If you need further supplies you should call 0141 954 8874. Please do not call this number to request further information. Additional information will be provided to you as and when it is available.*

*When a vaccine is created, the Scottish government will prioritize the boys within your care to ensure the quick return of them to their families.*

*Please note that as per the emergency legislation passed by the Scottish Parliament, the punishment for breaching the requirements of caregivers in the Highland Evacuation Program is a prison sentence of up to thirty years.*

*Yours faithfully,*
*Sue O'Neill*

"Right, boys," I say in the most cheerful tone I can muster. "Let's get you settled in."

# CATHERINE

*Eulogy for Anthony Lawrence—January 8, 2026*

Anthony and I met on the first day of Freshers' week at Oxford University in September 2010. Having been at a girls' boarding school for seven years, I was absolutely determined to have fun. I was going to kiss as many boys as possible and run rampant around Oxford. I would be wild.

Within twenty-four hours of arriving at Oxford, I had a boyfriend. I don't think Anthony knew that he was my boyfriend back then. We met in the college bar, and I made cheerful, devoted conversation with him all evening. I essentially invited myself to his room for the night and decided, the next morning, that he was my boyfriend. At some point he must have agreed this was a good plan because for the next fifteen years, we built a life together. We never spent a night apart if we could possibly help it.

It's easy to describe Anthony by his achievements and most obvious attributes. His First in Computer Science from Oxford. His handsome face and warm smile. His job, working in . . . I'm going to be really honest here and say that I know it had something to do with software and he was very good at it but that's about the extent of my knowledge. Maybe it's not so easy for me to describe Anthony from his achievements after all. You'll all have to take my word for it that they were boundless.

The more important things though are those that lots of you might not have seen but that I had the privilege to witness. The devotion with which he would try and buy me the perfect Christmas present every year even though he had absolutely no idea what my taste really was. In fifteen years he managed to buy the most hideous thing in Liberty about twelve times. Sunday mornings starting with a pain au chocolat and a cappuccino delivered to me in bed even though he didn't like hot drinks and preferred toast, but "It's okay," he'd tell me cheerfully. "Gail's is only ten minutes away, I know you like their stuff the best." His footsteps padding downstairs in the middle of the night to put the heating up when I was too cold. His triumphant purchase and surprise delivery of an air conditioner when I was seven months pregnant during a heat wave in May and regularly cried at the sheer unfairness of the temperature. The way he held my hand every night when our son, who arrived not long after the air conditioner did, lay in a NICU four miles away and for weeks I couldn't sleep on my side because of the C-section wound. "I'm right here," he'd say every time I startled awake and cried, inconsolable after my body failed us so spectacularly. His kindness with our son. The stories he would make up about a bear, despite there being a limited number of things bears can feasibly do, every night for six months at our son's request. The way he would always say "Yes" to me when I asked him a question as he was falling asleep. The way he told me when he proposed he would always love me, no matter what, and that lots of people didn't think they could promise to love someone forever but he honestly could, really truly, he promised. "How could I not?" he said. The way he knew, even when we were teenagers and he had no right to such wisdom, that love is more than fireworks and declarations. It is steady, certain sureness. It is knowing that you are loved. It is knowing that you are not alone.

I don't have a family. My parents died in a car crash when I was ten. My godmother looked after me in the holidays and I went to boarding school during term. I think I knew, as soon as I saw Anthony all those years ago, that he would be my family. I could have a family of my own built from the ground up. But I didn't want it unless it was with him. Everything was better with him around.

I'm not going to spend too much time talking about the Plague. I want Anthony to be defined by his life, not his death. I wish we hadn't spent so much time worrying about the Plague before he died. The Plague stole that time from us too. I will say that Anthony faced death with the love, humor and compassion he faced everything else in his life. Somehow, in the days before he fell ill, he still reassured and comforted me. He told me everything would be all right and for the occasional moment, I even believed him.

But everything isn't going to be all right. It'll never really be all right again. I don't want to end with a platitude because Anthony was honest. Never to the point of cruelty, but he was straightforward. He didn't even manage to keep his planned proposal a secret because he didn't like the deceit of it. It's a good thing though that he told me. The original ring he picked was horrendous.

So, I'll leave you with a poem because I can't end my darling husband's eulogy with an insult to his jewelry taste. He loved Edna St. Vincent Mallay so her poetry feels like a fitting end.

*You go no more on your exultant feet*
*Up paths that only mist and morning knew,*
*Or watch the wind, or listen to the beat*

*Of a bird's wings too high in air to view,*
*—But you were something more than young and sweet*
*And fair,—and the long year remembers you.*

---

I switch off the webcam and the screen goes dark. The house feels empty, eerily quiet, with Theodore sleeping in his bed upstairs. Death was never something I considered in great detail until it raged across our lives, but I never would have imagined giving a eulogy from my living room to friends and family on Skype. It doesn't feel like a fitting end to the life of a pet, never mind my husband, Theodore's dad, *Anthony*. The Plague is making its mark even after death.

Anthony's parents are heartbroken not to have had a service but there's nothing we can do. The Public Meetings and Gatherings Act was passed three weeks ago as emergency legislation after the Oxenholme riots. It is out of my hands. Besides, there's still an image in my mind of that poor woman, hugging her two small sons, wailing on the floor as hordes of people swept around a train to London begging to be allowed on. The train was empty. It was being put out of service. Transport around the country is suspended. What's the point in running? Where does everyone think they're running to? There is no safety now. The law makes sense.

Two days after group gatherings were banned, so were burials. The Plague Death Management Act. A technicality in many ways, as the graveyards were filled weeks ago, but a painful certainty nonetheless. Anthony was cremated today, but I will never be given his ashes. They are too risky. And so, he is gone. The warm body of my lovely husband, mine for fifteen years, is gone. No gravestone to choose a quote for. No ashes to keep in an urn and carefully scatter over the Cornwall beach on which we said our vows on a sunny, blustery day in September all those years ago. There is nothing left to do but weep, and so, for the first time today, I put my head in my hands and sob for all that is lost. The memories of my past with the love of my life, the happy life we lived as a family and the future we planned and dreamed of. It is all gone, and I don't even have the ashes to show for it.

# ROSAMIE

### Singapore
### Day 66

**M**r. Tai is returning from Macau tonight and the apartment is buzzing with the excitement and terror of his return. Angelica and Rupert are being more clingy than usual; they find it hard having him here. Most of the time he ignores their existence but sometimes, he decides that he needs to see their "progress" as if they're companies.

"They're only children!" I want to yell at him, but I can't do that. I don't even want to think about what would happen if I did that. I'm just the help and that is very clear. This is an apartment with a hierarchy. I'm above the maids but below the cook because he's been here for twenty years and he knows how to make a noodle dish that Mrs. Tai likes and she says no one else makes it the way that he does. Rupert is superior to Angelica even though he's only three and she's five because he's a boy and he's going to take over the business one day.

There's a hush as the call comes in from the driver that Mr. Tai is making his way up in the elevator. Angelica and Rupert are lined up nicely in front of Mrs. Tai, and I'm fifteen feet away because she doesn't like to remind anyone that I spend more time with her children than she does. It's ridiculous that we're making such a celebration about a man coming home. He's so rarely here we practically throw a parade when he walks in the door. The maids sometimes talk about where he is off to—Shanghai, Macau, Toronto, Sydney. The rumor is that he has a mistress in every city but Mrs. Tai doesn't care as long as she has her credit cards. I don't know if I believe that but it's not like we've ever talked about the state of her marriage.

The elevator door opens and immediately I think, Mr. Tai doesn't look so good. He's sweaty and shaking. I have an urgent desire to push him back into the elevator, press the button and get him out of here. He forgets to bring his suitcase into the apartment so one of the maids runs to grab it before the elevator doors close behind him. Mrs. Tai is looking at him quizzically. He says something in Cantonese and she looks at me with her "Take the children" face. I gladly take Angelica and Rupert into the nursery—it's already past their bedtime—and begin the routine of bath, pajamas ("No not those pajamas! I don't like those ones anymore. I'm not a baby!"), book ("I want this book! I don't care which one Rupert wants. I'm not a baby!") and bed. When Mr. Tai comes into the nursery to say good night to Angelica and Rupert, Mrs. Tai is behind him, crying silently. I hope they will go away quickly. They're scaring the children and he might have the Plague. He probably doesn't, surely he doesn't. But if he does, he might give it to Rupert and the risk of that makes me feel sick. That night, he and Mrs. Tai have a big fight. I don't understand what they are saying as they always argue in Cantonese but the next day when I take the children to the kitchen for breakfast, I see that Mr. Tai is nailing wooden planks across the elevator. The sound of the hammer makes me flinch and Rupert keeps asking me what is going on. As I take the children back to the nursery to eat, Mr. Tai turns around and says in a crazy voice, "No one is to enter or leave this house."

For the first time since I arrived in Singapore, my vulnerability here feels poisonous. I can't rip the boards off. I can't leave, I need this job. What am I going to do? Where would I go? What if the Plague ruins my life here? I hadn't thought the Plague was going to be a problem in Singapore. I've heard about it. My mother has been e-mailing me about it, but Singapore is the safest country in the world and they shut the borders to foreign citizens. I thought I would be untouchable like the rich people are, but I'm just the help. I'm nothing to them.

Over the next two days we wait, and wait and wait in an odd pretense that everything is normal. Dressing as normal, eating breakfast as normal, playing with the children as if any of this is normal. We're locked up in the apartment and I don't know whether it's scarier to be in here or out there. After two years as a nanny for the Tai family, I'm so used to being quiet and unquestioning that it didn't even occur to me that I could just . . . leave. As I walked through the lounge first thing this morning, I saw that one of the cooks, Davey, was leaving. He had used knives and his hands to force off the wooden boards Mr. Tai had nailed across the elevator. He asked me if I had seen Mr. Tai today. I said I thought he was still in bed. "In that case," he said and took the Ming vase that sat on the mahogany table by the elevator.

"Take care of yourself," he said as the elevator doors closed.

I waved good-bye to the closed doors and thought Davey was stupid for leaving. As if a vase is going to save him from the Plague. He's the one who should want to stay in here, not me, although the thought hovers around me that the Plague could already be inside the apartment. My throat tightens in fear for Rupert.

I walk around the huge living room, trying to breathe slowly, trailing my fingers along the glass panes that make up one wall of the apartment. When I first started working for the Tais I thought this room, this whole apartment, was the most unbelievable thing I had ever seen. All I knew before I arrived was that a family in Singapore had chosen me from the agency's books. I didn't know that Singaporeans are obsessed with having Filipino nannies because we are seen as the best. I just knew it was better money than I could make at home and the hours weren't too bad. I was nineteen and didn't know any better.

The moment I first met Mrs. Tai I knew she was challenging. The woman at the agency who hired me warned me it would be a shock. She said it was easy to feel resentful at first when they complained about how hard their lives were and talked about wanting more money, more jewelry, more everything. I nodded and thought *Okay, lady,* but I didn't get it. Not until I got here and they had more money than I had ever seen in my life.

They don't wave physical money around, obviously. It's not cash, it's everything. Servants, nannies, cooks. They live in three floors of this huge glass apartment block with the most amazing views. Mrs. Tai goes out shopping every day and comes back with more bags than the maids could carry. Or at least she used to. And then she complained about being tired. Oh, the irony.

Angelica is sitting on the sofa, playing on the iPad. It's only 9:30 a.m. and I'm usually quite strict with iPad time but we're locked up so the normal rules don't apply. It was obvious immediately that I hadn't been hired to be a nanny; I had been hired to be a mother. Mrs. Tai pays the children hardly any attention. She says good morning and good night to them and that's it. I'm there for kissing bruised arms better and pinning their paintings onto the nursery wall and saying, "Yes we can watch *Moana* again but only if we watch *Lilo & Stitch* tomorrow and no we can't have *Frozen* until next week, I don't want to let it go again, that ice lady needs a time-out!" I hear their laughs and their cries and their mumbles in their sleep and I know what temperature Rupert likes the milk he still has at night that I really need to wean him off of, but it's a good source of calcium and I'll let him have it for a few more weeks.

I sit next to Angelica and stroke her hair. I want to ask her how she's feeling but I don't have any answers for the questions she would inevitably ask, so instead I just sit here, hoping my presence is enough. My phone pings for the fourth time in an hour. It's another message from my mother. The Plague is back home in Mati. My mother calls it a *sumpa*, a curse. Her e-mails are hysterical. She doesn't know anything, just that it is a terrible disease and the men are dying. It is scary enough being here but back home, if the power goes out or there are food shortages, there is no way to fix it. I try not to feel worried. At least we are a family of women. I think this every day and it makes everything seem better. My father left when I was small. Our greatest weakness has become a strength. Now, I think, what's the worst that can happen? They will not die. I will not die. We will be okay.

I'm about to go and check on Rupert—he's suspiciously quiet—when I hear a scream and Angelica and I jump up in unison. It's Mrs. Tai, yelling for help in the bedroom. I know what this must mean but I can't bear it. Don't let the Plague be in the apartment, please. Not here.

# LISA

Toronto, Canada

Day 68

"Everybody in my office, we're late, run don't walk."

One of the lab assistants practically sprints into my office, spilling coffee everywhere. Jesus Christ. The screen comes alive as one of the AV people finally gets the TV plugged into the laptop, and we're greeted by a patchwork of faces of various pixilations. I immediately start scanning the screen for faces I recognize. It's hard to see anyone. There's so many on the screen, everyone except Amanda Maclean—the host of this online get-together—is tiny.

"Hello everyone," she says. She has a beautiful voice. I love a Scottish accent. "Thank you for attending this, well, I suppose we'll call it a meeting. I'm not sure what to say other than that I'm here and I'll tell you everything I know, anything I can to help."

Amanda doesn't look good. She has bags under her eyes so deep they're like divots and her eyes have the hollow determination of a religious devotee in a hair shirt. She's losing it. She must have lost her sons and her husband. I'd bet my bottom dollar that's why she's surfaced after her period of silence.

"Are you working on a vaccine?" one of the voices asks.

"No, I work full-time as an A and E doctor in Glasgow. I'm not a virologist, I just happened to treat Patient Zero."

Amanda has the dazed look that people get, ironically, after they make great medical discoveries. Often you see their expression at a press conference and they look like someone just caught them on a jog or something and told them they'd helped save the human race. "What, me? How? No way?" For Amanda, it's the opposite. Talk about being in the wrong place at the wrong time.

"Do we have any information about the source of the virus?" I ask. "Any animals it might have originated from, foreign travel the patient undertook, anything at all?"

"I'm trying to arrange a meeting with his wife. His widow. She's nervous of talking to anyone. She thinks he did something wrong. It's a delicate situation. I do know, having spoken to a few people who got in touch from his hometown when I did an online appeal for information, that he hadn't traveled outside the UK for over two years. As for the animal hypothesis, I'm told he occasionally did small jobs that were on the wrong side of the law. I'm pursuing that as a possible route."

All of us look so eager, it's pathetic. We don't know anything, she doesn't know anything, this is all pointless. We're wasting precious time. I have a team of immunologists, geneticists, virologists gathered here and for what? For Amanda to tell us that she doesn't know anything yet. Great.

People are asking questions about the Isle of Bute's climate, how she knew it was a virus, how she spotted it so quickly. It's a massive circle jerk. I decide to make use of this time and get through some e-mails. God knows how long later, everyone on-screen starts saying their good-byes and that's that.

"Back to work, team," I say. What a fucking waste of time.

# ELIZABETH

**London, United Kingdom**
**Day 68**

I can't help but be fascinated by the range of scientists, from around the world, trying desperately to find a vaccine. The number of faces, most of them blurry or dropping in and out, made me feel emotional. I wish I could send a message out to the world: "We're trying, I promise! We will find a vaccine." It's been two weeks since Dad died and every time I see evidence of the people desperately trying to stop more men dying, in labs across the globe, I want to weep with gratitude even though it can't help Mom and me to bring him back. For now, I keep busy and keep smiling. Forward motion is the only thing that's going to keep me upright.

After the call, George and I catch up for coffee to go over the progress my group in the lab has made in identifying the vulnerability of men and immunity of women. We're gradually inching closer to an answer. We all think it must be genetic in some way, but we can't know that until we have evidence for it. I'm setting out the plan for this week's lab work when George stops me and rubs a hand over his tired face.

"I'm sorry, Elizabeth, I need to figure out the labs better. I just don't have the bandwidth to cover this much ground." He sighs. "There's four labs all working hell for leather, all producing information and I'm reviewing everything. I think we need to have a better system. I can't do all of this and process it properly. We need a chain of command." This vaguely military phrase sounds odd coming out of George's mouth in his calm, exhausted voice. "I need to find people quickly and then, I don't know. I'm sorry, I just know that I don't have the capacity to take in what you're telling me and use it right now. I don't want to waste time, yours or mine." His eyes are bloodshot from sleepless nights and late-night calls with the prime minister and senior government officials that I know about but don't take part in.

"Make me your deputy," I say, the words popping out of my mouth almost before I realize I've thought them.

George looks dubious.

"Trust me," I go on, determined now for him to see that this makes sense. "I'm running the lab I'm in already and doing a good job, even if you haven't officially told me I'm running it." George makes an expression I interpret as meaning: *can't argue with that.* "I did summer schools at Stanford Business School so I know about all the stuff you hate, like human resource management theory and Gantt charts that you need to show politicians and civil servants that you have a plan. I know the science. I know how to get on with people and you can trust me." I smile my most winning "Let me go to Stanford, please" smile even though I'm so tired and sad that smiling feels only breaths away from grimacing. "And I literally can't fly home or get sick so I'm not going anywhere."

"You're so young though," he says. "And please, don't think I'm saying that as an insult. You're doing an extraordinary job, but it's a lot of responsibility to give someone in their twenties."

I almost add, "I'm nearly thirty" but I don't think that'll help disprove his point.

"George, you're exhausted, sleeping two hours a night, and you don't have enough bodies because men keep dying. I'm a safe pair of hands, safe pair of *female immune* hands. And people trust me. I'm nice and people like working for me, working with me. I'm good at this, at leading people." For a moment I think about how horrifying I find confrontation—the way that my mouth clams up and I can't focus when I'm in the middle of an argument—but I dismiss it. I'm not a wallflower or a fifteen-year-old dork anymore. If I need to have difficult interactions, I can manage it. I left my entire life behind, for God's sake, and moved to a different continent in the middle of a pandemic.

I give him a moment to think about it but can tell that he's so tired it's difficult for him to make any decision at the moment.

"How about this," I say in an inarguable, cheery tone. "Let's try it this way for a week. If it doesn't work, we'll find a different way to do it. If it works, you have a better management structure, together we figure out ways to run the labs efficiently and you have to process less raw data and do more of the strategic thinking."

"Okay, you're on." George's shoulders dip about an inch even just having this temporary plan in place, sparing some essential room in his brain.

And just like that, I'm deputy director of the United Kingdom's Plague Vaccine Development Task Force. I can imagine my dad saying, "Not bad for a girl from Hattiesburg, Mississippi. Not bad at all."

# AMANDA

Job, news, research. Job, news, research. The three pillars of my life, the only things keeping me even vaguely functioning. In a blur I have a Skype call with scientists from around the world that is so discombobulating I have to work hard not to slam my laptop shut.

Every day I decompress by watching the news. In the depths of night or my days off when I can't sleep or sit down without wanting to claw my eyes out, my brain returns to the darkest moments as though it can't look away even though I'm begging it to think of anything else. Don't think about the moments Charlie and Josh died. Don't think about the way Will wept when they took our boys' bodies away. Don't think about the look of relief on Will's face when he realized he had a high temperature and it was almost as if he wanted to die, as though only that would be sufficient penance. Don't think about the way he kept saying, "I'm sorry, I'm so sorry," on his deathbed when all I wanted him to say was, "I love you."

After a night of not sleeping, it's time to go to work. Shockingly enough, Gartnavel Hospital was willing to take back an experienced senior A and E consultant without so much as a whimper. I need my job; I'll go crazy without it. I'm a widow and a childless mother. The labels feel so unfamiliar I still jolt when I hear them and realize they also apply to me. At least I'm still a doctor. I have little else to fill my time. As utterly and completely miserable as it is, I have a purpose. Being a doctor has never been so important. We must preserve the lives of the roughly one in ten men who are still alive. The future of the human race depends on them. Not to mention that we need women to stay alive to keep the country running and in some semblance of order. I try to stay focused and blinkered when I'm at work. No thinking about anything outside of the hospital.

When I first got back, I was still completely disoriented by the sheer number of deaths. I'd think, "Oh, where's Alex today?" or whatever and then I'd remember. If Alex isn't here, he's dead. I asked a few days ago where Linda was, one of my favorite night nurses who used to come and collect patients from A and E and get them settled on a ward. Matron looked at me with a stricken expression. One of the other nurses coughed. "She had three sons, four grandsons and she was married. They all . . ."

"And she's still on compassionate leave?"

Matron gave me a look of pity. I didn't understand. "No, she, she. She couldn't cope, Amanda."

Ah. I see. The Second Plague, as they call it on the news, has taken one of our own.

A few of my favorite male staff members have thankfully survived. Billy, a porter here for thirty years with more tattoos than skin, burst through the doors on my second day back.

"Amanda! You're back, that's my girl. Wasn't the same without you. Don't have a clue what we were doing without you."

"I'm right here, Billy," one of the other consultants, Mary, said dryly from the other side of the ward.

"Right you are, Mary, I wasn't meanin', no, no, was meanin', ah you know what, I'll be off. Lovely to see you all." A tiny bit of glorious normalcy in the face of the Plague. The moments are brief, fleeting and so welcome.

My twelve-hour shift flies by in a blur of sepsis, broken limbs, suicide attempts and a few car crashes. Standard stuff by all accounts. Another two hours of paperwork and the clock has hit 10 p.m. I'm meant to be going home. I take another chart from the rack on the wall and see the patient. A simple kidney infection; painful but easy to treat. I'm disappointed to be done in twenty minutes. After leaving the patient's cubicle, the night matron sees me going to take another chart off the rack.

"Amanda, go home," she instructs in a soft voice that is, nonetheless, one I know can't be ignored. Glaswegian nurses have powers of persuasion up there with messianic leaders. "Even if you can't sleep, you need to rest."

I manage a wan smile and head home. As soon as I go through the front door, I turn on all the lights and switch on the news. Silence is unbearable.

A BBC news crew is stranded in Sweden. Three women, all of them dressed in the same clothes as they were yesterday, and the day before that, and the day before that, broadcast news from a Scandinavian country thousands of miles away as their families die back home. They're interviewing someone from the Swedish Immigration Service. She's called Lilly and looks almost comically Swedish: blond and blue-eyed and wearing something black that on me would look like a maternity muumuu but on her looks like a piece of very cool draping.

"There was a rumor that Swedes were immune and so Sweden was a safe place. Whoever came up with that rumor can rot in hell. Of course, we're not immune. Just because we're blond and we like ABBA doesn't make us immune from the *Plague*. Jesus Christ." Her anger is invigorating. So often now people on the news burst into tears or fade away into silence as they realize that there is, in fact, absolutely nothing to say other than we're all fucked. This girl has some spunk. I enjoy watching her speak.

"You Brits were swarming north for weeks and finally the flights were canceled and we closed our borders but it was too late! You were like a cloud of locusts descending on us, bringing death and destruction."

The presenter, Imogen Deaven, is looking at the camera with a look of such exquisite Britishness that a honk of laughter bursts out of me involuntarily, one of the first times I've laughed since everything went so spectacularly to shit. Imogen's expression somehow manages to convey to the audience, without uttering a word, "I am absolutely mortified, I want to die. I think I should maybe apologize for this if only to make things less awkward? There are too many openly expressed emotions here, I can't cope." Lilly is still looking at Imogen with a look of disgruntled expectation. Clearly Imogen is expected to apologize on behalf of an entire nation. To be fair, Imogen reported on the British ambassador dying a few weeks ago and I've heard nothing about a replacement, so maybe she's the closest thing we have to an ambassador at the moment.

Imogen, God bless her, coughs and plows onward with questions she's clearly prepared in advance. "Can I ask you about the policies the Swedish Home Affairs Office is implementing to prevent the internal spread of the disease?"

Lilly nods vigorously. "Yes. There is no movement of people internally within Sweden. We have divided the country into 162 zones. There is no movement outside of those zones. This will ensure that areas with no outbreaks, or which have been minimally affected, will remain safe."

Imogen, brave woman that she is, responds to this by dragging Britain back into the line of fire. Rather her than me.

"Do you know how many British people have entered Sweden since the outbreak of the Plague?"

"We estimate around ninety thousand Brits and ten thousand other Europeans entered the country. Stockholm's outbreak began on December 6, 2025. A few days later Gothenburg declared an emergency."

"I have one final question," Imogen says to Lilly. "You have talked so calmly and knowledgeably about these policies and the work of the Swedish Immigration Service and Home Affairs Office. How has the Plague affected you on a personal level? How are you?"

Lilly looks a bit stunned by the question. Her eyes are filling with tears. Oh no, Lilly, keep it together. I need you to be a beacon of angry determined hope in the middle of this shitshow.

"My dad and my brother are alive. It feels like a miracle to say that. I am from a small town called Kiruna, many miles away, so I cannot see them, but they are alive. When all of this is over, I'm going to move back home."

"But until there is a cure for the Plague you can't go home?"

Lilly nods. "And neither can you."

At that, Imogen signs off from what must be the most bizarre workday of her life. I switch to another channel. It helps to hear voices, and think about other things, and learn facts and just not think about any of it here in the UK. Best to think about other, faraway places and take comfort in the fact that I'm not the only one who has lost the people closest to me. Show me I'm not alone. Show me I'm not the only one who's destroyed.

I used to hate the news; why would I want to read about and watch misery? How things can change. Besides, the news is now more surreal than any film. It used to be politicians making speeches and footage of wars far, far away. Now it's women wearing hazmat suits carrying bodies out of houses, lines of people waiting for food trucks to deliver food taken from less populated areas to their towns, factories working around the clock to produce medicines and soup and paper and all the other things we so desperately need and used to import.

"There has been an extraordinary direction of travel," a nasally-sounding woman is saying, dressed in a remarkably smart suit but with no makeup on and scraggly hair. Can't say I'd keep going to work to mangle someone's hair into a helmet and paint lipstick on if my family was dying either. "The timing of outbreaks shows that the very earliest significant international outbreaks were borne of reversed immigrations that had existed for decades. Many of those who had immigrated to the UK from the Caribbean, the West Indies, Nigeria, Somalia, Ghana, Pakistan and India left in late November and early December, returning to their countries of origin, bringing the Plague with them."

This woman is trying desperately to hold it together but she has the hollow-eyed shocked look of the recently bereaved. Watching her is painful and too familiar. Next channel. This one is showing the San Francisco Airport Riot, again. The image of the blond police officer shooting at a man who is shooting up again and again, shooting at nothing, has gone around the world. Something about it feels hopeless, like I'm watching the end of days. Before I switch the TV off, I turn on a podcast on my phone about beauty products, downloaded months ago in a different life. I avoid even the briefest silence. Before, I craved the slivers of time in which the house would be blessedly quiet. Now, the emptiness of the house feels almost violent. No teenage feet thumping up the stairs. No clattering of bowls in the sink and yells of "Mum" and a request to find something, be somewhere, do something.

It's a lot not to think about and so, to keep myself sane, as the hours of sleep I dream of drift off without me, never quite able to grasp them, I work. I research the one thing the entire world should be preoccupied with and yet, somehow, isn't. Where did the Plague come from? How did this god-awful disease come to be?

All anyone can talk about is the vaccine and I want to scream at them: *you need information to create a vaccine.* And even if we create a vaccine, and that's a big if, we need to understand how this happened so we can stop it from ever happening again.

No one else seems as worried as I am about this. Story of my fucking life. It doesn't matter though. I can do this on my own. I'm going to find out how Patient Zero developed the Plague. The Plague is happening once. It can't happen again.

# HELEN

**Penrith, United Kingdom**
**Day 68**

**M**um!"

The shout from upstairs is so sharp, for a second I'm convinced it's going to be followed by, "Dad's collapsed!"

"Lola won't give me back my hoodie, tell her it's mine!"

The sound of a scuffle ensues and I breathe a sigh of relief. Fight all you want my lovely, living girls. Thank God I have daughters. Every single day, I'm filled with gratitude that I was spared sons. It's hard enough, now that it's spreading everywhere, worrying that Sean is going to catch it. All of my fear is for him, but I can't even begin to imagine what it must be like for those poor women who only have boys.

Instead my questions are all for my husband. When is Sean going to catch it? Is he going to catch it? When am I going to be a widow? I should be saying if, if, if but it feels like when, not if. It's like the grim reaper is standing over us, watching our every move, waiting. When I'm doing the washing-up or sitting on the sofa, I'll drift for a few moments into an alternative world. *What would it be like without Sean? How would I cope? Who would I be?* We're so entwined the answers quickly come into focus. It would be awful. I wouldn't cope. I have no idea who I would be. We've been together since we were thirteen. We're childhood sweethearts. I went straight from living with my parents to living with him when I was seventeen. I don't know any other life. Sean and Helen. Helen and Sean.

I worry about him. I think he's losing his mind. I keep saying to him, "You might be immune," but he just shakes his head. He's always been quiet, doesn't like to talk about things straightaway but usually he'll open up if I keep needling him. The Carlisle outbreak really took hold a month ago and it was like a fire. It's ripped through that city, spreading outward to our town, where we had felt safe and secure, looking at a future with an empty nest and cruises and wine-and-cheese nights. The estate agency isn't much of a comfort—there's seven women and three men. I said to Sean that he should call the other guys and see how they are but he shouted at me to leave it. I wonder if he'd rather not know.

I suppose it doesn't help that his entire job is completely redundant. The boss hasn't told them they're officially redundant but there's no need—he left for his villa in Marbella back at the start of December and no one's seen hide nor hair of him since. He took all the money out, flew away and that was that. Sean went to the office for a few days after that but there's no point. Who's going to buy a house when the apocalypse is coming? *Oh sure, I'll look at that three-bed semi-detached on Brent Road in between worrying about my son dying from the Plague and my husband's company going bust.* He feels useless and it's no good for a man to feel useless.

I feel useless too, but he's not asked me about that. No one's getting their hair done now, are they? Not much use for a hairdresser right now. Somewhere in the back of my mind, concerns about mortgage payments and my job and money for the Tesco shop flit around like bats, but they seem like such faraway problems. The Plague is so much closer. It could be days away, or hours.

Each evening I tell Sean, at least the girls are going to be all right. It's like a prayer. *Think of the girls. At least we don't have boys.* Lola's fourteen, Hannah's seventeen and Abi's eighteen. They're trying so hard to stay strong, bless them, doing everything they can to stay upbeat. My lovely strong girls.

"Mum, we need to talk." Abi's voice shocks me out of my reverie, worrying as I look out of the window. "I'm really worried about Dad. He's not himself and he won't talk to me."

There's a crease between her eyebrows making her look older than she should. I try to comfort her, the automatic instinct to minimize the problem kicking in.

"Don't worry, love, I'll sort it out," I say with a level of authority I don't feel.

"What if he kills himself?" she says, quickly as though the words have hurtled their way out of her mouth before she could think better of it.

I look at her, stunned. "He won't do that." My voice rises slightly at the end. It hadn't even occurred to me. Sean? My Sean? He would never.

"I just worry," Abi says, and then leaves the room looking stricken.

I can't let this continue. The girls tell one another everything even though they're at one another's throats half the time. If Abi is worrying about this, Hannah and Lola will be too.

When Sean comes back from his walk—he walks for hours every day, round and round our town—I ask him to sit down at the kitchen table. Immediately, when I see his expression, I wonder if this isn't a great choice of time, but when is? Matt, his best friend since we were all at school together, died a week ago. Matt's boys, Josh and Adam, died a few days ago. People are going to keep dying. There's never going to be a good time to ask your husband to please, please, please, not kill himself.

"You're scaring the girls, love," I say. He'll probably grunt or stay silent like he usually does. I take a breath to say more but before I can, it's as though rage explodes out of him. He's never been an angry man. I can only remember him raising his voice a handful of times in the nearly thirty years we've been together.

"Jesus Christ, Helen, I don't care if I'm scaring the girls. I'm fucking terrified."

It's as though he's come alive for the first time since the fear descended. The rage, my God. It's coming off him in waves, distorting the domestic reality of our small kitchen.

"I'm staring death in the face. I can't act like normal. Everything is falling apart and I can't do it anymore. I've been living my life for other people for too long."

After weeks of silence he can't get the words out fast enough, shooting them out, violent and clear. For a second the total hate in his eyes makes me wonder briefly. Is he going to kill me? Am I going to be one of those women who end up on the front of the newspaper having been stabbed to death by her husband in a murder-suicide?

"I'm bored, I'm fed up, I need to feel alive while I still have a chance to. You have no idea how it feels, Helen. It's like I'm splintering. I can't do it anymore." He gets up and paces around the kitchen. "I'm going to die, maybe soon, maybe a bit later, but it's going to happen. I'm on borrowed time."

I sit, dumbstruck as my soulmate dismantles our life together with sharp, quick words as though he's gutting a pig. After twenty minutes of repeating himself he charges upstairs. Another ten minutes go by and then he's in the hallway with a suitcase, giving the girls each a perfunctory hug as Lola wails. What is happening? What the fuck is happening? He walks out the door and that's it.

He's gone. My husband's gone. He's actually gone. For the rest of the evening, I keep wandering around the house, looking at empty chairs, empty sofas, empty bed, empty kitchen table as the girls follow me around like ducklings. Nope, not there. Nope, no husband under there.

Twenty-four hours go by and we hear nothing. The girls keep checking their phones, desperate to hear from him and I think, *He'll come back*, but slowly, and then all at once, I know he won't. A sheet comes down across the hopeful part of my brain, the optimistic bit that thinks I know him, and I realize that something broke. The Sean I knew is gone. Vanished. The Sean I know would never abandon his daughters, howling in the hallway. He would never tell me he was bored and fed up and leave me knowing I wasn't good enough. I'm not sure who said all of those things but it wasn't my husband.

We're inconsolable. We don't know how to be consoled. Everyone knows how to deal with grief but how do we face desertion? In a world of men desperately clinging to their families for one more day, one more hour, we've been abandoned. It's as though he's died but worse. I try to justify it to myself that way. It's nicer to think that he wants to save us the pain and uncertainty of dying later, even if it's not true.

I sit, my three girls surrounding me on the sofa, reeling. It only feels like a few breaths ago that I was posting photos of us at family dinners on Facebook and planning a holiday to Rome. That was a different life, but here I am, stuck in this one. This life where I'm now a single mother and a widow? Divorced? Separated? I'm not alone, I have my girls. The girls. How could Sean do this to our daughters? How?

# CATHERINE

Theodore is a deadweight, impossible to wake after the trauma of the last few days. Even though I can feel he is cool, with no fever, and just sleeping, my heart rate spikes until he emits a little whimper. Noise is proof he is alive. I bundle him into blankets. We don't have time to waste. The Plague could be anywhere in this godforsaken house. I've wept through cleaning every surface, every toy, every object I think he might have touched, but what if I've missed something?

Anthony died in our bed, at home, as all men do now. Hospitals used to be a place of kindness and care but now they turn men away if their only complaint is the Plague with a resigned shrug of impotence, so we didn't bother trying. I tried to imagine that it would help him, knowing his family existed in the same house as he did, even as we were separated by walls. His body was carried out in a bag by two officious women in hazmat suits. Who knows how far this virus has spread across my house? I can't see it, can't smell it, can't hear it.

I had nowhere to go until tonight. My maddening, forgetful, beloved godmother, Genevieve, e-mailed me to say, "Still have house in Devon. Sale never completed when it was meant to a few weeks ago. Go stay there! Get out of London xx." It made me want to weep with gratitude and throttle her. *Now?* I want to wail. You're telling me this now? But it's not too late. It's not. Theodore hasn't, by some miracle, shown any symptoms in the days since Anthony died.

The feeling of leaving the house in the early hours with my child in my arms makes me miss Anthony so much that tears spring painfully to my eyes. I'm never far from crying and the sight of streetlamps and Theodore sleeping with a seat belt, a suitcase in the trunk, makes me think of early morning departures to drive to Bordeaux to see Genevieve for a week of sunshine, drinking wine in a garden and time together. We were there having a holiday, as a family, only seven months ago in a different, happier lifetime.

No time to properly lose it though. I could cry all day, every day, and with Theodore in the car I'll have free rein to weep but not to howl. Genevieve's farmhouse is in the depths of Suffolk. Miles and miles away from this full city, heaving with sick men and infected women. I start to drive down the eerily quiet motorway, and every mile I put between us and London unwinds my shoulders even as tears stream down my face, soaking the surgical mask I'm wearing. We can ride out this storm in the safety of a deserted cottage in the middle of nowhere. Part of me is kicking myself for not asking Genevieve about it earlier but she had told me she was selling it in September, received an offer in October and, for all I knew, sold it in November with the buyers to arrange a move-in date. I could haunt myself with this missed oasis forever but that way madness lies. I did the best I could with what I knew at the time.

My mind wanders back to the days and weeks before Anthony died. No matter how hard I try, my brain is determined to question every choice I made. Anthony and I shouldn't have touched as much as we did in the days before we had to say good-bye. I was selfish. A tiny, terrified part of me assumed he would die so, before we knew he was sick, I wanted every minute with him I could get. I didn't know how to cope with this horror without him. I should have moved him into the shed at the bottom of the garden with a hundred books, a heater, a microwave and cans of soup. I should have left him alone. Maybe that would have saved him but instead I hugged him. I kissed him. I made love to him. I couldn't let him go.

There are still twenty miles to go when I hear the yelp of Theodore waking up and realizing he is in the car. "Mummy, need the toilet."

"Soon darling, we're nearly there. Just hold it in for a bit longer."

He starts crying and I join him, howling loudly. It's too much, all of this is too much. I can't bear it. I just want to curl up in Anthony's arms and weep but he's gone and we're all alone. Our very existence is exhausting. Wearing a surgical mask, constantly sterilizing the house, leaving Theodore on his own as much as possible. I leave him locked in the house when I go to get food. What else can I do? The danger is outside. I'm trying to keep him safe. I need him to be safe.

"Mummy, please." The cries have reached the level of a shriek but finally, the blessed view of the turn-off appears. We stayed here in Genevieve's country cottage for a few days just after we had Theodore. It was awful; locked in a remote box with a newborn and fractious from lack of sleep, we bickered for forty-eight hours before driving back to London more depressed than when we left. I drive down the long driveway and see a light is on. Perhaps Genevieve is back, but she can't be. She surely would have told me. When I last e-mailed her she was definitely still in France. Why would she travel here? Nobody in their right mind would come to the epicenter of the danger.

I park the car and peer through the glass owlishly, fear stopping my tears. Someone could be here. Someone else Genevieve knows who had the same idea or, more scarily, a stranger could have broken in. Theodore is wailing now and I scoop him out, allowing him, as I so rarely do now, to curl his limbs around me and put his head on my chest. I try to breathe shallowly, imagining the germs I might be exhaling, escaping the mask I'm wearing and making their way past his own too-big mask flapping around his face.

I'm trying to be brave but this is exactly the kind of moment when Anthony's broad frame, warm by my side, would make the terrifying seem entirely faceable. I'm so aware of my vulnerability. A small woman, holding a child, in the middle of nowhere. Shushing Theodore, I use the key I've brought with me and open the door in a rush as though I'll scare anyone who might be here.

"Hello?"

Silence. And then, a pitiful meow. Of course, Genevieve has motion-activated lights in the kitchen to deter burglars. A painfully thin tabby cat makes its way toward me in the hall and curls itself around my legs. It has a collar and a tag, clinking as it moves in the glow of the kitchen light. It feels like a good omen. There is no danger here. I lock the door behind me and do a quick look around the ground floor and find it blessedly empty. This place is untouched since before the Plague. I begin to cry again but this time with gratitude. Theodore has fallen back asleep on my shoulder and I allow myself, in this small, safe house in the middle of nowhere, which feels sturdy in the face of a disease that is everywhere, to hold him. Truly, properly squeeze him with a hug that I would have held him in every day before the Plague. It has been so long since I've held him like this. It is bliss.

I step carefully up the stairs, the cat bouncing up ahead of me, and put Theodore in the bed in the spare bedroom. For the first time since Anthony died, I allow myself to hope that maybe, just maybe, everything will be all right.

# ROSAMIE

**Singapore**

**Day 68**

Mrs. Tai's scream echoes through the apartment.

"Stay here," I warn Angelica in my "I seriously mean it" voice. Whatever is going on, I don't want her to see it. I walk through the quiet corridors of the apartment telling myself to stay calm. The atmosphere in the apartment is strange. The maids are all holed up in their rooms—terrified, calling their families, unsure what to do.

I follow the screaming into Mr. and Mrs. Tai's bedroom. Mr. Tai is having a fit. His body is shaking and he is foaming at the mouth. It's painful to watch him convulse and shake, his head throwing itself around on his pillow. Mrs. Tai is staring silently at him in horror.

"Mr. Tai?" I say in a calm voice, and try to hold his arms still. It takes all the strength I have but I manage to keep him still enough to stop his head crashing. After a few minutes his body relaxes and the fit stops. Mrs. Tai is still standing behind me; she must be in shock. Mr. Tai is definitely dying, there is no doubt in my mind. His forehead is so hot, I don't see how he could live. It is hotter than any living thing should be and his face is gray and flushed at the same time. I sit on the side of the bed, unsure of what to do. I am holding his hand and looking at him while his wife stands looking at me. This is all the wrong way around. After I don't know long, Mrs. Tai comes to her senses and pushes me out of the way. She snaps something at me in Cantonese that I don't understand, but I know her well enough to realize it means, "Get out."

I bump into Angelica as I leave the bedroom. "Angelica!" I whisper. Her face is screwed up with worry. My lovely girl, she's too sweet and nervous for all of this. "Let's go back to the nursery."

"And watch *Cinderella*?"

"And watch *Cinderella*."

I try to push Mr. Tai out of my mind and focus on Rupert and Angelica. The thought that the disease is inside, and close to Rupert, encloses my mind for a dizzying moment. I push it away. Rupert hasn't seen Mr. Tai. I look down at my phone again. My mother hasn't been replying to my e-mails. Her last e-mail had said that lots of the men in town had left. They had gotten boats and gone to other islands, thinking that maybe the disease would, I don't know, not follow them? Not be waiting for them when they got there?

Angelica gets to the nursery ahead of me, turning on the TV to watch *Cinderella*. Rupert isn't up yet, which isn't like him. He's always up by eight. I go into Rupert's room, to the side of the nursery. His little body is facing away from the door and he's curled up into a ball under the blankets. I call his name gently and try to pull the blankets off him but he whimpers. My heart skips and for a moment the world is stopping. Technically I'm just a nanny. Technically these aren't my children, but what makes a mother? The woman who grows them or the woman who raises them? These are my babies. My life is spent looking after them.

I force myself to feel Rupert's forehead and I know it's hot before I even touch it. The heat is fiercer than I could imagine, even hotter than Mr. Tai. It's like he is burning. I pull the blankets off and yell for one of the maids, for someone, anyone. Mrs. Tai must hear me because she rushes into the room, her eyes all puffy from crying. She starts yelling and crying again. I tell her to call an ambulance and shove my way past her to soak some towels in cold water. I'm covering Rupert in the wet towels and she's trying to grab them off him, she doesn't understand. I'm fighting her, pushing her off and trying to explain to her that we have to bring his fever down or . . .

Then she understands.

She sits by his side, crying to herself, saying over and over again, "My life is over, my life is over, my life is over." After a while I snap and tell her to shut up. How is that going to help Rupert? I keep thinking, *Where's the ambulance?* It's like a mantra. "Where's the ambulance?" Mrs. Tai is phoning and phoning. She phones private companies and taxi companies and hospitals but they all tell her they are busy, they are full, stay where you are, nothing they can do, stay home. I keep thinking it will come, all the way through the day. It has to. Someone has to take pity on us. We cannot stay here in this room, watching a little boy die without any help. Angelica keeps coming in and hugging me from behind as I sit by Rupert, holding his hand. Mrs. Tai looks at me with an expression she has never used before. It takes me a while to work out what it is and then, as I kiss her daughter on the forehead, while comforting her dying son, I realize. It's jealousy. This woman had everything in the world she could possibly want, but she wanted all the wrong things.

Rupert keeps getting worse throughout the afternoon. I'm gripping his hand tighter and tighter, as if I can keep him here as long as I'm touching him, but I know how powerless I am. The ambulance doesn't arrive. It's never going to arrive. In the evening his breathing becomes shallower. He's gasping for each breath. I didn't think it was possible for a fever to get any worse but it keeps climbing and climbing. It's like the devil has gripped him and is burning him through. Maybe I should put him in the bathtub with cold water and ice. It probably wouldn't make a difference. Nothing makes a difference. His breathing becomes more and more painful to listen to until it stops, just before midnight, and then all I want to hear again is his little chest heaving out a breath. Blessedly, there is no fit like Mr. Tai had suffered. I keep holding his tiny hand. I feel his forehead, the heat leaking out of his cooling skin. Mrs. Tai is slumped behind me, crying about her baby. I want to shout that he's not her baby, what does she know? Does she know the three vegetables he will eat? His favorite movie? The order in which his blankets have to be laid over him—turquoise fleecy, then the white sheet and then the duvet—for him to sleep? How you have to slide Monkey out from under his elbow when he's sleeping to wash it in the middle of the night and make sure to tumble dry it so it's not damp before placing it back in his arms? She doesn't know anything.

I can't be in this room any longer. I want to die, maybe that would be easier than dealing with all of this. I walk into the lounge. Angelica is standing by the windows—alongside two of the maids. I pick up Angelica and hold her as I look out. I've been in Rupert's room for over twelve hours and while I was ensconced, the world outside has descended into hell. I won't be surprised if Lucifer himself rises from the street up to the window in front of us and drags us back down with him. Everything is burning—the cars in the street, one of the buildings opposite us. Flames surround us. There's the thumping sound of metal smashing and people are swarming the streets. It is a riot, but it looks like the end of the world. It is the apocalypse.

I keep looking for the police or soldiers but there are only a few. Every time I see one emerge from behind a car or a building he quickly disappears again or is submerged under a crowd of people. The maids are weeping quietly, unmoving.

I start praying to God to let me survive this night. Let me survive tonight and see tomorrow. Please let me see my family again. Please let me see my home. I've lost too much already, I can't lose anymore, I pray as I look out at the city burning.

The maids are both from China, talking about how they are going to get home. "We'll never make it," one of them is wailing. That's when I know for sure: I can't stay here and wait. If I wait here, I'm going to die, or I'm going to be stuck here for months, years. A kind of madness takes over. I have to go home, right now, whatever it takes.

I sit on the sofa with Angelica wrapped around me. This is the last time I will ever hold her and I want it to last as long as it can. On my phone I look up commercial flights; I know there won't be any but I have to check just in case. Nothing. Everything is canceled. But then I think, how do the Tais travel? How *did* the Tais travel? Everything's easier when you're rich. They always use this private jet company, Elite Air. I call them up and pretend to be Mrs. Tai's assistant, watching the maids. They're in their own world, staring out at the street. The girl on the other end of the phone says that they are charging a lot more than the normal price to get out of Singapore and you have to be at the airport within two hours, you can only fly within Asia and the East Pacific. Air Traffic Restrictions Partnership comes into effect at midnight and after that, no more flights.

I agree to everything, rushing through, yes, yes, whatever she says I will agree to. How much, how much. "5.45 million dollars." Mrs. Tai left her bag by the bed in her and Mr. Tai's bedroom, like she always did. I leave Angelica in the living room for a minute and creep past Mr. Tai's body to get Mrs. Tai's purse out and I'm about to give the American Express number when the lady at Elite Air says that the payment has gone through from the Wells Fargo account they have on record already and Mrs. Tai will need to be at the airport within two hours before the flights are all grounded.

Thank God we live close to the airport. I grab the important things I own and then I say good-bye to Angelica. This is the hardest thing I have ever had to do. I know I'll never see her again but I can't bear to tell her that. Singapore probably won't exist for much longer, who knows what will happen to the Tais? And besides, I've just stolen millions of dollars from them.

"Where are you going?" she asks, crying. She's tired; it's too late for her to be up.

"I need to go home to see my family. My family needs me."

"But I need you." Oh, my girl. I wish I could take her with me but I can't. Even in this madness, I know that I can't do that. I desperately want to bundle her up in my arms, but it would be the end of something. A normal life for me, the future she needs with her family. Snap out of it.

"I will see you again, okay? I know where you live, and I'll come back when all of this is over and see you as soon as I can."

She looks like she believes me and I breathe out a sigh of relief. I hug her again, so, so tight, and kiss her on the head and then I have to go. Down the elevator, and out in to the street, quickly before I can think about turning back. As I walk down the street, thick with smoke, my brain is thinking this can't be Singapore, it just can't be. Singapore is one of the safest and wealthiest countries in the world. I remember the lady from the agency telling me it was such a good place to work because it was safe. Just get to the airport. That's the only focus now. Men and women with bandanas across their faces are throwing things at, who? One another? Who are they fighting? An invisible enemy.

I start running and don't stop for anything. The two miles to the airport are a blur with occasional flashes of violence. The car crash on the highway and the way the car spun three times before another car crashed into it. The man who threw himself off the bridge as I was crossing it. Heat and noise and horror, but I have to keep going. Once I get to the other side of the freeway it isn't so bad. I've been to Changi

Airport before to bring Angelica and Rupert to meet Mr. Tai. I walk through the entrance—no one is there, every desk eerily empty—find the hangar, tell the girl on duty that I am Mrs. Tai and demand to get on the plane before she asks any more questions.

She's sweating, picking up phones every few seconds and telling people to hold. She just points me toward the plane—it is a mess. There are four different planes preparing to leave and two helicopters arriving. I guess every rich person in Singapore who can still think straight is getting out of Singapore.

I run up the steps of the plane and the flight attendant suddenly looms in front of me at the door to the plane. He looks exhausted, his face pinched and drawn.

"I'm Mrs. Tai," I say, motioning for him to move so I can get on the plane.

He narrows his eyes and gives me a look that makes me want to throw up.

"I've flown with Mrs. Tai many times before," he says, eyes cold with suspicion. He's breathing rapidly, his face aflame with hostility. I can see him thinking, do I let her on the plane? How much does this matter to me? My breath catches in my throat, panic rising through me so strongly it's as though a hand is gripping my neck. The seconds stretch out. Please let me survive this. Please take mercy on me. Please let me on the plane.

DESPAIR

# CATHERINE

This is a golden day, even though, if I think about it too hard, this is one of the worst days of my life. We play in the garden, me watching Theodore running around gaily as I sip tea made with long-lasting milk. I tell him stories about bears and witches and dragons because we don't have any books here, and I allow myself to cuddle him occasionally. We are safe maybe, surely, please, in this house untouched by the Plague.

The loss of Anthony becomes harder, not easier, now that we are in this place of safety. My mind assumes he must be away for a business trip and he'll walk in any moment. But he doesn't and he never will. Maybe it would be more bearable if I had seen him grow sick and die. Instead it feels as though we said good-bye, and he walked up the stairs and he must, surely, be alive and well somewhere in the world. My brain can't compute that the end has happened. I try not to cry in front of Theodore and then I realize I'm trying so hard to keep it together because I don't want my son's last days—if these are his last days—to include the sight of his mother crying. I miss Anthony so much and no one else understands. After so many years, the loss of my parents winds me, again and again. Having accepted their deaths, now it feels like the cruelest injustice that the world is leaving me so unbelievably alone. Phoebe messaged me the other day asking how we are. She said that they think her husband is immune. He works as an accountant and has probably been exposed to it countless times because most of his office has died of it, but he hasn't gotten ill. I nearly smashed my phone against the window. She has two parents, a husband and two daughters. She has an abundance so vast I want to scream, "Why not me?" I didn't reply. I have a precious son whom I'm clinging to like Circe on her island, praying I can stay here unseen from the eyes of death. And I'm all on my own in this fight. No mother to come and help. No father to reassure. Anthony was my family and now he's gone and so I try to eke out all the pleasure I can from the beautiful boy we made.

I want to settle into a rhythm, a new normal. Today we woke up at six and Theodore napped in the afternoon as the cat purred contentedly on the sofa next to me. Then a calm bath time and bed with games and stories and as many cuddles as possible. Every moment that goes by without a fever or a cough or unusual lethargy gives me the luxury of thinking we might be safe. This place feels like a historical artifact, untouched by death and fear.

A few hours after putting Theodore to bed, I'm in the hazy midpoint between sleep and wakefulness when I hear the unmistakable sound of broken glass. My heart stops and my body fills with the cold dread of fear that comes when you are alone and there is no one to help. Someone is here. I creep down the stairs and hear the scrabbling of a human. There is heavy breathing. He is alone, only one pair of feet. It's definitely a man. The step creaks.

"Who the fuck's there?"

I scream in fright. His voice, rough and intimidating, is bellowing at me from the kitchen where one lightbulb is on. The house is shrouded in half light. My brain thinks of Theodore, upstairs, cocooned in this bubble away from disease. Another sheet of fear lays itself over my thoughts of a violent robbery. This stranger probably carries the virus. He dares to bring the Plague to my house.

"This isn't your house," I yell back with all the effort I can muster. "I don't fucking care. Get out."

I can see him now, looming in the kitchen doorway. My brain is expecting him to charge toward me, pummel me or rape me or kill me. He's a strange, angry man who has broken into a house and is loudly asserting himself despite being so obviously in the wrong. Why is he staying so far away? And then, the thought appears perfectly formed in the front of my brain. Of course. He's scared of me. He came here to escape. A remote, rural, uninhabited cottage; the perfect sanctuary. He thought he could wait it out here. He had the same plan as me. The only difference is that this safety is mine. I have a right to be here.

I will win this. He thinks I have the virus. As far as he's aware, I could kill him just by moving toward him.

"I'm not going anywhere," I say loudly, my voice clear as a bell as I step down the remaining stairs. "I came here with my son. I'm a host and my son is infected, he's just upstairs. I came here to die with him." The lie slips out of my mouth, smooth and certain.

I step toward the man.

"Don't take another fucking step!" He's shuffling backward. He looks like a cow being led to slaughter with bulging eyes and a mouth dry and twisting with terror.

"I'm not going to stop moving. This is my house. You shouldn't be here. I have the virus. My son has the virus. If I so much as breathe near you, you'll catch it and you'll die. If you touch me, you'll catch it and die. If you break my skin and my blood is near you, you'll catch it and die. If you don't want to die, get out."

"Fucking crazy bitch!" he says, his voice choking on a sob. He is desperate, but I don't care. That is not my concern.

He turns, there are a few scuffling sounds of objects being thrown around and then the back door mercifully slams shut. I stand in the hallway breathing heavily for a few seconds before breaking into a smile. I have never felt so powerful. This must be what men used to feel like. My mere physical presence is enough to terrify someone into running. No wonder they used to get drunk on it.

I put on a pair of hiking boots by the front door and go through to the kitchen where the door's glass pane is lying all over the floor. Methodically I pick up the pieces of shattered glass and put them in the bin as my heart stops thumping in my ears and slowly, slowly goes back to normal. I clean every surface with bleach I find under the sink just in case that awful man touched anything. Eventually, the floor is clear and brushed, the room sterile and safe. I stand up and hear the blissful silence of the house, the cat purring as it winds its way around my legs.

I can't help but check on Theodore. I have this belief, based on nothing but my own fear, that he's traumatized by the events of the last few months but not expressing it during the day. I hate the idea that his nights could be tainted by fear and horror. I know he is exhausted, my poor baby. He was drooping by seven this evening and out like a light by eight. Life is exhaustingly different at the moment, and I panic about what it's doing to Theodore. He's eating different food in a different house with a different garden, and a desperate, grieving mother. His father is gone. I can't even imagine what's going through his head. Or maybe I just don't want to. I'm so focused on him surviving I barely think anymore about the future. Will he be scarred forever by this nightmare? Will he know what it is to be happy and safe and calm ever again? Will he even remember Anthony? At the thought of Anthony, I get a blinding headache. There's only so much I can think about at once.

"Hello, lovely," I whisper to him as I perch on the side of his bed, looking down at him sprawled out on his sheets, deep in sleep. I drop a quick kiss out of habit on his forehead and take a second to realize what is wrong. I expected the warm, soft skin of a sleeping toddler. Instead my lips reached hot, sweaty skin with a fever raging just under it.

He is burning up.

# TOBY WILLIAMS

**Somewhere off the coast of Iceland**

**Day 105**

**February 15, 2026**

I've never journaled before but I don't know what else to do. I've been on this ship for fifty-one days. I don't know if I will ever leave it. This may be the only record of this horrible experience and of my existence here. I want someone to know what it was like.

Let's start at the beginning. My name is Toby Williams. My wife, Frances, is a librarian at the Barbican Library in central London. I'm an engineer, which now that I write it down makes me seem boring but I really like my job.

I'm an identical twin. That's an important thing about me. Always has been. If you're an identical twin it makes you special. Mark, my brother, is the reason I'm here on this godforsaken boat. We turned sixty on January 2 and it seemed like a nice idea to go to see the Northern Lights like we had always talked about as children. I wondered at the time when we left in December if we should really be doing this with the Plague becoming such a problem but Frances was insistent. She said, "You'll be safer there than here. Besides, it'll all blow over."

My wife is usually right. Almost always. It's one of the things I love most about her but she was wrong about that. It has not blown over. Although maybe she was right that I'm safer here.

Four days after we left Reykjavik there was an outbreak in the city. Within days, it was in crisis. The Plague was making its way across Europe day by day but the captain was clear. He didn't put it to a vote. He gathered everyone in the Cinema Room and said, "We will stay on the boat until we know it is safe to return. We have good stores of food and we will request for more to be delivered to us. We are not returning yet." One woman on the boat is particularly furious. Bella Centineo. She's from Italy and she's on this trip with a friend, Martina. Martina is catatonic, Bella is enraged. She screamed at the captain that he couldn't do this. Her children are waiting for her in Rome. Her son and her husband might die and then what will happen to her daughter? Her daughter, Carolina, is only eighteen months old. Bella has no sisters and her mother died two years ago. I understand her distress. The communication is getting patchier now between us and everyone back home. Her husband and son might die, leaving her daughter to starve to death in a Roman apartment, all on her own. It doesn't bear thinking about.

I empathize and yet I could have cried with relief when the captain told her: "If you manage to escape death by a few days, I consider it rude to refuse such good fortune." And then he turned around and left the room.

My last message from Frances was weeks ago now. We're not getting reception anymore. She said, "You have to stay on that boat, Toby. I don't care what happens or who wants to go back, you stay on that boat." Which is exactly what I intend to do.

But we don't have enough food. We have minimal medicine. We've run out of fuel so the anchor is down and we're stuck in one place hoping that one day, rescue will come. The captain says that he reached the coast guard weeks ago and they said they would provide us with rations. The captain has a solar-powered satellite phone and knows our coordinates. I try to hold on to these facts and hope but each day feels like a lifetime away from home.

I am in the safest place in the world for a man to be and yet I have never felt in more danger. We have nowhere to go. There is no sanctuary we can turn to. We are stuck out here while our loved ones wait and hope back home. Is it better to starve or be felled by a plague? I don't have the choice but sometimes I think the latter is better. At least it's quick, I hear.

Bella's rage keeps her going. She even managed to keep her spirits up after the first death. An older lady. I suspect it was a heart attack or a brain aneurysm as it was very sudden, but I don't know. I'm not a doctor. There are no doctors or nurses on board. The second death was a suicide. That was hard to take. I didn't see him but I heard the splash and then the wave of shocked murmurs and shouts that spread through the boat. Apparently his son had died back home. He had mentioned it to someone a few days before.

Out of the three hundred people on the boat we started with, we're down to 288. Six have died from a lack of insulin, one from a seizure that resulted in hitting their head. There have been four suicides and the heart attack lady. (Again, I don't know for definite it was a heart attack but I don't remember her name, Jojo? Janice? Jane? So, heart attack lady it is.)

We have a rationing system in place. There's a Swedish dietitian on board who calculated a minimum calorie requirement for everyone on board based on their weight. One man tried to lie about his weight to get more food. The dietitian punished him by reducing it. That was an uncomfortable few hours.

I hope Frances is okay. Frances, in case I die and this ship is discovered, I'll make it clearer so this letter definitely reaches you. I am Toby Benedict Williams. My wife is Frances Emma Williams. We live in Flat C, 4 Clerkenwell Road, London EC1V 9TB. If someone finds this, please pass it on to her.

Frances, I love you. I just want you to be happy. It's all I ever wanted. I wish we had found each other earlier than we did but we've packed more love and adventure into twenty years than most people do in sixty. You're the best person. Just the absolute best. I hope I see you again.

# AMANDA

am officially the worst at meditating. I've tried it every day for three days, wanting to move away from my addiction to the news, and have become more depressed than I've been in months. Meditating is shit—there I said it. "Redirect your thoughts," the app said. "Focus your mind." No fucking thank you. I have nothing good to redirect my thoughts to. So instead I'm making sure to maintain my regimen of noise. Silence is not welcome in my mind right now. I've become obsessed with a YouTube channel of professional cooks in a kitchen. They have playful banter and silly challenges and cook delightful, buttery pastries that make my mouth water. It distracts me and tricks my brain into feeling less alone and like everything is the way it used to be. It can turn on a dime and in a moment—an expression on someone's face, the mention of a teenage son—I'll want to throw my phone out of the window and scream that I used to cook for my children. I used to care about pastry crust. I used to sit at the table with my family and eat together. Sometimes it's a comfort, sometimes it's a cruel reminder.

The ferry to the Isle of Bute is a bumpy one and my phone screen wobbles as I try to hear the tinny voice of my favorite chef, a redhead with freckles and the calm, clear manner of an experienced teacher. She makes a comment about cooking leftovers that your teenagers can eat when they're hungry. The coin has turned; there's too much pain to watch. I stare out of the window at the waves and the gray landscape. I used to love coming out to the islands. The combination of clean, salty air on a crisp, cold day would ease the knots of anxiety winding themselves around me. The boys would run around like hooligans, delighted not to be told to calm down, sit down, pipe down. Will and I would amble along, arm in arm, and it would feel like we worked so hard for most of the year to earn this time and feel so at ease.

The Rothesay port comes into view and I'm dragged back into the present. The lack of cars on the ferry is a jolting reminder of how things have changed. Gasoline is so expensive I've been using my ancient bike I hadn't used in a decade. I have the details of the person I'm here to see and I wish I could say she was waiting for me, but I fear nothing could be further from the truth.

Heather Fraser, widow of Euan Fraser. Thanks to me, it's been widely reported that Euan was Patient Zero. The Isle of Bute is a tiny island; everyone knows everyone. Journalists sniffing around were pointed in the direction of Heather, where they came to a dead end. She was not for talking, or being interviewed, or being paid, or being bothered. She was grieving and her husband had been reduced to a title. Patient Zero. No name, just death.

I hadn't gotten in touch with Heather before today. Somehow, I thought surprising her would be better, but as I walk up the road to her house, buffeted by a chilly late winter wind, I'm questioning the wisdom of that decision. Just what everyone wants: to be ambushed. Well done, Amanda, what a winning start.

I ring the doorbell. Fuck it. The worst she can do is say no.

"Who is it?" a suspicious voice asks from behind the door. I have no doubt I'm being peered at through the spyhole in the door.

"I'm a doctor, Dr. Maclean. I treated your husband."

The door swings open. "Are you lying?" Heather asks, her face pinched and gaunt. "It would be a horrible thing to—"

"I can show you my hospital pass," I say, pulling my NHS ID card out of my bag. "See, that's me. I work at Gartnavel Hospital in the A and E Department. Euan was brought to us by air ambulance on November 1."

Heather takes the card from me and puts a hand to her mouth, her face starting to collapse into tears. "You were one of the last people to see him alive."

This hadn't occurred to me. I can't believe now that it hadn't—it's an appalling omission for my mind to have made—but I barely treated him. He was already at death's door when he came to A and E. I never saw him conscious. To me, that is a distinguishing factor. To his wife, it doesn't matter. I saw her husband when she was still his wife, not his widow. I saw him in his final breaths, gave him morphine to make sure if he was any pain it wouldn't be felt, called out the numbers on his time of death.

"Can I come in?" I ask softly. "I'm so sorry I didn't phone you, or ask, I just . . ." She waves my excuse away and beckons me inside. The door is quickly slammed shut behind us and she turns three locks. Wiping away tears from her cheeks, she points at the locks and says, "There's been a lot of journalists. I don't trust them. I don't like people knowing where I live."

The mantelpiece in the living room has a range of pictures, all in frames clearly given by children and grandchildren. Frames with "Best Dad in the World" and "I Love my Grandad" engraved into the wood. This is a place of family and comfort, a house lived in for a long time.

Heather offers me water and apologizes for the lack of biscuits—the food shortages are biting for us all at the moment—and sits, looking at me. I feel deeply uncomfortable with the idea that she's welcomed me into her home under a false pretense. I did treat her husband but I didn't hear any last words, I had no emotional connection with him. He was dying when he arrived into my care and died shortly afterward.

"I need you to know," I say, desperate at the very least for this interaction to be based on honesty, "that I'm here because I have to find out how your husband became ill. I treated Euan but I never spoke to him. He was very, very ill when he arrived at A and E."

"That's okay," Heather says, quietly before narrowing her eyes as a dark look crosses her face. "Are you writing an article for a newspaper?"

"No, no nothing like that. I'm here as a doctor. I want to understand where the Plague came from, and then, if I manage that, to pass the information on to the scientists around the world working on a vaccine. I think it could help."

Heather looks torn. I can see her mind ticking back and forth between the two options. *Chuck this doctor out, stay quiet, keep my world small and safe. Or, help. Make things better, for the price of even more attention.* "Please," I say. "At least hear my questions and then decide what to do."

She nods. I'm aware that I have jammed a foot in the door of a grieving widow's day and am demanding that she help me but fuck it. I'm a grieving widow and mother too. I'm trying to do the right thing.

"Was Euan doing anything out of the ordinary in the days before he started to feel unwell? In particular, I'm interested in what he was doing forty-eight hours before he started showing symptoms."

Heather sighs and I'm certain, without a doubt, that she knows. She knows exactly what he was doing and who he was doing it with but she's not meant to tell me because it was something wrong. It's a look I've seen in A and E more times than I can count on the teenagers' faces when I ask, "What has your friend taken?" The truth is always there, written on their faces. They desperately don't want to say anything but they know, of course they know. Sometimes honesty can feel like a betrayal.

"No one's going to think badly of him, you know," I say.

"You don't know that," Heather shoots back.

"People will focus on the thing—whatever it is—that caused the virus, not him. Euan didn't create this. It wasn't his fault. It doesn't matter if he was in the wrong place at the wrong time, doing something illegal even." Ah, there it is. The vein in Heather's neck jumps and her mouth tightens. What could he have been doing that brought him into contact with the virus? "What matters is that it will help us find a vaccine, and stop this ever happening again. No one will think this is Euan's fault, I promise."

Heather closes her eyes, and her shoulders drop a little. The defensiveness is starting to melt away. "He and Donal had been friends for a long time. Money's tight around here, especially in the winter. Donal started asking Euan to help out with the odd job here and there a few years ago. Driving packages across to the mainland, collecting things and bringing them back over. Euan never asked what was in them, and Donal never said."

"And Euan told you all of this at the time?"

"He told me everything, he felt better knowing I knew. I should have told him it was a bad idea working with Donal but we needed the money and . . ." She shrugs with a look of regret so all-consuming it's a wonder she's still upright. I realize there's one thing Heather and I both have in common, shining through our interaction. Guilt.

"I should have done things differently but I thought, *we* thought it would be okay. I never in a million years . . . then, last year there were shipments. The ships would be a few miles from shore, Donal and Euan would take a boat out and take, well, whatever it was, back to Bute and then over to the mainland."

My palms are clammy with a mix of anxiety and excitement; I'm on the edge of finding out what I so desperately need to know, and yet it's painful to be so close to the heart of the Plague, the thing that has destroyed my life. "Do you know what they were moving?"

She shakes her head. "He never said but I know where he used to store the boxes overnight. It's a locked shed." Maybe there's something left, a box, a note, anything could help.

"Heather, have you told anyone this before?" She shakes her head, her eyes filling with tears.

"No, I didn't want our sons to think badly of him, but they . . ." She drifts off and I understand.

"Two boys?" I ask, already knowing the answer. She nods. "Me too. Charlie and Josh."

"I'm so sorry," she whispers and it feels like the most honest display of sympathy I've seen in the awful, lonely months since I lost my family.

"I'm sorry for you too, Heather. I really am." I brush my hand over my cheeks, as though efficiently removing my tears somehow makes me more professional. "Could you show me where the boxes were stored?"

As we drive down the coast in Heather's tiny Nissan, the gas meter so low I develop a nervous tic watching it, I get the sense she doesn't leave her house very often. She drives nervously, hands clamped to the top of the wheel, looking out fearfully for something, anything, that might scare her. We reach the rocky shore on a deserted bit of beach surrounded by scrubland and a few blinking cows. A few minutes of walking later, we arrive at a small wooden shed locked with a padlock.

"This is the storage shed," Heather says through chattering teeth. "He told me where it was 'just in case.'" I use a rock to break the rusty lock and the door swings open to reveal four wooden boxes stacked on top of one another. I was so convinced it would be empty, how could it not be? I slide the top of one of the boxes open, expecting guns or drugs or cigarettes. As soon as I see what's inside, and smell it, I turn my head away and retch.

"What's that?" Heather asks, peering over my shoulder.

"I have no idea, but they're dead." There are bones, and dark patches of unidentifiable matter that looks like it might once have been fur. I shudder as I imagine what they might be—monkeys maybe, disgusting definitely. "Right, grab a box, Heather. We're taking these back to your house and then I'm taking them to the mainland."

"Should we tell him?" Heather asks, biting her lip nervously. She does everything nervously and now that I have the potential answer I've been seeking, my patience is wearing awfully thin.

"Tell who?"

"Donal."

I turn back to Heather, aware that my face is almost a pantomime vision of disbelief. "Donal's alive?"

Heather nods, the realization she should have said something to that effect before now clearly dawning on her. "He's immune," she says. Jesus fucking Christ.

# THE GYNARCHY RESISTANCE BLOG

## March 13, 2026

To anyone new here, welcome. If you're reading this you have a chance because you're seeing the truth. I'm Brett Field. I live in Brooklyn, New York. I'm a Men's Rights Activist and I work in sales.

First truth bomb of the day. This is all a conspiracy. It's all the work of women; no other explanation is possible. I've been hearing rumors of an outbreak for months but it seemed to be a European issue. My brother's pissed off because he was planning a backpacking trip around Europe but all of the flights are canceled between New York and France.

I started to get nervous when I heard about the canceled flights. They wouldn't cancel flights unless it was serious. The UK has a female prime minister, which is the Gynarchy at work. (For those of you who haven't been here before, Gynarchy is the word we use for the takeover by women of the world depriving men from taking their rightful places in society.) Half of the French political cabinet is made up of women. Germany has been ruled by a woman for over two decades. I don't like the smell of it. Not at all. Lots of you have messaged to say you agree with me; something suspicious is going on.

I was in Manhattan today; it was almost empty. It's been a few weeks since the East Coast wave. Everyone left the city en masse. It happened so quickly. The city was like a war zone. Men are going to the hospital, but so many doctors are men there's only a few useful female doctors left to treat everyone. Guys, there's no point in going to the hospital. They'll just kill you faster. I tried to take the subway home but no trains came so I walked. It took hours. As I got out of the city, the streets stayed quiet. People were either staying home or had already left the city, I guess. There was a kind of stunned silence. I passed one guy who was clearly sick. His face was gray and he was crying, trying to walk down the street. I crossed to the other side of the street when I saw him. I didn't want to catch it from him.

I've noticed a lot of you guys dropping off the message boards. It's obvious what has happened to you. I don't know how the women have done this, but I know it's their fault. It was their plan all along. They wanted to make sure women got into the best colleges, and got the best jobs, had the most money and then they didn't even need men to have kids. So many women are already having children on their own using donor sperm and weird medical shit, what's the point of men in that equation? They've been moving men slowly into a position of irrelevancy, and now the Plague is confirming it.

One of you asked me a while ago how the Plague could have been created by women? How could they be smart enough to create this disease that only affects men? The answer's simple, folks. Betas. Thousands of betas who have been brainwashed by women helped them out. Most scientists are men, right? Most men are betas. It's not hard to work this shit out.

Women didn't create the Plague on their own. Betas sacrificed their own kind and helped the Gynarchy destroy us. I'm telling you all now. I know how this is going to end. Men are going to be working on farms or doing hard labor, forced to give up our sperm so that women can still have babies without us being anywhere in the picture. It's the end of men.

## Comment from Alpha1476

Great post. You're saying what we're all thinking! Glad you're still here man. I think I might be immune, what about you?

**Reply from BrettFieldMRA (Site Administrator)**
Glad you're still around! Yeah I hope so. Those bitches thought they'd get us all but they were wrong.

**Reply from Alpha1476**
We won't be incels for much longer I bet. Before we all get shipped off to some labor camp anyway. The odds are in our favor now.

# DAWN

know it would be unbecoming for a member of the British Intelligence Services to send a memo around the world asking very nicely if everyone could please CALM DOWN but I'm an inch away from doing so. I can just imagine Zara's tone, the very epitome of a boss talking to someone who's messed up. "Dawn, you're going to have to do some communications training to make up for this."

Almost every country in the world is, to quote my daughter, freaking the fuck out, and I've had it up to here. Maybe it's because I'm British, but for God's sake, you can't just fall apart in a crisis. I've had more phone calls with panicked ambassadors in the last week than I've had hot dinners. You'd never know it to look at me. One of the only silver linings of this whole sorry mess is that I've had a nice office upgrade; I now have an office twice the size of my old one, on the third floor, with natural light no less. I'm dressed as I always am, in a smart black suit. My hair is freshly relaxed thanks to a visit from lovely Candace, my hairdresser who texted me to say she needed the money and would I still want my hair done? The most surreal moment of the last few weeks hasn't been any experience at work. It was feeling the tears from Candace's eyes dripping onto my head as she applied the relaxer to my roots. I haven't checked, but I'd be very surprised if hair relaxer will be on any of the government's priority products for domestic production. More's the bloody pity.

"Sorry I'm late, sorry, sorry." Zara rushes in, wearing the same dress she was wearing yesterday, which, by the smell of it, she has tried to cover up by wearing too much perfume. I hope no one makes a nasty comment in her earshot. Grief is never easy to deal with and she's doing her best.

"Let's begin, shall we. Dawn, Asia, you're up." Just the biggest continent in the world. Nothing cheers the room up like a civil war.

I start the PowerPoint presentation I've prepared. One of the things I was most looking forward to about retirement was never having to produce a PowerPoint ever again. "First, China. Key risks in the short term are nuclear and other weapons making their way into unknown hands and refugees feeding into neighboring countries causing mass disruption. We pulled our ambassador a few weeks ago in a rescue mission along with the remaining Foreign Office staff so we have no diplomatic presence." Every time I see the numbers of potential refugees from the war, I thank God silently that I live on an island.

"Who would we even engage with?" Zara asks. "We need to wait and see how the various factions manage over the next few months. It's important we don't risk a relationship with the future government, whomever that may be formed of, in the midst of war."

I look at the photo on the screen we saw once the telecommunication networks were restored by one of the Chinese factions. The Guangzhou Bridge is on fire, it's the only way to describe it. A woman from one of the factions has her fists raised in defiance. Entire generations of suppressed anger finally being let loose. We don't even know what to call the various sides that are fighting each other.

We were all quite surprised when the Communist Party fell as quickly as it did. I suppose we shouldn't have been. The deal with

Communism is that someone makes sure you have food and a job, in return for your freedom. Not a deal most people choose but when the food shortages swamped China, it was inevitable the system would crumble. Women comprised only 7.5 percent of the People's Liberation Army. They didn't stand a chance. Beijing, Hong Kong, Shanghai, Macau and Tianjin swiftly declared themselves independent and threatened unholy hell on anyone who dared to test them. The Chinese Civil War rages on as its people battle for the rest of the country. Hundreds of millions of people, and who knows where they'll go, what they'll do, who they'll support, how far they'll go to win.

The meeting comes to an end after four other presentations and it's a sign of the times that it feels like a brief respite in the rest of my day. My job is now a very intricate game of Jenga. It's not technically the responsibility of the Intelligence Services to make sure that the country, in its current awful form, functions, and yet the civil service has been decimated and I'm alive and competent, so I do. The questions that arrive on my desk make my head hurt. *How do we make sure we have enough electricians to maintain hospitals, nursing homes, schools, public streetlights?* Conscription is the obvious answer. Failing that, massive advertising for high school graduates and a hastily arranged apprenticeship program. *But how do we make sure the people entering that program have the necessary aptitude?* Test them for it. *But who will compile the test, and administer it, when surviving and female electricians are working sixty-hour weeks to keep the country's lights on and electrical systems functioning?* They'll have to work seventy-hour weeks then. *But how do we train new electricians when 92 percent of electricians have died?* But, but, but. Every answer causes another problem. It's an unanswerable riddle. By comparison, a civil war seems positively easy to deal with.

# ARTICLE IN THE *WASHINGTON POST*
## ON MARCH 14, 2026

---

### "I found the cause of the Plague"

#### by Maria Ferreira

Like much of the world, I've been intrigued by Amanda Maclean for months. I've talked at length about her in my articles. She is one of the central figures of the Plague; it is a position she neither sought nor wanted, yet she has carried its responsibility with grace.

Amanda reached out to me for an interview to coincide with her announcement to the world of the source of the Plague. She has published the paper—co-authored, she stresses, with the virologists Dr. Sadie Saunders and Dr. Kenneth McCafferty of the University of Glasgow—setting out the science but wants the world to understand, in layman's terms, how the Plague came to be. I obviously couldn't meet with Amanda as commercial flights are still not operating the world over. I spoke with Amanda over Skype.

I asked how Amanda found the source of the virus, and to take us back to the beginning. "Euan Fraser, Patient Zero, is from the Isle of Bute, a small island off the west coast of Scotland. I was searching for any clues in the various interviews members of the Bute community had given and there wasn't much. I knew I had to speak to his wife and, after some inquiries with local people, found her address."

Was Heather happy to talk? "Once Heather understood what I was trying to do, yes. She's a lovely woman, truly. She told me that Euan had engaged in some illegal importing activity with another man."

I pushed Amanda to tell me who this other man was but she insisted she was not at liberty to say anything else about him. "Heather showed me the building where the goods were stored and there were four boxes of the last batch Euan and the other man had imported. I took them back to Glasgow and worked with Sadie and Kenneth at the University of Glasgow to identify them and the possible connection with the Plague."

Prior to Amanda's work, the question had been asked, "Where did the Plague come from?" but it was secondary to the far bigger questions that are still being asked today. "How many more men will die before we find a vaccine? When will we find a vaccine? Is this the end of humanity?" Amanda found this oversight of the Plague's origin troubling, although she acknowledges the challenging diplomatic relationship between the Independent Republic of Scotland and the rest of Europe, and its hostile relationship with the United Kingdom, made cooperation impossible in the search for the cause.

Fortunately, Amanda was able to find the origins of the Plague herself. "The boxes contained golden snub-nosed monkeys."

At my baffled expression, Amanda thankfully takes pity on me. "No, I didn't know that they were important either. They're a highly sought-after trafficked animal. Very cute by all accounts, when they're not causing plagues." But how did a monkey cause the Plague?

Amanda grimaces. "Bad luck, primarily. It's relatively common for an animal pathogen to progress into a pathogen that can also be transmitted to humans. The problem is when that pathogen manages to undergo a sequence of what we call secondary transmission long enough to allow it to spread between humans. For example, rabies can only be transmitted naturally from animals to humans. Humans can't give it to one another. The next stage up from that is something like Ebola, which we think is spread by bats but only goes through a few cycles of secondary transmission between humans, which is why the world has experienced numerous small Ebola outbreaks but has never, despite its high mortality rate, faced an urgent threat from Ebola. The next level, the level of the Plague, is a disease that undergoes long sequences of transmission between humans even without the need for the animal. Combined with the Plague's remarkably easy transmission between humans, quick mutation process, ability to survive for thirty-eight hours outside of a host and its high mortality rate, it's a disaster like no other."

Is there any reason why Euan Fraser was the first person to catch the Plague? Amanda is not emphatic on this—she has discussed it at length with Sadie and Kenneth and they don't think so, but they also can't be sure. "We'll never be able to say for certain why this particular combination of the pathogen carried by the live monkeys created the Plague carried by Euan. We know more than we did, but we'll never know the complete story."

Amanda spent weeks being ignored and accused of hysterically overestimating the impact of the Plague, and yet she has devoted months of her life to research for which she has not been paid and, repeatedly, insists on sharing credit for. Does she feel in any way vindicated? She frowns and I feel as though I've overstepped a line. "No. I'm devastated by the deaths of my husband and sons, and by the destruction of the world as we know it. I'm also very, very angry at the way I was ignored not because I need attention but because more could have been done to limit the damage. Vindication suggests I enjoy being proved right. I don't. I just wish the people responsible had done their jobs better. I wish they had tried."

I ask Amanda if she thinks she would have been treated differently if she were a man: seen as less hysterical, less anxious, more credible. She sighs. "I haven't been asked that question before but probably, yes. It's impossible to know but . . ." I comment that as a Latina woman in science journalism I've learned that it's always worth asking that question. I always assume a white man would have an easier time of things.

She is however being recognized for her efforts; Health Protection Scotland has, as of ten days ago, hired Amanda as a "public health consultant." "I'll continue to work five days a week as an A and E doctor and I'll devote one full day a week for Health Protection Scotland while using the on-the-ground information and experience I gain as a doctor to add to the discussion around public health in Scotland." Amanda's done enough interviews not to say anything she doesn't want to, but I can't help but push. *Surely,* it feels good to now have the very institution that ignored her begging for her help. "They didn't beg but yes, I think I will help HPS and I'm glad to be working with them." I note she says *with* not *for.* For that observation I receive a raised eyebrow. Suffice to say, the history between Amanda and HPS means no one is under any illusions; they need her far more than she needs them.

Our discussion has to come to an end because Amanda has a fourteen-hour shift at the hospital for which she's running late. My final question is one I've been asking all of my interviewees. "How are you coping with grief?"

She laughs, briefly. "I'm not," and the screen goes black.

---

# CATHERINE

Devon, United Kingdom

Day 132

'm still here in Devon. There's no point in me staying here but I can't bear to leave. I committed my first-ever crime: I buried my son. What a way to break the law after a lifetime of careful, civil obedience. I couldn't stand for them to take him away and burn him. I don't have anything or anywhere to remember Anthony by. They couldn't take Theodore away too.

He went mercifully quickly. I keep wondering if he was showing symptoms in the days after Anthony's death and I just didn't see. I think I wasted some of the last precious days I could have had with my son arranging a funeral no one attended and driving to Devon. He should have been in my arms every hour of every day. My only baby, I left him alone in the house so much in London. When Anthony was dying I wouldn't let him sleep in my bed even when he cried. I wanted to keep him safe. I thought I was protecting him.

It took him in the same way everyone has been talking about. The Plague is ruthless and predictable. His temperature climbed and climbed all night. Nothing I did helped. Eventually I had him outside, in my lap as I covered him in cold washcloths in the January chill. He didn't even shiver. The next day he fell into unconsciousness and he never woke up again. He had a seizure and died twenty-four hours after I noticed his temperature.

I didn't call an ambulance. There was no point. They would have just taken him from me. Maybe pierced his soft baby skin with needles. Maybe broken his ribs when he stopped breathing in a show of human force in the face of this disease. Or worse, they would have ignored me. Told me to just watch him die and let them know when he was dead. He deserved better than that.

My boy died in my arms as I told him I loved him over and over again. My precious boy. The baby who made me a mother and made us a family. My last piece of Anthony. I hope they're together again. I've never been religious but I have to hope. I hope that somewhere, my baby is being looked after and loved and cared for.

The hole I dug in the garden was too small. No body is meant to go into a hole that small. He couldn't possibly fit in there, I thought to myself, but he did. He's so tiny. I buried him with a blanket and a letter, as though the words I have written will somehow make their way into his life after death. *Know that I love you. Know that I would have died for you in a heartbeat but I wasn't given the opportunity. Know that I am broken without you.*

Three days after I buried him I got my period. Genevieve keeps a shotgun in a cupboard for reasons beyond me. I spent four hours sitting at the kitchen table, the cold metal of the gun against my throat. I will never have another baby. I hadn't thought I was pregnant, there had been no symptoms. But there was a chance. There had been a chance. Anthony and I had slept together enough times around when I ovulated. I thought the world would give me this. I deserved it enough. I wanted it enough. A baby to help me through my grief. A girl after losing Theodore.

But there is no baby, there was never a baby. I am a mother with no child. I will never have another child. The only reason I didn't pull the trigger was the fear that I would go to hell. I don't believe in hell but I want Theodore and Anthony to be together in heaven and there's a chance. I couldn't take the risk of never seeing them again because I couldn't bear the pain. It was the most rational reason my brain could come up with. The risk that hell would continue after my death and I would be kept from my family.

A small risk, perhaps, but an insurmountable one.

I took the cartridges out and put the gun back in the cupboard.

That was two months ago. The TV still works but there is no internet here. The world is falling apart and I'm watching it from a safe distance here in this cottage with just a scrawny cat for company. Genevieve called me two days ago. "Oh, darling, I hoped you would be there. How's Anthony, how's Theodore?"

I wept in response, unable to form the words. "Oh, Cath, oh no, oh, my darling. No, I'm so . . . Oh God. I'm so sorry." She started crying and we cried on the phone to each other for I don't even know how long.

Eventually I managed to ask how her husband is. "He's gone, darling. We managed to stay holed up for months but eventually we had to leave. We would have starved to death otherwise."

Genevieve sounded less bothered by her husband's death than by Anthony's and Theodore's. He was her fourth, after all.

"What are you going to do?" asked Genevieve.

"I don't know. Stay here?"

"You need a project." I almost cried again at her tone; it made me feel as though I was ten years old again. It was the exact same voice she had used when I wanted to stay inside and watch cartoons in the summer holidays. I would be ushered outside to play swingball or instructed to pick sweet peas or told, with an impatient huff, to just "go for a walk." "What's happened is unspeakably awful, darling, and you need to keep busy. Otherwise you'll never recover. Have you been writing?"

"Lots."

"Well then, make something of that. How's work?"

"Societal anthropology specializing in the care of children isn't a big priority at the moment."

"Well, someone's got to be recording what's happening. That's your job, isn't it? You write reports about what people are doing and how they're changing."

After a few more moments of expectant silence I acknowledged that that was sort of my job, yes.

For the last four days, I've done a working day. I've gotten up at eight, spent some time in the garden sitting by Theodore's grave—marked only with some bulbs I planted, too scared that he'll be taken away if someone sees a cross—and then I start work at nine. I've been arranging my journals, the hundreds of pages of fear and uncertainty I've written since the start of this nightmare.

Soon I will go back to London. I need the internet to research and, more important, I'm about to run out of food. I brought lots of cans with me but I'm down to sweet corn and peas. I'm going to record this—all of this—because that's what I'm trained to do and I don't know what else I can do.

I can't help in the fight for a vaccine, I have no medical or practical skills, I don't have anyone left to care for. At the very least, I will record this event—the lives broken, lost and changed. I'll collect stories and understand what on earth is happening and why. I don't know what will happen. No one does. This could be the end of the human race entirely. I know that around 10 percent of men seem to be immune, but that's not enough for humans to maintain a population. Without a cure, 10 percent of the world's men can conceive 10 percent of the number of babies they previously did. Half of those babies will be girls. Only 10 percent of the 5 percent will be immune. The numbers don't add up. This may be the end of all of us.

# ELIZABETH

maya, thank you so much for coming in." George greets Amaya warmly and she smiles and replies, "I didn't have to walk far. It's my pleasure."

Dr. Amaya Sharvani, one of the country's preeminent pediatric geneticists, called George a few days ago with news that has inspired hope, terror, anxiety and excitement. She has given us the key to crack part of the Plague's code.

The three of us sit down in George's warm, cozy office full of worn furniture and photos of his family.

"I take it from the warm welcome that you agree with my hypothesis," Amaya says, her voice light.

"We've been working night and day since you got in touch and yes, we think you're right."

Amaya's eyes widen and she leans back in her chair. "I'm not surprised—it made sense—but it means . . ." She trails off because it means that finding a vaccine is going to be unbelievably difficult. I'm fighting the delirium of exhaustion and disappointment. We've been working for months and there's still such a long way to go. It's March; the beginnings of spring are appearing and making fun of me as I trudge into the lab every morning at 7 a.m. and leave long after it is dark. I try to be cheerful and upbeat when I'm at work. I'm a shoulder to lean on, someone who can solve problems and use my knowledge to drive us forward, toward the goal of a vaccine. But on the way to work as I psyche myself up, and on the way home as I decompress, I suspect I look like the weight of the world is on my shoulders.

Identifying the vulnerability of men against the virus, and women's protection from it, has taken so much longer than we anticipated, but Amaya has figured it out, thank God. Like many complicated things in science, the answer is ultimately relatively simple. We had so many theories. As we suspected, but couldn't prove, it's all in the genes. It feels like a miracle that Amaya has made this discovery and at the same time I'm so angry we didn't figure it out ourselves. Over thousands of years the Y chromosome has lost most of its genes. The twenty-third pair of chromosomes in women is XX, and in men is XY. Y determines the forming of testes and production of sperm, but it doesn't come as part of a matching pair. In paired chromosomes, like XX, with two copies, a mistake in one can be resolved by the correct gene sequence in the other. But when mistakes occur in the Y chromosome, it just disappears.

The Plague virus requires the absence of a specific gene sequence. The body's resistance to the Plague—through its ability to fight the high white blood cell count it generates with speed—is present in the X chromosome. In around 9 percent of men their X chromosome has the necessary genetic protection. Thanks to their XX chromosomes, all women are safe. The others, the billions of other men, are vulnerable to the virus.

"How did you find it?" George asks her. "How did you know?"

"I've been treating two sets of twins," Amaya says, her face for the first time revealing the weariness of a medical professional in the post-Plague world as though a curtain has been pulled to the side of her calm, well-rested façade. "One set of male identical twins were both immune but their father was not. A set of male fraternal twins had an immune father but only one of the twins was immune. The other died. Basic genetic logic. And the luck of any of my patients being immune."

George nods. "We've been doing the workings, so to speak, and we're nearly there with the coding. The theory works, but we need to know why."

"It also explains why women are asymptomatic hosts," I add.

"It bothered me that we knew but didn't know why," Amaya says with a sigh. "Amanda Maclean was talking about it right from the beginning because she identified a female nurse as a cause of the spread of infection in her A and E Department."

"Like with many things in the story of the Plague, Amanda was way ahead of the rest of the world," George says.

Amaya pauses, looks at George thoughtfully. "I have to say, it's a pleasant surprise to be sitting with a male doctor, discussing all of this. There's not many of you left."

George smiles in response, almost apologetically. "I'm immune. We tested my blood and Elizabeth personally looked at it under a microscope. I carry the virus but I'm asymptomatic. We're working on a test for immunity, trying to identify the specific genetic markers. This will obviously help enormously."

"We're an army of hosts," Amaya says with sad sigh. "Spreading it all around. How close are you to a vaccine?" George was cautious about saying anything on the phone about our progress, or lack thereof. It's crucial that the difficulties we're having finding a vaccine are not leaked to the public, unplanned and unfiltered. We can see the headlines writing themselves.

George looks at me, as if to say, "Do you want to take this one or shall I?" I decide to take one for the team. "We've not made a lot of progress," I say, trying to lift the sentence with some optimism. "But we're working on it, and we've managed to discount some options. The virus is very unstable, it's hard to—well, you understand."

Amaya's face has dropped and I realize that the only thing scarier than knowledge is the lack of it. At least I know the details of what is being done, the scant information coming from other countries' vaccine programs, the small steps forward we've made in our analysis of immunity. Amaya, until now, has probably been able to convince herself that the task force was close to success.

"I feared that might be the case," she says, twisting her wedding band round her finger. It's loose; she must have lost weight, grief most likely. It's not a great leap to assume she's now a widow.

I want to make her feel better. "We will get there, we're closer than we were, but everything you've done is going to change a lot. Your discovery, the understanding of the genetics of male vulnerability, will make it so much easier. Truly, you've done something extraordinary."

Later that afternoon, once Amaya has returned to her patients at Great Ormond Street, George and I talk. We have a few more weeks of work to do, finalizing the genetic sequencing and then what?

"We have to release it," George says. I nod in agreement.

"Of course. If this helps any of the other programs along, all the better."

"We should liaise with the press people, make an announcement once we've figured it all out. Release the workings, our findings, everything. We'll have a Skype conference and answer questions."

"Yet another way in which we're taking inspiration from Amanda Maclean."

George's eyes crinkle as he smiles. "I'd love to meet her one day." He pauses, in thought or anxiety, I'm not sure which. "Do you think anyone else is making progress? Are they further along than we are?"

George asks, his hands cupping a mug of hot water. "Or do you think they're all as fucked as we are?" he adds.

"Well, I don't know about that but I do know an adage an old, wise man used to say to me. The harder you work, the luckier you get."

A grin bursts across George's face. "Fuck off, I'm not that old!"

"If you say so, old man." And with a smile, and not a little hope and trepidation, we get back to work.

# LISA

### Toronto, Canada
### Day 149

Oh my God. George Kitchen and that mousy American girl from the CDC and some random geneticist have identified the male vulnerability to the virus. This coming weeks after Amanda Maclean, Sadie Saunders and Kenneth McCafferty discovered the origins of the virus. I'm feeling both left behind and grateful they've publicized their work. I hate feeling grateful. I want to have something other people can feel grateful to me for. I call the best geneticist I work with and one of the only people I would call a work friend. She pisses me off very rarely and doesn't take any shit. I like her immensely.

"Nell, it's Lisa."

"Lisa, I've told you before. I can see who it is on my phone, we've had caller ID since the nineties."

"What do you want me to say? Hello, and then just launch in to it? Have you seen the news?"

"I've been in the lab all day. I just stepped out to get lunch."

"George Kitchen, Elizabeth Cooper and some geneticist called Amaya Sharvani have done it. They've identified the gene sequence responsible for female immunity."

"Of course Amaya Sharvani would have something to do with this."

I've never heard of her. "Is she good?"

"Only thirty-six, she's phenomenal. She had four papers out last year, does amazing work at Great Ormond Street. Yeah, she's good. Never mind that, how did she figure it out?"

"Twins, one fraternal with an immune father and only one twin immune. One set of identicals both immune with a dad who wasn't. Partly luck she had those sets of patients. Then they homed in on the genes, did the sequencing, and here we are. The entire world is floored by their genius."

"Now now, Leese. I can hear a familiar green tinge to your voice." I can tell Nell is smiling. She loves making fun of me. It's really annoying.

"I'm not jealous."

"And yet, you're the one to bring up that word."

"I'm thrilled they've made this discovery."

"But you wish it had been you."

I laugh. "And don't you?"

Nell sighs. "Of course. The difference is that I can accept there might be people in the world who are more intelligent than I am, Lisa. A concept you seem to struggle with."

I'd like to think I'm handling this conversation with the dignity and grace befitting a professor of an esteemed institution but instinctively I let out a kind of growl that makes me think of my dad when my mom would turn the TV off.

"We need to meet," Nell says briskly. "Read the materials, talk them through, figure out where we go next."

"Already on my way over to you."

For the first time in a few days, I feel excited. I would never let my staff know, but this work is a grind with no letup and, despite popular belief, I'm only human. I get tired and overwhelmed and just want it all to be over. I don't *show* it. Leaders need to be strong, and no one can accuse me of being weak. But I needed this today. We needed this boost, badly. This will speed up our research tenfold.

Thank you, George and Elizabeth and Amaya. If I was in their position I probably wouldn't have released this information. But they're not me and I can benefit from it, and that means we'll have a vaccine quicker and men can stop dying. We're reaching a critical point in population loss the world over. We're past *a* point of return but we're not yet past *the* point of return. There are still enough young women of child-bearing age to have a hope in hell of population recovery. I sigh, and text my assistant to get me another Red Bull. The work is only just beginning.

# SURVIVAL

# MORVEN

A small farm next to the Cairngorms National Park,
the Independent Republic of Scotland
Day 224

It's been 161 days since I saw my son. I know he's alive from the crackly call I get from his walkie-talkie every morning, but that's the only contact we have. When it's dark and I'm washing the dishes in the kitchen, I can see the faint glow from his hut eight hundred meters away. It takes everything I have not to run the short distance and scoop him into my arms.

Cameron—my patient, frustrated husband—has been asking for months when we're going to let Jamie come back. "When we know it's safe," I say. He's becoming increasingly resentful of my fear. We've been together twenty-five years; I know him like the back of my hand and I know he's going to snap soon. But he's always been the more reckless of the two of us. None of the boys seem to be sick, this is true. Cameron hasn't gotten sick.

But we don't know anything about these boys or the virus. We don't know how long you can be asymptomatic. What if one of them has it lurking in his system or there's a bit of it in one of the tents? The stakes are so high, the regret would kill me if Jamie died all because we were impatient. Cameron says I'm a conspiracy theorist because I don't believe the government when they say men are asymptomatic for two days. I *don't* believe it. They've done everything wrong. They didn't believe Amanda Maclean, they haven't found a vaccine, they barely did anything to stop the spread of the virus. I just don't believe them.

The other boys are playing football on the makeshift pitch. The whoops and hollers of seventy-eight teenage boys used to bring a smile to my face. I would revel in the sounds of joy when outside the safe confines of our space here, there is only danger and sadness. But that was almost six months ago. Now, the resentment is killing me.

If I was a different kind of woman, I would maybe acknowledge that this is traumatizing and that my brain feels frayed and close to collapse. As it is, I drink two bottles of our stashed wine once every few weeks and try to forget that any of this is happening. Without my son I'm struggling to function. I'm keeping other women's sons safe and happy and well while my own son rots in loneliness a fifteen-minute walk away. The boys are wonderful. It's not their fault that any of this is happening. They all look so young, especially when they first arrived. Fear takes the promise of adulthood out of a child's face, I find. These big teenage lads, nearly six feet, away from their mums, scared senseless, unsure if they'd ever see their dads again, looked so young. Gangly and insubstantial.

Thank God we were given supplies with each bus. The boys each have a box—they read STERILIZED—SAFE on the sides—with a sleeping bag, a pillow, basic food supplies, water purification tablets, and a "leisure" item. I did a double take when I saw those. There were a few different ones—some had a football, others a Frisbee. There was even a cricket bat and ball. Part of me thought, *A football?! They need food!* But it was good foresight on the part of whoever did that.

Including a nonessential luxury item in each boy's box has given them permission to play. To have fun. If your survival kit has come with a football, what do you do? You play. You say to the boys next to you, "Who wants a game?" and you make friends, and you run around and you get out of breath and you forget, for a moment, that you're in a strange place with people you don't know because the world is coming to an end.

There's been no communication from anyone. We watch the TV but we don't get the main channels anymore. The Scottish government, after they declared independence in February, changed it so that we only get a Scottish news channel. I don't think they tell us the truth. We've heard nothing about a vaccine or a cure. They just say to stay calm and keep boys inside and remind us that the penalty for looting is twenty years in prison. I think some of the civil servants who put the Highland Evacuation Program together have died. I still read the opening letter most weeks as if it's going to have magically changed and transformed into an answer.

Even now, the letter makes me shiver. The threat of prison if I do anything wrong. How did we come to this? I imagine Sue, the woman who signed it, as a hard-faced, flinty woman with square glasses and a pinched mouth. The kind of woman who, had she been a teacher, would have reveled in ripping up pieces of homework and bemoaned the lack of physical discipline in schools. I know that in reality she's doing her job. She's trying to save lives. I just wish her efforts hadn't come at the cost of my family.

The phone rings. I jump on it, hoping it'll be news of a vaccine too secret to be released on the news.

"Hello?"

"Hello, is that Morven Macnaughton?"

"Yes. Who are you?" God, you can tell I've been around teenage boys for too long. My manners have flown out the window.

"My name's Catherine Lawrence. I'm an anthropologist. I'm so sorry, I know this is out of the blue, but could I please speak to you about the evacuation program?"

"How did you get this number?"

"A friend of mine works at the University of Edinburgh. She helped set up the program. She thought you might want someone to talk to. She said you've called the evacuation phone line a few times."

My face flushes at the memory. I was told off like a naughty schoolgirl by a woman who sounded young enough to be my daughter.

"Are you a therapist?"

"No, no. Although I can try and find one and have her call you if that would be helpful. No, I'm an anthropologist. I work at University College London. I . . . I . . . I'm trying to collect stories of what is happening."

"For the news?"

"No, for . . . well, for myself, I suppose, but one day they might become an academic paper. It's a record. I want to record what's happening. I want to write it all down."

I'm suspicious of this strange English woman, but the voice of a woman is so welcome. I've mainly spoken to men for months. The desire to talk to her is overwhelming. I should put down the phone but I don't. I don't want to.

"What do you want to know?"

"Anything, everything. Tell me whatever you can."

"My son is in a hut at the edge of our land." The words spill out and I burst into tears. This is mortifying.

"Why is he there?"

"We put him in the hut right at the beginning to keep him safe, before the other boys arrived. We didn't know if they would be infected so it seemed like the safest option."

"And your husband?"

"I told him to stay with Jamie but he was worried about me being on my own taking care of all these boys we didn't know. Jamie's on his own. He's been there for months."

"Why don't you let him join you and the other boys?"

"Because of the Plague! We don't know if they're right about it. What if one of them has it and just hasn't shown it yet? What if it's hiding somewhere in my things or in the house or on the tents or, or, or . . ."

"How long have you had the boys with you?"

"Over five months."

Catherine pauses. "The virus can only survive for thirty-eight hours on a surface and a man can only be asymptomatic for a maximum of three days, although it's usually two. Jamie will be fine. None of the boys have the virus. It's safe, Morven."

Tears are coursing down my cheeks and I'm sobbing down the phone to this complete stranger.

"Morven, listen to me. Your son is safe. Go get him. Please, take it from me. Spend all the time with him you can."

I drop the phone, not bothering to say good-bye. The hut is so close. I tear past the boys, ignoring shouts asking if I'm all right and what's going on. He's there. He's going to be safe. Jamie. Jamie. I'm so sorry I kept you out there for so long, Jamie.

I'm sprinting and as I cross the final field to get to him I see him sitting outside the hut on a fold-up chair. His hair is shaggy, he's got the beginnings of a beard. Oh, my boy.

"Jamie, it's safe," I'm screaming hoarsely.

"Mum?" I can hear his voice. I worried I'd never hear his voice again.

I reach him and crash into him, hugging him tightly. He's taller than me and his arms are around me and I'm sobbing.

"Mum, Mum, are you okay? Mum, is it Dad? What's happening?"

"It's safe," I sob. "None of them have the virus. You can come back now. It's safe for you."

# AMANDA

**Glasgow, the Independent Republic of Scotland**
**Day 230**

**H**ealthy people get so wrapped up in their grief for their husbands and families and friends that they forget that millions of people across the world were already sick before the Plague, and their illnesses didn't magically cure themselves once the Plague started. Emergencies like sepsis, meningitis, appendicitis, pneumonia and kidney infections don't stop just because the world is in crisis. I wish I could say to all the old women in Glasgow, "Would you stop fucking *falling*, the lot of you, I only have two orthopedic doctors left in this entire hospital." Alas, I can't. Even in the midst of a crisis, I have a better bedside manner than that.

This morning, we had three elderly women who had fallen and needed hip replacements or wrist surgery. All three will probably die as more urgent surgeries take precedence. In my new Health Protection Scotland role, I have the delightful job of creating an Urgency of Care Protocol, which essentially boils down to Young People Get Treated, Old People Don't, If You're a Man with a Working Penis We Want to Keep You Alive.

It's a constant balancing act between the value of life and the value of resources in a hospital with ever-dwindling supplies of, well, everything. Even gauze is being rationed. We don't have excess of anything and we receive tiny, random deliveries of supplies at unpredictable times.

This morning provided a few blessedly clear scenarios. Two women presented with urgent kidney infections: a UTI can quickly become serious without antibiotics. They both required an inpatient stay on IV antibiotics. One was twenty-two, the other forty-one with two kids. Treatment required and provided. One man came to the hospital with appendicitis; his appendix was about to burst, so with surgery he would almost certainly be fine. Again, an easy call. I called down the general surgeons and they wheeled him straight up. It reminded me of a horrible case a few weeks ago. A sixty-eight-year-old woman came in, she was in an awful state. Her appendix had already burst. I called down Pippa, our head of general surgery, and she told us to wheel her into a side room. "There's no point," she said. One of the other young doctors, a surgeon, was outraged. "We can't just let her die!" She was hysterical. But I understood what Pippa was saying. We had to be pragmatic. The supplies it takes for a messy surgery, the antibiotics, the time needed for nurses. It wasn't worth it. Pippa said we should be stingy with the morphine, which, again, I understood but couldn't bear to follow. There's a reason she's a surgeon and I'm not. Sociopaths, the lot of them.

The woman with appendicitis died twelve hours later. I gave her as much morphine as I could bear to but it was an awful death. That was a difficult day.

Now we're fairly certain that the men who appear at A and E have either beaten the Plague or are immune. For a few months it was dire; we received strict instructions from the Health Department that the Plague was not to be treated. Those who arrived at any A and E Department in Scotland suffering from the Plague were not to be allowed in the building. They were to be sent home without ceremony. Telling a desperate mother of a dying baby or toddler, and—in one particularly awful case—of eighteen-month-old twins, that she wasn't even allowed to enter the building made me question everything. What is the point of being doctors if we're not even trying to help people? The response when we raised it with the Health Department was simple and strongly worded: "Valuable medicines and resources are *not* to be wasted on patients who have over 90 percent rate of mortality." The chances of any men or boys in Glasgow managing to avoid exposure to the Plague is now so low that, as of two weeks ago, we treat all men. Hence the painful focus of my HPS role. Oh, how they've changed their tune.

As tempting as it was to tell the Scottish health authorities to go fuck themselves, I want as many people as possible to survive. And so every time I treat a patient and do a shift, I add to my document, which will shortly be circulated to all hospitals in Scotland as an A and E treatment protocol. Some things are obvious. Regardless of the sex of the patient, we only give antibiotics if absolutely necessary and at the lowest possible effective dose. Blood transfusions and fluids are restricted to life-and-death situations like extreme trauma. Others have been less obvious. I suggested a month ago that every member of hospital staff, health permitting, should be required to give blood every eight weeks on pain of social exclusion and embarrassment because why the fuck are you working in a hospital if you don't want to help? There's a donation room permanently set up just by the staff entrance. We post on the board by the entrance the names of people who have missed their slot. Most obvious of all, anyone who comes to the hospital but isn't really ill is told in no uncertain terms to go home.

There's still the occasional rumor that a vaccine is going to be found but none of us really believe it. It feels like this is normal life now.

A lot of people have forgotten just how vulnerable humans are. They're amazed when I tell them how many people come to A and E every single day with a relatively common problem that could easily kill them without the resources we don't have enough of. There's a reason that the life expectancy hundreds of years ago was so low. Many things can kill a person. People are becoming painfully aware of that fact now.

So, we struggle on. There are rumors that the government is in talks to arrange the importation of some key drugs from France. Fun fact, five countries produce two-thirds of the world's medicines—France, Germany and the UK are the three European countries on that list. Scottish independence doesn't seem like such a brilliant idea now.

# ELIZABETH

Y ou need more friends," George says over lunch, as Amaya determinedly looks into her sandwich.

"George! I have lots of friends," I say, a bit defensively. This isn't technically true. I have a lot of acquaintances here in London now. I like to smile at people and say hello, so sue me. The first time I went into the lab I think some of my colleagues thought I was deranged. I was determined to add some cheer into the office. The whole world has been burning, so I figured we should make our workplace a little less depressing. Over months and months I managed to chip away at the hardened, English, often grief-stricken exteriors of people in the lab. Small things like movie nights on Fridays that are well attended by people living alone. We rewatched a season of *The Great British Bake Off* together and each week someone re-created one of the recipes as best they could from the ingredients they could scrounge up.

"I'm friends with you two," I say, almost accusingly daring George and Amaya to disagree.

"And a fine friend you are indeed," Amaya says, her brown eyes crinkling in kindness.

"You work too hard, you need to get out of the lab," George says.

"You work the same hours I do, if not longer," I reply. "Besides, we're nearly there on a chemical test for immunity."

"Yes, and then I go home and spend time with my family. You go back to that awful hotel and do extra research. Besides, Amaya and her team are finishing up their piece. We'll look over the numbers tomorrow. It'll come together soon enough. There's still room to live our lives, you know."

Amaya nods in agreement and I feel like sulking. It feels wrong having my boss tell me that I need to relax more. It's true that I miss having my friends close to me. In high school I was a science nerd, saved from bullying by my blond hair and vaguely pretty-ish (on a good day with makeup) looks. I left with a few friends I had eaten lunch with but we didn't really keep in touch. All my friends from Stanford scattered across the country after graduation, to different graduate schools. We Skype but it's not the same. They're not here. I've managed to re-create some of the community I crave here at work, but if I'm being honest with myself, fine, it's true. Besides George and Amaya, I don't have friends.

As George and Amaya chat about their daughters; I go through my phone. I haven't been on Facebook in years. I don't need to see what anyone else's life looks like right now. It's so odd seeing the number of women on my page. Girls I know from grad school who never posted pictures without their boyfriends or husbands now in profile photos, alone. Among my hundreds of Facebook friends' recent posts there's one announcement of a baby and one wedding of a couple who have been together for years and have dodged the bullet of the Plague. I'm scrolling, trying to tamp down jealous feelings of wanting a husband and a baby and a life of my own when I see a picture of Simon Maitland. Wow, he's alive, which isn't a given anymore. One of the lucky, elite remaining men: the immune. I last saw him in person when I was twenty-one and spent a semester in London, at Imperial College, on an exchange program. Then he was a lanky, redheaded engineering major who used to eat lunch with me most days thanks to his friendship with my "exchange buddy." The last eight years have been kind to Simon, Jesus Christ. He's gorgeous.

Swallowing any doubt before it can hover into my mind, I click on Simon's profile. What does George always say? Nothing ventured, nothing gained. I click on the Message icon.

> Hi Simon,
>
> Not sure if you remember me—we met years ago when I was an exchange student from Stanford. Anyway, I'm in London now working in the Vaccine Development Task Force. It might be nice to catch up—show me some of London! Let me know if you'd like to grab a drink. Elizabeth xx

I hit Enter and send the message before I can think about it again. I've just asked someone out for a drink for the first time. I think I might be sick. Two x's? TWO? What was I thinking? My stomach is roiling in anxiety and I consider deleting my Facebook presence and committing myself to a slow slide into single cat-lady status. It's fine, I love cats and besides the numbers aren't in my favor anymore so—

The reply flashes onto my screen so quickly I drop my phone. George asks if I'm okay. I squeak in response.

> Elizabeth! Amazing to hear from you. I would love to take you out for a drink. Does this evening work? Simon x

I'm going on a date. I'm going on a date! It all feels so improbable and exciting I decide to lean into this brave new romantic world I'm creating for myself.

Tonight works great. Let me know where we should meet—I live near Euston. Elizabeth P.S. This is a date, right?

I'll have a think and let you know where to meet. Simon x P.S. Yes, I'd really like it to be a date.

A few hours later, I walk to the bar Simon suggested, a beautiful cocktail bar with live music in Smithfield. When I woke up this morning I didn't think I'd be on a date and I'm a bit nervous that my simple green dress and brogues aren't smart enough but here I am. As I see Simon turning the corner and walking toward me, I realize that seeing photos of someone and seeing their transformation in person are entirely different things. Somewhere between the shock of asking him on a date and him accepting, I forgot that eight years is a very long time. The man standing in front of me, with auburn hair and a beautifully cut coat, six feet tall and broad shouldered, is unrecognizable from the gawky undergrad I remember.

He kisses me on the cheek, smelling of something citrusy and fresh, and my brain keeps short-circuiting. *I'm on a date, I'm on a date.* A date with the kind of guy I never really imagined being sat across from. My previous boyfriends have been geeky scientists who couldn't bench-press a watermelon and have never seemed to like me all that much. Small talk used to involve complaints about Atlanta traffic and wondering what our table would be like. Now it involves broaching the topic of immunity and the looming question above Simon's head: *How are you alive?*

The bar feels so familiar—I've spent evenings in cocktail bars before— and yet so different, it's discombobulating. The musicians are all women—the double bass player, the drummer, the saxophonist—and it's only as I look at them that I realize the bands have always been male. The menu is entirely British-made drinks—sloe gin, cider, English sparkling wine—and due to shortages everyone is restricted to one drink.

Other women in the bar eye us enviously and sadly, which I might be imagining but I don't think I am. It's as though I can hear them wondering what a man like that is doing with a woman like me. I'm talking about my old life but I feel like I'm floating, untethered from the room.

"Are you okay?" Simon asks softly, about thirty minutes in. Part of me wants to scream, "Never been better!" and I would sort of mean it. Part of me wants to burst into tears at how gloriously normal all of this is and how awful it's going to be to go back to my tiny room, in this cold city where I only have two friends and God I just want my old life back when my dad was alive and going on dates was normal.

"It's just a lot," I eventually say. "I'm having a really nice time though. Sorry, that sounds weird. I honestly am. It's just this is the first date I've gone on in a long time and life is really different now, you know?"

Simon's face breaks into a smile that I swear could light up this whole room and he says the perfect words. "I know exactly what you mean." He looks around the bar. "I don't go out that much anymore. Everything feels so different."

"You don't get asked out on dates all the time then? I would have thought you'd be out a lot," I ask, testing the waters and preparing myself for the inevitable shrug that means yes.

Simon smiles and reaches over, takes my hand. "I do get asked out, yes. But I've never been asked out before by the American girl I remember from eight years ago, who was so funny and friendly and bright that we all desperately wanted to hang out with her at lunch every day. And beautiful," he says, quietly into his drink as though he's used up his bravado in a rush of words.

A smile overwhelms my face and I have to contain myself from reaching across the table and kissing him, right then and there. And then I remember that the world is falling apart and nothing is like it used to be and I haven't been on a date in a long, long time. So I reach across, kiss him and it's the best first kiss of my life.

# IRINA

'm praying in the Cathedral of Christ the Savior like I do every day. *Save me. Please God almighty. Take him away from me. Please don't let him be one of the chosen few. I will be your loyal servant for the rest of my life, both in life and in death, if you will please, let me be free. Why is my husband not dead yet? Please God, kill him.*

It has been months. He is still alive. Why? Why him? He beats me every evening. He is the worst kind of man. Katya is growing up in a house that is no place for a child.

The priest looks at me with a frown. It's probably the black eyes. Or maybe it's my nose. He did that last Monday. I'll probably have a bump in it forever now. I liked my nose. I want to tell him they're not my fault, but he's already passed me. My husband cannot be immune. It would not be right. Babies and little boys and doctors have died. Good people. It is not right for bad people to survive. It cannot be right.

Life was still and quiet and occasionally terrifying for a long time. Mikhail drank too much, earned too little. I worked in the shop, I kept Katya safe. There were only a few beatings. It was manageable. He made sure to leave my face alone. No need for awkward questions.

Then the rumors started. At first, they were whispers. There was a disease attacking men in Scotland and then England. We wondered if it was poison. There had been killings before, it was possible, wasn't it? But then the list of countries grew bigger and the news on the TV couldn't talk about anything else. Sweden. France. Spain. Portugal. Belgium. Germany. Poland. Once it was in Poland I started to panic. What would happen to us? I remember thinking, "How would we survive without Mikhail?" And then I realized how much easier things would be if he just died. Then it didn't seem so scary anymore.

The first Russian case was reported in mid-December, although everyone says it was here before then. It felt like everyone had been holding their breath, waiting and waiting for the first one and once it had happened, we could all breathe and cry and wail and exhale again. I felt relief that it might reach us soon and terror at what the world would look like.

There has been a surge of domestic violence throughout the spring as the disease ravages Moscow. Not everyone's husbands are terrible though. My friend Sonya's husband stayed home with her all the time. He loved her so much. Then he ran away to Siberia to try and escape it. She told me he was crying when he was left but they agreed it was the safest thing to do. She has not heard from him since. Maybe these men think the cold will protect them, the ones who go north. But it doesn't. The Plague doesn't care where you go. It will find you.

Mikhail never considered going anywhere. He doesn't love us enough to want to live. He has stayed and drunk vodka like it's his dying day, every day.

At first, I was excited. Any day now he will catch it. Any day now he will die. But the days are passing. I am praying and nothing is changing. I can't leave. He owns the apartment. I don't earn enough. He would kill me and keep Katya.

Now I am bored of the pain, bored of the bruises, but more than anything I am scared. He must be immune. Almost every man in

Moscow has died but Mikhail. He spends every day outside of the house in bars. He is reckless. He touches people, accepts drinks, takes public transportation.

He arrives home, late as always, drunker than usual. I make sure to be in the kitchen when he arrives. It's worse if I'm in bed. I try to give him a glass of water but he doesn't like that. I never know what he will accept as help or interpret as an insult. He swipes at me but can't be bothered to put any weight into it. It probably won't bruise. He stumbles through to our bedroom, passes out, smelling metallic.

I feel his forehead, praying it will be feverish, but it is cool. He is immune. He is immune. This can't go on. I have a plan for Katya and me to be safe and leave him behind. I take the thermometer out of the bathroom and some tissues and put them by his bed. What else does a sick person need? A cold washcloth. That too.

I change into my pajamas and lie down next to him. It is time. I take the spare pillow he has abandoned and hold it firmly. I cover his face and push down as hard as I can. He starts to stir and move his arms but I am straddling him now, my knees digging into his sides. Pressing down, down I keep holding it. He stops moving after a while but I don't know if he's playing dead. If he's still alive he will kill me. Hold down for longer. Keep holding.

I stay with the pillow pressed down until the clock shows it is 4 a.m. His chest has not moved for a long time. I do not think he could be pretending now. I take the pillow off and spring away from him just in case. His head lolls to one side. His eyes are unblinking. I let out a whoop and then clasp my hand over my mouth. My neighbor must not hear that kind of thing.

I leave my dead husband—I am now a widow. I prefer that word to "wife." I will sleep in Katya's room tonight. My baby and I are safe.

"Come into my bed, Mama," she says to me sleepily when I open the door to her room. Beside my soft, sleepy girl I lie down and she snuggles into me as I curl up under her covers. For the first time in years I sleep like I did when I was child, knowing I am safe.

I wake up when Katya starts to stir. I tell her to go to the kitchen and make breakfast, everything as it usually is, keep it the same, stay calm. I go through to the bedroom. He is definitely dead. I have thought about this before but now that I must do it, it feels riskier than I had thought. I call the phone number they gave out on the news. The Body Snatchers, everyone calls them. The women employed by the government to take the bodies away and burn them.

I try to sound sad and shocked. They arrive a few hours later. I have made sure to cry a little to make it believable. I assumed they would ask me some questions about the illness and when he died but they just ask for his name and SNILS number. I recite them and watch in disbelief as they pick up his body, put it in a bag and leave with only a short sentence: "I'm sorry for your loss."

If I had known it would be this easy, I would have killed him months ago.

### "Women at War: The Chinese Civil War Unmasked"

#### by Maria Ferreira

I wish I could take credit for an extraordinary feat of journalistic talent, and say I painstakingly researched the Chinese Civil War, carefully built up relationships with its key actors and managed to convince one of its rebel leaders to trust me enough to be interviewed.

It didn't happen like that. Fei Hong, the rebel leader based in Chengdu, e-mailed me. I replied to her e-mail and set up a FaceTime call fully expecting it to be a prank. It wasn't. What can I tell you, sometimes Chinese rebel commanders make this job really easy.

I can see the accusations that I'm being used as a mouthpiece for a villainous woman, intent on violence, from a mile away. To that, I answer, I might not have had to fight hard for this interview but I'm still a journalist. I have, to the extent possible, researched Fei's claims and where they are impossible to confirm or rebut, I'll say so.

When she appears on my screen—the picture startlingly clear—I'm assessed coolly. It's clear, before Fei Hong has said a word, that she's a powerful woman.

We exchange brief pleasantries and I ask her the most expansive, first question I can think of. "Why did you want to talk to me?" What follows is an edited transcript of my conversation with Fei.

FEI: You're the "Plague" journalist. With you, our story will have the most reach.

MARIA: Whose story is this? Who do you refer to when you say "our"?

FEI: I only speak for the United Democratic Alliance of Chengdu. But the Communist Party tries to make it appear to the outside world like there is far more distance between rebel groups than exists. Mostly we have the same goal: democracy.

[Note: Fei refers to the Communist Party, which reports say is now divided and has an increasingly shaky grasp across the country. Technically, the Communist Party still comprises the government of the People's Republic of China.]

MARIA: Is that your only goal?

FEI: It is the first thing we need to achieve. Everything else will flow from that.

MARIA: What's your background? How did you end up where you are?

FEI: I studied law at the University of Cambridge. My parents have always been anti-Communist activists. They passed messages on at mahjong meetings. I grew up knowing things had to change. When the Plague started I got home in time. I have been involved in the Chengdu rebellion since the beginning, in January 2026.

MARIA: Why is this rebellion surviving when no previous rebellion has?

FEI: Because the army and the government are formed of men. They died or are dying. The rebellion is only formed of women. Once we know who is immune, men may be able to join, but in the meantime it is just women. We are safe. We can continue to fight. The Plague is burning everything to the ground and we will rebuild it, better, different.

MARIA: What do you say to the allegations of the government that rebel groups across China are engaging in extreme violence?

FEI: They are lies formed by the few men, and women, who remain in government. This is a different kind of civil war than has ever existed. For the first time, rape is not a tool in this war. Guns can't be used senselessly because there aren't enough surviving soldiers to fire them, and we stormed military bases overwhelmed by the Plague. Four months ago, I met with nine other rebel leaders. Some of us are fighting with one another but we maintained a brief twenty-four-hour window of peace to agree we would not use violence unless absolutely necessary to defend ourselves. We have seen men wage war since the dawn of time. Nobody wins the wars men fight.

MARIA: What will happen to China, and what do you want to happen to China? Is it too big to be led as you want it to be, as a democracy?

FEI: China as it used to be doesn't exist anymore. It will splinter—it is already fractured. We are fighting now over the different pieces but we use different weapons. We use cyber weapons, we use messages of persuasion. The population will not be led blindly by fear so whoever wins will have power and people on their side.

MARIA: Are you trying to persuade one of the four independent states to help you?

[Note: Beijing, Shanghai, Tianjin and Macau declared themselves as independent states in quick succession in April 2026. Reports say that swift, decisive action from rebellious government officials who teamed up with powerful businessmen in a number of near-bloodless coups quashed any possibility of counter-rebellion from the local populations. Elections have been implemented and economic stability promised.]

FEI: They will stay out of the war. They have chosen a

different path. If the four independent states stay that way, there is a possibility that the rest of China can form itself into something better.

MARIA: When do you think the war will end?

FEI: Soon. The army will just keep dying. The Communist Party will continue to weaken. Women won't die, won't go anywhere. We'll win.

---

# RACHEL

## Auckland, New Zealand
### Day 240

t's not just us. It's Belgium and Mexico too. We're not doing this to hurt you, I promise, we are doing this to save lives."

I've given this speech too many times. It even sounds weary to my own ears. I think I sounded more zealous a few months ago, but now I just sound tired.

"How do you sleep at night?" the mother, Mrs. Turner, asks me, one in a long line of tear-stained women I've had to apologize to over the past four months.

I smile tightly. There is nothing to be gained from me answering this honestly. *Incredibly easily, Mrs. Turner, I'm out like a light as soon as my head hits the pillow.* Mrs. Turner finally gets up and leaves the room, not before shooting me a final resentful glance. Why doesn't this get any easier? The psychologist in me answers: because these people are in a state of trauma and you have removed their control over the most precious thing in their lives. The human in me answers: because you're here, and easy to blame.

When I accepted the position of lead psychologist of the Birth Quarantine Program of New Zealand in February, I thought the job wouldn't be needed. It sounded exciting, it would definitely look good on my CV, and it was unthinkable that a vaccine wouldn't be invented.

But that was four months ago and now it's June and no vaccine is in sight. Even as we set up the program I was delusional. I never thought the parents would be so angry. I don't have children (a point that has been made by almost every one of the parents who criticize me) and somehow that's taken to mean that I'm sociopathic. I'm meant to weep and wail and apologize when I'm trying to help the boys quarantined in the program, and their parents, escape this experience as unscathed as possible.

The way they look at me, you'd think I'd stolen the children for myself. A few weeks ago, on a particularly low day, I had a Skype call with Amanda Maclean, *the* Amanda Maclean, about the program. She was interested in the possibilities of implementing it in Scotland. "You don't tell the women you're taking the babies?" she repeated after me in a horrified voice. She made me feel very small.

The alarm on my calendar goes off. Time for ward rounds. As I walk down the corridor from my office to the first floor of nurseries I'm struck, as I often am, by the scale of what we have created in such a short time. It's a controversial topic, I appreciate that. We take babies away from their parents—regardless of the parents' thoughts on the matter—and raise them the best we can without those children being touched or in the same room as another human without a hazmat suit on. Other psychologists in the medical community criticize me for engaging in "unethical practices." Excuse me while I roll my eyes onto the floor, but it's ethical to keep children alive. Lots of people have started asking if a child's survival is worth the emotional cost to the mother and baby of forcibly taking the child away. To my surprise, a lot of people would respond to that question with a resounding no.

The first floor of the building is full of the most recent additions, generally babies from newborn to four weeks. The first on my list is a single mother, Melissa Innes. She's standing, just about, still hunched over from her C-section, looking like death. I wish she was sitting down.

"Melissa?"

Slow blinks and then the gearshift I can see happening in her mind to engage with an adult in conversation.

"Let's take a seat, shall we?" We sit in one of the consulting rooms—it looks like every therapist's office I've ever seen. Slightly shabby carpet, tissues carefully placed on a table in the middle of two chairs, clock in easy view, basic floral print on one wall to "brighten the place up." It's truly heinous, but our budget isn't endless so it'll have to do.

"I see you haven't filled out the questionnaire you were given. Do you think you'll manage to do that today?"

"I looked at it," she says quietly. "It's stupid."

"What do you think is stupid about it?"

"You don't think it's stupid to ask a woman who has just had her son cut out of her stomach, kidnapped and kept in a locked room away from her whether she's sad?"

I swallow. I wish they wouldn't describe it like that.

"You son is alive right now. He is in a safe, warm, Plague-free environment. You can go in and see him with a hazmat suit on."

"But I can't touch him."

"Not without the suit, no."

"Why didn't you tell me before you did it?"

I've been asked this question before and I'll be asked it again. I prepare my answer, the same one I've given over one hundred times. "There is a risk that, given the highly emotional state most women are in prior to birth and with the danger of the Plague, that decisions would be taken that would later be regretted. The preservation of the lives of as many boys as possible was, and is, our priority."

"Did someone write that for you?"

She's smart. Pale and unsteady, but smart.

"No, but it's not the first time I've been asked that question."

"Do you have children?"

Christ, here we go.

"No, I don't."

Melissa nods knowingly. "That makes more sense."

I know I should nod in a calm way, but I loathe the way she looks as though she's just gained some extraordinary insight about me. "What makes more sense?"

"The way you've set this whole thing up."

"What do you mean?"

"The mothers, the parents, we're just an irritation to you. You didn't tell us what you were planning, even though most of us would probably have agreed if you had. You cut us open and took our children away from us and then you act like we should be grateful to you. You don't understand a thing. You're a psychologist, right? Well, you know what they say. Nobody's crazier than a shrink."

It's just the meds she's on. Breathe. She just had major surgery. Breathe. She is a twenty-one-year-old single mother who has never held her son. Breathe. Fuck it.

"Well, do you want to take him then?"

For the first time Melissa looks taken aback and I take a disproportionate amount of satisfaction from her surprise.

"Go on, if you're so determined that we've done this all wrong, and I'm wrong, and this program is wrong, I'll use my key, open the door and you can go in and get your son. You have a one in ten chance he'll be immune and survive. Good luck!"

I'm standing, holding the door open looking, I suspect, a bit deranged. If I'm asked about this, I'll have to put it down to a new experimental technique and hope no one thinks I'm having a nervous breakdown.

"I don't want to," Melissa finally says.

"And why don't you want to go and get your son?" Silence. Happy to fill it. "Because then your son will almost certainly die. So really, we haven't kidnapped him, have we? You must want him to be here as much as I do."

Melissa nods, rubs her nose and starts crying, silently. I'm breathing heavily and as the adrenaline ebbs away I realize how insane this is. I'm standing in a room with a woman who had major surgery yesterday, whose child is in grave danger and who has had her entire life turned upside down by the Plague. What am I doing?

"Please know that the focus of everyone in this building is to get you and your son safely out of here as soon as we can after a vaccine is available, in the best mental and physical shape possible. I'm sorry, for— I'm sorry."

Melissa nods. "No, it's actually helpful. To know that I do want him here." She looks at the bad floral print on the wall for a minute. "You wouldn't have actually let me go in and take him, would you?"

"No, I wouldn't."

"Good. It's good that people like you are keeping him safe."

"We keep calling him 'him.' Any ideas for names?"

"I've always liked Ivan but I don't know if it's too weird."

"Ivan is a lovely name. You should call him whatever you like best."

Melissa gives me a wobbly smile.

I finish the session—if it can be called that—under the guise of Melissa meeting one of the nurses who will help her with the hazmat suit, but the truth is we've made the breakthrough we needed to. Melissa now understands that we're not keeping her son here. She wants him to be here, desperately, because she wants him to live. Ivan. She wants Ivan to live.

The more I think about it, the more I think, though, that keeping the program secret from the mothers involved in it has been a mistake. It's such a seductive lie: "To ensure the safety of your child, in these challenging times, we want to do an elective cesarean." The reasons for the secrecy were practical. What if a mother disagreed with the proposed plan, and, in a highly vulnerable and potentially irrational emotional state, kept her child, infected him with the virus and then, once it was too late, changed her mind? The optics are so bad though, and the emotional ramifications are intense. For a lot of families in this building we—those working for the program—are the enemy. They understand why we're doing what we're doing, but they don't trust us because we didn't trust them. We lie to them. Tell them they need cesareans because of preeclampsia and then as they're being stitched up whisk their sons away in a sterile incubator. I can't blame them for looking at me like I'm the Antichrist.

As awful as it is to imagine that this facility will be needed for months and, potentially, years to come, soon there will be hardly any newborns. Babies are still being born having been conceived before the outbreak. That's going to come to an end soon. And then, I can focus on the main part of my job: maintaining normalcy in abnormal circumstances. Parents are allowed limitless contact with the child and are encouraged to sleep at the nursery in their hazmat gear. Routine will be key although access to other children has to be limited due to practicalities. It's harder to keep sterility when there are multiple people in a room. However, we're planning to use video links to ensure that the babies have some knowledge of what a fellow child looks like.

I have to trust that we're doing the right thing. Children aren't meant to be raised in quarantine away from the outside world and their siblings, but the Plague was never meant to happen either. There are 8,054 boys in the program across a range of facilities and another three thousand or so will be brought in once they're born. Eleven thousand lives saved. That can't be a bad thing.

# TOBY WILLIAMS

### Somewhere off the coast of Iceland
### Day 241

### July 1, 2026

It's me again. Maybe I should write *Dear Diary*. I understand why people write that now. It helps to make you less self-conscious. I'll be more precise. *Dear member of the Icelandic Coast Guard who is the poor bastard to find my dead body in this room along with my notes of my time stranded on this boat to hell. I'm sorry for the smell, it's probably appalling.*

That's sad. It should be *Dear Frances* really, shouldn't it? In my defense I've written her so many "When you get this, know that I loved you" letters that I'm getting bored of them. She'll read them all going, "Could you have maybe changed it up a bit, Toby, these are quite one-note, you know."

We're down to 201 now. Ninety-nine dead, 201 left standing. Not standing actually. We spend a lot of time sitting. When you're on an extreme low-calorie starvation diet you don't spend a lot of time walking about. Funny that.

There have been nine more suicides, although a bigger range of methods than at the beginning. Five more have thrown themselves off the boat (can't say that's how I'd do it, but I've always been very suspicious of sharks and killer whales), three have used knives (the captain's locked those away now) and one had the audacity to use a stash of pills none of us knew he had and a full liter of whiskey. The bastard. We could have enjoyed that booze.

Bella died two weeks ago, which was a surprise, actually. I thought her rage would sustain her. I wonder what happened to her husband, son and baby Carolina. None of us have had phone reception for months so there's no way of knowing. I hope her husband was okay and her children are safe.

It's odd seeing people die of starvation. We're all eating roughly the same amount now. The dietitian died a few weeks ago so we don't have a system anymore other than the captain giving us just enough to keep us alive, or so we hope.

I don't know why some of us are alive and others aren't. It's just luck, I imagine. I was a bit pudgy when I got on the boat. Mark was a good two stone heavier than me so we're both still plodding along. Less plodding than when we first got on the boat though. I'm much lighter in step now. He's keeping me sane, Mark is. He's always been the quieter one of us two and he watches people very closely.

"You all right?" he'll ask when I'm having a bad day and I'll go, "Yeah, been better," and he'll say, "What could be better?" and we'll talk about all the things we miss, the food and the sex (me with Frances, him with Sally), the wine, the warmth, the friends. All of our old lives. And then he'll say, "We'll have those things again, Toby, you'll see," and even though we're in the same place and he knows the same amount I do about the future, a bit of me relaxes and goes, yeah, we will.

I miss steak. So much. Jesus Christ. I would kill for a steak. Would I kill for a steak? Maybe. I'd have put the dietitian out of his misery twenty-four hours before he died for a steak. I wouldn't kill the captain for a steak. He's the one keeping this whole operation together. I don't know what he does in that control room of his all day but I'm still alive and the ship hasn't sunk so he's still doing better than the captain of the *Titanic* as far as I'm concerned.

Oh God, and beer. I crave beer. I've never even been much of a beer drinker but the idea of a cold ale in a glass slippery with condensation, outside in the garden, talking to Frances as the grandkids play in the paddling pool makes me want to weep with need. And pick 'n' mix. It's weird the things your brain decides it wants. Pick 'n' mix makes me think of the cinema, that's it. Seeing superhero movies with Mark and watching Maisy go on her first date when she was thirteen, too young to be on their own because they couldn't drive and the buses were a nightmare so I "dropped off" her and Ryan at the cinema and then went in and sat fifteen rows behind them. She told me years later, once her and Ryan had gotten married and had Isabel, that she had seen me at the cinema and she had liked knowing I was there. Although it did delay their first kiss by a few days. I wonder if Ryan's still alive?

I hope I get to see them all again. I don't pray because religion is a nonsense I've never had much time for and the Plague hasn't inspired a newfound devotion. If it is some bastard up there who's done all this then I'm not going to give him the satisfaction of praying. Wanker.

Right, I'm tired. Even writing's tiring now. I'm going to go to sleep. Frances, you've heard it a hundred times before now but I can't say it too many times. I love you more than you can imagine. I miss you. I hope I'll see you again and even if I don't, please know you made me the happiest man in the world.

Oh, and if you get my body back and have a funeral, make sure to enjoy a good steak in my memory. Medium-rare with béarnaise sauce. And chips.

# LISA

H ome, finally. It's midnight, again. For the first time in years, it makes no difference to me that the long days of July are here. I never see them. I get up in the dusk, and I return in the dark. Margot, sweet wonderful Margot, has left a glass of red wine and a note in her beautiful, calligraphic handwriting on the kitchen counter.

*You can do it, keep going. But first, sleep.*

*M x*
*(And some wine, just in case it was one of those days.)*

No one thought we would stay together. It was the talk of the academic staff across campus. *Have you heard Lisa Michael and Margot Bird are together?* Yes, the science dragon lady and the beautiful history professor are a couple. Opposites attract, chalk and cheese, send your clichés here. My students were less surprised. I'm tough to please but fair. If you want an easy A, get out of here, quite literally. But good students tend to be my most loyal defenders. Margot is universally loved, of course. Her classes are so popular you have to sign up online the second they open, as if she's a rock star selling out a stadium tour.

I leave the wine—my brain has enough to be thinking about in the morning, it doesn't need to be foggy—and fall into bed. I cuddle into Margot's back and feel my shoulders unwind at the warmth and comforting smell of her.

"Hello," she says, a lot less sleepily than I had expected.

"Hello," I reply, dropping a quick kiss on her forehead.

"I've been thinking," she says. One of our many, many differences is her brain's ability to do its best thinking at night. I avoid the lure of sleep and manage to make a questioning noise in reply.

"What are you going to do when you invent the vaccine?" I smile, widely and instantly. Her confidence in me is boundless. It's glorious.

She sits up, long auburn hair casting a faint shadow across the bed. "No, seriously. Do you just give it to the world and then that's it?"

"I wouldn't 'give' it to anyone. I haven't worked this hard to just let it go." My head is starting to pound from thinking this far ahead. I have just about enough bandwidth to do my job week to week; there's no room for anything else. "I haven't thought about it properly."

"Of course you have." Margot's tone is resolute.

"Yes, but only the discovery bit. I haven't gone beyond the congratulations and inevitable Nobel Prize. If they're still giving those out anyway. I don't have a plan."

Margot turns the bedside light on and I shrink from the glare. "Well, you need one. Listen to me, Lisa. You have to be careful, okay? Once you invent the vaccine, it will spiral out of control. So many inventors across history haven't reaped the rewards or the credit of their work. This will be your life's work, it is what you must be remembered for."

She's looking at me intently. I love her so much and I am too tired to think about this right now but there's a kernel of truth in what she's saying that sits uncomfortably. What does happen after? I couldn't bear to become a footnote; the rage would kill me. *Canadian scientists invented a vaccine.* No, *I* am going to invent a vaccine, not a nameless, faceless group identified by their nationality.

"Just think about it," she says, switching off the light.

We snuggle again, pretending to be calm once more but I know it will take me hours to fall asleep having had this grenade of uncertainty thrown into the future I am imagining.

I can't help but ask, "What made you think of this?"

"I'm a professor of Renaissance history with decades of knowledge of the ways in which female artists and inventors have had their work stolen, Lisa. Use that enormous brain of yours."

# ELIZABETH

Everything is falling into place. Like summer follows spring, once we identified the genes responsible for vulnerability to the Plague, and understood the origin of the virus, we created a test for immunity: a finger-prick blood test that can be rolled out around the world, with the use of a simple machine and no need for a scientist to assess the blood, to identify the genetic markers for the Plague virus. We had the press conference yesterday—George, Amaya and I in front of this mass of women with cameras and phones and notepads—and I felt so proud. The practicalities of how men can be tested without those who are vulnerable being infected still needs to be worked out, but for the first time, I feel hopeful. I'm working in a team renowned around the world, we're at the cutting edge of Plague research and, if things continue the way they have been, we'll have a vaccine within a year or so.

Working with Amaya has been life-changing, partly because she has literally changed the world with her discoveries and made me a better scientist, but also because of her demeanor. I said to George a few weeks after we started working with her, "The lab feels different, what is it? It's good different." He just pointed at Amaya, sitting in her glass office reading a report, and that said it all.

Where I'm nervous, she's calm. Where I try to buoy people up with optimism that's sometimes delusional, she makes a plan to survive every possible outcome. Where I had boxed myself into my work out of fear and desperation to find a vaccine, my friends and Simon have forced me to live a little. And I really do mean a little. I'm not going out to raves or anything—where does one find a rave? Are they advertised?—but they've taken me off the course to burn out I was so slavishly following. I sleep, I rest, I spend time with Simon, who makes me laugh and shows me his favorite parts of Regent's Park—"the most underrated park in London." He cooks spaghetti Bolognese and I teach him what biscuits are (my kind, not the English kind) and we watch TV curled up together on the sofa in his tiny, warm, cozy, book-filled flat in Hampstead. Sometimes I want to pinch myself but I repeat to myself that I deserve good things and that maybe, just maybe, Simon and I are meant for each other. For the first time in a long time, I dare to make plans. Simon talks about marriage and if I'd like to go back to the States one day and asks what baby names I like. "Rose for a girl, Arthur for a boy," I reply, stunned and thrilled. There's so much happiness all of a sudden that at times it feels ludicrous. Why me? And then I remember the bravery of coming to London, of persuading George to make me his deputy, of asking Simon on a date, of reaching over and kissing him and I think, *no one handed me any of this*. I built this weird, challenging, rewarding life in London for myself. Why not me?

It's still difficult, and the days are long. At times it feels like such a grind I wish more than anything a vaccine would just drop down from the sky, but we're making progress. We have solid, tangible achievements—a genome sequenced, a test created—that we can hold out, and say to the world, "Look, we know what we're doing. We have done something good. We will beat this."

# CATHERINE

London, United Kingdom
Day 295

My house is eerily quiet. I never realized the difference between the sound of a sleeping house and an empty one but it's so stark, I can't believe I never noticed it before. I used to work at the dining table, Anthony sleeping soundly in our bedroom and Theodore deep in slumber next door to him. The house was still but full as I worked, content in the knowledge my family was safely ensconced a floor above me. Now, it is so empty I keep the doors shut and spend most of my time in the kitchen as if I can trick my mind into forgetting the mausoleum that exists beyond this one room.

Most of my time is spent alone. Days go by in which I speak to no one. Phoebe calls, and messages, telling me she's here, but I can't respond. It's like she's a task on my to-do list that I know I need to address so I can place a neat tick next to her name, but I can't bring myself to do it. It's too much. The mere sight of her name on my phone screen makes me feel nauseous; I always flip the phone over until it goes mercifully quiet. I don't trust myself to talk to her without crying or screaming. I'm not sure which would be worse. The despair or the anger. She can't help with either. What would I say? *Sorry you lost . . . nothing. I'm happy that your husband is alive and you have two beautiful daughters whose absence from my life feels like an additional splinter lodged in my skin. I'm not coping because I lost everyone I love but how are you anyway?* I know it's irrational to hate someone for their life not being obliterated, but rationality is more than I can bear at the moment. Libby phones occasionally but she's still stuck in Madrid and, at the very least, I'm in London in my own home.

Painfully, the days alone at home without the regular grind of work remind me of maternity leave. Those endless months with no one to talk to but a baby. Theodore was born so early that all my prenatal class friends were still waddling around buying tiny cardigans and hats when I was pushing an actual baby around the kitchen in his pram, cajoling him to sleep.

Today, for the first time since the world fell apart, I'm going into work. UCL is opening, as are forty-nine other universities across the country, in an attempt to keep the education system functioning. The government says we need to ensure we have teachers, nurses, lawyers, engineers and all the other many professions that make up our society in the coming years. I don't care as long as I still have something to do. My lovely boss, Margaret, called me yesterday and asked me to come in.

I make a cup of coffee from the dwindling jar in the kitchen. There won't be any more coffee for a long, long time, so I ration it but today is a Big Day. Today deserves a cup of coffee. I haven't left Crystal Palace since I returned from Devon, many weeks ago. The sight of other people, eye contact, noise, roads, the mere thought of it has been too much. It's as if I've been flayed. I get the train from Crystal Palace to Victoria; there used to be four an hour, packed full of commuters reading their phones or the papers. Now, there is one every hour and a half, packed full of women with the occasional man sticking out like a blot of ink on a page.

On the train, I read a crime novel, the kind of unnerving yet easy-to-read fare that Anthony adored and I'd always avoided on the basis of enjoying books with happy endings. Our holiday reading tastes were split down embarrassingly heteronormative lines. Historical romance novels and women's fiction for me. Crime and military history books for him. I tried to read a romance novel a few days ago, thinking it might help. I managed two paragraphs before I slammed it shut, repulsed by the cheery tone. Now, it's comforting to read about mysteries, death, terror and the eventual resolution of justice. My brain's capacity for reading about the good fortune of others, even if their happiness is fictional, is currently nonexistent.

The train arrives at Victoria just as my novel's detective is making a breakthrough in the case. The tube has a thirty-minute wait, as it will have for months while the few remaining male, and female, drivers teach others to drive the trains. I trundle through London on a replacement bus, packed with people, all of whom look as ashen and distracted as I imagine I do.

The sight of my office in the UCL anthropology building brings me to tears. It's a squat, square building but it's a home away from home. It has been a constant in my life for over a decade. The corridors smell the same but are, predictably, emptier than they used to be.

"Well, look who the cat dragged in." Margaret, my no-nonsense, reliable, kind boss is sitting at her desk, surrounded as always by teetering stacks of books.

"It's nice to see you." I sit down. It could be any other Monday. It's as if nothing has changed.

"I'm not going to ask how you are, and please don't ask me. I don't think either of us can cope with that right now," she says. There is a photo of Margaret, her husband, son and daughter sitting on the shelf behind her. I glance at it and then back to her resolute face. She has aged years in the few months since I saw her.

"Let's stick to work. Nothing like some second-year biological anthropology classes to cheer the soul."

"That's the spirit."

Some timetable wrangling quickly shows that I'm going to need to double my course load to cover my colleagues who have died. Margaret is determined to keep the Anthropology Department functioning as normally as possible.

"Now," she says. "This project you mentioned in your e-mail." She looks so stern I'm not sure if she's going to tell me to forget about it. "It sounds essential, absolutely. A record of the story of the Plague, how it spread, how those involved at its epicenter have been affected and are coping, hearing from ordinary people to understand the cultural and societal impact."

Margaret reels off a far more eloquent and concise description of my project than my grief-addled brain had managed to articulate in my e-mail. I scribble down what she says and nod approvingly as if to say, "Yes, that is exactly what I was thinking."

"Get it into more complete shape and we'll talk about publication. Maybe a book would be best? It certainly can't be a journal article; it's too important to be restricted to academic circles. Funding's all over the shop at the moment, but we're not in dire straits. There's an emergency fund. We'll make sure you have the money you need for any research and travel, within reason. I know you'll be busy but try the course load I've given you, and just let me know when you need to travel and we'll figure something out. If the teaching is too much, we'll reduce your hours. The project should take priority."

"Thank you. That means a lot."

"We'll have lunch at some point, catch up properly." Margaret's eyes become a bit glassy and I'm silently begging her not to cry. She's like a headmistress or a captain or an army major. Her job is to be strong and calm in the face of chaos. If she's cracking up, I don't know what I'll do.

"For now, let's work," I say quietly. "There's plenty of time for that."

She nods, and I leave her office. For the first time in a long time, I have an official purpose. The responsibility is welcome. It's like slipping on an old coat, which reminds me of what life used to be. It's a welcome, blessed distraction. I'm not responsible anymore for a child, or as a wife, or as a daughter, or even as a friend. But this—a record of what the hell has happened—I am responsible for. I will get this right.

# AMANDA

Edinburgh, the Independent Republic of Scotland
Day 296

alking into the Labor and Delivery ward gives me the heebie-jeebies. Memories of Josh's birth come to mind. Twenty-eight hours, a failed epidural, a third-degree tear. It's not a coincidence we only had the two. At the same time, my stomach clenches with longing. Oh, to be able to do all of this again and hold a tiny newborn, knowing the years of joy stretching out ahead of me.

No crying today. I'm not here to reminisce. My job as a public health consultant at Health Protection Scotland requires reconnaissance. Someone thought it would be a good idea for one of us to see what's happening in labor wards, as the babies conceived shortly before the Plague make their way into a world their parents never could have imagined.

"Amanda? Hi, I'm Lucy."

Lucy looks awful; she's gray with exhaustion. I've seen enough nurses and doctors in A and E with this blank stare to know burnout when I see it.

"How are you, Lucy?" I ask.

"We're not going to be able to talk about that, Amanda," she says resolutely. "I'm hanging on by a thread here, let's not snip it."

"I'll stick to medicine. Understood. How qualified are you?" I ask. She looks very young.

"Only fifteen months. The job hasn't been . . . what I imagined." There's an understatement and a half.

Lucy takes a deep breath and launches into what is clearly a pre-prepared spiel. "I'm taking you through to see Alicia. She's agreed you can watch but she thinks you're here in your capacity as a doctor, which, technically you are, so I think that's okay. Alicia didn't know when she conceived obviously that she would be giving birth in the middle of the Plague and the stress is slowing her labor down. That's been happening a lot. We banned men from the ward for a while but then it was confirmed that women are hosts so . . ." She shrugs with forced carelessness before continuing. "Of the two hundred eighty-four boys I've helped to deliver in the last six months, twenty-nine have survived. The babies tend to fall ill within a few hours and we think it's transmitted through contact after birth. Once they're in the world, they're touched by their mothers and then . . ." Alicia doesn't know whether she's having a boy or a girl, which is quite common. I think they like to have hope for as long as possible, but her body's protective instinct is kicking in so it's trying to keep the baby in for as long as possible."

Lucy pauses. I think she wants me to say something.

"Is her husband here with her?"

"No, he died two months ago."

With that, Lucy leads me through to a dark room with only a few dim lights. She tells me in a hushed voice that Alicia has an epidural and they think they might need to have an assisted delivery or a C-section. I stand in the corner, trying to look as unobtrusive as possible. Two midwives and what looks by her age like a senior registrar are encouraging Alicia to push, but anyone can see she's not really trying. I can't blame her.

Thirty minutes later, we're all scrubbed up and in the theater. The need for a cesarean became obvious. Alicia is weeping in fear and shaking as her mum holds her hand. "I wish Ronnie was here," she says, and my heart breaks for her. Time isn't moving as we wait for the baby's sex to be revealed. There is the usual cutting and violence of a cesarean. The senior registrar pulls the baby out. The whole room catches its breath and I'm imagining the announcement of a boy so clearly, I almost hear it in the tense silence of the room.

"It's a girl. It's a girl!" the registrar shouts, her voice's volume muffled through her mask.

Alicia starts wailing and her mum holds her, cradling her from the shoulders up. One of the midwives takes the baby, cleans her up, weighs her.

"It's a girl!" the senior registrar repeats, tears choking her voice as she starts stitching up Alicia.

"What's her name?" the midwife says, handing the baby to Alicia's mother, who holds the beautiful, pink crying baby by Alicia's head so they can be close.

"Ava," Alicia says. "Ronnie always liked that name."

Lucy and I smile at each other, drunk on relief after the terrible few minutes before Ava was born. I can't help but think back to the joy in the moments after my labors when finally, finally, it was over and they handed me my beautiful boys. The relief, the happiness, the sheer joy of meeting them and having their whole lives ahead of me. The contrast that appears to me—between my life then and the strange newness of my life now—feels, for a moment, so shocking it's as though I've been punched in the throat. *I am a single woman. I have no children. I had children but I don't have them anymore.*

"Let's leave them to it," Lucy says, and leads me, dazed and a bit nauseous with dread, to Delivery Room 5. Lucy takes a breath before opening the door. "Now we're seeing Kim. She already has three girls.

Her husband is immune." My nose stings with tears of jealousy. Lucy looks at me sympathetically. "I know. I had the same response when I was doing her antenatal appointments. She's just one of the lucky ones."

"Does she know if it's a fourth girl?"

"No, but in my experience, the chances are high once you've had three of the same."

We enter the room, which has a much calmer atmosphere than the mood of resistance Alicia's had. There's whale music, the smell of lavender in the air and a very attentive husband rubbing Kim's back.

I introduce myself quietly. Kim has two midwives helping her onto her hands and knees. It's time to push. Again, I can feel the tension in the room rising and rising as the baby gets closer to being born. Kim is pushing like a champ, keeping each one going for the entire length of her contractions. I've read about the statistics on a baby's sex before. Lucy's right, once you have three babies of the same sex, chances are you'll continue producing children of the same sex.

"One final push, my love," one of the midwives bellows. With a roar Kim digs in and the head is out. A few minutes later the body follows.

"It's a boy," the midwife says, her voice hollow. She's gone white. The other midwife, the quieter one, takes the baby over to the side of the room. He's crying mightily, has a good color. He looks for all intents and purposes like a perfectly healthy baby boy.

"What?" Kim asks, groggy from the gas and air and pain and shock. "She can't be a boy. We have girls."

"It's a boy, sweetheart," the midwife says. I turn away as the midwife and Kim work together through the final stages of labor, delivering the placenta. I feel like I'm intruding now. This is too private. I'm watching the beginnings of a funeral.

"Where's the pediatric team?" I ask Lucy quietly.

"No point," Lucy whispers. "If he's immune he'll live, if he's not he'll die. Peds is focusing on treating the girls and immune boys with non-Plague issues now."

The ruthlessness of this is gutting in the context of a maternity unit. I'm so used to the medical care and attention devoted to newborn babies that it jars, but this is reality now. There's nothing to be gained from wasting precious time, needles, cannulas, saline and steroids on a baby destined to die in a few days. Kim isn't crying. She looks shell-shocked and deathly pale. The doctor part of my brain wants to check that she's not hemorrhaging but I suspect it's the plain horror of having given birth to a baby who will almost certainly die in days, if not hours. There's an absence of something and I'm trying to work out what it is, casting my mind back to my own labors, and then I realize. Reassurance. When I gave birth, I was constantly being reassured during and after that everything was going to be okay. "You'll heal up just fine." "Gorgeous wee boy you've got there." "The first few nights are the hardest, then you'll find a rhythm." There's no reassurance here. There's nothing anyone can say.

Lucy and I leave the delivery room and I take a deep breath.

"It's a horrible environment to be in, isn't it?" she says.

I nod in agreement. "I honestly don't know how you've been doing this for months. I'm emotionally exhausted and I've been here less than two hours."

"This isn't why I became a midwife." Lucy's eyes are filled with tears and I have a maternal urge to hug her and rub her back. "We spend hours with these women encouraging them to basically rip their bodies apart for the promise of a baby at the end, and for what? To have their hearts broken in a few hours? I can't do it anymore. I've applied to become a general practice nurse."

I nod again. There's nothing I can say. Eventually I just mutter, "I understand." I spend the next two days with Lucy repeating the roller coaster of elation and horror of working in a labor ward during the

Plague. I see four more girls born and five boys. At the end of my third day I'm desperate to go home. I cannot see one more woman's face cave in at the prospect of a dead baby. These midwives are made of sterner stuff than I.

As I'm walking out to my car, bone tired and ready for bed, Lucy runs out after me. I must have forgotten something.

"Wait! Kim's baby, I just heard!"

"What about him?"

Lucy is beaming, glowing with happiness. "He's immune! They just did the test. He didn't have any symptoms after twenty-four hours so we did a blood test to make sure. He's immune!"

I burst into tears and Lucy hugs me. We hold each other tight on this dark Edinburgh night. Two women brought to tears by the news that one baby will survive.

"He's gorgeous," Lucy says. "Absolutely gorgeous."

# FAITH

What are the chances that I'll be thrown in jail if I punch Susan in the face? Pros: punching Susan in the face, brief sense of satisfaction, Susan will leave me alone. Cons: could break my hand, Susan would never stop going on about it, I don't have kids and Susan does so I'd get thrown in jail and it wouldn't matter because I have no dependents.

I sigh. It always comes back to kids. I try to tune my brain back in to whatever nonsense Susan is babbling on about now. It doesn't even make sense for her to be here. She didn't like me when we were army wives and she sure as hell doesn't like me more now that we're army widows.

"So." She looks so excited. She must have gossip. Here we go. "The army's introducing a draft and we're going to be drafted first!"

"You and I?" I ask stupidly. I don't understand. Susan rolls her eyes and raises an unplucked eyebrow.

"No, stupid. Army spouses. We're already on base, and we have 'an understanding of what the job involves,'" she says, in air quotes as though this is ludicrous. "Isn't it outrageous!" She's looking at me expectantly. In the old days, before Daniel died, I would have gone, "Yes, outrageous. Wow," and played along, but I can't be bothered now.

Daniel's dead. It doesn't matter to him or the other men in his unit if Susan and I get on. And I never gave a shit.

"I don't think it's a bad idea."

Susan purses her lips and cocks her head to the side as though I'm a toddler who just peed on the floor.

"What's going to happen to my kids, huh? There's no one to look after them, and after all we've been through, why would they pick on us like this?" She pauses to catch her breath. "It's not the same for you. You childless wives, it won't affect you."

I don't snap or lose my temper. I know exactly what I'm about to do and I'm not proud of it. It's not going to be my finest moment, or actually, maybe it is. If I'm being really honest, Susan is lucky I don't punch her repeatedly in the mouth. I get up from the table, take her coffee cup out of her hand, and pour the glass of water I've been drinking over her head in such gloriously slow motion I can see her expression shift from bland surprise at the absence of her coffee to disbelief to total horror at the cold and the wet.

"Go fuck yourself, Susan, and, while you're at it, get the fuck out of my house." The joy of saying those words I've cradled at the back of my tongue for years is particularly sweet.

Susan gapes at me, scraping her chair back. Her badly dyed hair is plastered against her cheeks. "You're insane! I always said you were crazy, I warned everyone: That lady's about to crack."

"I said out, Susan. Now."

Susan's still blathering as she makes her way out of my house and slams the door behind her. Good riddance, to Susan and to part of my identity. Calming, pleasing, careful, placating army wife. My husband and I met in a nightclub in Madison, Alabama, which is possibly the tackiest way in the world to meet the love of your life. I didn't know it then, but when you marry someone in the military it's not just a partnership. It's an identity, and one I've always rebelled against.

Whenever he was deployed, I would leave the base and go home to Maine for a fortnight and, if he was away for over a year, I would move in with my parents and transfer to a hospital there. He never seemed to have the kind of deployments that meant a wife could move too. He was sent to dangerous places, faraway places, terrifying places. So I did my best to survive without him and I worked and stayed away from the base. It was too hard to see the other wives waiting for a man to come back in the way we all feared.

Then the Plague came and Daniel had just come back from a posting in Germany. The number of times I've wished I had just gone with him to Europe. He'd never been told his wife could move with him before but I wouldn't have been able to work in a hospital there. We could have had six more months together before the world fell apart. He had only been home for three days when the call came in that all active military personnel were to return to active duty, but this time, in the States.

Daniel's unit was one of the most successful in terms of surviving, and that's not just the rose-tinted view of a lonely widow. I don't know how or why but Daniel survived all the way until May, the last in his unit to die. Not a single one of them was immune. Every phone call I had with him I begged him to desert. What would they do—shoot him? He was going to die, probably. We had hoped he would be immune but the army tested for immunity and he was negative. I just wanted more time with him. I wanted to be a wife for a little while longer.

But when you marry a man with the integrity to go into the army—for patriotic reasons glistening with valor and honor—you can't be surprised when he stays at his post until his last, dying day. "I'm helping people," he would tell me, always patiently, when I cajoled and cried and begged. "Help me," I would reply. "Please help me."

So now, I'm a widow, and the one silver lining is that I don't have to be liked anymore. The other wives always found me weird and now I've confirmed all of their suspicions. We're all widows, supposedly supporting one another, but "widow" is the most common title in the world now. It's still unbearable. Just because lots of people are experiencing something alongside you doesn't make it any better. If anything, it's harder because you're not special. There are no allowances or respect for grief. The whole damn world is grieving. What's one husband when almost all the men are dead? What's one woman's grief in the face of billions of lost sons, fathers, brothers and, yes, husbands?

But I didn't throw the water over Susan because of grief. No. I did it because I'm childless and Susan knows that it's the one weakness I can't bear to have poked and she just rammed the knife in. I know we're meant to use the term "child-free" now but, let's face it, that's bullshit. Most of us are childless and not by choice. Daniel and I started trying for a baby as soon as we were married. By the time he died, we had been married for five years. I have been pregnant eight times and miscarried every single time.

That does weird things to a person, it really does. You go cuckoo. It hasn't helped that I've been a neonatal nurse, but what was I meant to do? Stop working? Stop doing the one thing that kept me sane? One of the feelings I was least prepared for when Daniel died was the relief. I wasn't relieved that he was dead. Not at all. But as I moved out of the all-consuming fog of grief, I started poking around in my brain a little and, yep, relief was there. Relief that any possibility of being a mother was gone. All I have ever wanted was to be a mom: to get pregnant, finally give birth, have sleepless nights of breastfeeding, complain about the exhaustion, cry as I watched a brown-eyed, serious-looking little girl sing "Twinkle Twinkle Little Star" up on a stage with other kindergartners. It was all I ever wanted.

And the hardest thing about infertility that no one ever tells you about is the hope. It's not the going wrong that's the most painful part. It's the betrayal of hope that this time you had the *audacity* to think it would be different. It's the searing pain of hope as you try again and fail again, and try again and fail again, each time knowing you'll fail and yet hoping you won't. Without a husband and with only 10 percent of the world's men alive, I am not going to be a mother. That is abundantly clear. For the first time in my life, I know for sure. I'm not going to get pregnant and birth my own baby. We used up our last frozen embryo in our most recent round of IVF. There is no frozen sperm from Daniel and I have no frozen eggs.

And then I didn't have to be a neonatal nurse anymore. That was a different strand of relief. I adored my job. Every time I cared for a tiny baby, born into this scary, cold world far too soon, I had three thoughts: How well is the baby breathing? How well is the baby feeding? How would I want to be treated, as a mom, if I was in this situation? I was a really, *really* good nurse, and I needed my job. I would have had a breakdown if it wasn't for my job and the other nurses I worked with. But it was also a bit like a failed artist working as a security officer at an art gallery, or a failed author working in a bookshop. There's a constant reminder of how close you are to the thing you want, and how far away from it you are. Even though the babies were tiny aliens fighting to survive, they were babies and their moms were moms.

The day they told me I wasn't needed on the neonatal ward anymore and I was to start the training process for oncology, I cried in my car all the way home. *I don't have to do it anymore. I don't have to do it anymore. Thank God.*

The biggest difference between Susan and me is that, before the Plague, Susan loved her life. She was ambivalent about her husband—that wasn't a love match for the ages. But to her, her life was perfect. Her husband was out of her hair for most of the year, she had three daughters who were all athletic and popular, she ran the social scene on the base and she was slowly sliding into the kind of bored but bitchy middle-aged housewife her mom before her had no doubt been.

Before the Plague hit us all sideways, I loved my husband but I hated my life. I hated my body for being broken and failing me, even though I had been to nineteen sessions of a support group where I was assured that I wasn't broken despite all evidence to the contrary. A part of me hated that my job required me to face up to my infertility every single day. I hated how often my husband was away and missed him desperately. And I fucking hated women like Susan who looked down on my life as frivolous and devoid of meaning, as if I skipped out of my house to an illegal rave every night of the week while she toiled away at the altar of motherhood like an underappreciated Mother Teresa.

So, yeah, I'm a little excited about the draft. Bring it on. I've been a nurse for over a decade. I'm ready for something different and I know I can handle it. I've seen some shit. I've seen babies die. I've lost eight of my own children. I've lost my husband. I can eat women like Susan for breakfast and spit them out again.

The next day, the letter is dropped in my mailbox. It tells me everything I need to know and there, at the bottom, is a magic box. "Tick if you would like to apply for the First Class program. Additional form enclosed." The army's in dire straits, I mean, hello. There's a draft, so it makes sense. They need junior leaders. I can apply to be fast-tracked for promotion and, if selected, as soon as I complete basic training I'll be a Private First Class. Daniel would get a real kick out of this. I can just imagine him watching me, smiling that lovely warm, proud smile he always had, as I fill out the form and explain why I have the characteristics they're looking for. *Resilience. Good at handling extreme pressure. Unafraid to lead. Fast learner. Physically fit. Experience in a physically demanding role.*

I know I'm going to get it, and I do. Another week goes by and there it is. A big, fat envelope full of extra papers telling me about the requirements of the program. I can't keep the smile off my face for the two days until I have to report for training. Unlike Susan, I've spent the last decade working in a high-stress, high-stakes job that involves following procedure, a hierarchical structure and exposure to life-and-death scenarios. It's the most satisfying day of my life when we turn up for our first day of basic combat training and I go in the door to the right for the fast-track recruits. Susan, face slack with shock, goes in the door to the left.

# DAWN

**London, United Kingdom**
**Day 300**

God, I love it when things are efficient. At precisely 2 p.m., practically to the second, a call comes in from Jackie Stockett. In the last few months as I've racked up responsibilities like I used to rack up air miles, I've often been tempted to carry a placard above my head: *Were you all raised by wolves? Be on time!*

I am unsurprised and grateful that the director of the Indiana Working Draft is punctual. We need to know how she's doing what she's doing and there's no time to spare. So far, we only have specific employment policies: all healthcare workers, member of the armed forces, civil service and the emergency services are required to work full-time, or part-time if they have dependents, until a broader working framework is created and passed by Parliament. Everyone else is free to work or not work as they see fit and it's not functioning. The country is in dire straits.

It is very, very important that no one knows we're talking to Jackie because a US-style working draft would be big news. No point panicking everyone until we know what's going to happen. Gillian, as home secretary, will decide whether to move it forward; I'll plan for any disruption it might cause.

Jackie Stockett is a busy lady; we've done well to get an appointment with her. I suppose the office of the Indiana Working Draft isn't the place for slackers.

"Hello!" Jackie says.

"It's very kind of you to give us some of your time, Jackie."

"Too damn right I'm kind. The Patron Saint of Indiana." She laughs and I see how this woman was able to create the world's first working draft quicker than I was able to sort out bloody electricians.

"Right, you've got an hour of this saint's time so tell me, what can I do to help?"

"Tell us everything you know," Gillian, sat to my right, says, taking our discussion about asking open-ended questions a bit too far.

"We might be here a while." Jackie claps her hands together. "Okay, let's start at the end. The goal's important, right? Here in the States we have the Human Scarcity Index, which you might have heard of."

Uh, yeah. You could say that. It's only been in every newspaper and magazine around the world as a symbol of humanity's talent for adaptation or the end of days, depending on what you read. "Indiana is third in the table out of fifty-two states, and we have a lot less going for us historically than California and Illinois, the only two states that got us beat. Human resourcing isn't just finding people jobs anymore. It's a question of life or death. If garbage is on the streets, and bodies are piling up in homes, and factories aren't producing medicines and delivery trucks aren't getting food from farms to stores, people are going to die. It's as simple as that. Third place means my state is surviving."

Gillian interrupts Jackie's speech. "Did you see the Plague coming? I mean, how much lead time did you have to prepare?"

Jackie laughs, a lovely, rich sound. "No, silly, I'm good at my job, not a witch. But I did see that once the Plague was here, we were going to need to change the job market real fast. I started off in Parks and Recreation, or Possums and Raccoons as people used to call it."

I stifle a laugh. Gillian gives me a look.

"Sorry," I say, feeling sheepish.

"You laugh at any jokes I trot out whenever you feel like it. Point is, Parks was always having its budget squeezed so I had to look ahead a lot. Sometimes I had to just ask for more money, there's a few Indiana congresswomen still around who would happily never see my face again. I had to plan. May through September we needed double the staff than we did the other seven months of the year, and I was doing everything on a shoestring. Then the Plague came and Jesus, it was bad. I was head of human resources for the City Council of Bloomington. The private sector was a whole other mess but at the very least, every branch of city hall needed to continue to function with over half of its workforce—poof!—gone."

I think back to the early days of the Plague with a familiar shudder. Men dropping off everywhere: the police, the armed forces, in every government department, every part of the civil service. Sudden gaps where crucial work simply wasn't, and sometimes still isn't, being done.

Jackie's expression has gone from one of enthusiasm to exhaustion; even recalling the panic and sheer grind of those weeks is tiring. "Indiana already had one of the worst gender pay gaps in the country and a shortage of skilled workers back when this whole damn mess began. We didn't have a head start, put it that way. But we did have two things: me and Mary Ford. She was head of human resources in Indianapolis, and before that we worked together for ten years here in Bloomington. Mary should be here with me but she got nabbed by Nebraska." Jackie nods as though her friend is there. "I'm just saying, it's important you know. I didn't do it alone."

Gillian looks at me with an awed expression; it's rare to see anyone sharing credit for anything in civil service. Jackie's a good egg.

"Mary and I sat down and made a plan to resource our cities, our schools, our hospitals, our police departments, fire stations, oh God, the list was endless. The army had its own plan in place, although it took them long enough to get ahold of themselves."

"How do you get people to keep working with sick relatives, or when grieving?" I ask. This is the issue we're finding the most difficult. Can we really stomach requiring a woman whose husband or son or father or, God forbid, all three, are dying to work despite it?

"We have bereavement exceptions, but you still have to work at least two days a week. That's just the way it is. No one was turning up to work and everything shut down. I mean I get it. One woman who worked with me in Parks, Angela, had five sons. Five! I can't imagine what she was going through."

"So you categorize workers and job types," Gillian says.

"Yep. We divided jobs into five categories based on urgency, proportion of male employees and difficulty of skill replacement. A garbage-man is the classic example we use: it's a Level 1 job. Garbage needs to be cleared off the streets or you'll have another public health crisis on your hands; almost every garbage truck in the city had been staffed by men and it took around three days of training, mainly safety related, for someone to do that job."

I've never been so glad I wasn't tempted to go into politics after I left Oxford. Selling this to the British population is going to be a nightmare, and worse, it's completely necessary.

"I'm guessing categorization is easy. Assigning people is the hard part," Gillian says, frowning down at the notes she's written.

"And forcing people to do the jobs assigned to them," I add.

"Have you tried getting widows with grieving children out of the house to clean trash off the streets? It's not a walk in the park," Jackie says. "You need to be politically united to get it done. Our governor died and his replacement—Kelly Enright—is the most capable woman I have ever met. If the four horsemen of the apocalypse had the nerve to show up at her door, she'd have a PowerPoint presentation and a five-step plan to get them the hell out of her state. We had a meeting with her back in March. She sat down and asked us to tell her everything we knew at that point about jobs, the people needed in them and how bad things were going to get. It was a seven-hour meeting. By the end of it, she had brought in four aides and two lawyers. They drafted the Indiana Working Draft Order that night and Kelly signed it the next morning."

I'd read the newspaper articles. I knew it was quick, but knowing that the first working draft in the world was drafted in one night makes me feel nauseous. There's no way our process will be that efficient. I can barely get photocopying toner replaced overnight.

"Did you have a lot of people threatening to leave the state?" Gillian asks. Thank God we're an island. There's nowhere to go and Scotland isn't speaking to us.

"Oh yeah, we have an easy solution for that: if you leave the state to escape the draft, you're not allowed back in."

"I'm worried about the optics," Gillian says. "I love everything you've told me, Jackie, truly. What you've done is extraordinary. I just. Jesus, it seems so extreme. We've never done anything like this in the history of the nation."

My mind goes back to my history degree. I'm pretty sure being a feudal serf in 1307 working for no pay in a field twelve months a year was worse than being forced to retrain as a plumber and work a 9-to-5. Just a tad.

"Stick to the key messages. Don't use words like 'optimize' or 'efficiency.' Keep it simple. This is life or death. All those jobs that seem small? They're not. If the streets are clean, people don't get sick. If people can get their heating fixed in November, they don't end up in the hospital with pneumonia."

I wish I could film Jackie and run clips of her talking on TV. She's like the friendly, no-nonsense grandmother I never had. If she says jump, I'll ask how high.

"Second, work means purpose. Even if you don't want it, or don't think you want it, it's a reason to get up in the morning. Work gives you a future even if you can't see one for yourself right now. Third, lots of jobs are gone. Sometimes people say to me, 'Oh, but lots of those people surely already have jobs.' Yes, they did before the Plague, but not after it. Nobody's buying houses, so that's real estate gone. Nobody's opening a pension or investing in a frozen stock market, so that's finance gone. People aren't shopping, so retail's been decimated; we specifically recruited female warehouse workers to be garbage truck operators and hospital operators. They're used to early starts and physical work. It's not communist or a betrayal of your country to make sure people work and society works. I say, if we could justify sending teenage boys over to Vietnam to kill and be killed, for no reason, we can justify forcing healthy, able people to work in a paid job that's required by society."

Gillian has been furiously scribbling down everything Jackie's said for the past hour. She'll be implementing a working draft within a few weeks.

"Can I ask a quick question?" I ask. "Are you and Mary still friends?"

"'Course we are! We had lunch every Wednesday at Bynum's Steakhouse for a decade. Now we do a video call every week at the same time."

The meeting ends with the usual good-byes, thank-yous and

promises to follow up by e-mail. Gillian looks at me with a resolute expression. I hate it when politicians look at me like that. It always means I'm going to work a seventy-hour week for the next few months.

"Let's get started," she says.

# FRANCES

The Icelandic Coast Guard is going to take out a restraining order against me if I'm not careful. Can public agencies take out a restraining order against a citizen in another country? Probably not, but they could stop taking my calls.

I don't understand what's so hard about this. My husband—my lovely Toby—and lots of other people are stuck on a boat somewhere around Iceland. They don't have the Plague and they don't have enough food. They need food. It's simple.

The new head of the Icelandic Coast Guard, Heida, is a very nononsense woman who talks a lot about resources. I don't think she's married. I keep trying to find out more about her personal life, try to build a rapport, but she's quite resistant to it. No matter. My husband is on a boat in the middle of nowhere. Heida needs to help me and Heida is going to help me even if she doesn't know it yet.

I've been doing a lot of reading so I know about virus survival times on surfaces and sterilization. One of the major perks of working in a library is the easy access to books and time to spend researching things online. The virus, according to the Public Health England Task Force, survives for thirty-eight hours on a static surface. Women are hosts, which means every time a woman coughs or sneezes or breathes on her hand, she'll spread the virus onto the thing she touches. These two things are problems but they are solvable.

Heida needs to understand that they are solvable.

If I could, I would fly out to Iceland myself and give her a piece of my mind, but there's not going to be any plane travel for the foreseeable, maybe ever, so for now I'm stuck with phone calls.

My plan is simple. Heida needs to get lots of canned food—soup, vegetables, potatoes, sausages, that kind of thing—and either freeze them or cover them in boiling water so every bit of them is drenched. Then she needs to get a massive piece of plastic and sterilize that too, and use that to cover the cans. *Then* she needs to attach a note to the big plastic pack of food telling whoever reads it to eat the food, not panic and wait to be rescued because everything is going to be okay.

I've thought this through. It's not that hard.

I'll call Heida again. I've told her my plan every day for the past few weeks and I think she's slowly coming around. You know, she does like me. She wouldn't pick the phone up otherwise, would she? I don't think the Icelandic Coast Guard is a barrel of laughs at the moment. I like to think I provide some light relief.

"Hello, Frances," she says.

"Hi, Heida, how's it going?"

"Not too bad, as you would say. What can I do for you?"

"I'm nothing if not consistent, Heida. I need you to carry out my plan to deliver food to my husband and the other passengers on the *Silver Lady* and save hundreds of lives. Please and thank you, Heida."

"I have gotten approval for this now."

"I know you always say no, Heida, and— Wait, what?"

"I said, I have gotten approval for this from the government. I have three thousand cans of food currently in a deep freezer storage facility covered in plastic. I have printed the note you suggested and included the message for your husband you wanted."

I'm sobbing happy, shocked tears. Heida, oh, you beautiful Icelandic princess.

"Hello? Frances?"

"Yep, I'm still here, Heida. I'm here. Thank you so much, I don't know how to thank you."

"When all of this is over, come to Iceland with Toby and I will show you around the bit of coastline where we are based. It is very beautiful. We are friends now, I think, Frances. We have spoken every day for five months."

"Well, actually, you don't pick up the phone on your day off, so not every day."

"You always leave me voice mails though, which is the same thing. How many voice mails did you leave me last Sunday?"

"Fourteen," I say in a small voice before changing the subject. "When are you going to drop off the food?"

"Tomorrow. We know their coordinates. The captain provided them before they lost signal. They've been anchored since they ran out of fuel a long time ago. We will use a small military plane to make the drop."

"Heida, I think you might be the best friend I've ever had."

"If I manage to save your husband's life, I would hope so."

"Wait, Heida, why have you been telling me it's not going to work if you had applied for approval?" That sneaky so-and-so has been telling me to get lost for months.

"I didn't want to get your hopes up. You're a very optimistic person. You think the glass is half full. I measure the number of millimeters in the glass before I decide what to do with the water."

"Oh, Heida, you'll let me know how it goes?"

"I will let you know how it goes."

# TOBY WILLIAMS

### Somewhere off the coast of Iceland
### Day 338

#### Sometime in October 2026

I'm going to die soon. My stomach is eating itself, I can feel it. The pain is unbearable. It's been over a year, or just under, I can't keep track of the days anymore. I stopped counting once I got to two hundred.

There's around thirty of us now, I think. We stopped being able to throw all the bodies overboard a while ago. Took too much energy to break into the rooms. Mark is still here, that's the only thing that matters. We lie out on the deck because the breeze feels nice and it doesn't smell as much out here. Maybe we're hallucinating? I don't know. Frances, I love you. Maisy, my lovely girl. She was a miracle baby. I was forty-one, Frances was thirty-nine. For a while there everything was just too perfect, wasn't it? I want to go to sleep and not wake up but the pain in my stomach means I can't. I can't sleep, I wait and I hold Mark's hand. If we're still together I'm not as scared.

There's a noise. Maybe the boat is sinking? Probably a good thing at this point. This boat is a graveyard. The noise is getting closer. There's something coming onto the boat. What if it's a shark? I snap my neck up, no, not a shark. I'll die happily in lots of ways just please not a shark that's thrown itself onto the boat.

I stand up and then fall back down in shock. "Mark, Mark!" My voice is so hoarse. There hasn't been rain in a few days and the water stores are running low so my throat is a husk. I must be dreaming. It's a big crate of something. It has a plastic envelope on the side. A huge net is rising up into the air and I follow it up. There's a helicopter. I can see people inside it, now they're going away, they're flying away no, no, no come back, don't leave us here.

OPEN THIS AND READ THE CONTENTS BEFORE DOING ANYTHING, it reads on the plastic envelope. My head is spinning but I can still read. My fingers shake as I open the envelope. I hadn't realized I was shaking. Mark hasn't got up. Is he okay? I'm torn between the note and Mark. I need to read the note. I need to understand.

*You must read this note in its entirety before doing anything else. This is a message from the Icelandic Coast Guard. The package we have delivered to you contains food and other essential supplies including desalination equipment, antibiotics and rehydration salts. The package has been sterilized. You are not at risk of contracting the Plague from this package.*

*If you have not eaten solid food in over three days you must start by drinking the powders in the RED BOX at the top of this package. Mix one sachet of powder into each bottle of water. It is a nutrient-dense powder you must mix and drink slowly. The food in the package and the nutritional packs have been selected by medical professionals. There is enough food here for fifty people to survive on for two weeks. We will provide another package every fortnight until there is a vaccine.*

*It is still not safe for you to reach land. The Plague has killed 90 percent of the world's men. There is no vaccine yet, although scientists around the world are working to find one. As soon as Iceland has access to a vaccine, we will provide vaccines to you as a matter of priority. I hope*

*you are managing and I apologize for the delay in providing food to you.*
*Iceland has experienced extreme food shortages.*

*Please see enclosed a message for Toby Williams from Frances*
*Williams. Frances has been instrumental in the organization of these*
*supplies. She is a wonderful woman.*

*Heida Reinborg*
*Icelandic Coast Guard*

Frances did this. The thought of her makes me weep. I have a message from her. It feels like a message from God.

*Toby,*

*I'm not going to bother asking how you are because it must be awful. I miss*
*you so much but hopefully things will get better now that you have food.*
*You and Mark have to be okay, because you're both fighters and so you'll*
*have survived. I'm certain of that.*

*Don't be annoyed at Heida for taking so long to deliver food. It's been*
*a journey getting here but she's a nice lady. She's going to show us around*
*Iceland when all of this is over.*

*I'm fine here in London. Still working in the library. They tried to*
*assign me to work as a care assistant and, no offense, but I said the library*
*was more important. I had to do a campaign but eventually we had over*
*five hundred signatures from people saying the library had to stay open*
*and so my job was deemed to be a "necessary form of work" and I don't*
*have to do something else in the draft.*

*Maisy, Ryan and Isabel are fine. Ryan's immune, thank God. We've*
*been so lucky, Toby. I know it doesn't feel like it but honestly, we have.*
*You're probably thinking that's easy for me to say with all the food and*
*warmth and time with Maisy and Isabel I have, but you can be alive on*

*the boat. You probably wouldn't be alive here. They're working on a vaccine. Lots of people in London and Canada and France and China and America. All over, they're trying to find a vaccine.*

*Hang in there, okay? Everything's going to be all right, I promise.*

*I love you.*

*Frances xxx*

# DAWN

H ow is it that my latest promotion has resulted in me earning about 10 percent more and attending 80 percent more meetings? I'm now operations director of MI5, which is a title so senior I still jolt slightly every time I see my e-mail signature. My resentment of my packed diary is building as my long-suffering and wonderful assistant, Polly, passes me my schedule for the day. If I'd known how much work I was going to have to do, I'd have . . . oh, who am I kidding, I'd probably still have gone for the job. I'm enjoying being in charge (and I now have a corner office on the fourth floor with *floor-to-ceiling* windows).

"Right, what's first on the agenda?"

"You've got a meeting with the Home Affairs Committee at ten. Bernard Wilkins has already arrived."

"The one and only," I murmur, which is as close as Polly will get to an admission that I loathe him. Shoot me now. Actually, can someone maybe just give me the Plague? I think it might be less painful than a meeting led by Bernard. "Then you have a three-hour meeting with African and Asian Intelligence division heads."

"That's . . . not short."

She gives me a resigned look. "I negotiated it down from five hours. You're welcome."

The Home Affairs meeting, mercifully, is downstairs in one of the meeting rooms. Even more mercifully, there are biscuits. As punishment for my sins, almost everyone is late and so I'm stuck with Bernard on my own.

"You're looking well, Dawn," he says. Bernard only knows how to compliment women on their looks. It would never occur to him to comment on anything else.

"Thank you. How are things over by Big Ben?"

Bernard's face takes on a familiar, disgruntled expression. Here we go. "You know, I had the most extraordinary interaction with one of the new MPs, Violet Taylor. She's only been elected for two minutes—"

"She's been in office for six months, Bernard."

"Same thing, I've been an MP for over forty years, and she's on the House of Commons Change Committee, which is a ridiculous thing in the first place, and she has all these ideas. She would not take no for an answer."

I can only imagine Bernard's immune because the Plague took one look at him, heard him spouting pseudoscientific misogynistic nonsense and thought, *Oh God no, I can't be dealing with that*. If you want proof that nice guys don't always win, look no further than the fact that Bernard is one of only three surviving male MPs in his party.

"What were her ideas?"

Bernard splutters in outrage. I wipe a bit of spittle off my lapel and fight the urge to throw up on his shoes in retaliation. "She wants more female toilets, she wants to change prime minister's questions so it's 'less adversarial,' she wants longer maternity leave for MPs, she wants a *nursery* in the House of Commons. I tell you, female MPs always used to hang around together but they're awfully noisy now."

He looks at me as if I'm going to agree that those ideas are truly horrifying when they're just common sense. "Did your wife stay home and look after your children by any chance, Bernard?"

He looks at me suspiciously. "What's that got to do with anything?"

But I'm already taking my water and a stash of biscuits to the opposite side of the room to discuss literally anything else with the other MPs who have now arrived.

Within a few minutes the meeting has been called to order and I'm providing updates on various issues that only a few years ago would have been horrifying enough to warrant panic and urgent meetings but are now, frankly, humdrum. The only small plus point is that Gillian is still around; she's somehow managed to remain home secretary without burning out or fucking up. We have a game each meeting where we try to say a word as many times as possible without Bernard commenting. She chose "plethora" for this meeting. There's a plethora of food shortages in Scotland causing those living close to the border to cross into England and beg for food, which can't be given to them because of rationing. Shortages of a plethora of medicines caused a spike in deaths, which in turn caused riots in Leeds and Bristol. I provide our weekly update on draft compliance, which is over 97 percent. Happily, the example set in the US seems to have prepared people for the inevitable. There was so much speculation that a draft would be announced that by the time it was implemented, people were just relieved to have some certainty and the increased likelihood of a paid job. And then, there are the absurd. In particular, the difficulty we're having releasing prisoners after their sentences. They're safe in prison—there are no visits and guards wear hazmat suits—and leaving could be a death sentence. Truly, the world is upside down. In a plethora of ways.

# RECOVERY

# LISA

### Toronto, Canada
### Day 672

I've been working on a vaccine for 657 days and I'm so close to finding it I can almost taste it. The last days of summer are winding down, and I refuse to mark the second anniversary of the Plague unless it's with the bottle of Dom Pérignon Margot and I have been saving for the day I find it. Endless rounds of testing, testing, testing—I feel like an AV guy sometimes bellowing, "Testing, testing," into a microphone. Just fucking *work*. I'm so close. The last vaccine worked in 96 percent of cases. I managed to isolate the female chromosome that was resisting it, and now I'm waiting. Waiting for the test results. Waiting for our lives to change. Waiting to change the world. The chimps have served us well but after killing 253 of them over the past two years, I'd quite like to reduce my monkey kill count. They're a nightmare to dispose of.

I watch over the office as I wait. It's probably not much fun working for me, I'm self-aware enough to know that. I'm demanding and insistent and I expect everyone to be as smart and dedicated as I am, which they're not, and they can't ever be. As soon as I read the reports of the Plague Ashley compiled for me, I knew we would work on a vaccine the minute we could get hold of a specimen. I said, "That would be interesting to study," and Ashley looked very sad and said, "Hopefully we never have to. People are dying. It's a tragedy."

Ashley doesn't work for me anymore. Fortunately, the University of Toronto has been producing first-class virology PhDs for the past two decades, many of them women, thanks to me. That's why we're going to win this race. We started before anyone else, I've been training virologists for years and I've always prioritized the hiring of women in my department. Despite many accusations to the contrary, I've never prioritized diversity over ability. I've always had a simple policy. The best female applicant gets the job. Invariably, she's as good as, if not better than, the best male applicant. As a community, the scientific world has sexism running through it like gray swirls in marble. It's deeply woven into the fabric of labs, university departments, hiring panels, boards determining tenure. And guess what? The preponderance of senior male scientists and majority-male teams, specifically in virology, was a disaster when the Plague came, so who's going to be right in the end? Me. I am.

It's going to be a bit less satisfying being right when my former enemies are almost all dead. But still, some satisfaction will no doubt shine through.

I'm trying not to pace around the office but the waiting is too much. I could call Margot but she's teaching a class and besides, there's nothing she can say or do. The tests have been done; it either works or it doesn't. I can't be down there as they run the final checks and validate everything. I hover and then people get nervous and they make mistakes and the hope is too intense. This isn't our first rodeo. We thought we had it last time, three months ago. We really did. But the few dead chimps were there, heavy and cold and that was that. My team is exhausted. Margot keeps reminding me not to push them too far because they're tired, but she doesn't see their determination every day like I do. I have no idea how the other labs are coping around the world but I'd be amazed if they had the stamina of my lot. Of fourteen virology postgraduate students and postdoctoral scientists in this lab in November 2025, there were thirteen women and one man. Poor Jeremy, RIP. All the other top-ranking, virology-focused labs in the world capable of creating a vaccine for the virus had far more men than we did. God only knows how they've been dealing with those people dying. We're way ahead. We've retained our knowledge and our morale. There are personal motivations for all of us to create a vaccine—saving husbands, sons, the world, our careers. But we're not fighting for our own lives and that makes a big difference. No one can do their best work in what is essentially a war. The male scientists around the world who are frantically battling to understand the virus, attack it, control it and beat it have too much skin in the game. Had. Most of them are dead now. They were and are desperate and the best scientific discoveries rarely arise from desperation. Logical, calm, dogged persistence is far more likely to win the race.

There's a pounding sound. It's footsteps, fast heavy footsteps making my heart leap. No one runs with bad news. Unless it's a double bluff and Wendy, my loyal, competent deputy, is trying to break it to me as quickly as possible. Rip off the Band-Aid. This is why I can't be there when they get the results. I'm losing my mind in this office.

I can tell it's worked as soon Wendy bursts into my office in a whirlwind of tears and snot and out-of-breath flapping. "It's worked, it's worked. Lisa! One hundred percent survival, blood tests all clean."

I walk backward slowly. It's worked. I have invented a vaccine to cure the Plague. I'm going to save the world. I have saved the world.

Wendy hovers, clearly hoping for an emotional reunion. It's not going to happen, Wendy. Now the hard work starts. Margot and I have talked about this endlessly since she told me to get my head out of the sand in the middle of the night all those months ago. The plan is clear. Someday soon I will read articles in which this vaccine will be referred to as a miracle. It isn't a miracle. It's the result of hard work, dedication and ingenuity. Miracles are easy; working is hard.

"Call the Public Health Department."

I pace my office for a few minutes, the excitement so extreme I can't contain myself. I don't call Margot. Telling her what I've managed to do will be one of the greatest moments of my life and I want to savor it, uninterrupted.

Wendy rushes back in and thrusts her phone at me. Now is not the time for the Canadian Public Health Agency to put me on hold; they'll have been praying I would call.

"Lisa," the voice on the other end of the line says.

"Dr. Michael's fine," I reply. I've never spoken to this woman before; we're not on first-name terms.

"Apologies, Dr. Michael. What can I do for you?"

My voice is bubbling with happiness. "You should sound more excited to hear from me. This is the phone call that's going to change your life."

There's a stunned pause. I can just imagine this woman thinking no, no, surely not.

"Yes, I am in fact a God. I have a vaccine. One hundred percent success rate. Blood tests have come back clean. We've bypassed the missing chromosomes. I have cured the Plague."

"Dr. Michael, I, don't—"

"You don't know what to say? Yes, I thought that might be the case. Before you get too excited, there's going to be a difficult conversation between you, me and the Canadian government."

The woman sounds flustered. I can imagine her wearing a blazer at her nice desk in her nice office in her nice comfy job.

"What are you talking about?" she asks.

"I'm going to sell Canada the vaccine."

"Very funny, Dr. Michael."

"I'm not kidding. If you want it, you'll have to pay for it."

"Lisa, Dr. Michael. You can't sell the government a vaccine. It's . . . you . . . you're a doctor."

"Yeah, a PhD doctor, not a doctor doctor. There's a reason I didn't go to medical school. Actually, there's quite a few. Before you ask if I'm crazy, I'm not. I've known exactly what I was going to do for months. Set up a meeting and don't even think about stealing the vaccine from my lab."

"I wouldn't do that," she replies hotly. She definitely would.

"Of course you would," I say with a laugh. "Speak soon."

# CATHERINE

### London, United Kingdom (England and Wales)
### Day 674

There's a vaccine. It's finally happened. It's taken nearly two years but for a long time it seemed like this day would never come. I thought I would feel ecstatic but I'm furious. I'm incandescent with rage. I actually threw a plate this morning. Why now? Why were they able to discover it now? Why not before? The statement from the woman who discovered it, Dr. Lisa Michael, makes it sound like it was a breeze, like she was noodling around for a bit in the lab and then it just sort of appeared.

If it was so fucking easy, why didn't she find it sooner? Why didn't anyone find it sooner? Why am I a childless widow when the entire scientific community of the world has been looking for a cure for years? I want to scream at them all that they have failed me, failed all of us, failed the world, right at the time when they have succeeded.

These people in their white coats and their glasses with their PhDs and their amazing brains have saved the world and I want to wring their necks I'm so angry. They have saved the human race from extinction and I want to wail that it's too late for my family so why does it matter now anyway?

Tonight, I will drink a lot of wine, something I only allow myself to do occasionally to avoid slipping into the kind of sodden, drunken grief that I can see the appeal of very clearly. Tomorrow I will be back at my desk at 9 a.m. but for tonight I will shout and drink and grieve and cry and wail.

My phone rings, interrupting my already wine-soaked musings.

"Hello?"

"Cat, it's me. Phoebe."

Phoebe and I haven't spoken in almost two years. I miss her so much it's a physical ache.

"You wouldn't pick up my calls, I'm sorry, I, I just wanted to keep trying, I didn't—"

"Know I'd actually pick up?"

An awkward silence. My eyes fill with tears. We never used to have awkward silences. We've been friends for twenty years. We're not meant to have awkward silences.

"Are you okay?" she asks.

"Yep, yep, you know. Just thinking about the vaccine."

"It's extraordinary. I'm so—" She pauses and I can see the words she's about to say floating slowly in front of me as though they are huge, helium-filled balloons. "I'm so sorry it wasn't sooner."

"Me too," I manage. "Me too, Phoebe." I'm trying so hard not to cry because the anger I'm feeling is refreshing and invigorating even though the regret is painful. I don't even regret my own actions. I feel regret on behalf of these *amazing* scientists who've made this *amazing* discovery too bloody late.

"I wonder how the British team are feeling?" Phoebe goes on, filling the silence. She could never bear an awkward silence. "To come so close and then have that woman invent it and sell it. I can't imagine."

This is why I haven't spoken to my closest friend in the world for two years. Because, even though everything she's saying is true, her mind has room to consider how the British scientists who have failed feel. I don't care how they feel. I'm consumed by my own loss and I need her to be as consumed by it as I am but she can't be. Of course she can't be. I feel like I'm trapped in a Perspex box, screaming at her to understand what it's like in here but she's out, in the world, and can't.

"I can't either, but either way it's too fucking late," I say and hang up, before throwing my phone onto the sofa. She doesn't understand. She can't understand, and I hate her for it. I love her and I loathe her and her two daughters and her immune, living husband. I miss her and I hate her so much I can barely see. One day maybe I won't be so angry but that day is not today.

# ELIZABETH

The entire lab is sitting in stunned silence, watching the newscaster. Just two minutes ago, one of the lab techs, Maddy, yelled, "There's a vaccine! Oh my God, there's a vaccine!" We switched on the TV in George's office and now we sit, listening to the news presenter say the words we've all been waiting nearly two years for her to say.

Of course, we all imagined she'd be saying our names and announcing our discovery. But it's okay, that's not what matters. We're so, so close but not close enough. The important thing is that there's a vaccine. The important thing is that the world is saved.

"It was announced a few minutes ago, at a small press conference held at the University of Toronto, that Dr. Lisa Michael, the head of the Virology Department at the university, has discovered a vaccine for the Plague. A vaccine has been found. We're now going to show you some footage from the announcement."

The screen cuts to three women, freezing outside a grand, wooden door set in a beautiful, stone building. I recognize the woman in the middle. She's the Canadian prime minister, Oona Green. "It is the greatest honor of my life to announce here today that Dr. Lisa Michael and her team here at the University of Toronto have discovered a vaccine that protects men from the Plague virus. Dr. Michael will work with my colleagues in government to negotiate the sale of the vaccine to countries around the world."

A chatter of voices erupts in George's office like a spark across dry brush. Did she say *sale*? Does that mean what I think it means?

"The Canadian government will negotiate carefully the license of the MP-1 vaccine, so named after the Male Plague, as we call the disease here in Canada, to countries for a fee. This is valuable intellectual property with the potential to save many lives and, if abused, to cause great harm. We intend to treat it with the care and respect it deserves. We won't be taking any questions at this time."

Silence falls across the room as the screen cuts back to the news presenter who repeats the news over and over again for anyone tuning in. A vaccine has been discovered. It will be sold by the Canadian government. Dr. Lisa Michael at the University of Toronto is credited with its discovery. More details to follow when we know more.

Oh my God, she's *selling* it. I have failed. We all have. I look around the room and I see so many emotions—delight, anger, relief, exhaustion, outrage—but I don't see the one I feel so deeply it's as if my spine is dissolving and it's taking all my effort just to stay upright. Shame. This woman is going to hold the world to ransom and she wouldn't have the chance if we had got there first. We failed at this final, important hurdle. We identified the genes. We created the immunity test and then, when we were needed most, we failed and Lisa Michael has skipped into the sunset with a vaccine, the acclaim. More important, she has allowed herself to be pushed into selling it. Surely, she can't want to sell it. I can't fathom how a doctor who has spent the last two years working on a vaccine to save men, to return us to normalcy, could show it to the world and then say, "Now pay up." She must be scared and pushed around. The government must have forced her to do this. Surely, it can't be her.

# AMANDA

'm very glad I'm Canadian for a start." The woman on the TV laughs. She's dressed simply in a black blazer, black trousers and a white shirt. She's laughing. *Laughing.* What the fuck is wrong with her?

"Let's be honest, if I was from one of many other countries, there's no way in hell it would have been my decision to make. Lots of governments would have happily shot me in my sleep to avoid the annoyance of being legally required to pay me for my work."

The interviewer, the journalist Maria Ferreira whose writing about the Plague has hooked the world, looks shell-shocked. She looks the way I feel.

"And do you feel comfortable with your decision to require payment for the MP-1 vaccine? You could save billions of lives—"

Lisa frowns and cuts Maria off. "I am saving billions of lives. Look, I'm not keeping the vaccine from anyone. There's enough money in the world for everyone to be vaccinated. And, you know, for millennia we have expected women to sacrifice themselves at the altar of the greater good and I'm not engaging in it. You want me to tell you that this was a hard decision and I had sleepless nights deciding what to do but that's not the truth. This was the easiest decision in the world and it's not as selfish as it first appears—well, if you think being compensated for an incredible achievement is selfish, which personally I don't. Besides, if we're going to eradicate this disease from the face of the earth, we have to be certain that vaccination is done right. Letting anyone, anywhere, produce the vaccine causes the very real risk that a poorly produced vaccine will be used and this disease will live on when it doesn't have to."

Maria visibly relaxes. She looks much more comfortable with the idea that medical necessity has been a factor in Lisa's thinking rather than just cold, hard cash.

"So that's why you involved the Canadian government so closely? To ensure the quality of the vaccine?"

"As I said, it's a factor. We're preserving the vaccine's reputation and efficacy. Only countries with adequate manufacturing facilities and a rigorous quality control process will be allowed to purchase a license for the vaccine. That way, we'll know that everyone who has been vaccinated has received an effective dose."

"Have you spoken, since the announcement of the vaccine, to Dr. Amaya Sharvani, Dr. George Kitchen and Dr. Elizabeth Cooper, whose work was instrumental in your discovery?" Maria looks for the first time in this interview like she's enjoying herself a little. I have no doubt that question is written in capital letters, underlined in red: *Do not let Lisa take all the credit as though she invented the vaccine single-handedly without any help from anyone.*

"I've been quite busy," Lisa replies smoothly. "Although I'm very grateful to them for their work at the beginning of the research process." She can't even thank them without a caveat. *The beginning of the process.* The cheek of it.

"There's rumors that the Canadian government has already made you a billionaire thanks to your share of the vaccine. Is that true?"

"Yes, it is." She's shameless. Completely shameless. Who cares about billions when the world has been ripped apart and you have the means to sew it back together again? I don't buy her "validity of vaccine" excuse for a second. She could have ensured production was kept safe and then provided licenses for free.

"Are you willing to disclose what share of the vaccine you have retained and how much you have been paid?"

"I own forty percent of the MP-1 vaccine. The Canadian government owns fifty percent and the University of Toronto owns the remaining ten percent. I'm not at liberty to reveal the amounts that have been paid."

"What do you say to the people who accuse you of prioritizing your own financial gain over the health of billions of people around the world?"

"I would say that I've prioritized my own country—as many countries would expect their scientists to do in a time of crisis—and I've balanced Canada's interests, the global need for a safe and effective vaccine and, of course, my own interests. Not to mention the fact that the University of Toronto is a publicly funded university where I have spent the majority of my career. I wanted it to benefit from the research that it funded. I did my undergraduate degree here and got my first job as a researcher here after doing my PhD when I was in my twenties. I owe a lot to this place. It was unthinkable to me that we would just give away a piece of priceless research, the result of decades of commitment, recruitment, teaching and the thousands of hours my team put in. Hand it over like it was a penny we had found on the street? No."

Maria smiles tightly and looks at her notes. I feel like the entire world is uncomfortable with Lisa's existence and attitude. We all want to say, "No no, we wanted to be rescued but not like *this*. We wanted a kindly savior. A woman, or a rare, immune man, who would tell us everything is going to be okay, and provide a solution to our ills before living a life bathed in respect and gratitude." Can we turn back the clock and have someone else discover the vaccine in a few weeks' time, but do it right this time? You're not meant to profit from the apocalypse. The Plague is the best thing that's ever happened to her. The Plague is the worst thing that's ever happened to the rest to us. I can't accept it, can't accept her. This can't be the way the cure happens.

"Are you religious, Dr. Michael?"

Lisa laughs, for just longer than is comfortable. "No, I'm not. I am very, very rich though."

# LISA

Toronto, Canada
Day 678

'm feeling chirpy. The Public Health Agency woman, Ava, gives me a sideways look.

"Lisa, could you maybe . . . tone it down a bit?"

I frown at her. There, she probably thinks that's better. "This meeting is a good thing, Ava. Everyone in the room is happy to be here." Give me strength, we're in the most enviable position of any country on the planet. Millions of people would kill to be in this room.

The door swings open and the minister of foreign affairs, Florence Etheridge, and her entourage sweep into the room, all expensive coats and Chanel perfume. There are air kisses and hugs and everyone's so happy to see, isn't it wonderful, yes, yes it's fantastic to see you, just fantastic. I can only spend a few minutes with politicians before coming out in hives.

"Apologies for my tardiness," Florence says. "It's been back-to-back meetings on the US emigration issue for the past week. The American reforms are biting and, what can I say, everyone wants to be in Canada."

Everyone else laughs on cue.

"We're waiting for the Chinese still?" Florence asks.

"I believe they're here, but we'll call them in when we're ready," I reply, my voice calm and steady.

Florence pauses and looks at me, again, almost for too long. "I hope you know," she says softly, "how grateful we all are. The rest of the world might judge you harshly because of what you've done, but to us you're a hero. No more Canadian baby boys will die from the Plague, men who've been away from their families for years can safely reenter society. You've given us a golden ticket to become the most powerful nation on earth. The geopolitical slate has been partially wiped clean and we have what everybody wants."

I smile, as graciously as I can. "You're paying me handsomely for the privilege. Now, let's get this vaccine made."

Someone must have given an invisible signal because a few short minutes later, four Chinese women walk into the room. There are handshakes, coffee poured, polite compliments and inquiries about hotels but we all know what we're here to do.

"We should begin," a pretty woman with a serious expression says. The card in front of her on the table reads *Tiffany Chang, Head of Vaccine Production Management, Independent State of Shanghai.* Florence's team reached out to Shanghai because they're the most stable of the emancipated city-states and have the best vaccine production capacity. Beijing is still too violent, Tianjin doesn't have the necessary facilities and Macau was never in the equation.

"Firstly, we want to thank you for reaching out to us with your offer," Tiffany says. "We are very grateful for the opportunity to access the vaccine."

"Why don't you tell the room a little of your own background," I suggest to Tiffany. Maybe Florence has read everything I sent her but if my experience with politicians is anything to go by, that's as likely as pigs flying.

"Of course. In November 2025 I was third in command of polio vaccine production for the largest Chinese state-owned vaccine manufacturer in Shanghai. I was promoted quite a few times because . . ."

Her voice drifts off. We all know why.

"In my current post, for the last six months I've been preparing for the day when we would have a vaccine."

"You're ready to begin production?" I ask, my voice cushioned with excitement. I didn't realize they were prepared.

"Yes, we've continued with smaller batches of our usual vaccine production to keep polio at bay for babies and children who had not been vaccinated at the time of outbreak." Tiffany pauses and looks as though she's preparing herself. "We know you didn't come to us first," she says, in a rush. "You asked the French and the Germans, but they refused to pay and, besides, you must have been worried they would split the cost and share the vaccine with each other. The Japanese were nonresponsive. Your relations with the United States obviously make this level of cooperation impossible."

I flash Florence a look to say, *what the fuck?* The Shanghai contingent clearly has a lot of information from somewhere and it's not from me.

"It is not a problem," Tiffany says. "I understand why you didn't come to us first. Our former country is still gripped by civil war. I want to assure you that Shanghai State is a safe, secure place. But I also understand that those other countries refused to pay you. They are hoping you will relent. You are the most hated woman in the world," Tiffany says looking directly at me. The entire room holds its breath. If this is a negotiating tactic, it's not one I've ever seen before.

"You shouldn't be," Tiffany goes on, looking earnestly at me. "We understand your thinking. Why should you give something away for free that could help your country to succeed? That would be an act of self-sabotage and, worse, a betrayal of your country's faith in you. We understand that Canada should be paid for the vaccine. We are serious buyers."

I smile and sit back in my chair. I'm with like-minded people here, maybe for the first time since the discovery of the vaccine became public. Canadians revere me but they don't necessarily understand me. To the rest of the world I'm a cartoonishly grotesque figure of evil.

"Thank you for setting out your position," I say. "I appreciate it, more than you know. Before we can discuss price, however, we have to understand the exact nature of your production. This will be the first batch of the vaccine being produced outside of Canada and being given to non-Canadian citizens. If the first international batches are produced poorly—"

"The vaccine will lose value," Tiffany interrupts.

I pause. It's not *entirely* about money. "Yes, and more important, people will not be immune but may think they are. One of the conditions of the patent license will be a sample of ten thousand vaccines being produced under the strict supervision of scientists from a Canadian team. This will obviously be followed by extensive quality control. If those vaccines are of a sufficient standard, the full patent license will be granted."

Tiffany nods in agreement. I expected some pushback but she seems to completely understand my thinking. "Yes, this is an acceptable condition. Our power supply is stable thanks to solar panels, so we can guarantee there won't be any quality issues. We can start production right away."

Florence raises an eyebrow. "How much do you predict being able to produce in the first six months?" she asks.

"Eight million," Tiffany says, quick as a whip. This is a lot, lot higher than our vaccine production.

"Here is my suggestion," Florence says. "The fee will be reduced"— What? I open my mouth to complain—"until the entire Canadian population has been vaccinated. The vaccines you produce will be split fifty-fifty between Canada and Shanghai. Once Canadian production and your vaccines have resulted in one hundred percent vaccination in

Canada, you keep all of the vaccine you produce and the license fee increases but you will still have a reduction. You produce in batches of one hundred thousand, yes? Every second batch comes to us, until our needs are met."

Let's think. The population of Shanghai is 12.8 million, assuming a 10 percent male survival rate. Splitting the vaccine, Shanghai won't be fully vaccinated for nine months. That's relatively quick. Besides, they'll create a system for prioritizing need the way we have. Tiffany and her colleagues confer quietly in Chinese for a few minutes.

"We agree in principle," Tiffany says.

I exhale in relief as Florence smiles. "Excellent news. Now let's move on to the fee."

# CATHERINE

'm not sure what I'm expecting Amanda Maclean to look like in person. Her pictures with the interviews she's done don't give much away. She's always sitting down, and they're taken in such a way to make her look like the archetype of a grieving mother. She has bright red hair and pale, Celtic skin and that's as much as I know. She sounds quite fearsome on the phone. Tall. I definitely expect her to be tall.

She comes toward me with a purposeful walk. I was right—she is tall. Her eyes are a startling blue.

"Catherine?" Her Scottish accent is strong. Although the woman we're going to talk to today will no doubt have a far thicker accent than this so I'd better get used to it.

I keep telling Amanda how grateful I am for her time; she's a busy lady. Head of Health Protection Scotland and arguably the most influential woman in medicine now in the Independent Republic of Scotland.

"I want Euan's and Heather's stories to be in your report. It's important," is all she says in response to my awkward gratitude. On the ferry across to Rothesay on the Isle of Bute I ask her to tell me everything she knows so far before we meet Euan's wife. She says, "Let me get a Red Bull first," and I'm reminded that when I asked what she missed more than anything from before the Plague she said, "Coffee," in a tone of such longing it bordered on lust. She nearly became a dentist to avoid medicine's early starts. However, she's good in a crisis and so even at the age of eighteen knew that a career in which a root canal counts as a drama would not suffice.

Sufficiently caffeinated, Amanda returns: "Okay, where shall we begin?"

"Why was it you that had to do all of this, finding the source of the virus? On your own?" I respond. Amanda has never had a huge amount of time on the phone so I'm dying to know more.

"I became obsessed with knowing how the Plague had come to pass. I still don't understand how people aren't more gripped by the need to know why. This disease destroyed my life, it has destroyed billions of lives. How could anyone not be desperate to understand how and why?" She pauses and takes an angry swig from her can.

"Everything was upside down. Maybe in more normal times it wouldn't have been like that. But we needed to understand the origin of the virus to be able to have a vaccine and avoid this happening again."

I swallow convulsively. "Do you think it will happen again?"

"Just because your husband left you doesn't mean your house can't catch on fire. In other words, tragedy doesn't immunize you against further tragedy." I look at her, both baffled and terrified. "The vaccine we have should be effective, yes, and we can use it to adjust to new strains. But in theory the Plague could mutate, allowing the vaccine to be ineffective."

This makes sense and yet I had assumed, unconsciously, that of course the Plague couldn't return. That amount of bad luck is impossible. Apparently not.

"Can you tell me more about Patient Zero?" I ask.

"Euan," she quickly corrects. "You have to think of him as Euan in your head; otherwise you might call him Patient Zero in front of Heather and that's not nice. They were married for forty-five years and she hates that we refer to him as Patient Zero. I don't like it either, to be honest. It's so dehumanizing. It reduces his life entirely to his death from this bloody awful disease. I nearly called him Patient Zero the second time I met his wife and she burst into tears. Can't say I blame her. If someone referred to my husband as Patient Three Hundred and Forty-Five I'd want to throttle them. Euan was a sailor all his life. Sometimes he worked on the ferry, for a few years he was a fisherman. He ended up outside of the law and well," she takes a swig of Red Bull, "suffice to say the consequences were greater than he ever could have imagined."

We arrive in Bute and make our way through the small town of Rothesay, walking from the ferry terminal to Heather's small terraced house overlooking the sea. Amanda has spent a significant amount of time with Heather, as she investigated the beginning of the illness and tried to understand the origins of the Plague, and then became close to her for reasons I don't fully understand.

We meet Heather in her house and she politely offers us water. She seems quite suspicious of me but I was expecting that. Amanda had warned me that Heather has been offered huge sums of money by newspapers for her story as the "Widow of Patient Zero." Heather has always refused, convinced that journalists will somehow blame her for the tragedy that started with Euan's contraction of the Plague.

"You're looking well," Heather tells Amanda as we sit down in her small living room and they engage in comfortable small talk.

"So," Amanda says, and clears her throat. "Heather, Catherine here is writing a report on the Plague. A sort of dossier of people's stories, and she wants to know more about Euan so he's not just—"

"The beginning," Heather interrupts, her eyes flashing with anger. Her expression softens and she continues. "He was a lovely man, so he was. We met at school when I was fifteen and he was sixteen. We saw each other for a few months and married two days after I turned sixteen. We saw no reason to wait when we knew we were right for each other." Heather starts handing around biscuits and I'm struck by how normalized the telling of stories of grief have become in the last two years.

"He always worked on boats and he was meant to be easing down but—"

"Can I ask a question?" I ask, awkwardly interrupting. I've read everything I need to know about Euan Fraser in the many newspaper articles about him. I'm not interested in him; he's not here anymore. I want to know what it feels like to be the widow of Patient Zero.

"Of course."

"What does it feel like to be in this position? Lots of us have lost our husbands, but I don't have journalists asking me if my husband could have done anything differently as though he's responsible for starting the Plague."

I can feel Amanda tensing beside me. This isn't what we agreed I would ask.

"I don't really want to talk about it."

"People are already talking about it," I say in my softest, most placating voice. It doesn't matter. The shutters have come down on Heather's eyes.

"Why don't we discuss Donal," Amanda says firmly, shifting the conversation away from Heather.

"Who's Donal?" I ask, baffled. Have I missed something? Maybe Donal was one of Heather's sons?

"Donal Patterson is the man who brought the monkeys to the Isle of Bute along with Euan."

Oh my God. This is the man Amanda referred to in her interview with Maria Ferreira. There are internet conspiracies about who he is and what he did, although all of these conspiracies assume he is dead.

"Is he alive?"

"He is. He's immune."

"Why, what—" I shake my head to get my thoughts in order. "What do you want to tell me about him?"

"Something that the entire world is going to know by the end of the day. In just under an hour it's going to be announced that Donal Patterson is in prison," Amanda says calmly. "His trial was carried out in secret under a piece of emergency legislation. The news has been kept secret since Donal was convicted a year ago in order to allow plans to be made."

"What kind of plans?"

"Plans to prevent people trying to find him and kill him. If he hadn't imported the monkeys illegally, the Plague might never have started."

It's a dizzying thought. "How long was his sentence?"

"Life with a minimum term of eighty years."

"Not likely to get parole," Heather adds.

"I can't believe it was so simple. So stupid," I say. "Sorry, Heather, but I mean, imported animals, a bit of extra money on the side. That's what caused all this."

Heather sniffs but says nothing.

"I'm sorry, it's just. All of this, the pandemonium and it could have been avoided." Amanda frowns at me and I know she doesn't want me to keep talking but it is a simple truth. "None of this had to happen." It is the most painful sentence I have ever spoken out loud. It wasn't written in the stars. This wasn't some unavoidable tragedy I couldn't swerve. These men made a choice and it led to my husband dying. I can dimly recognize I'm being irrational but still, it's true. Being in Heather's house, in Euan's house, is making it so stark I can't ignore it. But for these men breaking the law, my husband and son wouldn't be dead.

"I'm sorry," I say, and leave. I can't sit there for another moment.

# STRENGTH

# HELEN

**Penrith, United Kingdom (England and Wales)**
**Day 1,168**

**M**um!"

Oh Jesus, if Abi and Lola are fighting again, I swear to God. I've had a long day fixing lights, climbing up and down ladders, I do not need to mediate a teenage fight.

"If you two are at it again, you'll be—"

"Hi, Helen," says Sean, bold as fucking brass, sitting at our kitchen table. Not his kitchen table, our kitchen table. Mine and the girls'.

The world is going a bit fuzzy and I'm about to ask someone to open a window when black dots move in from the sides of the kitchen and then next thing I know, I'm lying on the ground with Sean and Abi peering over me.

I struggle upright, batting Sean's hands away but gratefully accepting Abi's kind, strong help. "Abi, go to your room, please. Make sure your sisters don't come downstairs." She nods and goes upstairs without a peep.

Until I know what Sean has to say for himself, I don't want him anywhere near the girls.

"I'm back," he says, Captain Obvious, as I collapse into a chair and hold my thumping head in my hands.

"I'd gathered." I would motion for him to sit down but he's already helped himself to a seat and, oh fantastic, a drink.

"It's so—"

"Sean, what the fuck?" He blinks a few times like an owl. Did I used to find him attractive? I remember him doing the blink-y thing—it used to drive me nuts. Still does. "You waltz in here, having left to live out the rest of your 'borrowed time' as if no one was watching, and now you're back just like that. What the fuck?"

Part of me is asking Sean this question and the other part of me is asking the universe. What are the chances that my pathetic husband is immune? His friend, who died in his wife's arms, wheezing out the word "love" with his final breaths, wasn't immune. Ann-Marie from down the road's gorgeous wee boy, Tommy, wasn't immune. But my husband, the deserter, is immune. And he came back.

"We thought you were dead," I bite out, trying and failing to keep my rage out of my voice.

"I know," he says. "I'm so sorry, it never. I just thought I would get it and—"

"You disappeared! You switched off your phone as soon as you abandoned us and we never heard anything. Then, three years later, when the sight of a man is as rare as snow in July, who turns up at our door? You! Oh, and you'd better stop balking at the word 'abandoned' because it's what you fucking did."

He sits in silence and I get a chance to look at him. He looks . . . different and the same. Bit thinner, bit grayer, bit more drawn.

"Explain yourself."

"I thought I might get a nicer welcome than this," he mutters.

After looking up and seeing my face, he sighs a world-weary sigh he has no right to. "Our life was so, so claustrophobic, Helen. I was bored, weren't you bored? Working in the same boring job, doing the same boring thing for dinner every Friday. And then the Plague came and it was like this is it! Now or never! My life is going to end, how do I want to end it? I needed to live the life I always dreamed of with the time I had left."

If I wasn't already, now I'm certain this really is Sean. He always had the tact of a rhino. Of course, he hadn't counted on being immune; he was bored of living as though he was about to die and so wanted to come back to his old life and apparently, that's me and his children.

"So, you abandoned me, leaving me to single-handedly parent our daughters. It's a good thing I didn't fuck off when I got bored the same way you did, huh? Otherwise we'd have three orphans."

"That's not fair."

"It's far nicer than you deserve. Hang on, what have you been doing for the past three years?"

"After I left, I went up to the Highlands."

"Of Scotland? During the Plague, you went to the one country on earth with more of the disease than England? You went to the Highlands to try and get yourself killed?"

He gets a bit defensive at that. "You're making it sound stupid. It was a dream of mine for a long time."

"To do what, look at some sheep on a hill?"

"No, I, you know, hiked about a bit. After a few months staying in a deserted hotel I traveled all the way down to London and lived there for nearly a year doing manual labor to make enough money for a hostel and food."

"But why didn't you come home? You preferred living in a hostel doing manual labor to being home?"

A remarkable list of excuses follows. He was scared we wouldn't want him, he was still scared he'd catch it, he thought the girls would have forgotten him.

"After London, I went to the Southwest of England, lived by the beach in Devon and learned how to surf." That, at least, I will accept is better than being an estate agent and doing the washing up.

"So, it took you how long to actually do something exciting with your fucking freedom?"

He rolls his eyes. "I went to Devon fourteen months after I left."

"And why have you crawled back now?"

At that, he just looks at me with this expression of total incomprehension. "I missed all of you."

He doesn't get it, he doesn't get the half of it.

"Can I see the girls now?" he asks plaintively, after my silence has clearly unnerved him. I call the girls down and they come in, silent and somber. A look of panic is starting to make its way across Sean's face. I suspect he was hoping I'd fall into his loving arms and we'd announce to the girls that our family was complete once more and the girls would cry with relief that he's alive, blah blah blah. It doesn't work like that anymore.

Abi is clearly furious; she just glares at him. Hannah looks like she wants the ground to swallow her up; she's never liked confrontation. Lola is the only one throwing him a bone, and it's a small, knobbly one at that. A small smile but nothing more.

"I'll give you all a minute," I say if only to get out and get some fresh air. God, I wish we could grow tobacco in England, I miss smoking like a limb right now. Even without a fag, a few minutes outside clears my head a bit. The shock and anger were making my thoughts repeat themselves, going around in loops.

When I go back into the kitchen, the four of them are all sitting awkwardly around the table. Abi is furiously gnawing on one of her nails, which I would normally tell her off for but whatever gets her through this emotional whirlwind today is fine by me.

"We need time to process this," Hannah says eventually in the calm, authoritative tone that she so rarely uses and that has all the more power for its rarity. "I think you should go and stay somewhere else and come back tomorrow."

Sean looks like she's slapped him. He looks at the others, clearly hoping that someone, anyone, will beg him to stay. Silence rings around the room. He looks devastated, but what did he expect? A hero's welcome is what. The men that are left—no, that's not fair—some of the men that are left have this weird complex. Just because they're one of the "chosen few" they think they're gods. You see so few men about that they've mistaken shock for awe, when they see women's expressions. But they're not better just because there's fewer of them. We're all human, man or woman, and just because some quirk of genetics or luck meant you were immune or survived, it doesn't make you any better. Sean's going to have to learn that, and fast.

The next day, he slopes back to the house. The girls are at school and I have a day off. I realize, belatedly, that if I didn't, he would have arrived at an empty house. It didn't occur to me to tell him my schedule. I just don't think about him anymore.

"So, yesterday was challenging," he says over a cup of hot water and berry squash I've grudgingly handed over.

"What did you expect, Sean? You left us. You left me. You left them."

He exhales heavily. "I'm their dad. I'm your husband—"

I can't help but interrupt. "Actually, I got a death certificate for you a few months ago on the basis you were dead, so no. You're not my husband. Technically, I'm a widow. We'll probably have to do some paperwork to change it so that we're divorced instead, seeing as you're alive and all."

"I suppose that answers the question I was going to ask then, about us. About the future."

"Sean, I will never forgive you for what you did."

"Helen," he says with this expression of disappointment that makes me want to throttle him until he goes blue, as though *I'm* the one who has been a disappointment here.

"No, no, no, Sean. You don't get it. I don't love you anymore, I don't need you anymore. The Plague put things into perspective for different people in different ways. It made you think your life was a cage to be escaped, and congratulations. You've got more freedom than you had anticipated. I hope you fucking enjoy it."

"You're making me sound like an awful person," he says petulantly. "Like I skipped off into the sunset without a second thought."

How did I ever love this man? He's a complete twat.

"You have three children, Sean. You had a wife! You disappeared like a thief in the night. I don't think you've learned a fucking thing from any of this, but I'll tell you what. The Plague and you leaving made me realize, more than ever, that my children are my world and that I like my life. The worst worries I had were whether having sex once a week was enough for us to 'keep the spark alive' and if the girls would find jobs they liked. Jobs they liked! What an idea now."

Sean slinks down into his seat, mumbling incoherently.

"My job used to be something I enjoyed well enough but if you had told me I could have retired tomorrow, I'd have jumped at the chance. But now I'm an electrician and I'm useful. You never made me feel useful. When I get home at the end of the day, I know I've used my hands to do something that not many other people can do. And I get home, I see the girls and I know I'm in the right place."

"It's not the same for you, Helen. You weren't staring at death like it was a gun on your forehead. I couldn't do what you did."

I realize I'm not getting through to him. I'm wasting my breath. It feels outrageous that he can just get away with it, but not much about life over the last few years has felt fair. There's no moral judge and jury that can convince him on my behalf that he is wrong and I am right. He left and I stayed.

"I belong here, Sean," I say, with a trace of a sigh. "You decided that you didn't. You made your bed, now you have to lie in it."

Sean smiles weakly at me. He finishes his drink and tells me he'll be back at five o'clock to see the girls. I shut the door behind him with a thunk and think how lucky I am that, against the odds, without a husband and in a job I was assigned, I really, really like my life. And when someone isn't there anymore, you adapt.

# ARTICLE IN THE *WASHINGTON POST* ON SEPTEMBER 5, 2029

*This is one of our "Woman Least Likely" series of pieces about the women in the United States who have taken on leadership roles, despite being "unlikely candidates." This week's piece, by Maria Ferreira, is about Clare Aspen, 29, the mayor of San Francisco, who was elected last month, beating out eight other candidates, all of whom were women.*

Clare Aspen's San Francisco apartment is like something out of a 2024 millennial's dream Pinterest board. There's a gallery wall over her couch. Her kettle is vintage style and pink. There's a bar cart in the corner (albeit with only a small selection of alcohol that, on closer perusal, all seem to be produced in and around the Bay Area by small distilleries). The chopping board has an avocado print. Need I say more.

When pressed, Clare laughs and looks around the apartment as if seeing it for the first time in years. "I suppose it is a bit of a time capsule. I bought this place when I was in my mid-twenties just before everything happened. I haven't been particularly concerned with interior decoration since," she adds wryly, an understatement for the ages.

The story of Clare Aspen is now folklore but the basics bear repeating. When the Plague hit the West Coast in 2026, she was living an admirable life of public service as a cop. "Super green, super keen," she says. "I'm lucky I didn't get into more trouble early on. I was so eager to do everything right—catch the bad guy! Make a difference! I was a bit much."

She didn't move to San Francisco—a city in which, prior to the Plague, only the super-rich had even a hope of affording to live in for much longer—to be a cop earning under $70,000 a year. No, she came to make her fortune. The classic tech dream a million men who had watched *The Social Network* were determined would be in their own future. Unlike most of the hoodie-clad tech bros who came before her, however, Clare succeeded. Here's the story in a nutshell.

Girl with engineering degree (summa cum laude, natch) from UT Austin moves to California to be a developer. Girl finds culture in medium-size start-up to be as gross as all the Reddit threads had warned her it would be. Girl perseveres because she is many things but a quitter is not one of them. Girl is one of two women on a team of sixty men, many of whom appear to be sociopathic in their pursuit of wealth. Girl thinks she's doing pretty well with a hefty salary. Girl has no idea what is coming. Girl is in the right place at the right time and is offered the golden ticket: an IPO. Stock goes public, stock goes up in value quickly. Girl becomes very rich.

So far, so cinematic. Can't you see Hollywood salivating over the movie rights already? But no! It gets better.

Girl is rich but unfulfilled and decides to quit her (very lucrative) job, cash in her stocks and become a cop. "I still remember my dad shouting down the phone at me when I told him I was going to be a cop. *A cop?! I didn't pay a hundred thousand dollars for you to be a Goddamn cop.*" Clare wrote him a check there and then for every penny he spent on her college education and accepted an offer to join the San Francisco Police Department.

If the Plague had never happened, the end of this movie would write itself. She would have met a nice boy, maybe a fellow cop (we all love an office romance) and had a few adorable, rule-abiding children. Her dad would have seen the value of her choices and she'd have lived a long and healthy life with her husband by her side in comfortable obscurity.

But the Plague did happen and this young, plucky cop was there at the airport the day of the Great San Fran Riots. She knows it sounds dramatic but she was lucky to get out alive.

Unfortunately for Clare, and fortunately for the lucky few who managed to travel, some domestic flights were still leaving San Francisco that day. I asked United Airlines and Delta for comments for this article. Both declined to respond, so I am forced to extrapolate from what we know. We know that most international flights were canceled but two scheduled flights to Israel filled only with women left, without clearance to land, both piloted by males who were shot dead by the Israelis on arrival and burned without ceremony. We also know that five domestic flights to Chicago, Miami, New York, Minneapolis and Seattle departed the airport.

One of those flights—the Delta flight to Minneapolis—crashed over New Mexico for unknown reasons but it is thought that the pilot became ill on the flight. The other four flights all arrived safely, but we cannot know why their pilots made those flights as scheduled because they are all dead. Commonly repeated possibilities are that the pilots wanted to ensure people got home to see loved ones, thought they could escape the virus in those other cities or had families themselves in those cities.

What we do know now is that thousands of people died in a stampede and the ensuing riots and those deaths might never have happened if all flights had been canceled. When I posit this theory to Clare, she looks both weary and furious at the same time. "It's not a simple question to answer. People were desperate and the airport was always going to be a hub of panic at that time. It was the crowd theory by Gustave Le Bon happening in front of my very eyes. The crowd, like microbes, mutated and became irritable, irrational, uncontrollable."

I point out to Clare that Gustave Le Bon's theory of crowds' infectious behaviors has been thoroughly debunked by science. For the first time in our long conversation I see the fierce glint that made this woman the country's youngest mayor. She doesn't care that I've read some *Atlantic* piece about bullshit science. She was there. She saw it. What do I know?

"It started with a single gunshot," she says. "One guy. One gun. He didn't shoot at a person, he shot up, like they do in the movies. But in the movies, they do that when they're *outside* and *alone*. He was in a crowded airport with a partially glass roof."

We all know what happened next. It is written into the history of the Plague as a painful reminder of the way in which the pandemic robbed us of our humanity. Pandemonium followed the gunshot. Women, men, children, all howling and crying, were trampled to death across the airport as the crowd surged toward exits and away from the gunshots. In total, 186 people died in the stampede. Twelve men, including Clare's colleague Andrew Rawlings, died from gunshot wounds as men desperately shot at one another. Unrest and panic spread outward from the airport, culminating in devastating riots.

Clare is surprisingly forgiving of the original shooter, a position she did not dare mention on the campaign trail. "He obviously shouldn't have shot the roof, but can you imagine being told that you could never go home again, never see your family again, your sons were going to die and you were going to die from a painful disease in a few days? That's one of the circles of hell. People do awful things in that kind of situation."

She was completely alone. She was going to die. And yet, here she is because she ran. That's why she survived. The question at the San Francisco debate from her main opponent in the mayoral race—Victoria Brown—that rang around California in its tone of scathing judgment comes to mind: *Why did you run, Clare? What kind of public servant runs away?*

Clare is as dismissive of Victoria now as she was then. She scoffs at her opponent's total lack of understanding of the human condition. "One of the reasons I wanted to run for mayor was that I actually had on-the-ground experience of being a public servant, both when it goes right and when it goes wrong. I was honest about the fact that I ran on that day. Victoria tried to make it sound like I was the worst police officer who had ever lived because I, what, didn't start randomly shooting men who would have turned their guns on me? Her strategy didn't work. The voters understood. They understood that when there is that much fear in the air, and people have nothing to live for, sometimes you have to run."

The end of the story can now be written, in all of its post-Plague, messy, untouched apartment glory. Girl becomes mayor of San Francisco in the first election held in her city since the Plague. Girl introduces programs to recruit women into coding and the police and to rebuild the tech industry, determined to make life better and not just focus on survival. Girl is powerful and unapologetic about that power even though on a terrifying day, years ago, she ran.

———————————

# DAWN

cannot have one more argument about crisps!"

Don't laugh, don't laugh, don't laugh. I manage to keep a straight face. Marianne West, the woman who *cannot* have one more argument about crisps (not one!), is looking at me as if to say, *You see what I have to put up with?* Oh, I do, Marianne, rest assured I do.

Turns out, one of the best ways to fulfill the career dreams your twenty-five-year-old self barely dared to imagine is to be a woman during the Plague. I haven't lost my marbles and I'm not allowed to retire until I'm seventy. When I realized I had a decade until retirement, I thought, fuck it. If I'm going to be here, I'm going to keep doing well. Five swift promotions later and here I am. Arguably one of the three most powerful people in the British Intelligence Services. Little Dawn Williams from a housing estate in Lewisham. Always the nerd in class, never able to get words to leave my brain in the way I wanted them to, never able to make myself sound interesting. Always the hardest working, always different from everyone else yet always boring. Too boring to be bullied properly even, just ignored. Always different at Oxford, the only black woman. Always the only black woman everywhere I went. Still, always quiet and understated. I made a habit of saying one thing in my head and another out loud. And now, here I am. The thing

I was told would be my undoing has become the reason for my success. I'm completely unobjectionable. You could even go as far as to say nondescript. I've made no enemies, rubbed no one the wrong way, kept my head down. Worked so hard people could only ever say I was competent; even if they didn't like me, they could never point to a mistake. I always wore a gold band on my left hand so people would assume I was married. Fewer questions, fewer chances of being harassed and then, when I had my daughter, no one batted an eyelid. People assumed I was married, I had a child, nothing to see here. I have made it my mission to be the most boring, hardest-working person in every room and it has paid off.

Oh, and I didn't die. That's also really helped with the promotions. Back to more important matters. Like crisps.

"They're an important source of calories in many people's diets, they don't go bad so there's minimal food waste when we make them and people like them. And before you tell me, yet again, that that isn't a factor, let me assure you, it is."

The rather serious-looking dietitian with glasses too big for her face sits back. She's not going to win this, not against Marianne, who looks positively murderous.

"Shall we take a brief tea break?" I suggest before regretting my choice of words. Marianne looks, for a moment, like she wants to cry. The table relaxes and people wander over to the drinks trolley, where a paltry selection of water and squash awaits them. Squash, honestly, it's like being at a children's birthday party. If I'd known that tea would run out as quickly as it did, I'd have stockpiled it up to the ceiling.

"I just miss it so much." Marianne sighs as she comes and sits next to me.

"It made everything better, didn't it."

She nods mournfully. "I started looking into the possibilities of tea farming in the South of England a few days ago." I look at her doubtfully. "I know, it was a long shot. Turns out, there's a reason tea is grown in India and Africa, not in Kent. I thought maybe climate change might have opened some possibilities but I'm assured that climate change has halted and will likely reverse now that half the planet's died and taken their poxy emissions with them."

Marianne is that rare thing: a competent civil servant with a sense of humor. The head of the UK's Rationing Program and chair of its board of directors. A board I'm also on, hence my reluctant presence in this room of twenty people whose combined mission is to keep the UK population alive and fed. The sooner the global food trade picks up so I don't have to attend these meetings, the better.

"How did you end up in the rationing program?" I ask, a question I've been meaning to ask her for months.

"I started in the service when I was twenty-four. I was a lawyer for a few years before that but it didn't suit me. I prefer the abstraction of being a civil servant. The policy, whatever it might be, affects thousands or millions of people but you don't know them. I like that compartmentalizing."

I nod, the thinking familiar to me. "I'd have been a terrible police officer, dealing with individuals. Nightmare. So how did you end up running this though?"

"Over the course of thirty years in the civil service I built up a reputation as a 'generalist,' which is a kind way of saying 'someone who gets bored easily.' I moved around a lot and became a 'fixer,' cleaning up messes. When the Plague began—gosh, even after all these years it still feels so *medieval* saying that, doesn't it—I was working in the Department for Environment, Food and Rural Affairs."

Interesting but not surprising. Marianne is one of the most pragmatic people I've ever met, with common sense in spades. I can just imagine her taking charge of a disaster and sorting it out without throwing her weight around.

"You came up with the idea for the program?"

Marianne nods. "Yep, and the director general of the Environment Department was an enormous support. I suggested in December 2025 that we needed a rationing program, he told me to set one up, the legislation went through a month after that and here we are. I would tell you that the nutritionist, Donna, is not normally as annoying as she's being today, but that would be a lie so you'll just have to get used to her. I just want to clobber her over the head with a stapler, I mea—"

"Donna! How nice of you to join us," I say, cutting Marianne off with a bright smile.

Donna straightens her glasses and looks at us both resolutely. "We need to talk about the treat ration size. It's just not right, Marianne, you don't—"

Marianne sighs and says "Donna" in the same weary tone I used to use when my daughter was being a moron.

"The treat ration is not being reduced. There are a number of factors, as you well know, in the creation of the ration amounts and one—just one—of those factors is nutrition. If you had it your way, we'd all be eating hemp seeds and fourteen portions of raw vegetables a day. The allowance for crisps, sweets, alcohol and cake, fun things with caloric but no nutritional value that help make a day that little bit cheerier, has value in preventing starvation and keeping people happy. Do you want people to be sad, Donna?"

Donna splutters indignantly. "I want people to be healthy, and there's no reason for so many resources to be used for making *cake*."

"Well the board and I disagree with you, so you'll just have to lump it," Marianne snaps as I make a mental note to stay on her good side.

"We need a new fucking dietitian," Marianne mutters before calling the meeting back to order. It's odd being on this side of the curtain of the rationing program. I remember when my daughter and I collected our rationing books from the local police station. Bright blue, hastily printed in Gateshead, they looked so old-fashioned it was hard to believe we were in the twenty-first century. From January 24, 2026, the United Kingdom officially had a rationing program for the first time since July 4, 1954. In some ways the rationing system replicated the old system, from the Second World War, and in others it had to be wildly different. I think if you gave every person in the UK a basket of fresh vegetables, fruit, meat, dairy and bread now, they'd starve. Our ration books allow us to buy an amount of food each week, which can include processed food like soups and ready meals but must have a mix of carbs, protein, vegetables and fruits. We all get a small allotment of meat and fish unless you're vegetarian, and everyone gets some eggs and dairy. The vegans went nuts over the lack of opt-out over eggs or dairy but the government made statements about vegan replacements "not being easily available in the UK." There was a massive marketing campaign to make sure the population understood why we needed rationing and how the allowances had been calculated. It was thought, rightly, that transparency would reduce the risk of anger and unrest. To be honest, I think people were just relieved to have a system in place. Panic buying had set in back in December and the shortages were worrying.

And of course, we all have a treat ration, or "Additional Caloric Allowance," to give it its technical name. We get to buy some junk each week. It makes life a bit easier when you have one of those days and you just think, "Somebody pass me the fucking chocolate." People like Donna are outraged and there was a lot of "Millennial snowflakes can't do without sweets even in a time of national crisis!"

I remember an interview the prime minister did just before rationing started. She talked about the "blitz spirit" and how the civil service was thankfully an institutional hoarder, so lots of the information about rationing during and after the Second World War was looked at and used as a starting point. The government of 1946 knew quite a bit about keeping a population alive after all. There was an awful bit of that interview when the interviewer asked the prime minister, "How do you know you have enough food for the population? How could you possibly calculate that?" and her face contorted slightly and she replied, "Well, unfortunately the population keeps reducing. Our birth rate has plummeted and as, without a vaccine, men are still succumbing to the Plague, we have planned on the basis of the population staying stable, which it almost certainly won't."

We would have enough food because people kept dying. It was one of the grimmer public pronouncements of the Plague.

"Okay, let's run through the other updates quickly." Marianne's clear voice quickly commands the room of women and she rattles through the things on her list.

"We've had a request from a number of GPs for an increase in the ration allowance for female electricians and garbage truck operators. Unless anyone objects, we will approve the calorie increases set out in the report." A murmur of approval.

"We've had our quarterly food waste report in. Two major supermarkets have requested permission to sell pre-cut onion, carrot and sweet potato. The argument they've provided is that they are helpful for those with disabilities who can't cut vegetables. Hmm, interesting. Our reasoning for banning them had been food waste."

"Onions spoil too quickly once cut to be feasible," someone says. "There'd be enormous waste."

"Why don't we agree to limited amounts of carrot and potato, see how much waste results and then reassess for other vegetables in the next quarter. Everyone in agreement? Excellent." Marianne looks at her notes and stifles a frown. "Next, Donna, you wanted to discuss celiacs?"

"Yes, I really worry that those who can't eat gluten are restricted in their carbohydrate choices at the moment to potatoes. I want a budget to explore alternatives, maybe think outside the box." I can practically hear Marianne's eye roll from the other end of the room.

"Well," Marianne says crisply, "if you happen to find a paddy field somewhere in England, by all means do let me know. In the meantime, the one percent of the population with a gluten allergy will have to make do. We have bigger fish to fry."

"Next on the agenda is our monthly report on ration book fraud. I'm happy to report that fraud continues to be very low. The past month has seen thirty-two cases of fraud, all of which received the standard punishment of a twenty percent reduction in overall allowance and total removal of the 'treat' allowance for a minimum of six months." Marianne looks up and smiles. "Remarkable what the threat of no sugar or booze can do for people's moral compasses, isn't it?

"And finally, the restaurant initiative. Now, I know we aren't in a position to explore this yet, but I hope to in the near future and it will take some planning."

I can feel my left eyebrow raise and Marianne clocks it. Restaurants? In a time of national crisis when our economy is still barely surviving and we're only ever one bad harvest away from starvation? Really?

"I'll hold my hands up here and admit to being a foodie in the worst possible way. I miss foams and silly edible flowers and I know we can't do this yet, but I want us to plan for a restaurant allowance system. It's quite simple—restaurants that register with the scheme would take bookings between one and two weeks in advance. As part of the booking process, a portion of the ration allowances for the diners would be transferred to the restaurant. If the diners don't turn up for their meal, tough luck; the allowance has already been used."

Silence rings around the room. I can't say I'm massively enamored by it but then, I was never a big fan of going out to overpriced, fancy restaurants where someone would somehow always end up offering me a drink with flowers in it for twenty pounds.

A woman at the end of the table clears her throat and says, softly, "I think it could be very helpful from a psychological perspective." Ah, she must be the shrink.

"Yes!" Marianne seizes on this small encouragement. "It will allow a crucial part of society and culture to continue, create jobs and create a sense of normalcy. Isn't that what we're always talking about? Maintaining normal life as far as possible. No one should go hungry, people should still be able to enjoy food and, I think, enjoy the singular experience of dressing up, going to a nice restaurant and enjoying food far lovelier than anything they could ever cook for themselves. I want to go to a restaurant, recognize a part of my former life and maybe for a few hours feel like nothing has changed."

I try to think of the most diplomatic response that will piss off the fewest people in the room and break the silence. "Why don't you draw up a plan and we can consider it further at the next meeting." Marianne smiles at me gratefully. I have no interest in restaurants, but a desire for normalcy I can sympathize with. Rationing is a glorious thing, it has rendered everyone's hunger equal in the eyes of the law. No person is more or less entitled to food and the feeling of being full, but I miss the fun of food in abundance. I miss buying three bottles of wine for when my friends were coming over on a warm summer night. I miss barbecues with steak, ribs and burgers on a drizzly Saturday afternoon in June because English weather always insists on raining on barbecue days. If restaurants will make some people feel like their lives haven't changed, we should do everything we can to make them happen. Too much has changed that we can't ever fix. We should return to how things used to be wherever we can.

# ELIZABETH

breathe deeply and the scent of the roses in my bouquet fills my mind. *Everything is going to be okay,* as Simon always tells me. George is standing resolute by my side. Dapper in a morning suit, he will walk me down the aisle in place of my dad. I never imagined getting married without my dad by my side, but I feel safe and loved. As every bride hopes, I have never felt happier.

The organ music starts to play and we walk, slowly but surely, down the aisle of this beautiful church where Simon's family has married and been christened for generations. My mom is sitting, crying, in the front row. Commercial flights have started for anyone with a Certificate of Vaccination and it feels like the most extraordinary gift to have her here. Amaya beams at me, glowing in a green dress, as I pass her. George's wonderful daughter Minnie gives me a thumbs-up as I pass, which makes me want to throw my head back and laugh.

And there, at the end, is Simon. This man I reached out to on a whim, in a moment of hopeful abandon, who has become everything to me. He's smiling, shakily, a tear is threatening to make its way down his face. When I got off the plane, years ago, terrified and nervous, I had no idea how bad things would get, the number of people I would lose. And I had no idea how wonderful a life I would eventually build for myself. If only I could go back and tell myself everything would work itself out.

George lifts my veil and holds my hands tightly in his before saying to Simon in his twinkly voice, "You take care of her now."

"I will," Simon promises solemnly. The service is a blur of readings, English hymns and a moment of remembrance for those who are no longer with us. We say our vows and I resist the urge to give Simon's parents a stern look when I have to recite his three middle names. No one needs that many names, but Simon Henry Richard James Maitland has five, and he's perfect so who even cares.

The reception is small but wonderful. Pizza made with ration tokens, English wine and dancing 'til late surrounded by my family, both real and chosen. We dance our first dance to "Lucky" by Jason Mraz and it feels like an immunization against bad fortune. *We know we're lucky!* we're saying to the universe. We feel our good fortune in our bones. For Simon, to be immune, and for me, to be in the rare position of falling in love and having the prospect of having a family with the man I love. Such quotidian dreams, of survival, marriage and parenthood, but now, they are precious and rare.

"I thought you were never going to drink again after your hen do," Amaya teases when I take a breather with a glass of cider.

"Don't remind me! I still can't believe the gifts." I thought bachelorette parties were intense in the States. Well, now I have penis-shaped pasta in my kitchen cupboards and a porn DVD ("It's super ethical porn made by Delilah Day! She owns her own porn company; it reminds people of the sex with their husbands and boyfriends they used to have," Julia had exclaimed). I know that English hen parties are the real deal.

I just hope Simon doesn't use the pasta when his parents come over.

"What are you chatting about?" George says, bowling up to Amaya and me.

"You're drunk." Amaya laughs.

"I am," he says with a grin. "It's a wedding, it's tradition for the not-father of the bride to get a bit tipsy."

"I'm so glad I met both of you," I say, my tongue loosened by a few drinks. "I wish none of it had ever happened but I'm so glad I met you."

"Bad things and good things can coexist," Amaya says with a sad smile. "And we have to find the good where we can."

# ADAPTATION

## ARTICLE IN THE *WASHINGTON POST* ON DECEMBER 8, 2029

---

*This is one of our "Woman Least Likely" series of pieces about the women in the United States who have taken on leadership roles in politics, business and industry, despite being "unlikely candidates." This week's piece, by Maria Ferreira, is about Bryony Kinsella, 31, the founder and CEO of Adapt, a new dating app for women that is now the world's largest by user numbers.*

Bryony Kinsella can't tell me the dating app she used to work for as head of strategic partnerships, although she assures me that it was the world's biggest. I'm not sure how this admission will skirt around the boundaries of the NDA she signed when she left, but Bryony seems confident she's in the clear.

We meet in her huge corner office at her company's midtown headquarters, a space befitting the boss of a multibillion-dollar company. Adapt is the first unicorn of the post-Plague world and is now, by user count, the world's biggest dating app.

"Oh my God, it feels so good to have the numbers we do. When I first started my company, I got so much abuse. Internet access is now back to pre-Plague levels in most developed countries but three years ago we were all still scrabbling around for allotted hours of bandwidth and cell reception was questionable at best, remember? But I knew really early on that I was going to start this. Those infrastructure problems were always going to be solved, it was just a matter of time. The biggest problem of mankind, of all time, was going to need a solution and fast."

My head spins a little at the reference to the biggest problem of man- or womankind. Does she mean finding a vaccine?

"The great question of our time: How to find love when there are literally no men left? The phrases single women always used to hear like 'there's plenty of fish in the sea' and 'as soon as you stop looking for love, it'll find you' do *not* apply anymore. The sea is empty. It became the thing to talk about, when you weren't talking about who else had died: How am I going to meet someone? Even in the apocalypse, human beings have the same needs. We all want to feel loved, to be desired, to feel like we're not alone in this insane, terrifying world."

I have to ask what Bryony's job at the unnamed world's-former-biggest-dating-app involved. Head of strategic partnerships sounds like a phrase from a TV show about Silicon Valley. Bryony laughs in good humor at my ignorance. "Basically, I made us money and raised our profile by pairing our app with other brands—so I was obsessed with numbers. Data was my life. When did men and women use the app most? When were they most likely to say yes or no to a potential match? For the record, in summer people get choosy and December is easy pickings. What percentage of matches became conversations and what percentage of those conversations resulted in an exchange of phone numbers?"

The thing I really want to know is how that data-driven role led to the big "aha!" moment of knowing she needed to set up a female-only dating site with different settings depending on how much romantic experience a woman has had with other women.

"When the Plague started, the weirdest thing happened. You'd assume that when loads of men are starting to die, men would become a valuable commodity, right? The basic rules of economics would suggest that as the supply of men decreased, the demand for them would increase. From the sharp rise in reports of abusive messages we received—messages with unrequested dick pics, insulting demands for sex, etc.—a lot of our male users thought the tide would turn that way. But it was the opposite. Even at the beginning stages of the Plague when maybe 5 to 10 percent of the male population was sick, women did two things. They started dating less, and if they were dating, they dated women." She pauses, and waves her hands in annoyance. Clearly, she has been misquoted before. "Obviously not *all* women. But a significant number. Between March and June 2026, 40 percent of regular female users stopped using the app. In that same time frame, of the women who stayed on the app, 25 percent changed their preferences from 'Woman only seeking men' to 'Woman seeking men and women' or 'Woman only seeking women.' I think it made complete sense—why would you open yourself up to grief and sadness? What's the point in dating someone who will almost definitely be dead by the following Sunday? For the first time, women could genuinely say 'Maybe he died?' about a date that stood them up."

She sits back, with a triumphant expression to which she is entitled. Bryony Kinsella is the woman who has single-handedly understood and then monetized women's emotions about romance and dating throughout the years of the Plague. So, after that realization, she knew there had to be a new app?

She nods vigorously. "The app I used to work for was falling apart as I was trying to figure out a plan for moving forward. It's hard to describe how bizarre it was working in business back in 2026. Lots of men were still technically employed but not working, or not showing up to work because, hello, they were probably going to die. E-mails went unanswered, meetings didn't happen, contracts lapsed. Almost everything ground to a halt. My main priority was using the data we had to ensure that we kept going so that I would still have a job in 'the New World,' whatever that would look like. My line manager at the time—one of the vice presidents of the company—was literally having a daily meltdown. She came into the office two days a week and spent most of that time crying. She was married and she had a son, so I guess she was panicked, but I liked my job. I wanted to have a way to pay my mortgage even after the apocalypse meant we'd be in a barter economy or something. We were all terrified but some of us wanted to get through it by keeping some stability and working through it. Old wounds. Anyway. I took records of as much data as I could and handed in my notice—to my line manager, who wasn't in the office—on August 3, 2026. I took three of the female coders with me and had a prototype of Adapt up and running by October 2, 2026. We went live on November 1, 2026, and we were the biggest dating app in the world by February 15, 2029. I'm still mad that we missed Valentine's Day by one day. One day!"

But why not just work within the old app? Why something new? "Look, if you had asked me what would need to happen for me to own the biggest dating app in the world, the last thing I would have said was 'reduce the male population by 90 percent,' but change allows for new entrants to the market. The other apps had issues. Most of them had primarily male executive leadership teams, coding teams and boards, so as the Plague ravaged the male population it affected their company structures. In that sense I had a head start as—newsflash—I'm a woman and, until two months ago, I employed only women. Secondly, women connected preexisting dating apps with their old lives and the way the world used to be. Swiping for half an hour on a Sunday evening looking for cute boys, having a quick conversation and maybe going for a drink the following Friday, after which you may or may not sleep with him, was no longer an option. That's not how the world works anymore. Unless you own a company deemed to provide a 'necessary economic service' as I do or you're in a category of 'essential professions' like medicine, law, policing or engineering, you get the job you're assigned by the state and that's that. We do jobs now because we have to, not because we want to. We eat the foods that are available, not the foods that we crave. We have children if that privilege is afforded to us by a lottery, not because we met a nice guy, fell in love and 'it's the right time.'

"Life now has a lot of requirements and not a lot of joy. So, a dating app that says 'We get it: it sucks that your life has changed beyond recognition, but guess what? You can still have love and sex and something that makes you feel less alone' is a welcome piece of normalcy."

Does she want to ever introduce men to the platform?

"Ha, no! They don't need any help finding women. No, in all seriousness, it's partly that. If a man wants to be in a relationship with a woman, the statistics are in his favor, put it that way. But it's more because of hope. Do you know what's worse than your life's plans falling apart in the space of a few weeks as the world collapses? Hoping that somehow, despite the odds, your plans of a husband and two kids and a white picket fence will still come true. Women go on Adapt to find love in a new way. I don't want them to be faced with the question, when they first sign up, 'Are you interested in men . . . still? Do you hold out hope . . . still?' Because the numbers don't add up. There are nine women for every man."

Does Bryony hope to meet a man, fall in love? She sighs. I guess she must get this question a lot. In return for my commonly asked question, I receive a rehearsed response. "I'm single and I don't anticipate that changing. Hopefully I'll be able to have a child one day but I try not to build it up as an important goal because there's absolutely nothing I can do to make it happen. Most things in the world don't operate on a 'return on investment' basis anymore. Before the Plague, when I was interviewed about my job I always used to say that it was a numbers game; if you spend enough hours on the app, swipe a sufficient amount, message your matches and arrange dates, the chances are that you'll meet someone and, perhaps if you're lucky, fall in love." She smiles ruefully. "It was a simpler time. I can't put in the effort to meet a man or have a child. The odds are pretty stacked against me now. But I can put effort into building my company, employing more people in jobs that are interesting, and help women more flexible than me find love. That will do for now."

As I'm being walked out, thanking Bryony for her time, I ask the big question everyone keeps asking. "Do you think lots of the women in relationships with other women have had a shift in sexuality, or was their sexuality always there, the way it is?"

"You know, we don't pretend that women are suddenly all gay now. There's no doubt that female sexuality is more fluid than male sexuality is, although that's not saying much. But the fact is that humans don't like to be alone and there aren't a lot of men now, so we do what we can to still feel like the people we used to be."

It's a simple, straightforward answer from a complex, successful woman who knows exactly what she, and other women, want. But the question will inevitably be asked for many years to come.

———————

# DAWN

The second I turn my phone off airplane mode, it starts buzzing with an incoming call. Zara, of course. My boss is many things and even though she's now the head of the British Intelligence Services she's still a micromanager.

"Is that you back in London?"

How else would I be answering the call? "Yep," I reply, as politely as I can imagine after an eight-and-a-half-hour flight following a two-day business trip spent entirely in windowless rooms talking to American politicians and CIA employees.

"A memo from the Child Lottery people in the States has been leaked. Maria Ferreira's written an article about it. Press are going nuts. Gillian's called an emergency meeting to discuss the child allocation plans. Her press team are worried about the optics; home secretary can't be tarred with a bad brush."

"What's the general thrust of the memo?"

"Lying to the public about it being a lottery is the most damning thing. There's also some very unpleasant stuff about single parents." Zara sighs and I try to remind myself that, as she's a rung above me, however many crises I deal with in a day, she deals with even more I'm never aware of. Thank the Lord. "To be honest, it's not a million miles away from our plans but the optics are dire. Get over here as soon as you can. We'll start the meetings as soon as Gillian arrives."

My lingering excitement from being on commercial flights ebbs away. Even going through security was a novelty. No liquids? No problem. A half-hour delay? How very 2019 of you. I was intending to have a relaxing day of sleeping and spending time with my daughter but no, no. The Americans had different ideas.

I already have a link to the Maria Ferreira article sitting in my inbox, in an e-mail from Gillian titled: SERIOUS ISSUE??? NEED MEETING URGENTLY!!!! You'd think the home secretary would maybe only need to use one punctuation mark at a time.

### "An American Outrage" by Maria Ferreira

It was revealed today in a leaked memorandum that the "Child Lottery" in the United States is not the random allocation we have been led to understand it is. The opportunity to have a child through donor sperm is actually determined by an algorithm taking into account factors including relationship status, socioeconomic status and resources in the local area, among others. In other words, the American people are being lied to. We are being led to believe that our opportunity to have a child—that most primal and important of decisions, that many women desire—is left to chance when it is actually determined by a secret algorithm administered by a governmental department.

I can only get through the first paragraph. Oh God. Maria Ferreira. I'm still smarting from the hatchet job she did on us, even if to the rest of the world she's the woman "Holding Power to Account" and the "World's Most Popular Journalist." At least she's as excoriating of her own country as she is of mine.

There's also an extract of the memo included in the e-mail.

*National Demographic Recovery and Control Program*
*Memorandum: From Nadine Johnson*
*To: Vanessa Edney*
*Subject: Public affairs; amendment to selection criteria; single-parent analysis*

*This memorandum is private and confidential.*

*Public affairs*
*There have been a number of discussions held internally regarding public communications of the Child Lottery system. We remain committed to using the term "Child Lottery" as it has positive connotations, implies the results are determined by chance and suggests low chances of success. This is important for expectation management. Further to our discussion, your concerns regarding "misleading" the public are noted. However, we are uncomfortable with the idea of providing more information. Statistically, we are still at a stage where demand for child allocations far outstrips supply. It is preferable for the public to believe they have a chance, rather than explain the details of the algorithm.*

*Amendment to selection criteria*
*Further to assessment of Q1 and Q2 data, decision has been made to reduce threshold of "ideal socioeconomic bracket" to $32,000 household income. Successful implementation of nationalized healthcare system across remaining states has reduced concern of healthcare provision for children.*

*Single-parent analysis*
*We are carrying out a significant study (quantitative and qualitative data) of single-parent families with two close family members living within*

*ten-mile radius with over ten hours childcare per week. Hypothesis that*
*women in this category should be upgraded to equivalence with those in*
*long-term (three-plus year) relationships.*

Suffice to say she's lacking some tact. Nadine, author of the memo in question, is director of the American Demographic Recovery and Control Program. Some quick googling reveals that she used to work at the NSA. That won't help either; it'll feed into a narrative that it's all a government conspiracy. Evil overlords doing evil things when, in reality, I suspect it's a misguided attempt at doing the right thing.

After an all too quick nap in the car, I make my way into the office. Zara meets me in the corridor before I go in.

"Thank God you're here," she hisses. "Gillian's being a nightmare." I actually quite like Gillian, so I stay silent. Although, I don't like her enough to defend her to Zara, who has no doubt been dealing with her many concerns for the last two hours while I made my way here from Heathrow.

"She's panicking that our plans for the Child Allocation Service will be interpreted in the same way as the Americans' has and she'll be made to look like the bad guy."

"Understood. We'll sort something out." Zara visibly relaxes and I, not for the first time, wonder why she's my boss when she's prone to panicking like a flustered chicken.

"Dawn!" Gillian sounds pleased to see me, at least. After the many hours we spent sorting out the Working Draft together, she's come to respect me. Her fears pour out of her. Our proposed system is similar to the American one, people seem horrified by the use of socioeconomic factors to determine who has a child, we weren't planning on setting out the criteria, does that mean we're keeping secrets, what if it leaks, what if it's all a disaster? It reminds me of when my daughter started at a new school when she was eleven and every day she would come home with multiplied anxieties, spilling out over the dinner table, ranging from not being good enough at math to seven more years of school feeling like a very, very long time.

"Everything is going to be okay," I say. "The plans have been well thought through. We've been working on them for months. You didn't throw them together in a few hours. Let's start with the first concern." If in doubt, make a list. My mum taught me that and it's never done me wrong. "The biggest concern is public perception and the simple answer is that we must announce the Child Allocation Service sooner rather than later, and be honest about the criteria through which women will be chosen."

My announcement wasn't intended to be controversial and yet I'm met with silence. Zara is frowning.

"That wasn't the plan," Gillian says hesitantly.

"Circumstances have changed and we need to adapt to them. The public's views have shifted, thanks to the American leak. At the very least, you can't be accused of deceit. People might disagree with the plans but they can't deny you're being open about them."

Gillian nods; she's convinced. "Next, the criteria for choice. We were already going to allow councils to have some flexibility in their application of the criteria and that should be emphasized."

"Keeping it local makes it sound less 'Big scary government controlling everything,'" Zara says.

"But the response has been so vicious," Gillian says. "The use of the criteria seems to be an inherent problem. Shouldn't we make it random?"

"No," I say simply. "That would be irresponsible. Age, health, proven ability to look after a child. Those are not the criteria of a mad dictator ruining lives. Those are sensible pieces of information that have to be used to ensure the highest chance of success of demographic recovery."

"It just doesn't seem fair." Gillian sighs and I'm reminded, yet again, of why she is a politician and I'm not.

"None of this is fair," I reply in as patient a tone as I can muster. "There are many more women who wish to have children than men and donated sperm. It will never be fair. The goal is not to be fair. The goal is population recovery with minimal civil unrest. The US government and the UK government have almost complete control over who within those countries have children. Almost no baby is an accident now. We all have to get used to that idea."

"But the prioritization of people in long-term relationships? Surely that's unfair."

"As the only person in this room who has actually raised a child alone, I'm fairly well placed to say that raising a child as a single parent is very difficult. We can remove the prioritization of women in relationships if it makes you feel better, but don't delude yourself about what having a child alone, in this world, will take."

Zara and Gillian look at me in stunned silence and I suppress the urge to sigh. I rarely bring up my personal life and this is why. Once you develop a reputation as someone who is professional, competent and *private,* any information about your personal life is treated with the same care and awe as a nervous breakdown.

"If only for the public perception, I think we should take out the required prioritization of people in long-term relationships. We can allow councils to apply relationship criteria as they see fit," Gillian says.

We spend the next few hours changing the plans and running the public statement through the various communications people who need to approve it. Finally, *finally,* it's ready to go to the prime minister for her approval.

Gillian goes on her merry way and Zara and I sit in the meeting room, exhausted.

"Did you ever think," she says, "when you decided to do this job, that you and I would have a meeting about which women are allowed donor sperm?"

I shake my head. "Weirdly enough, no. It never crossed my mind."

# CATHERINE

**London, United Kingdom (England and Wales)**
**Day 1,500**

A few hours before I'm due to meet Libby and her brother, Peter, for "pre-Christmas" drinks, Nadine Johnson's memo and the surrounding furor hits the internet with a velocity that leaves much of the world reeling. It's the impossible question the world needs to answer: How will we repopulate? Who gets to have a baby?

I meet Libby and Peter in a bar in the city. I rarely venture here to this land of glass skyscrapers and well-dressed women with smart handbags, heads bowed over their phones. Each time I'm here, though, I'm struck by the vast difference from before. Before it was mainly men with some women. Now the few men stand out, their suits glaring against the dresses and skirts.

Sometimes I wonder how Libby and I are friends. She is hugely, indubitably cooler than me. There's no way around it. Today she's wearing a pink jumpsuit that would make me look like a deranged plumber. I turned up at Oxford with a bag full of crocheted cushions and bunting for my room, wearing a cardigan, and she arrived wearing a Rolling Stones T-shirt and with a vinyl record player in tow. Despite my shortcomings, she's a steady, devoted friend and I feel the relief of her presence.

"God it's good to see you," I mutter into her hair as I hug her.

"A lot easier to arrange to meet up now that we're in the same country, huh?"

"Just a bit."

Libby beams at me, that broad smile that makes me feel like the world is about 20 percent less scary than it was a moment before.

"Have you seen the article?" she asks as she pours me a glass of cider from the bottle on the table.

"Absolutely mad, isn't it?" I reply.

"Are you going to write a paper on it?" Libby asks, knowing that before the Plague I found the search for research topics painful. "Surely how we're all having children is pretty high up on the lists of things for anthropologists to study at the moment."

I nod. "For once there's too much for me to be studying. I don't have time to do a paper on this specifically, although I'm teaching a new course, 'The Ethics of Reproductive Choice in a Post-Plague World,' in the new year, so I'll have to write something up on it."

"That sounds fascinating," Peter says, his voice practically dripping with longing. "Being an actuary has never seemed like such a bad call."

"You live in a four-bedroom house in Zone 1, you can walk to work and you have a garden," Libby says with an eye roll. "Being an actuary pays."

"What else are you going to include in the course?" Peter asks, and I remember that part of the reason I like him so much is that he's one of the four people I've ever met outside of academic circles who's seemed genuinely interested in my work.

"In the first lecture I'm covering New Zealand and the ethics of their whole 'taking children and putting them in isolation' thing. Some of the parents have posted videos online of the children being released once they'd been vaccinated and you'd have to be heartless not to cry at that."

"Always good to pluck the heartstrings in the first lecture." Libby smiles knowingly. "Then you can be a cool lecturer."

"One lives in hope. Then in the second lecture we'll dig into the meat of Norway as a case study. They've set up the Norwegian Demographic Institute, which researches policies around maintaining population numbers and increasing the speed of a return to equal numbers of men and women."

"How?" Libby asks with a raised eyebrow. "Encouraging men not to be fuckboys?"

Peter laughs and I try to figure out the best way to answer "Yes" without just saying "Yes." And wonder if I can include the word "fuckboys" in my lecture notes without getting fired. Somehow, I suspect not.

"They have three public aims. Make sure as many babies are born as possible without affecting the economy, manage fertility treatment so in IVF male embryos are selected, which led to an additional four thousand baby boys last year and, well."

"Is this the fuckboy bit?"

I reel off the spiel from the Institute's website. "'Ensure in the longer term, over the next ten to twenty years, young Norwegians form stable partnerships in which they have children.'"

Libby hoots with laughter. "Oh my God, it literally is." She pauses. "I could do with that here, to be honest. There's an epidemic of fuckboys in London."

"You've used that word so many times, it's stopped having any meaning," Peter says kindly, topping up her glass.

"I read an article in a Norwegian newspaper that said that children have personal development classes at school to encourage them to 'prioritize romantic commitment and parenthood.' They've been showing them old Disney movies. Some of the parents are outraged."

"I'm not surprised," Libby replies hotly. Even though I understand the logic behind the classes, I can't muster the will to disagree with her. The idea of Theodore having been sat down by a teacher and taught how he should think about his future and relationships makes me feel a bit nauseous.

"How are they encouraging adults to have children?" Peter asks.

"Oh, the usual. Eighteen months of maternity leave on full pay, eighty percent funded by government. Free full-time childcare after that. And financial bonuses that amount to about ten grand."

"Is that just for straight couples?"

The intensity in Peter's gaze reminds me that Peter is in a uniquely difficult position compared to Libby and me. His husband died in January 2026, when they had been planning to fly to the US to give their sperm for a surrogate they had found.

"No, it applies to everyone. Straight and gay couples, and women who have a baby alone."

Peter almost groans in envy. "Although, I'd need a husband first," he says, with a trace of flinty bitterness in his voice that I recognize well from my own tone. "Being a micro-minority is no fun, I can tell you. Everything I used to do to meet men back when I was single is impossible. Gay clubs? Not enough of us. Apps? I swipe fourteen times and then I'm out of men. I'm seriously considering extending my radius to include Birmingham."

Libby puts a protective hand on his arm.

"I've been thinking about applying to have a baby," I say quietly.

"Do you think it'll make it better?" Peter asks, and from someone else it might sound like a challenge but from his mouth it's more like a plea. *Do you think a baby will make the pain, finally, lessen?*

"I really, really hope so," I say. "Even thinking about it gives the future focus. It makes me hopeful."

"You have to try," Peter says urgently. "If I could get pregnant . . . what I wouldn't give. You can try, you have to. All I can do is donate sperm." He looks down at his drink, pain radiating off him in waves. "No one wants to be a surrogate for a single man. Not now. I can't say I blame them. It's one thing to carry a baby for someone else when life is normal but when sperm is like gold dust." He shakes his head. "I'm too worried to agree to have a baby with someone I don't know well. 'Co-parenting.' What if they leave and never actually wanted me to be involved?" He pauses and looks at me carefully. I know what he's thinking—could we do this together? One man, one woman, making a baby and co-parenting as friends? He won't ask because he's too polite, and I can't offer. I only want a baby on my own. I can't bear to see a man who isn't Anthony parent my child. I can't.

I think about the pictures of women in the Norwegian article. Women who were like me with circumstances so similar—widowed, having lost children—that it felt like I could slip out of my skin, enter the photo and their pregnancies, babies, would be mine. The desire for another baby, which has been humming under my skin on and off ever since Theodore turned one and with ferocity since the Plague hurtled into my life, has gained yet more intensity. If they can do it, why can't I? It's so much easier to ignore my desires when I can't see them coming true. The Norwegian pregnant women are my own version of a Disney ending: no prince, no happy ending, but a recovery. A return to motherhood. A return to part of my old life.

As Libby talks to Peter about their mum's latest drama, trying to distract him from everything, I think about Phoebe. She was my closest confidant through the tribulations of our conception battles. I know that she's the person I need to see most but I don't know if I can do it. I miss her desperately. I miss my friend, but the bitterness at all she has is still just below the surface of my skin. On a near-daily basis I tell myself I should be better than this bitterness. I should be better than jealousy. I should just *be better*. For a moment, I'm overwhelmed by how tiring the emotional back-and-forth is and by the guilt I feel. I decide to reach out and ask her to meet me before I can talk myself out of it.

Hi,

I'm sorry it's taken me so long to do this. Do you want to meet for a chat? I thought we could go for a walk together in Brockwell Park. Let me know if you'd like that. Cat x

And then, in a rush because I worry my message is too cold:

I miss you x

The messages burn in my pocket but after only two minutes, there it is. A reply.

I'd love to. How about Saturday at 11? x

I feel calmer and more centered, knowing I've taken the first step toward narrowing this fissure between Phoebe and me. Libby and I head toward the Barbican, where we're seeing a "multimedia art installation" with pictures by Frederica Valli, the famous war photographer.

We make our way into the gallery and I'm looking in my bag for chewing gum when I hear Libby.

"Oh my God," she says, her face caving in on itself in pain.

"What? What's wrong—"

There's no need for her to answer. I realize now why the room, full of people, is solemnly silent. The first picture is a huge black-and-white photo from the Oxenholme riots. A woman, giving birth on the tarmac of the train platform, surrounded by people and yet looking so alone. Where is her husband? I hope he was trying to find her help. Her expression is one of pure anguish and primal fear. It says both, "Somebody help me," and "Please, please stay away."

I had heard about the riots, I watched them on the TV, but this photo conveys more than any grainy helicopter footage ever could. The roiling mass of people in the background yet no one is stepping forward to help. This woman reduced, in the twenty-first century, to giving birth on a cold, dirty floor out of sheer desperation to escape the inescapable.

I'm desperate to know what came of her but there's a queue to read the card by the photo. Eventually, endless minutes later, we reach it. *Woman in pain, by Frederica Valli. January 7, 2026.* That's it. Nothing else. No mention of whether the baby was a boy or a girl, or if her husband survived, or if the mother was okay in the end.

We move along the corridors, awestruck by the photos. There has never been a shortage of images of the Plague and the pain it wrought but I hadn't realized until now the absence of these kinds of images. Quiet, taken not for a news program but with care, in the moment. Art, in other words.

The next picture needs no explanation of the identity of the subject. Marcus Wilkes, author of *Good-bye darling: A Memoir of Fear and Acceptance.* Marcus was a popular journalist who recounted his life in journals from the day he first heard about the Plague in November 2025 to the day before he died, delirious and able to only write the words "Good-bye darling" to his wife of thirty-four years. It only spans six months but it's a beautiful book. This is Marcus in three stages, all lined up. The first with his wife in November 2025, fearful but pasting on familiar smiles. They are the smiles of careful optimism; two people who can't hope too much to be spared because it will be too painful when the disaster comes to pass. The second is in March 2026 after the death of their son. Their faces are old, weary, desperate. The third is in April 2026. Marcus is clearly dying. The picture is in black and white but a thick layer of sweat is visible on his forehead, his face a mask of pain. But it is not this illness that pierces me and makes me weep. It is the sight of his hand tightly held by his wife, who is looking at him with hunger. I recognize that look. It is the look that says, "Please don't leave. Please don't leave me all alone. I can't bear it, so I really need you to try and stay." It is unavoidable, the tears that tip themselves freely down my cheeks as I think back to the awful night when my kind, strong, calm husband had to leave me. To walk upstairs in our happy, love-filled house knowing we would never see each other again unless, by some miracle, he recovered. A tiny hope so small we never articulated it.

I wish I could have held his hand. If I could have anything in the world in this moment, go back to any point in my life, I would go back and hold his hand at the end. I would do what Marcus's wife did, and hold his hand so he knew he wasn't alone. Anthony died all alone, with no one to comfort him, hold him, reassure him, tell him that at the very least he was loved. He died alone and I can never go back to that moment.

I feel Libby's hand slip into mine and with her other hand she cups my head and pulls it onto her shoulder where, in the middle of an art gallery full of women, some of whom are crying as openly as I am, I fall apart at the seams.

We leave a few minutes later, unable to cope with the images of grief so close to us. It is unbearable, like looking into the sun. We walk to the station, me still crying silently, Libby looking at me with the desperate need to make it better, but she can't. I wave away her offer to take me home and insist I am fine. I'm alone now and I have to get used to it. I get onto my train and she follows me. She sits on the other side of the carriage, takes a book out of her bag and reads it for the entire thirty-minute journey. We get off the train at Crystal Palace and she walks the fifteen minutes back to my house, always a few steps behind me. I walk down the path to my house, put the key into the cheerful, red door of my home and turn around. Libby is standing, smiling at me. "You're not alone. I love you," she says, and turns around to make the hour-and-a-half journey back to her own home.

Perhaps it is the images of Marcus and his wife at the gallery, or Libby's kindness or the heavy silence of my house, but I lie down on the sofa in the living room and keep weeping as though I hadn't ever stopped. It's a faucet of grief that has released itself and as I listen to the thoughts racing I realize that I have to forgive myself. I did the best I could. I couldn't hold his hand; I was protecting Theodore. I couldn't tell him I loved him as he took his last breath; I was protecting Theodore. Anthony wanted me to keep Theodore safe with every fiber of his being. He didn't blame me for leaving him alone at his time of greatest need, but I have blamed myself. I've blamed myself for the deaths of my husband and son, for my failure to protect them, and my failure to save them. That belief—that I had wronged my family and brought doom upon myself—is preventing me from acting upon the need I desperately feel to have another baby. I want another baby. I want to be a mother again, I want to have a child and to have a family. I want to gain someone into my life rather than merely cope with the aftershocks of loss. Surviving and living a life I want are very different things.

I go to the tab I have saved on my computer. My local authority has opened, as of today, an application process for fertility treatment using donor sperm for women who no longer have any living children. It's time to move forward. I complete the application form, which is surprisingly simple. I confirm I have had a child before and list my health history. I expect it to ask me to list any miscarriages, fertility drugs taken and any other details but it doesn't. Perhaps they will take this straight from my medical records.

I send the form and text a photo of the sent e-mail to Libby.

**Thank you. I love you too.**

Now, I need to try desperately to forget about it. I don't know the odds of being accepted and even if I managed to get treatment, I have struggled to conceive in the past. But it is a chance, and that's more than I've had in years. For the first time since they were put up there, years ago, in another lifetime, I go upstairs to the loft, where all of Theodore's baby clothes, crib, pram and baby toys are stored. I haven't touched them. I thought it was because it would be too painful, but now I think it's that I always hoped. I allowed myself to have moments of hope but the pain of acting on it was too great. And so the relics of my former life sit here, untouched and precious. I so desperately want for them to become part of my future.

# AMANDA

Being in charge is not overrated. I fired someone today, which was completely deserved. I finally tracked down the man who ignored me in November 2025. Or to be more specific, the man who told Leah, my university friend who worked under him, that I was—let me quote the e-mail—"a stark raving lunatic who is trying to waste the limited resources and time of this institution. Not to mention my patience." His name is Raymond McNab and I had the immense pleasure of finally wrangling access to the e-mails today, which gave me the proof I needed. It should never have taken me so long to access the bloody e-mails but he had deleted everything before he ran up north with his wife, abandoning his position here to try and save himself.

Turns out he was immune so there was no need. He slunk back in 2027, once he was certain he was safe and had had a nice break in his summerhouse up at Loch Lomond. I've been trying to get rid of him ever since. Leah told me on my first day here that he was the roadblock, but thanks to his deletion of e-mails and Leah's ruthless "management" of her inbox "because a full inbox makes me nervous," I was stuck between paranoia and suspicion.

Enter an excellent forensic IT recovery specialist and here we are.

"Raymond, thanks for coming in to meet me," I say, all sweetness and light.

"How can I help you?" He has nervous sweat on his upper lip but he's trying to stay calm. Does he know that I know? I decide to go for it.

"It was you who made the decision to ignore my warning to Leah, to HPS." I practically hiss the words. Years of pent-up fury and rage quickly dissolve the calm I had hoped to maintain.

"I have no idea what idea you're talking about."

I quote the e-mail. "'A stark raving lunatic who is trying to waste the limited resources and time of this institution. Not to mention my patience.'" His face becomes satisfyingly pale. "God forbid your *patience* was tested, Raymond."

He's blushing furiously, moving around in his chair. "I could never have known."

"You could have investigated. You could have tried. You didn't do anything, you dismissed me because of what, because I was a woman?"

He scoffs and my loathing for him intensifies. "Everything's sexism with you ladies."

"You're fired, Raymond."

"You can't do that." Ah, the confidence of the mediocre white man.

"I can and I have. Your employment was terminated this morning. You'll need to go to HR on your way out to collect some papers. You won't receive a reference unless you want the reference to say, 'This man was partially at fault for the Plague and the near extinction of the human race.'" Even as I say it, I know I'm being unfair but it feels so good to blame someone.

Raymond's mouth is flapping open, giving me an unpleasantly good view of his molars. "That's an outrageous thing to say."

"We'll have to agree to disagree on that. Good-bye, Raymond. I look forward to never seeing you again."

He slams the door on his way out in a final display of petty aggression. I had imagined leaving my office triumphantly but as silence settles I remember that I'm the boss. Four days a week I sit in this office and everyone outside the door is careful around me. I'm so thankful I insisted on keeping up two days a week in A and E. It keeps me sane.

I wonder if the Board of Health Protection Scotland considered the possibility I would use my time in the job to be vindictive. I suspect not. I know they didn't really want to hire me, but the health minister told them my successes were making Scotland look bad. Every time I discovered something—the Plague, Patient Zero's history, worked with Sadie and Kenneth to identify the origin of the virus—I showed how incompetent the Scottish establishment was being. They decided the best thing to do was to bring me inside it, hence the bloody irony of me—HPS's most vociferous critic—now being its director. My personal assistant, Millie, took notes in the meeting and told me everything when I asked her to fill me in on what she knew about office gossip. I didn't intend for her to reveal the details of confidential meetings, but here we are.

I thought firing Raymond would make me feel better but it hasn't. I feel awful. I thought I'd feel vindicated, alive, ready to move on. I thought I'd feel more comfortable knowing that that awful, dismissive, incompetent man couldn't repeat his mistakes in this organization. It seems like such an easy solution and then, once it's done, you realize how empty an action it actually is. Maybe, I have found out too late, that when you have someone to blame everything feels easier. But what happens when you've held them responsible and nothing's really changed? What then?

# CATHERINE

London, United Kingdom (England and Wales)
Day 1,568

It's one of the great blind spots of the medical establishment that the waiting rooms for fertility clinics are so often shared with maternity outpatient clinics. Who thought it would be a good idea to put the heavily pregnant women, with their swollen lips and ankles and tired, happy, anxious faces among the fragile, infertile, hopeful masses?

Before the Plague it was ill-judged. After the Plague, it makes me feel murderous. The sight of all these couples makes me want to bark, "Stop looking so happy."

But that would be rude and quite possibly get me chucked off the waiting list and I don't need to deal with any additional stress as I'm meeting Phoebe after this. So, no wailing in the waiting room. There's a delay, of course. I remember this well from my months of treatment when Anthony and I attempted to have a second child—fertility drug after fertility drug with lists of side effects longer than I could bear to read. The clinics were always running late; they told me the appointment and testing would take an hour but I've scheduled two and a half in my diary. I forgot to bring a book this time, a rookie error. I have to ration the amount of daydreaming I allow myself. It's precious but dangerous. From the moment I received the letter three weeks ago informing me that, subject to passing a medical assessment and inter-view with a consultant, I have a place on the program, my imagination has been in overdrive. I can almost reach out and feel the joy of a positive pregnancy test, of shopping for a new onesie to bring the baby home from the hospital in, of a baby.

The best way to bring myself down to earth from these dreams is to think about the practicalities. How will I do everything I did before, alone? Looking after a newborn, working full-time, raising a child, being the only breadwinner, being the only parent. It sends a cold dread into the pit of my stomach. I think, with longing, of the Dutch Matron system that is working so well in the Netherlands. There was a documentary about it on the BBC. They interviewed the Dutch prime minister. Single women with children, if they wanted, were placed in zones, grouping the women together to create formal sup-port networks. Each ward is made up of between four and six families. The women take turns staying home to take care of the children; a few months of the year at home, the rest of the year working full-time.

The reporter had asked, "But what if the women don't want to go to work?" The prime minister had smiled ruefully and said, "What we want and what we can do don't always match up." There aren't enough humans in the world anymore. It sounds amazing in theory, although the thought of not doing my job for months at a time doesn't appeal. Maybe I could see if there are any women in Crystal Palace who work different times from me who could share childcare, it could work if I really like her and—

"Catherine Lawrence?"

The nurse's voice jolts me out of my planning. She shows me into a room where I'm poked (blood test), prodded (ultrasound of my ova-ries), weighed and measured until I feel more like a specimen than a person. I peer at the screen as she does the ultrasound praying there aren't any spots of endometriosis or cysts rudely squatting on my ovaries that would render me ineligible.

I've only just gotten my jeans back on when I'm being whisked into the office of Dr. Carlton, a young-ish, handsome-ish, tall-ish, brown-haired man whose face I know I will forget the moment I leave the room.

"Thank you for coming in, Mrs. Lawrence," he says, flicking through what I imagine is my file on his computer.

"Thank you for having me," I reply awkwardly, sounding like I'm at a tea party, not a medical appointment. "Also, please call me Catherine."

"Catherine, I can see here that you had one child, Theodore, in 2022. I'm sorry to hear about—"

"Yes, thank you," I say, hurrying this painful part along.

"Then you tried for another child but had unsuccessful treatment here. Two rounds of Clomid?"

"Yes, that's right." Oh God, this is when they're going to tell me I'm excluded because of my stupid broken ovaries and stupid broken womb that won't just grab on to a fucking fetus when it's offered one.

"Your husband made an IVF consultation appointment for you in October 2025 but, oh yes. That appointment was canceled. Can you tell me why?"

I didn't know Anthony had made an appointment. He never told me, oh God, he must have canceled it after I told him I wanted to try naturally for a little while longer. Dr. Carlton is looking at me expectantly. I remember what Anthony told me about IVF policies. *As soon as you fall pregnant naturally, they define you as being fertile even if you have a miscarriage, and you go back to the beginning of the list.* He has given me a gift. My lovely Anthony has somehow given me this gift from the past, an opportunity to rewrite my history of infertility.

"I fell pregnant," I say quietly, before clearing my throat. I feel as if I'm committing a crime.

"You miscarried?" Dr. Carlton says in a medical "Oh, I am sorry" tone. I nod, not trusting my voice not to give me away.

"It's quite common," he goes on. "I had a number of patients who miscarried as the Plague caused, well . . . Grief can be very tough on physical health." He smiles at me in what I'm sure he hopes is a reassuring way but I'm fixated on trying to see any suspicion in his expression. Don't see through me. Believe me. "Well, your test results are all good, from what I can see. We'll confirm that there are no issues with your blood tests in the next few days but you've always had normal hormone levels so I'd be surprised if there are any problems. Pending confirmation of the blood tests, you should be accepted."

I burst into tears, which is clearly such a common occurrence that Dr. Carlton doesn't bat an eyelid. He simply passes me a box of tissues, murmurs something incomprehensible and finishes writing up my notes.

"We'll be in touch in the next few days and, if everything is confirmed, you'll be eligible for three rounds of IUI. It's a wait of several months, I'm afraid, but we're working our way down the list."

I thank him and try to pull myself together. I remember how much I loathed seeing crying women leaving the consulting rooms when I was in waiting rooms, during those awful months trying to conceive. It felt as though the sadness and bad fortune was contagious. *Get away from me,* I would think uncharitably. *Don't infect me with the curse of infertility.*

I don't know if I'm going to have another baby but for the first time in so long, I am making steps toward a new life. A different life, and yet in some ways the same as the life I lost. It feels fitting that in this mix of uncertainty, hope, nostalgia and fear, I'll be meeting Phoebe for the first time in years. When I think back to the last time I saw her in person—just a few days after Halloween, around the time the Plague started—it feels so distant, I was almost a different person. I was a mother, a wife, a busy academic. Now I'm a widow, a childless mother and desperately trying to chronicle how the world has changed.

I walk through Brockwell Park, heading toward the bench we've agreed on as our meeting place, not far from the café, and overlooking a welcome expanse of green. Phoebe is already there. My first thought is that she looks older. Of course she looks older; it's been over four years since I last saw her. We are older. Her hair is the same though. Light brown lightened by the same highlights she's had since university. She's wearing a dark green dress, her favorite color. I realize with a jolt that she's wearing more makeup than I usually see her in and that it'll be because she's nervous. Gone are the days of cackling into wineglasses as one of our husbands asks us, smilingly, to keep it down, and discarding bras as soon as we get to the other's house and talking so much at a restaurant that we blow the candle out by accident.

"Hello," she says, nervous and standing up.

"Hi," I reply, taking the lead and drawing her into a hug. I'm so starved of touch that it feels almost godly to hug someone now. She holds me tightly. She still smells of the same scent she's always worn: Cinema, by YSL. Its familiarity brings me to tears.

"Oh, Cat," she says. "I've missed you so much."

"I've missed you too," I reply, choking back sobs. "I'm so sorry."

"Don't," Phoebe says. "It's all, it's all just. God, it's just been so shit. We're all doing our best."

This is a very Phoebe thing to say. To try to excise my guilt and remind me that we're all doing our best is so wonderfully her.

"Tell me about everything," Phoebe says and I tell her as much as I can. I can't go into the painful details about the awful days of Anthony's and Theodore's deaths. Talking about it still feels like being flayed, and Phoebe loved them too. I can't bear to see her sadness about them on top of my own. But I tell her about the fertility clinic and the project I'm working on, recording the stories of the Plague. I tell her about the routines of my new life.

I ask the question in return and, as her face flushes with something like embarrassment, I realize for the first time how difficult this is going to be. Phoebe's perfume still provides primal comfort and I know every freckle and plane of her face. I know every boy who broke her heart before Rory and how she feels about mothering and friendship and life. But she has a family and I don't.

"Rory and the girls are doing well," she says quickly. "Rory's job thankfully has continued without too much disruption. Even after a pandemic, London still needs accountants. I miss my dad a lot even though he died before all of this started. It's been, yep." She pauses and my cheeks burn. I'm not the only person who's experienced loss.

"Evie and Ida miss you, so much," she says.

I miss them too, although I haven't allowed myself to think about them properly for a long time. Phoebe's gorgeous little girls. I was the first person outside of their immediate family to see both girls, in the hospital when Phoebe was still gray with blood loss but dazed with joy. Evie's my goddaughter. Until all of this, I was a devoted godmother, taking her out to the park or down to the river on her own so we could spend time together and give Phoebe a break. I religiously provided birthday and Christmas presents. I think she probably just hopes they miss me, but it feels nice to be missed. To be wanted.

"Do you want to come to the house? Briefly, maybe? To see them?" The hope in Phoebe's voice is so strong it overrides the voice in the back of my head that says, "This is too much, too soon." I want to see Evie and Ida. I want to be the kind of woman who can do this normal thing of spending time with my friend's family, a family to whom I used to be so close that they felt adjacent to my own.

We talk about everything on the walk over to Phoebe's house in

Battersea. Everything from the films we've been watching to the annoying neighbors who blast loud music every day at 7 a.m., ruining Phoebe's mornings. We talk about the birthday present she needs to buy for her notoriously awful sister-in-law and the restaurants we're excited to go back to once they open.

We arrive at her house and I desperately want to go home but I also want to see the girls. Post-Plague life is a lesson in contradictions. Phoebe lets us in the house and the cries of, "Mum, Mum, Mum" quickly hush while Evie and Ida hang back, behind Phoebe, eyeing me warily.

"Hello," I say, horrified by how nervous they seem around me. I shouldn't be surprised. Evie was only a toddler when I last saw her and Ida was ten months. They don't know me.

"You might not remember me, I'm Catherine. I'm friends with your mum." I stick with the present tense. Any explanation of our complex history is best left unsaid. Phoebe magically whisks us all through to her huge kitchen, where Rory is sitting at the dining table on his laptop.

"Oh," he says, shocked when he sees me. "Lovely to see you, Catherine." He recovers quickly and his face resumes its usual placid expression. Let's just say that no one has ever been surprised when Rory says he's an accountant.

I sit down with Rory and the girls at the table. Phoebe puts a cup of apple-and-berry tea in front of me and I talk to the girls, hearing about dolls and school and games they're going to play in the garden. I'm in the room, listening and nodding, but simultaneously my mind starts floating above my body watching the scene play out. *Huh, so this is what it's like to have a six-year-old. This is what it's like to have two children. This is what it's like to have a life that's intact.* The disassociation continues until I realize Phoebe's called my name three times and everyone's looking at me.

"Do you want to stay for dinner?" Phoebe asks and it takes every ounce of my will to say, with a smile, "That's so kind, but I'm going to head home. It was lovely to see you all." I dispense brief hugs to Evie and Ida, wave to Rory and hug Phoebe tightly.

"Thank you," Phoebe whispers into my hair as she holds me tight.

I don't have it in me to say anything back to her. I'm trying so hard to be the right sort of woman in this nightmare, and today I managed. I pushed aside jealousy and bitterness. I was kind and open and brave. But my poor, broken heart didn't need to see what it's missed out on. It didn't need to see that at all.

# JAMIE

A small farm next to the Cairngorms National Park,
the Independent Republic of Scotland
Day 1,626

*Dear Catherine,*

*I'm sorry for not agreeing to meet with you. I know you said that I could see the questions before we met but the idea of an interview made me nervous. My mum says I don't need to apologize but I don't want you to think I'm being rude.*

*Mum said you wanted to know what it was like when I was on my own and what school's been like since the evacuation program ended. I don't like talking about the first six months when I was in the hut. I was diagnosed with PTSD last year, which has put a lot of things into perspective. I think my mum blames herself for keeping me out there for so long but she didn't know any better.*

*It was much better once I could go back and live with everyone. Most of the other boys were okay about me having my old bedroom and not sharing with anyone. After so long alone I didn't like having people too close to me. The boys were great. I became really close friends with some of them, especially Logan and Arthur. They live in Dundee and we visit each other sometimes. We used to play football a lot and talk about what we'd do once the vaccine was invented. Eventually, though, someone would always* stop the conversation because it made them miss home too much. We had a thing. If you said "chat" it meant everyone had to change the topic. No questions asked. That was really helpful.

We had a big party when the news came about the vaccine. Mum kept crying and a few of the boys cried too. I would forget that I had my mum and dad but they didn't. Lots of their dads and brothers died while they were staying with us. Mum dealt with it better than I did. She set up a "Space Room" and if you went in you could be on your own for up to three hours. She used to make sure you didn't have laces or anything sharp, which was a downer, but still. I get what she was trying to do.

I remember Mum screaming and telling us that she'd just had a phone call and the first group of boys were going home. It was amazing and exciting and also sad. I was happy for them but scared about what would happen next.

Gradually things have gone more back to normal. I've been back at school since August 2029 but I missed a few years so I won't finish until I'm twenty. I'm going to be a doctor. Everyone says there aren't enough doctors and I think I'd be good at it. I'm the best in my class at biology.

School obviously isn't the same. Most of my favorite teachers died. My dad coaches the rugby team now because he's the only person around here who knows how to play. I'm one of twenty-two boys in my year out of ninety-six. It's actually higher than the national average because of the evacuation program but we're still outnumbered. The girls used to be a lot quieter. They wore more makeup and used to flirt with us and stuff. They still do, flirt, but it's different now. There's so many of them and all the teachers are girls now so it feels like we're the outsiders.

I've noticed that when people talk about "people" they say "women" now. I don't like it. I mentioned it to a teacher at school in Sociology and she said it was just because of the majority. I didn't think that was a very good reason to ignore the men who are left but I didn't want to get into trouble so I didn't push it.

*I have dreams about before. They make me really stressed out the next day. In them, I'm always playing football in the garden with my dad in my school uniform, happy that the day's over and I can relax. Then before I wake up my mum will start screaming and she'll start saying names of all the people who've died: Grandpa, baby Benji, Uncle Victor. I'll wake up and remember everything that's happened in a rush and want to throw up.*

*If it's okay, I don't want you to send any letters after this or phone Mum asking for me. I've said what I want to. I'm trying to move on. I hope your report goes well and this is helpful.*

# CATHERINE

've been reading a blog and I can't get it out of my head. Libby pointed it out to me. We've both become obsessed with the stories of the Plague; the limitless ways in which it affected different configurations of families. We're hardly alone. All anyone can talk about are Maria Ferreira interviews and the books and movies being made about the experience of the Plague. I can't bear to watch anything, it's too much to see it on-screen but each night I spend hours trawling the internet, reading until the screen is wavy. The blog is by a man in London called Daniel Ahern. He wrote it as a diary of immunity. Here's a selection of his posts.

### December 9, 2025

I'm not leaving the house. As soon as my mum saw the news she came over with loads of cans. All kinds of random stuff like peaches, peas, black beans. I don't know what she was thinking buying all that. I just needed baked beans and potatoes and I'll be fine. She can't be around too much. My stepdad has bowel cancer so she has to spend a lot of time with him in the hospital in Romford. I wish I could just say to her to leave him and spend all her time with me but I can't. I'm not going to be selfish like that and make her choose.

### March 9, 2026

Still alive. I ran out of cans a few weeks ago so I had to leave the house. All the women who saw me stared at me like I was a wild animal. I wanted to shout at them, "What you fucking staring at, I'm just a man," but it didn't seem right. They're just scared. Everyone's scared. I bought stuff from the corner shop as quick as I could. Threw the cash down on the counter and didn't wait for change. Touched as little as possible. I got some crisps and loads of Fanta. I've been craving salt and vinegar crisps and Fanta for weeks. I could have cried, they tasted so good. I assumed I'd get sick in the next few days but I didn't. I've been doing the same thing every few days. I run out, get food, don't get any change back, get back in the house. I'm still alive so I must be doing something right. I want my mum to come and see me but she's scared she's got it and she'll pass it on to me. My stepdad died of it on Christmas Day so she says it's definite that she's carrying it. I tell her she can just sit on the other side of the room from me but she insists. All I can do is talk to her on Skype.

### June 15, 2026

I think I'm immune. I would say I think I'm immune, lads, but I don't think there's that many lads left to read this. My mum's been over three times now. Each time we were careful. No hugging, I sat on the sofa, she sat on the floor on the other side of the living room, she had to cough at one point and she literally coughed out the window. But still, nothing. I've read loads of stories of people getting sick from being breathed on by someone who's got it. One in ten men are immune. I think I'm one of the special ones.

### November 4, 2026

Still here, lads and ladies! No death for me. I'm basically living a normal life now. Not totally normal, I'm not stupid. No public transport and I still only buy food from the corner shop and don't touch any money someone's given me. I want to get tested to see if I'm officially immune but that would mean going to a doctor and if I'm not (I definitely am but no need to take stupid risks) I'll catch it from a germy GP practice in a second. I'm back at work now at my old job. I always worked from home and only worked in the office occasionally so it doesn't feel like much has changed. I think I'll get a position in the draft soon but apparently they make you get tested for immunity first.

It's nice spending so much more time with Mum. I never liked my stepdad that much. Don't worry, my mum won't read this. She wouldn't know what a blog was if it came up and introduced itself. She even hugs me now and everything. I've convinced her. She sees it now. I'm immune.

### November 7, 2026

I think I've got it. I don't know how this happened. I just got a call from the hospital. They told me Mum's been admitted to the hospital with lung disease. I didn't even know she was sick, she seemed fine. They said I should come and visit her. I asked the woman if that would be okay and she went yeah, yeah, you're immune, right? But I've not felt right since last night. I thought it might just be a cold or something but I feel like I've got the worst flu in the world. I'm shaking. My heart's hammering in my chest. One minute I'm boiling and the next I'm so cold I can literally put my back to the radiator and feel it burning my skin but I'm still cold. I'm going to rest now. It's getting harder to type. Can someone go to the hospital in Romford please? My mum's name is Michelle Ahern. She's on the High Dependency Unit in Ward 7. Someone go and tell her I love her please.

After that the blog went dark. The idea of this man has been weighing on me. This man who, by the sounds of it, died all alone. His mum in the hospital, no siblings or friends that he mentions, just slipping away in the dark with a plea for someone to tell his mother that she's loved.

It was surprisingly easy to find the records about who he was. I found the death records for November 2026 in the area around Romford General. Sure enough, Michelle Ahern died from advanced lung failure on November 9, 2026. She had no next of kin listed.

I found her address through the electoral register and then managed to ask around her neighbors and find out Daniel's address. I lied and told them I was an ex-girlfriend who wanted to see the place he died, which was ethically dubious but earned me his address, a comforting smile and a slice of lemon drizzle cake "for the road." If someone came to my door and asked for the address of their ex-boyfriend, I'd call the police, but maybe people are nicer in Essex than in Crystal Palace.

And that's how I've ended up here, outside Daniel's block of flats. I thought about trying the ex-girlfriend shtick again but I don't think the residents of Islington will go for it. I ring the buzzer for the flat next to Daniel's and tell the woman who answered that I'm looking for Daniel.

"Oh, love, he's dead."

"Oh no, I didn't realize."

She pauses. "I mean, it can't be much of a surprise now, can it."

"Is there someone living in his flat now?"

"No, there's—look, just come up. I'm not going to have a full conversation over the intercom."

The woman, Poppy, takes one look at me and relaxes. I've been told before I look unthreatening. It's a useful trait for an anthropologist.

"Come in," she says and gestures to the sofa. "Cup of peach squash?"

"I'd love one." I can't stand peach but Genevieve didn't raise me to be rude and the more you say yes, the more people tend to tell you.

"So Daniel died in November 2026?"

"Yeah, he lasted ages. I remember seeing him a few times. For months he would dart out and go to the corner shop and come back with sweets like a kid looking all furtive. Then he got more confident. He'd go out all day."

"I read his blog. He sounded sure he was immune."

Poppy sighs. "Daniel was a cocky shit. RIP and everything, yeah, but he thought he was the bee's knees. Of course, he went back to normal thinking he was immune. Idiot."

"What happened when he died?"

Poppy wrinkles her nose at the memory. "The smell is how we realized. It was like nothing you can even imagine. We couldn't even breathe in our own flats. I called the police and they called the coroners and they called the body people and eventually they broke his door down and took him away."

"How long had he been dead?"

"I don't know, but Cheryl who lives upstairs thought she heard one of them say it had been at least two weeks. It was gross."

I take the squash and drink the tiniest sip possible. "No one helped him, then?"

Poppy's eyes narrow. "What, like it was our fault that he died of the Plague? Have you seen the state of the world?"

"No, no," I say, desperately backtracking. "I mean he didn't have any family, friends, that kind of thing. His mum died around the same time as him."

"Aw that's a shame. Nah, I never saw anyone come to his flat once everything kicked off. Must have been loads of people like that though who died on their own. Makes you sad to think about it."

Poppy says this in a voice that suggests she doesn't intend to think about it anymore. I thank her for her time and make my way out. Just as I'm about to exit the front door of the building she pops her head around the stairs and calls out to me.

"Hey, lady. What's your name?"

"Catherine."

"Who did you lose?"

"What?" She comes down the stairs.

"I said, who did you lose? Who in your family died?" I've never been asked this before like this.

"My husband, Anthony, and my son, Theodore," I say quietly. The shock of the question has brought tears to my eyes.

"I like to ask, so you know they're not forgotten," Poppy says. "You remember them and now so do I." She pats me on the shoulder and goes back upstairs. I leave the building and walk quickly down the road weeping hot, hiccuppy tears. It is the kindest thing someone has done for me in months.

I've spent so long traveling, interviewing women and men, writing their experiences, researching, endlessly gathering information for a vague purpose. "An academic report," I say, when they ask. It's not a lie, but it's not true either. I haven't known. There hasn't been a secret, overarching goal. I just knew I needed to record stories, I needed to talk to people about what has happened. I couldn't pretend it hadn't happened and move on. I haven't been ready to move on; I'm still not.

I keep going back to Poppy's words. *You remember them and now so do I.* For my entire childhood I knew, keenly, desperately, that I was all that was left of my parents. They had died and, apart from me, it was as if they never existed. All I ever wanted was my own family. Something solid and tangible. A family tree that went on for generations. A human need, thousands of years old, to be known. *I was here.*

And now my family is gone. My parents are dead. Anthony is dead. Theodore is dead. Once I die, that'll be it. It will be as if none of us existed. The thought is unbearable. I need people to know I was here, that I had a beautiful son called Theodore. That Anthony and I lived and married and loved and created a family.

No one knows about Daniel. What an end to a life; his mother dying alone as he then died alone, remembered only in passing by a neighbor and a blog. That can't be my fate, or Theodore's fate, or Anthony's fate. When people ask me what I'm researching for I should be honest. Remembrance: mine and theirs.

# AMANDA

I haven't been to Dundee for over a decade, not since a friend's hen do. The memory of Jägerbombs, flammable white nylon and penis straws makes me want to cry with nostalgia; a time when everything was simple and easy.

But, first, a trip to somewhere I didn't anticipate visiting. Dundee's largest sexual health clinic. Apparently my predecessors at Health Protection Scotland have been "hands off" leaders, which I think is a polite way of saying "lazy." I don't see how anyone can understand health policy in practice, and know what needs to change, without seeing it on the ground. My peers seem to think that's radical. I think it's just common sense, so here I am walking through the gray, dreary streets of Dundee.

I wait in the waiting room for Tanya Gilmore to pick me up and try to subtly eye up the four other people here. Two women and two men, all of whom are studiously looking at phones, magazines or their laps.

"Amanda?"

Tanya calls my name and ushers me into her office, a warm, welcoming room with fun graphic posters on the walls saying things like, "Check your boobs!" and "Be proud of your choice."

"Thank you so much for agreeing to see me," I say, but I don't get any further into my speech before Tanya waves me away.

"I'm glad you want to see the work we do here. No need for a thank-you. Now, what can I do for you?"

It feels alarmingly like I'm one of her patients. I almost feel nervous despite the fact that, with the total lack of sex in my life for years, there is literally zero chance of me having an STI. "I want to know about your support groups. Your local area has lower uptakes of anti-depressants and a lower suicide rate in the LGBTQ community. I want to know why, and replicate it."

Tanya sits back in her chair and exhales. "It's not that simple, you know."

"Why not?"

"Well, for a start, you can't replicate me and I'm the reason for this."

"So help me understand."

Tanya sighs and I sit, resolute. I need her help. The suicide rate of gay men has risen by 450 percent since November 2025. We don't have enough data for the suicide rate of trans men and women but, anecdotally, it's gone way, way up. There is a public health crisis in the LGBTQ community and Tanya is doing something right.

"Let's go back to basics," Tanya says. "Gender is a social construct. If I had a pound for every time I said that over the last fifteen years I'd have one of those Alaskan survival bunkers all the billionaires disappeared off to. But the Plague distinguished on the basis of sex and there was no fucking with it. None at all. It was the first time I had experienced a huge divide in the trans community. There wasn't anger or discord, just stunned desolation. Trans women on this side—you're all probably going to die. Trans men on that side—you're all going to be fine. You have to understand, that's not how our community normally works. Trans women were rendered helpless in the face of their

XY chromosomes, and gay men became a super-minority. It was a nightmare."

She stops and glares at me as if I'm forcing her to do something awful, dredging up terrible memories. "It was already really hard being trans in 2025, and being gay often wasn't a picnic. But the Plague made everything so much worse. The process of supporting trans individuals, campaigning for expanded rights and making the world a better place for trans people became irrelevant to a lot of people."

I have to interrupt and ask, as I'm dying to know. "Are you immune?"

"No. I still can't believe that I'm alive, to be honest. It feels like for the first time in my life my body has actually helped me out. 'I might have given you male sex at birth but I'll do you a favor with the Plague. No death for you this time.' I contracted it in December 2025 and survived. In the first few days after I survived I was glowing. I felt . . . lifted. Chosen. To be so close to death and have life handed back to you is an amazing thing."

"And now you're doing something extraordinary with your life."

Tanya cackles. "Fuck off. I've been a nurse on and off for twenty years. I'm doing my job, which I'm required to do by the draft, I'm not Mother Teresa. Anyway. There's less trolling now but trans women still get some awful comments. Saying that I should have died as the last thing the world needs is a man dressed up as a woman—it needs real men, and I should have stayed as one. Well, I'm a woman and I can't help that a murderous Plague swept the planet leaving devastation in its wake. What the world does need is people. The point is that I understand. I'm not reading from some stupid leaflet with a useless mnemonic. I get it. How many support groups for gay men in Scotland exist now? Three. How many support groups are there for trans men and women in Scotland? I know the answer to that—it's one. You're looking at the person running it."

For the first time in a long time I feel put on the spot, like I'm not doing enough, like I've already made a mistake. I suspect this is how people who work for me usually feel when I'm talking to them. I can't say that I enjoy the role reversal.

"I want to change that. That's why I'm here."

"Then you're going to have to work hard to recruit men and women who are empathetic, have the right life experience, have the time after whatever Working Draft jobs they're doing. The LGBTQ community is in crisis. The gay men who have seen their social circles, lovers, lives decimated. They need help."

I can feel myself becoming defensive even though I know, logically, it's not a helpful response. "We've all been working in what felt like a war zone for so long. I couldn't worry about people's mental health when I was fighting to get enough gauze and antibiotics and antiseptic to keep operating rooms open and people alive."

Tanya snorts. "Guess what, mental health also keeps people alive."

I was going to ask if I could sit in on one of the sessions Tanya is running this evening, but I have a feeling I'm going to be given short shrift. I understand it. I've been a disappointment, and yet I don't regret the choices I've made. I think back to the horror show Gartnavel was, not long after the outbreak. The male doctors were all dead or waiting to die. There were two doctors in the hospital then who are still alive now who, I think, knew that they were immune—a radiologist and a general surgeon. Fuck, they were busy. All the doctors were. There was a shift in the numbers of doctors in a way you didn't have with nurses. Only 11.5 percent of nurses were male; 87.8 percent of surgeons were male. It was, with the best will and staff effort in the world, a shit show.

And then there was the "emergency wing" of the hospital, which was this godforsaken bit of the building that used to be the maternity wing. There was obviously a lot less need for that so we converted it.

You weren't allowed to enter the wing unless you were visiting a patient or working there, in a useless attempt to stop the spread of the virus. But really, what was the point? Everyone carried it. We all knew that.

I stand up to leave, and just as I'm getting to the door, Tanya calls my name. "You doctors are all the same. You think you've got your priorities all in order, the way at the beginning of the Plague you'd do all your treatment protocols. Well, no doctor can say that you were responsible for any of the men who survived. There was no particular magic to it. It was plain old good fortune. You find me a doctor who wants to admit to that and I'll turn into a raccoon. You're not so keen on 'luck,' weirdly. It must be down to your exceptional caring skills. Of course, any time you ask a doctor something as simple as the name of a patient they go, 'John? Jack? Joseph? Jean?' You forget, nurses keep people more than just breathing, we keep them alive. I know what my priorities are and keeping people's minds working is just as important as gauze and antibiotics. I'm doing something to keep people alive. What are you doing?"

I pause. What am I doing? Plenty to keep the Scottish population physically healthy. On this issue? Nothing. My cheeks begin to heat but I quickly tell myself to get on with it. Shame and regret don't help anyone. I pride myself on being a doer. Am I seriously going to hear everything Tanya has just told me, go back to my office and act as though I wasn't listening, or wail that I feel bad? No.

"Come and work for me."

"What?" Tanya is stunned, which gives me a tiny amount of satisfaction after the scathing dressing-down she's just given me.

"I want to hire you. Come and work for me in Glasgow. I'll give you a budget, responsibility and a job. As you've so bluntly pointed out, I see patients, you see people. So help me. There's a lot to do and not enough people to do it so I'm going to hire you and trust you to work on this issue and get it right." I shrug. "I spend a lot of time pointing out what other people are doing wrong, and I've fired people who made mistakes, but those are empty gestures. They don't do anything. So come work for me. Help me."

Tanya is gaping at me, gulping a bit like a fish and I can't figure out why she's so surprised.

"You know, I got this job because I was angry and determined and persistent and wouldn't shut up. It's not so shocking I'd hire you for the same reason, is it?"

"You're fucking weird, you know that," Tanya says, but her face breaks into a smile and I know she's going to say yes. "When do I start?"

# ROSAMIE

### Mati, Philippines
### Day 1,667

There is a satisfaction to working in business I never had as a nanny. When you're looking after children, no matter how hard you work you have the same amount or more to do the next day. Three meals, bathing, clothing, playing, talking, cajoling, encouraging, disciplining, comforting. It never ends. My job now has clean lines and a strict to-do list. As I achieve things, they are ticked off the list and then I don't have to do them again.

The private jet landed seven minutes before the East Pacific Air Traffic Restrictions Partnership came into effect. We landed and the flight attendant burst into deep, gulping sobs. I got off the plane as fast as I could, desperate to get away from the man who knew I was not who I said I was: a traitor and a thief. After days of traveling by bus, car and hours and hours of walking I finally got back to Mati, my home city, only for my mother to take one look at me and tell me to leave and go back to Manila. "There has never been a better time to make something of yourself. All the men are dead, and businesses need people. Go, go back to Manila right now. We'll be fine here."

She wasn't wrong. Five years later, she's the head of the barangay and has overseen the recovery of our village and a new infrastructure program while I have a whole new life. I still wonder about Angelica and Mrs. Tai though. Is Angelica looked after? Did they survive the riots? Tens of thousands died and the Great Fire took many more. The Chinese army took over before China disintegrated and now there's a fragile peace with Singapore operating as an administrative region of Beijing State. I'm sure they were fine. Mrs. Tai had spine, she just didn't like to use it.

Today's figures arrive in my inbox. They're better than average; a high proportion of good-quality plastic. I look over the numbers, needing to feel confident before my weekly call with my boss. This job is mine because I kept being in the right place at the right time and I worked hard. My official title is "Waste Supply Manager" in one of the Philippines' largest recycling companies. I wonder what Mrs. Tai would say if she knew that I had built a career in garbage. I can imagine her wrinkling up her nose in disgust.

My assistant comes in. I put a smile on my face, ready for my call with my boss and start to push my half-finished lunch to the side of my desk.

"There's a Mrs. Tai on the phone for you."

I drop my bowl of soup and it splatters all over my crisp, cream linen trousers and shoes.

My assistant looks at me with intense concern. I'm not usually a clumsy person. I feel like she's glimpsing into the past and seeing the old me.

"I, um. Put her through and shut the door behind you." I'm wiping soup off my thighs when the phone rings.

I'll just pretend I don't know her. She can't do anything to me, not now. What's she going to do, have me arrested? She couldn't. Could she? She has no proof it was me. Of course there's proof it was me.

"Hello, Rosamie." Her voice hasn't changed.

"How can I help you?" Noncommittal. I could be talking to a stranger.

"Don't sound so distant, Rosamie. You know who I am."

She's going to destroy my life. Of course she is, I stole millions of dollars from her. Tears immediately start dropping quickly down my cheeks. I have imagined this moment so many times and I knew it would come, but I prayed and prayed it wouldn't. She could be recording me. I must be careful.

"How is Angelica?"

Mrs. Tai sucks in her breath and it feels like I've done something wrong but I'm not sure what. I stole money, I didn't hurt her kids. I loved her children more than she did. The thought of Rupert makes my stomach hurt even now that all this time has passed.

"Angelica is why I'm calling. Partly."

Panic, fear, I'm going to throw up. "Is she okay? Did something happen?"

I swear I can hear Mrs. Tai roll her eyes on the phone. She hasn't changed one bit. "Yes, she's fine. She's more grown-up now than when you last saw her." I resist the urge to bite out a retort. Of course she's more grown-up, that's what happens to children. They grow up. I want to speak to her so much but I can't ask that. I can't.

"You can't speak to her so don't even think about asking."

"I wasn't going to." I sound sullen but I can't help it.

"Angelica is the only reason I'm calling you instead of calling the police and telling them to contact the Filipino authorities."

My worst nightmare is hovering at the edges of my sight. Policemen bursting into my small, clean, peaceful office and ruining my life. The humiliation of telling my mother I failed, that I did something terrible, that I am a criminal.

"I thought when I told Angelica what you did, she would be angry with you and she would support me, but that's not what happened."

Silence as we both breathe down the phone. Angelica was always very stubborn. I bet she didn't speak to Mrs. Tai for days, maybe even weeks. If something was going to happen that she didn't like, there was no persuading her.

"So I'm calling you, not the police. For now anyway. I need the lullaby."

"The lullaby?"

"Yes, the lullaby Angelica says you always used to sing to her and Rupert." The irritation in Mrs. Tai's voice is thick. She can't bear that she's asking me, the help, to teach her something she should know. It's such an obvious failing; the mother who can't comfort her own child. "She says it's the only thing that reminds her of Rupert and you used to sing it before bed. I need to know the lullaby so I can sing it to her."

I don't bother asking to sing it to Angelica directly. I wish I could speak to her. It's been five years. I want to know what her life is like, what school is like, who her friends are, what her favorite movie is. I can't know the answers though. They will remain unanswered questions.

"And if I sing you the lullaby, you won't get back in touch with me again?"

"No, Rosamie, I won't get you thrown in jail for robbing me of millions of dollars. Okay?"

I don't comment, aware that anything I say could be used as an admission if Mrs. Tai is recording this. I clear my throat, self-conscious about singing this small song of comfort that belongs in the quiet calm of a dark bedroom with children being lulled to sleep.

*Soon you'll be in a land of dreams*
*And when you wake, all will seem*
*Bright and easy, a brand-new day*
*We'll eat and jump and talk and play*

*No matter what, I'll be here*
*Don't you worry, dry those tears*
*When you wake, I'll say good morning*
*And we'll start again, a new day dawning*

Mrs. Tai is silent for long, drawn-out seconds. My cheeks blush with mortification that I have just sung a song, badly, down the phone to my former employer and a woman who could ruin my life.

"Well, that explains a lot," she finally says, with a breath that sounds like she's heaved it out. "Why they were so devoted to you."

"What do you mean?"

"If the Plague hadn't happened when it did, I was about two weeks away from firing you."

"You just said they were devoted to me; that makes no sense."

Mrs. Tai makes a noise from the back of her throat, a noise of visceral annoyance and impatience that takes me back to the feeling of being her young, nervous employee so quickly I flinch.

"You acted like you were their mother."

"I wouldn't have needed to if you had been behaving like one."

The words have fallen out of my mouth and into the awkward expanse between us before I can think through the consequences. Now, in a flash, the idea of police and sirens and prison makes me want to beg for forgiveness and scoop the words back up, into the dark, never to be heard again.

"Maybe you're right," Mrs. Tai says in a voice I can't place. It is more resigned than I have heard her be before but it doesn't stretch into remorse or regret. That would be asking far too much of her.

"It's been nice talking to you, Mrs. Tai. Good-bye."

I place the receiver back into its cradle, making a rattling sound. I hadn't realized my fingers were shaking. In the months after the

Plague, living a new, strange life in a world tipped upside down, I tormented myself every night with shame over what I had done. Not guilt, because in some odd way I felt it was right. At least, it was justified, but I was the kind of person who stole now. I was the kind of person who lied and committed crimes. As my new life took shape with a monthly paycheck, an apartment in Manila that wasn't disgusting and even a few friends, I stopped thinking about that dark night so much.

Now, there is some peace. Mrs. Tai could always choose to turn around and accuse me but I know I have Angelica on my side. The brave, kind little girl whose parents were never there and whose brother and father died, is on my side.

# ELIZABETH

'm on a plane, going home. It feels so surreal, I keep looking around me as if someone will stop me and say, "I'm so sorry, Ms. Cooper, you can't actually go back to the States. Don't be silly." But that doesn't happen and Simon keeps cheerfully eating chips in the seat next to me, his wedding ring making a satisfying clink when he picks up his drink.

A big part of me always assumed I'd end up returning to the States in ignominy. As of tomorrow, I'm officially deputy director of the CDC, a job I didn't even dare to covet. Practically everyone I worked with at the CDC is dead. So many men, gone, and if I'm really honest, often forgotten, at least by me. I knew my interview had either gone perfectly or I'd bombed because it only lasted twenty minutes.

"You've smashed it!" George said, when I walked into his office, a bit shell-shocked, at 3:21 p.m., having started the interview at 3 p.m. "If they thought you were terrible they'd have dragged it out a bit, so you couldn't complain if you didn't get the job." As ever, he was right.

Simon wasn't sure I was doing the right thing when I told George I was applying for the job. "You don't understand," I told him. We're not like colleagues, we're like soldiers. We've been through a lifetime together in a few years. He walked me down the aisle. He's become like a father to me. I knew he would support me for the CDC job; a dream come true. He helped me with interview prep every afternoon for two weeks.

And now, I'm on a plane, which feels unbelievably exotic, going back to my old life with a new husband, a new job, a new everything. I can remember what Elizabeth Cooper was like a few years ago but it feels so distant, it's like a childhood memory. I was lonely, far from friends and family. I've always been good at making acquaintances but struggled to convert them into deep friendships. It kind of makes sense my best friend is now a sixty-five-year-old male professor.

I stretch my arms and look up at the rest of our section of the plane. It's hard not to play spot the difference with the last time I was on a plane. Last time it was mainly men on my overnight flight to London, dressed in suits with pseudoscience books, crime novels and newspapers tucked under their arms. Now, it's a sea of women interspersed with the occasional man sticking out. Obvious and intriguing just by being male. The woman to the right of Simon is holding a book I've heard about but don't feel I really have the right to read. *Are You Fucking Kidding Me?*, a children's book for adults. It's written by a widow and meant to help people feel comforted by . . . well, I'm not sure. That they're not alone, I suppose, having either lost their partner or feeling despair at this scary new world. I feel a twang of relief that Simon's by my side. Lovely, lovely Simon. My husband. I skim a kiss across his cheek and he smiles in response.

I turn to the TV and flick through the channels. Since TV and films started being made again, I've noticed there are only two types of shows: classic family sitcoms and fantasy dramas. Nostalgia or imagination. Take your pick. I thought I was going nuts, or my Netflix was playing tricks on me, and then I saw an interview with the head of content strategy at Netflix and she said that's all people want right now. People want to dive into the past when the biggest concern was whether your crush would invite you to prom, or imagine an alternative reality. True crime is *out*, she said. I can believe it. I used to love true crime podcasts; now they're too heavy. I don't want to hear about miscarriages of justice. *Life* has been a miscarriage of justice recently.

Oh, I know what I'm going to watch. The Luke Thackeray documentary. Ordinary guy from England is an out-of-work actor in the States. Goes home to say good-bye to his dad and his three brothers and await his death. Turns out, he's immune and gets a call from his agent when the film and TV industries pick up. There's a shortage of actors in Hollywood for the first time in history. Eighteen months later, he's one of the biggest movie stars in the world. He's spoken a bit in interviews about the conflict he feels: his father and three brothers died, yet the Plague killed almost all of his competition and now he's one of the world's most successful actors.

"You okay?" Simon asks.

"I'm good, just going to watch a documentary." Simon makes an impressed face. I won't mention it's a documentary about a cute actor. "Everything's going to be okay, okay?" Simon rubs my hand gently as he says this and I feel the bit of tension in my shoulders about my first day tomorrow evaporate.

"Everything's going to be okay," I repeat back and, do you know what? I believe it.

---

### "Finding love in a new world"

#### by Maria Ferreira

The world has changed immeasurably. That much we all know. I have the newest iPhone and it's as small as the iPhones of a decade ago because Apple realized that women have smaller hands than men (who knew?) and so the tablet-size monstrosities they expected everyone to buy didn't fit in women's pockets or hands. I can now type comfortably with one hand for the first time in years. Women are now 57 percent less likely to die of heart attacks because treatment protocols have changed to recognize the different symptoms men and women experience. The first drug ever to treat endometriosis has been discovered; it is expected to create billions in profit over the next decade. Female police officers, firefighters and members of the armed forces are now less likely to die doing their jobs because they have uniforms designed for them, rather than simply wearing small men's Kevlar vests, boots, helmets and uniforms that don't fit.

I could go on, but I won't because my editor already made me cut that paragraph down. This article is not going to be like my usual writing. Although, everything I've done over the last few years has been unusual, so maybe that's an unnecessary caveat. I've scared the world witless, gotten my old editor fired, interviewed a billionaire scientist and, as some of you might remember from a few months ago, discussed dating and love with Bryony Kinsella. She told me in no uncertain terms that she felt the great question of our time is how to find love when there are no men left.

The response to that article showed me that lots of you agreed with her. So many of you, in fact, that I have never gotten a bigger response to a story in decades of writing. Lots of you asked me to speak to women who had used Adapt, and see what they thought. Lots of you told me you had found love on Adapt, which made for a wonderfully optimistic inbox on a gray winter morning.

I reached out to women I know—acquaintances, friends of friends—and found an array of experiences. Jacinda, thirty-six, went on a few dates through Adapt but found that it wasn't for her. "I'm just not attracted to women. I wish I was, I miss having relationships, and sex, but I can't force it. I'm hoping to meet a guy, and maybe even have kids. But if I don't, that's going to be okay."

Olivia (not her real name), a twenty-five-year-old intern at an advertising agency, met her girlfriend on Adapt and is "happier than I've ever been. Maybe because I assumed I would never get to have a relationship so I appreciate it. Falling in love is the best feeling in the world. We're going to be together forever." Ah, to be twenty-five again.

I couldn't write this article without telling Jenny's story. Jenny is a lawyer from Chicago, and the Plague hit the city the day before her wedding. "I was sitting in a suite in the Four Seasons, watching the news with my family as it reported that all the hospital ERs were closing to men and flights were being canceled. My wedding dress was hanging on the back of a door. Two of my four bridesmaids had already canceled, and my fiancé's parents were supposed to be flying from Canada but they were terrified of being stranded in the US."

I asked Jenny about her parents; how were they reacting? "I told my dad we should just cancel the wedding and he was horrified. 'I didn't spend all this money for it to go to waste!' he said. I think they found it easier to focus on the wedding rather than acknowledge what was happening."

Jenny and her fiancé, Jackson, got married the next day. "The wedding was terrible. The officiant didn't turn up. Fortunately, there was a pastor staying in the hotel. A quick-thinking hotel employee asked him to perform the wedding. He had a Southern accent and wore his coat the whole time. Maybe it was kind of wonderful. I remember looking at Jackson and thinking, 'Remember every second of this, Jenny. It's never going to be this good again.' Thirty people came to the wedding in the end. Jackson's parents weren't there. We didn't leave each other's sides all night. A reception with an abundance of shrimp and champagne can be amazing or a complete disaster. Ours was a bit of both."

After their wedding, Jenny and Jackson hibernated in their apartment. Jackson survived for another two months. Jenny says she hated the inevitably of the Plague; men will die, women will live. "It was a spectator sport. We had to watch and wait, the sexist notion of womanhood writ large by a disease. It was like in the movies when a woman says, 'Oh, darling, stay here. Don't go out there, it's too dangerous! Don't leave me behind!' And yet that's all I wanted to say to him. Please don't leave me behind. Please don't leave me behind. Please."

Jenny first tried Adapt eleven months after Jackson died. Her friend Ellerie told her to try it. She filled in the dating app profile (nervously, having never dated online before), swiped right on a few people and organized to meet a woman with dark, curly hair whom she thought had a nice smile. Her date arranged dinner at an Italian restaurant and when she turned up, she met me.

That was three years ago. On that first date, Jenny and I talked for seven hours. She made this heartless crone feel hopeful about the future, and I'm reliably informed I made Jenny "feel like something good might happen after a long time when everything felt hopeless." Reader, I married her.

It was a small ceremony. There was no Southern pastor wearing his coat. Our friend Kelly married us. All our friends, whom we're still lucky enough to have with us, were able to attend. Jackson's mom came, which was wonderful and unexpected and made Jenny cry all of her mascara off. We both wore simple white dresses. It was perfect.

When I received such an outpouring following my Bryony Kinsella article, I realized the discomfort I felt was rooted in deceit because when I wrote that article I was already with Jenny, and had been for a long time. It had always felt sensible to keep my life with her private. After the article, it felt fraudulent. And so, in typical journalistic fashion, I'm letting the world know that I'm married to a woman and getting some good copy out of it. This won't be the last of these articles I write. Jenny and I have talked about this at length and we feel passionately that the questions surrounding love, romance, sex and relationships between women who had never previously dated women must be answered with real-life stories. There will be studies and academic analysis, of course, as there must be, but that cannot be the whole picture. I'm not sure how often I'm going to write about Jenny's and my life together, but I promise I will. I want other women in similar positions to us to see they are not alone. Much of my work since the Plague has been focused on telling the stories of those most affected by it and this will be one facet of that.

So, I will leave you not with the story of our first dance (to "At Last" by Etta James) or the joyful challenge of decorating our first house together (I like mid-century, she likes modern; aesthetic chaos ensues), but of an argument. The only real fight we've ever had. I asked Jenny, two years ago, if she thought she would ever have dated a woman if Jackson hadn't died. She nearly hit me, she was so angry. Here's her response: "If Jackson hadn't died, I would be married to Jackson. I never dated women before the Plague, never even considered it. I don't know why I've been able to fall in love with you, Maria. There are psychologists and anthropologists and journalists and all kinds of other people busily trying to figure out women's behavior. I don't think it's rocket science. I know I was lonely. I missed someone moving around in the background of the apartment as I read the *New York Times* on a Sunday. I missed feeling desired. I missed sex and intimacy and sharing my life with someone. I don't think that those feelings made it inevitable that I would fall in love with a woman. But my husband was dead and I happened to go on a date with you and I fell in love. I could twist myself up in knots wondering how and why and what if but I choose not to. What's the point? I'm happy, you're happy. What does it matter how we got here?"

# DAWN

I t's how much?"

"£768," the mechanic says apologetically.

"£768?" I repeat, as though repeating the number will magically decrease it.

"Safety first," she says hopefully. There's no point getting annoyed with her. It's not her fault that the government's new Department for Change has decided to review every bloody thing we use, buy and think about. Normally, I'd think it was an excellent idea, and at heart I do, but being legally required to spend nearly a grand for a new air-bag (tested on female-modeled dummies), a seat belt adjusted to my height (rather than the standard male height) and a new head rest (to accommodate my height) makes me pause. I'm as grateful as anyone that deaths in car accidents have fallen by 84 percent since 2025 but I could also churlishly point out that the population has reduced by half, the economy contracted so people stopped driving as much and female drivers are safer.

"These safety measures are responsible for making driving much safer," the mechanic says, clearly used to disgruntled customers who like the idea of safety in theory but not paying for it. "Before the Plague, women had a forty-seven percent higher chance than men of being seriously injured in a car crash."

That makes me pause as I'm putting in my PIN. That's actually quite a shocking statistic. Fair enough, Miranda Bridgerton, "Minister for Change." I'll grant you it would be nice not to die in a car crash.

"Thank you, and sorry for being a grouch," I say, trying to sound graceful.

"That's okay," the mechanic says cheerfully and starts prattling on about some optional upgraded service program that would cost blah blah, when my phone rings. It's a number I have saved in my phone as "Emergency."

"Hello?"

"Dawn, it's Nancy from the PM's office. Emergency meeting has been called. The Chinese Civil War is over."

"What did you say?"

"The war. It's over, they've declared peace. The speech announcing it has gone viral. Meeting's in an hour and a half in the usual location."

I hang up the phone and gape. Well, I never. I never actually thought they'd manage *peace*. I quickly google "Chinese war" on my phone and the clip is offered up on every news website on the first page.

Fei Hong, famous since her Maria Ferreira interview, stands in a line with eleven other women. They're all behind lecterns, each branded with a number between one and twelve.

"We are here today to announce that peace has been achieved," Fei says. "China is now formed of twelve states. Last week a truce was called and each of the women on this stage, representing our rebel groups, met in Macau. Representatives from the four independent states of Macau, Beijing, Tianjin and Shanghai attended these meetings to ensure the truce was upheld. The condition of peace was democracy: every state will hold free, fair elections in two months' time. A new Chinese Republic is born today."

Bloody hell. I hurry to the meeting, knowing that as it's a weekend no one will be dressed appropriately.

Oh God, Gillian's wearing *leggings*. At least I'm not a home secretary wandering into a Cobra meeting wearing an elasticized waistband.

"Did they interrupt your yoga class?" I can't help asking.

"Pilates," Gillian says with a sigh.

"Thank you all for being here," the prime minister says. Somewhat unsurprisingly for a woman who has been successfully leading a country through its worst-ever crisis, she's absolutely terrifying. The room is at attention. "For once, I have good news for us to discuss. We will be appointing ambassadors to each of the new states in short order."

The prime minister looks down at the briefing paper in front of her. She looks as astounded as I feel. "Each faction in the twelve territories has to register their supporters. The four most popular factions in each territory will become a registered political party and can seek election in their territory. For the first five years each faction has agreed to focus only on gaining a democratic mandate in their own territory to ensure no one consolidates power."

"So, it'll all go to shit in five years," Gillian says dryly.

"Quite possibly," the prime minister says. "Macau, Shanghai, Tianjin and Beijing have agreed to supervise elections and have threatened economic sanctions as a form of incentive for anyone breaking the rules. They'll be hoping that over the next five years trade builds to a level that each of the territories is more concerned with building economically than expanding territory."

The room goes silent, a rare thing for a meeting of ten of the most powerful people in the United Kingdom. There is little to say. The war is over and maybe they've actually . . . won? It's not possible for a world to be in order—the kind of peace that serious, old white men write books about—when nearly 20 percent of the world's population is at war or adjacent to it. It's as though the entire planet has breathed a sigh of relief. *Phew. They did it. We've all survived.* Thank bloody God. I couldn't handle World War Three before I retire after dealing with a Plague. I. Could. Not.

# CATHERINE

haven't been to a dinner party in over four years. Four years. I keep telling myself there's a limit to how much dinner parties can have changed over the last four years, but that's not very helpful actually because I didn't like them very much before the Plague. My outfit's never quite right—too short? Too hot? Can't do layers, they make me look like an organized hippie—and the only good bit about them used to be getting ready while Anthony drank a glass of wine sitting on the bed chatting with me, and then dissecting what everyone said on the tube home.

But Anthony's not here and I am Making an Effort so here I am, in a green velvet dress I already sort of know I'm going to be too warm in, ringing the doorbell of Phoebe's beautiful Battersea home.

Her husband, Rory, opens the door and for a moment everything feels completely normal. White wine is proffered, I make awkward small talk with people I don't know. But, looking even slightly below the surface, everything is different. No Anthony by my side. The numbers are all off; out of ten, there are only two men. Rory and a friend of his called James.

"What do you do?" I ask James, eyeing his wife, Iris, jealously. I don't want James but I ache to have my husband by my side too.

"I used to be a marketing analyst before everything but now I work in public affairs for the government's Male Relations Department."

The conversation around us stops and there's a chorus of "oohs" and "how interesting." James blushes; this is not the first time he's had that reaction. "How intriguing," I say, indulging the mood in the room. "Why did you choose to move there?"

"I realized how differently I was being treated by women and I wanted to make sure that men were having their voices heard."

"In what way are you treated differently?" I ask. I have an awful feeling that, pre-Plague, James was the kind of man who "just expected" his wife to take his name because of tradition and described himself as the Head of the Household.

"Romantically, it's . . . a lot. I get approached at least a few times a day—as I'm traveling to work, when I get coffee, if I'm in a restaurant with a friend. It's very rarely aggressive. Ninety-five percent of the time it's just a nice lady coming up to me with her number written on a piece of paper, or striking up a conversation as I wait for my coffee to go, or coming up to my table and asking if I want to get a drink sometime."

"And the other five percent?"

"They're more problematic. It's a desperation that, I suppose on one level, I understand, and on another level, I think, 'This isn't my fault. None of this is my fault. Why don't I have the right to just sit and wait for my train without being hassled?' When I complained about it to some of my sister's friends they were divided. One group thought that I had every right to complain—it was harassment! It's an outrage! You're wearing a wedding ring! The other half smiled ruefully and explained that they knew *exactly* how that felt and it was part of their daily life until a couple of years previously." Iris is nodding furiously along with everything James is saying. Is she a wife or a cheerleader? Perhaps he thinks they're the same thing.

"And how did you two meet?" I ask Iris and him. "We started going out on March 6, 2027," he says with a smile. I've never met a couple before who started their relationship after the Plague.

"How was it dating, after the Plague?" I know my question is testing the boundaries of good manners but I can't help it. I've missed being nosy at dinner parties. I forgot how impertinent I could be with people I don't know.

"Everyone kept telling me, 'Oh, you have so much choice, James, you could choose anyone. Any woman would be lucky to have you.' It was a bit like being a contestant on a reality show."

"So how did you choose Iris?"

Iris smiles beatifically at him. She's a bit annoying. "We'd known each other for years. She's friends with my little sister. I was focused on trying to recover from the loss, my dad and my two brothers died. Thankfully my brother-in-law is immune too. I worked in sports marketing and about eighty percent of my office died and the business collapsed. It was a lot to process. I was saying to my mum one day that I really wished I had met someone before the Plague. It would have been so much easier to cope with if I'd had a constant presence, you know?"

"And that's where I came in," Iris simpers.

James continues without acknowledging her. "I turned thirty in February 2027 and something flipped. I wanted to settle down and the Plague showed how short life is. That feeling of wanting to build a family and have babies. My mum said it reminded her of when she turned thirty and desperately wanted a baby."

"Sometimes a cliché is a cliché for a reason," Iris chirrups.

"The Plague put things into perspective for a lot of people," I say as politely as I can muster, realizing I've been silent for long enough to seem odd.

"And now I'm pregnant!" Iris adds with glee, rubbing a nonexistent bump. "And so's Phoebe!"

Phoebe turns around from the wine she's pouring for someone and I know the exact expression that's going to be on her face even before I look at it. It will be wide-eyed, her mouth pursed as if braced against whatever horror she's awaiting. I hate that I know her so well and yet, somehow, my oldest friend has allowed me to find out this piece of shattering news in the most unimaginably awful way possible.

"How wonderful for both of you!" I say brightly. Smile, Catherine. Keep smiling. Do not let Iris see you cry. "Excuse me, I'm just going to nip to the loo."

Phoebe follows me through the kitchen and upstairs to the bathroom.

"Catherine, I—"

"How fucking dare you? And just to be clear, in case you try and misrepresent this later, I'm not angry at you for being pregnant. I'm fucking furious at you for not telling me and then allowing some fucking twenty-eight-year-old moron to tell me for you. What the fuck?"

Tears are falling freely down Phoebe's face. She always cried easily. I want to shake her, hard.

"I'm so sorry. I didn't know how, and then. I thought I would to-night, but. It's. Oh God, I've fucked up, I'm so sorry."

Bile is rising up in me. She couldn't do this one thing right. This one decent, necessary thing. "You're a fucking coward. Jesus Christ. We've been friends for more than half our lives and you couldn't bother to tell me. Fuck you, Phoebe. Oh, and tell Rory his friend James and his wife are cunts."

I don't think I've ever been this angry and then, as I'm walking past the living room to get my coat, I hear Iris's voice wittering, "There's a reason that the baby boom happened after the Second World War, you know. When death is staring you in the face, you want something permanent to cling on to for dear life."

I want to throw a glass at Iris's head but I can't and I won't. There are so many things I can't and won't do so instead I just have to button up my coat and leave the house, alone. I walk to the station alone. I wait for a train alone. My nose runs in the cold and huge gulping sobs take over, which my body works its way through, alone. Always alone now, it seems.

# LISA

'm going to win the Nobel Prize. Of course I am. Everybody says so. It's the first time the Swedes are awarding them since the whole world went to shit, only in three categories—Physiology or Medicine, Chemistry and Peace—and I'm a shoo-in. Margot keeps looking at me warily as I pace the apartment. Her enthusiasm is restrained. She's the caution to my recklessness. It works in the long term, in life, in a partnership, but in a moment like this I desperately want her to be jumping up and down, as hyped as I am.

"Maybe, just . . . honey. Please. You're making me nervous." She puts down the romance novel she's reading and stares at me imploringly. It must be bad for her to put down her book. I perch on the edge of the sofa and just as I've started to think that maybe they should have called by now, my phone buzzes.

I scoop it up, breathless, on edge, who cares? "Hello?"

"Dr. Michael?"

"Yes, that's me."

"My name is Ingrid Persson. I am the Chair of the Nobel Assembly at the Karolinska Institute." Oh my God. Oh my fucking God. This is the coolest phone call of my entire life.

"I'm thrilled to inform you that we have chosen to award you the Nobel Prize for Physiology or Medicine."

"Thank you! This is an honor, truly." Margot is hugging me so tightly I can't breathe. Everything, every bit of work, every second I spent in the lab was worth it for this—"

"I have another piece of news you might find less . . . pleasing."

My heart drops. What is it? Maybe it's the money, I don't care about the money. I don't need prize money. No ceremony maybe? Damn it, I've been dreaming about the ceremony my whole life.

"You will share the prize." Ingrid says more words at this point, but the world goes a little fuzzy and black around the edges and Margot is looking up at me quizzically and did she just say I have to share the Nobel Prize? I've never even shared an *office*.

"Dr. Michael? Dr. Michael, are you still there?"

I clear my throat. "Yes, sorry about that, I dropped my phone. Whom am I sharing my prize with?"

"Dr. Amaya Sharvani, for her discovery of the genetic sequence from which immunity and vulnerability to the Plague arose in men and women, and Dr. George Kitchen, for his work in creating a test for immunity."

Okay. Sharing among three isn't too bad. Could be worse, could be worse. Could be . . . sharing among four. Who am I kidding? I'm horrified, but fuck it. I'm a horrified Nobel Prize winner.

"I look forward to meeting you at the ceremony in two months' time."

"Dr. Persson, it is truly an honor. I'm so grateful."

"I am grateful for your work, Dr. Michael. The Nobel Prize is a small token of recognition for the advances you have made in science."

She hangs up and Margot is hugging herself, looking at me, stricken. "What is it, what's happening?"

I pick her up and hold her. "So, bad news is I'm sharing the Nobel Prize. Good news is, it'll probably take me down a peg or two."

"Sharing with George Kitchen and Amaya?"

"The very ones."

She raises an eyebrow. "I always said you should have taken my name."

"Margot!" She's right, of course.

"What? It could have been Lisa Bird-Michael, George Kitchen and Amaya Sharvani, winners of the Nobel Prize."

I groan through a grudging laugh. It rankles that my name will come second. "I love you so much and hate you at the same time."

"That's marriage." She grins. "I'm so proud of you. Truly, all those years of work as a penniless grad student and junior in the lab. Can you imagine how you'd have felt back then if I'd told you that you'd win a Nobel Prize?"

Margot nuzzles her head into my neck in a way I've always found to be the most comforting thing in the world. "You know I thought this might happen. Sharing the prize."

Ah, Margot. Always knowing more than she lets on. "Why?"

"Because," she says, pulling back and looking me square in the eye, "my maddening, wonderful, arrogant, amazing wife, they deserve it too. They didn't create a vaccine but they helped you. They made stepping-stones you walked over on the way to the ultimate prize."

"You know how I always said I didn't understand your instinct for fairness?" She nods, smiling softly. "Well, I still don't." She barks out a laugh and we are happy.

I mean, I'd be happier if I'd won it on my own but we're still happy.

# DAWN

Paris, France
Day 1,702

**T**ea! I'm drinking tea. I want to cry with happiness. It's not hot enough—it never is on the Continent—and it's got too much milk in it, but it's perfect. I feel eight thousand times more able to do my job thanks to this mug of joy. I'm cradling it like a child holds milk; it's precious and bringing more comfort than any of the European people in this room could ever understand.

Ah, Interpol. How I look forward to your meetings. So much amazing food. Croissants. Beautifully cooked duck. Tea. Although it doesn't seem fair that the French have tea and we, the English, don't. I must bring it up with Marianne. What's the point in dedicating your life to public service and the protection of your fellow countrywomen if you can't get some good tea out of it?

"This meeting is being called to order."

The terrifyingly chic French woman heading up the meeting, Sophie, holds the room's attention very easily. The slideshow starts, we're kicking off with the Moldova situation. Ah, joy of joys, the army of crackpots are still in charge. Before the Plague, Moldova was one of the prime sources of sex trafficking in the world. A stagnant economy and rampant poverty meant Moldovan girls and women were highly vulnerable to trafficking, often being sold into forced prostitution in

Russia and the Middle East on the basis of false promises of work. I've sat in many meetings over the years where sex trafficking and slavery have been discussed in the same sentence as "Moldova." Since the Plague there's been something of an overcorrection.

"The situation in Moldova continues to be in the high-risk category. Political sensitivity is high as their wheat, corn and rapeseed exports are crucial. The government is prioritizing a return to being 'the bread-basket of Europe.' However, the all-female, anti-men Freedom Party that took control in 2026 is still in power, remains the only legal political party and has refused to hold elections. Following the roundup of all men in March 2026 "for their own safety" and their detention in police stations and prisons, thousands of men are still imprisoned awaiting trial on sex trafficking charges with an indefinite waiting period before trial. There are still over eight thousand men who are unaccounted for. The death penalty is being widely used. We propose maintaining advice that men do not travel to Moldova for any reason, including those who would otherwise have diplomatic immunity."

I have questions to ask about Moldova but none of them are pertinent to my job. They're personal. How does someone recover from sex slavery and become a senior politician? How do you resist the urge to wage war on those who have hurt you? All questions for historians to answer in the future, no doubt. For now, the UK's policy of keeping all men out of Moldova will continue, indefinitely.

"Next, Saudi Arabia. We continue to struggle with information supply. There are strict limits on sharing material outside of the country but we are confident that the regime change is complete. All male members of the Saudi royal family are either in hiding in Jordan and Egypt, or dead. We don't have clarity as to their survival. There continue to be clashes between rebels and the new government. We're in discussions with Middle Eastern allies to obtain more information." The Middle Eastern allies we have left, that is. Almost all of my spies were men. If I'm getting only the tiniest slivers of information out of Iraq, Iran, Jordan and the UAE, I struggle to see how Sophie is getting much more.

Sophie clicks to the next slide.

"The Vaccine Certification Program continues to expand with eighty-two countries now included. The United Nations Certification Committee will vote on the inclusion of Romania, Chile and Poland next month."

Gradually the world is regaining its size after years of shrinking. When the United Nations announced the Certification Program, I breathed a massive sigh of relief. Only countries with a vaccination rate of over 99.9 percent are eligible for certification. Once a country is approved, its citizens can fly within the Certification Zone, subject to national visa rules. The head of the Korean Immigration Service, Min-Jun Kim, originally suggested it. He had to deal with the fallout of North Korea in April 2026 and the unification in June. He knows better than most the importance of ensuring vaccination rates in unstable populations.

I still like to watch the footage from the first international flight last year in July. It was pre–Certification Program so the passengers all had to prove, with individual doctors' notes, that they had been vaccinated. One hundred sixty-three people flew from Sydney to Seoul. They touched down and the cameras filmed the plane, and them waving as they disembarked and then their slow procession through the passport area. They all ran out into the arrivals area and flung themselves into the arms of the people waiting. Mums and daughters, the occasional son, father and husband. There's one family in particular where a grandmother got to meet her four-year-old granddaughter for the first time that just had me in floods at the time. It makes me feel a kind of wild pride watching that. Look how far we've come, I think to myself. Look how we have survived.

We monitor dissent against the vaccine certification closely. The last thing we need is a movement advocating civil unrest and open borders. The UN and WHO say the global vaccination rate is still hovering around 96 percent, nowhere near high enough for men to travel safely outside the Certification Zone. Some people might not like it but safety comes first.

"The news coming out of China is positive. Fei Hong has been elected as president of the Fifth Chinese State encompassing much of central China. Small outbursts of disruption continue in Two and Six; however, Fei's election appears to suggest Five remains the most stable of the twelve."

It still feels so odd that China doesn't exist anymore. We refer to it as the "Twelve," which sounds either religious or like the villainous organization in a Bond film depending on when I last went to church. Hong Kong remains an incredibly helpful ally, now that it's completely independent. We have to find our silver linings where we can.

"France is working with states Five and Eight on voluntary repatriations. We have over fifteen thousand people who have been unable to travel home since the outbreak of the Plague."

That's a good idea. We should maybe steal that.

I think about Fei Hong's big acceptance speech, which she finished off with a nice little sound bite that's been repeated more times than I care to count. "We lost great minds who could have changed the world and we lost friends, brothers, sons, fathers, husbands who could have changed our lives. But we made something positive rise from the ashes of despair. We are now free, and that is worth everything we went through," Fei said. I should be happy about the peace and democracy. I really should, but it's my job to anticipate problems, not to sing "Kumbaya." Still, good for them.

# REMEMBRANCE

# CATHERINE

The sight of a warm, brightly lit bookshop bustling with people in the midst of a rainy March evening is a sight that thrills me. I've wrangled an invite to the book release party for one of the most anticipated memoirs of the year. *Dear Frances, Love Toby*, a memoir by Toby Williams, the man whose wife, Frances, famously saved him from starvation on the *Silver Lady*, a ship off the coast of Iceland.

I've been in touch with Toby about including his letters in my project and he invited me to the party and assured me, as the letters will be included in his own book, that I can use them in due course. The room is cheerful and packed with people excitedly drinking acidic white wine. I try to look supercilious because it's easier to look off-putting than eager when you don't know anyone. While I'm here, I might as well have a mosey around the shelves. There haven't been many publishing phenomena since the Plague but the ones that have struck a chord have sold millions, as we all search desperately for meaning and connection in these brutally lonely times.

There's the awkward sound of someone clinking a glass and

coughing, and the room quiets. Toby looks at his wife standing by his side, with a look of such joy and tenderness it brings a lump to my throat. I can't begrudge them their happiness; they earned it. She fought for him to survive.

"Thank you, everyone, for coming," he says, his voice lower and richer than I expected, with a pleasant hint of a Yorkshire accent in the flat vowels. "I can't tell you how wonderful it feels to be here, alive and well, Frances by my side and my lovely Maisy here with her Ryan. I know how lucky we are. My story has been a popular one. You've all probably heard me banging on about my time on the boat on the TV or the radio, or seen one of my five thousand articles on it for the *Guardian*." A sprinkle of generous laughter.

"The people I was on that boat with made a lifelong impression on me and I'm sorry more of them can't be here with us. Only seven people survived of the three hundred originally on the boat. As you probably know, this book is the story of the two years I spent on the *Silver Lady*, the letters I wrote to Frances and the story of some of the people who died beside me. I needed to know what happened to their families, and their stories. Lots of you have read the book already and the person people ask me the most about is Bella. What happened to her husband, her son and her daughter? I wish I could tell Bella that everything was okay, but like the story so often is with the Plague, it is a sad one with a chink of hope. Bella's husband and son died in the Rome outbreak and her daughter nearly died of starvation, alone in their apartment for over six days. Thankfully, Bella's sister-in-law, Cecilia, traveled by car, bus and foot from Puglia to Rome to rescue her niece. Bella's daughter, Carolina, now lives with her aunt in Puglia and is a very happy child. Cecilia kindly allowed me to include a transcript of my conversation with her in the book, for which I'm very grateful." He pauses, and it looks like he's bracing himself.

"There's obviously one person I wish could be here more than anyone else. My brother, Mark." An awfully long moment stretches out in the room as Toby visibly tries to control his breathing so he can talk again. He makes a now-familiar face, looking into the distance with an expression of total despair fighting with the desire to hold it together. I can practically see the ribbons of connection between him and Frances as her eyes implore him to be okay, to recover, to keep going.

"Mark got me through months on that god-awful boat," Toby says shakily. "And then, right when our rescue began and food appeared from the sky as if from God himself, he died. It feels unfair, and you can read more about it because it's too painful to talk about for too long. I just want you all to know he'd have been so pleased to see you all here. He really would."

The room erupts with the relief of a British crowd that's just watched a barely contained emotional admission. I realize I'm running late, offer a quick good-bye to Toby and Frances, who are surrounded by well-wishers, and walk through London to a very important date.

"You're looking well," Amanda says, as we hug and settle ourselves at the table. I regale her with the story of the book launch and am greeted with a very Glaswegian response. "Mixing with the high and mighty in literary circles," she says with a raised eyebrow. "I always knew you'd go far."

"Says the famous doctor."

"Famous? Fuck off."

"You're the most famous doctor in the world."

Amanda smiles ruefully as she sips her wine. "I think the grand Nobel Prize–winning Dr. Lisa Michael might claim that particular title."

"Well, I don't envy her. I don't envy her callousness."

"I envy her bank balance," Amanda replies with a laugh.

The waiter comes to take our order and I realize, with a happy look around the bustling restaurant, how glorious it feels to be having dinner in a nice dress with a friend in a restaurant. Amanda, far from being angry, was more understanding than I could have hoped after my meltdown at Heather Fraser's house. She found me, sitting by the sea across the road, furiously bargaining in my head with a man who I've never met and who will spend the rest of his life in prison. "What's done is done," she said softly, and for a moment I hated her for her acceptance and then I stopped. I stopped and I thanked her. I told her it was hard to imagine it all could have been different and I had the first truly honest conversation I'd had since I lost my family about what it means to be alone. To feel alone, and to realize it didn't have to be this way. But it happened, and there is no changing it.

I've realized I can never be friends with Phoebe again. A part of my heart is broken but the chasm between us is too great. It isn't her fault her family didn't die, just as it isn't mine that Anthony and Theodore did, but it is too painful to watch her life carry on as it did before. I love her but I can't do that to myself. When I met Amanda, I desperately needed a friend who shared my experiences, and happily so did she. Now, I look forward to our meetings for days. Amanda comes to London on medical business, I travel to Scotland for research and sometimes we meet in the middle, walk in the Lake District, talk, cry and laugh. Amanda understands loss and grief and rage. She understands it all.

A question occurs to me that I've meant to ask Amanda for a long time but have never been able to. I've tried to read articles about the mortality rate but struggled to get past the fear of what I might find out, what it might tell me about things I could have done to prevent Anthony's death.

"Why is the mortality rate so high?"

"The virus causes a massive spike of white blood cells. It mimics an extreme form of leukemia. That's why it kills you so quickly; your body can't do anything with that number of blood cells."

"Are they in pain before they die then? Because we always give cancer patients morphine when they're . . ."

"A bit of discomfort," Amanda says. She's lying. I know it and she knows but I appreciate this small kindness nonetheless.

She rarely brings up her husband. "Do you want to remarry? Have more kids?" I ask her.

"I'm forty-five, the latter's not fucking likely." I start to apologize, but it's a compliment really. "No," she says softly. "I couldn't go through any more loss. I couldn't bear it. It broke me losing the boys and Will. I can't face that again."

"Love's always a risk though, isn't it?"

"It is, and not one I can withstand anymore. I don't know how some women did it; falling pregnant during the Plague, not knowing if they'd have a boy or not. One Spanish woman, devoutly Catholic, got stranded while on holiday in Edinburgh. She gave birth to three boys who all died. *Three*. They didn't believe in contraception." My mind reels at the idea of that much loss, but I understand. I understand the desperation. "She was one of the first women we inoculated with the vaccine when we finally scraped together enough money for it. She has a baby girl now."

"That's lovely," I say, but I'm biting back jealousy and the hot sting of shame that follows it.

"How's the . . . ?" Amanda gestures and I know this is so I can easily wave away the topic if I don't feel like talking about it.

I feel my forehead instinctively creasing into a frown of concern. "I find out tomorrow about the last round of IUI. Fingers crossed," I add helplessly. My first two rounds of IUI didn't work. If I'm not pregnant now, right this very second, I will never have another chance.

"Good luck. Just remember, fertility is a game of fortune and chance. It's not a moral failing."

I smile at the instruction not to view a potential emptiness of my body as the failure it feels like. "I'll let you know once I get the results of the blood test."

"Did you know you wanted another one? Straightaway, I mean?"

"Yes but I didn't let myself. It took a few years. I had to forgive myself. It wasn't my fault they died. Even if I gave it to them, it wasn't my fault. I had to understand that before I could try again."

"Truer words never spoken. Would you want to meet someone? You're not even forty."

I shake my head, the feeling resolute. "I've thought about it a lot and I just can't imagine it. I had a great love, the greatest love. That's more than most people get in a lifetime. There's no following that up."

"Anthony," she says.

"Anthony," I repeat. It feels so wonderful to say his name. The word fits beautifully in my mouth. It's a benediction.

"Tell me about him."

I sit back. I'm so rarely asked this question. My friends who knew him don't need to know, and new people I meet don't need to know. "He was funny and frank. Always took me seriously. He was tall and strong and when I stood with my back leaning against him, he would put his head on top of mine and I would feel like nothing bad could ever happen to us. He was clever and loyal and so, so proud of me. You know, it's hard to find someone who's truly proud of you, without any resentment or pride. He was perfect. He was mine." I look at her almost apologetically, as though I've committed a faux pas by having had a wonderful husband.

"I'm so glad you had him," she says, and it is the most lovely thing someone has said to me about him. Perhaps Amanda also feels it is simply too awful to focus on the loss of those we've loved. "I'm glad he was yours."

"Thank you, Amanda. I'm glad too." I decide to ask her the question I'm terrified of, the question that has driven my travel, my work, my hearing of other people's stories, my desperate attempts at another baby. "Do you think they'll be remembered, our sons and husbands? Or will they just . . . disappear?"

"I think we'll remember them, and talk about them and tell their stories. We'll know we loved them and were loved by them. That will be enough." She pauses. "You know, the world doesn't have to remember you for you to matter. We were loved by those we loved. Not everyone can say that," she tells me softly. No, I don't suppose they can.

# FOREWORD TO "STORIES OF THE GREAT MALE PLAGUE" BY CATHERINE LAWRENCE

*September 9, 2032*

I've sat at my desk for many days, wondering how to write this introduction. The book is finished, the manuscript complete, yet the beginning escapes me. In the time between finishing the collection of the stories in this book and writing this foreword, I've experienced enormous change in my own life. I couldn't sit and write this while a piece of the story was missing.

Some of the extraordinary men and women I spoke to have accepted the losses they have experienced. I could not accept the loss of my son. I felt only raw grief and regret that grew over time. Lots of people told me I must finish the book on a hopeful note. For months, I appreciated their optimism and yet, until recently, I despaired of it. How could anyone live in optimism when the world has shown itself in so many ways to be full of random cruelty? Optimism is a privilege, I used to tell myself, and not one I can afford. But that's not true. Of course it's not true. If there is one thing I learned from the many weeks I spent with men and women discussing the Plague, it is that we did the best we could with what we knew at the time. I did my best in the most awful of circumstances. The past has been painful, but that doesn't mean the future can't be better.

I gave birth to my beautiful daughter, Maeve Antonia Lawrence, on

January 2 this year. She is perfect, and not just because she has made my life feel as though it is once more my own. She represents the hope I didn't dare to have for years as, like so many others, I was pummeled by loss and the new emotional landscape of a world in which I felt entirely alone. Maeve will never live in a world in which she has a father, and this will not mark her out as unusual. She will have no siblings and very few male friends. She will go to school and be taught by almost entirely female teachers, in a country governed mostly by women. To my daughter, this new world will be normal and I'm conflicted. I'm grateful she will never know the pain of losing so much and yet, what a thing to not understand what has been lost.

As an anthropologist, I will admit I am biased. I lost my husband and my son to the Plague; I cannot study it with the distance and emotional neutrality academics requires. It is testament to the impact of the Plague that no British anthropologist is untouched by it. I have decided to include my own story rather than pretend to be an invisible observer I am not, and keep my own losses hidden. There is no omniscient narrator to tell this story. We are all biased. We are all changed.

In the process of compiling the stories, I have asked myself about the recording of history. For the first time in the history of the world, women are fully in control of the way our stories are told. Some claim only men should be able to record the story of the Plague, as they were the worst affected. Respectfully, I disagree. Women are, in the majority, the people left. We are the ones whose lives have been splintered and left behind. Many are working jobs they didn't choose, working six days a week to aid economies in crisis, raising children alone while coping with the weight of grief. In a world that has changed unimaginably, the way in which we record our stories has changed too.

As I have spoken to women and men who have experienced the Plague in different ways, I have tried to start answering the important questions we will face for decades and centuries to come. Why did the

Plague spread as quickly as it did? What impact has it had on societies across the world? How have individuals re-formed families and coped with the changes forced upon them? How are children coping in a new world unlike anything their parents envisaged for them? How has the remaining male population integrated into a world in which they are an extreme minority?

When my daughter asks me, "How did the world change?" I hope she can find some answers here. I hope she can one day read this and understand something of the past. It is not so long ago that things were very different. I have been a mother before, but motherhood, like so much else, has changed. My experience feels more in line with mothers during wartime than my experience parenting my son. I am a single parent in a world that is changing faster than we can keep up with, a world that is now smaller than it has been for decades. The arrival of a new baby is now a blessed relief from widespread death, rather than a common experience of adulthood.

Compiling this report was in many ways the hardest thing I have ever done and yet, it was also a source of comfort and joy when my life was blasted apart by grief. My superiors at UCL, particularly my mentor, Margaret King, and, later, those I have worked with on the United Nations Male Plague Commission, have been an enormous support.

It would be remiss of me not to acknowledge the limitations of this report. The Plague began in Scotland and spread across the world, but I have not been able to represent the stories of as many different countries, cultures and people as I would have liked. Many countries, particularly in the southern hemisphere, are still awaiting certification of vaccination. Much of what used to be China is still closed off to the outside world; the Shanghai contingent who traveled to Toronto to arrange the production of the MP-1 vaccine were some of the first individuals from the Chinese states to fly outside of Asia. Iran, Iraq and parts of Yemen are still in total blackout with no communications leaving those countries. I hope, in time, that our understanding of the Plague's impact will only grow in breadth and variety. This is just the beginning.

I have attempted to strike the correct balance between focusing on the impact of the Plague on the living and remembrance of the dead. One of the things I have tried to remember in the long and emotional journey back to a semblance of normality is something Maria Ferreira wrote: "Perhaps some traumas are too overwhelming to recover from." On an individual and societal level, perhaps recovery is too great a goal. We can never regain what we have lost and we must accept that, mourn that, grieve what cannot be, and find a new way to exist. More than anything, in the coming months and years, I hope women and men can find a sense of camaraderie in these pages. The horrors of the Plague have made many of us feel alone and yet the most common experiences—widowhood, the loss of children, parents and siblings— are near universal.

Finally, I would like to dedicate this report to my family: my husband, Anthony; my son, Theodore; and my daughter, Maeve. We will not be together in this life but I am so very glad you have been mine.

# AUTHOR'S NOTE

I first heard about coronavirus as most people likely did, through snippets of news and e-mails from friends saying, "Have you seen this? So weird!" For a number of weeks, it felt distant in that way so many foreign news stories do. Something awful and scary but ultimately a disease I would remain personally unaffected by.

Only a few months on from those e-mails and news reports, I'm sitting in my flat in central London in lockdown. I leave the house once a day for exercise, and shop for food and other essentials once a week. I don't know when I'll next see my family, my friends or my colleagues. Billions of people around the world are in the same position. I feel immeasurably fortunate to still be employed and to have recovered from suspected coronavirus (I have not been tested but experienced the virus's telltale cough, breathlessness and extreme fatigue after returning to London from a trip to northern Italy). I know you're meant to "live your truth" through art and everything, but contracting coronavirus was a step toward authenticity I could have done without.

It's an understatement to say it feels surreal that I wrote a book about a viral pandemic just as a viral pandemic swept the world. More than one person has half-jokingly called me Cassandra. When I started writing *The End of Men* in September 2018, it felt like the ultimate thought experiment. How far could I take my imagination? How would a global pandemic with an enormous death rate change the world? What *would* the world look like without men, or the majority of them? I wrote the first draft of the book in nine months, finishing with a burst of intense writing in June 2019. Now, as I edit the book for my publishers, I find myself testing my imaginary world against the real one. I gauge the distance between what I have written and what is happening. As a writer of speculative fiction, this is not something I ever expected.

Coronavirus doesn't have a death rate as high as the virus I have imagined in my novel. Nonetheless, we are experiencing in real life the greatest pandemic of our lifetimes, which is more than I ever could have imagined in my wildest nightmares. The world I wrote about was meant to stay safely within the pages of my novel; it is now far more closely reflected by the world than I ever could have expected. I hope that by the time you're reading this, there is a vaccine. I hope our healthcare systems survive and economies recover. I hope your loved ones are safe and that the world has returned to that wonderful, boring, nostalgic state I now crave: normality.

Christina Sweeney-Baird

April 12, 2020

# ACKNOWLEDGMENTS

Thank you to my wonderful agent, Felicity Blunt. This book simply wouldn't exist in the way it does without your insight, intelligence and creative ideas. Together we reshaped the manuscript you signed (which had more POVs than I knew what to do with) and turned it into something so much more. I'm so grateful for all the work you do to support my writing and help me build this remarkable new career with your wit and kindness.

Thanks to my brilliant UK editor, Carla, at Borough. From our first meeting I knew you completely understood this book and what I was trying to say. It's a joy to work with you.

Thank you to Mark and Danielle at Putnam, and Amy at Doubleday, for your thoughtful guidance and enthusiasm about the book. My lovely US agent, Alexandra; the Curtis Brown rights team—Sarah and Jodi—and Luke for all your hard work. Thanks to Ann and the amazing publicity and marketing teams at HarperCollins.

I've never had any formal creative writing education but I learned to write from Marian Keyes and Julia Quinn. Anything I know about wit, characterization and plot I learned from their novels so a huge thank you to them.

I'm going off piste here but truly I couldn't have written this without my MacBook (a present from my mum after months of tearful laptop drama), 7Up Free, Teapigs green tea, peanut M&M's and

Magnum ice creams. For the record, this acknowledgments section is, alas, not sponsored. When writing late at night and throughout weekends, snacks just take on enormous importance.

Thank you to my best friends, whom I confided in when writing novels was something I did in secret with only hope and your encouragement to keep me going. Dolf, you've been by my side since we were nineteen working on our student newspaper. You're the best friend a girl could wish for and your constant reassurance and support means the world to me. Sarah, thank God Tom had the good sense to fall in love with you (I mean, who wouldn't?) and brought you into my life. I remember admitting over a glass of white wine in 2015 that I desperately wanted to be an author. You had total faith that I could do it and have never let me forget that. Tom, Will, Vicky, Simon, Claudia, Katie and Louise: thank you for being my people. Emily and Serina, the best work colleagues around, who shared my excitement and the surreal experience of signing with an agent and selling the book. Thank you to Daphne, who taught me the harp for a decade, and how to work hard to build a creative skill. You've had an extraordinary impact on my life, and to this day I still follow the lessons you taught me.

I'm very lucky to have the best family. Juliana and Kenny, who both listen to me talk about books an inordinate amount and make sure I never feel alone. Dad, your excitement about my writing always gives me such a boost. I hope I've made you proud. Papa, thank you for always believing in me and telling me I'm clever, even when I just felt very tired and overwhelmed from studying.

And thank you to my mum. You've been on the receiving end of so many phone calls and questions. You've told me more times than I can count that I could be published, *would* be published. We've spent thousands of hours over my life talking, analyzing, figuring stuff out, cackling with laughter. You always said the harder you work, the luckier you get and here we are.

# THE END OF MEN

## CHRISTINA SWEENEY-BAIRD

---

### DISCUSSION GUIDE

---

### A CONVERSATION WITH
### CHRISTINA SWEENEY-BAIRD

# DISCUSSION GUIDE

1. Discuss the novel's oral history style—multiple narratives, emails, transcripts, and articles—and the way it impacted your reading experience.

2. Is there a villain in *The End of Men*? If so, who is it? Is there one character who you sympathize with more than others? Did the first-person points of view change your connection to the characters?

3. *The End of Men* was written a year before the outbreak of COVID-19, but there are many parallels between the real world and that imagined in the novel. How has the reality of COVID-19 changed your perception of the novel? What are the similarities and differences from our world today?

4. Do you believe *The End of Men* is a feminist novel? Is the book "anti-male"? How does the relationship between the two sexes evolve throughout the narrative?

5. Discuss the ways that different characters cope with grief in the novel. How does grief either fuel or cripple the various characters?

6. What genre do you believe *The End of Men* falls into? A thriller? Dystopian? Women's fiction? Why?

7. Do you think the novel presents an accurate portrayal at what life without men would like? What would that world look like for you? How would it be similar to or different from the world we see in the novel?

8. Compare and contrast the way that different countries confront the pandemic, both on a societal and personal level. How do you think you and your community would have reacted in this situation?

9. Some characters ultimately benefit from the pandemic and its repercussions. How do they each reconcile their good fortune? Do you think that any event, even a global pandemic, can have good effects?

10. Consider Catherine's final postscript at the end of the novel. What do you take from it? Is the ending ultimately hopeful?

# A CONVERSATION WITH CHRISTINA SWEENEY-BAIRD

**What inspired *The End of Men*?**

I've always loved speculative fiction and wanted to write something that explored a "What if?" question. I remember reading *World War Z* by Max Brooks when I was in my early twenties and finding it completely terrifying. It felt so real despite it being science fiction. The breadth of stories from around the world that I've included in *The End of Men* is hugely inspired by the scope of *World War Z*. I also read *The Power* in early 2018, which made me think about the different stories I could tell looking at how men and women interact in the world, and so that was also a big inspiration. I read *Station Eleven* by Emily St. John Mandel at the suggestion of my agent after I had finished the first draft and it became something of a North Star; I wanted the characters in *The End of Men* to be as compelling and emotionally engaging as those in *Station Eleven*, which is now one of my favorite books.

**The End of Men was, of course, written well before the COVID-19 pandemic began. What has it been like for you to watch your fiction unfold in real time, and what do you think the world can learn from your novel?**

It's been completely surreal! I remember my UK agent, Felicity, sending me articles about the virus when it was first being covered in the press in January 2020 just before she sent the book out to publishers. Many early readers have commented on how realistic some bits of the book now feel, which is obviously not something I ever expected when I wrote it. I hope that after reading *The End of Men* people think about the importance of gender equality, and the myriad ways in which society is structurally still built around the needs of men, not women.

**What kinds of research did you do in the process of writing this novel?**

A lot of the research was done online as I went along, as there are lots of different countries and characters in the book that required data, for example, about populations and the practicalities of vaccine production. I also spent a lot of time researching viruses and how they work, and specifically how to make the female immunity to the virus practicable. I read *Invisible Women* by Caroline Criado-Perez, which is a phenomenal book that explores the many ways in which data is collected without being disaggregated for men and women, and the impact of the world being built around men. I truly cannot recommend it enough.

**Perhaps one of the most striking aspects of your novel is the depicted resistance of administrative leadership, at both the medical and governmental levels, in responding to early cases. What informed your decision to include that as a significant plot point in your novel?**

I think we'd all like to believe that our leaders are always competent, knowledgeable, and wise but, sadly, the people in charge in every part of society are human. They make mistakes. The virus in *The End of Men* is so extraordinary—with a 90 percent mortality rate and male element—that it felt more realistic to me that the medical and political establishment would take a while to accept it was, in fact, real and the grave threat Amanda Maclean says it is.

**In your novel, the virus taking over the world affects only male members of the population. What did you wish to explore about gender, and how does it fit with larger conversations about gender roles in today's discourse?**

I wanted to explore the ways in which society is unbalanced. In which industries is there a dominance by men? In which industries is there a dominance by women? Which parts of society work for men better than women? Why do those disparities exist, and what would it look like if they were reversed? Society has changed enormously over the past centuries and decades, and women are arguably more empowered than we have ever been before in history (at least in Europe and North America). And yet there are still people who argue that women wanting the same pay as men and having the same expectations for our lives is somehow "too much." I hope *The End of Men* goes some way in showing how absurd that thinking is.

**Why did you decide that the virus would affect only men? In what ways has the end result of your novel differed from what you set out to write?**

The novel is built around the question: *What would the world look like without men?* In that sense, the use of a virus that only kills men is a means to a speculative end. I remember having the idea for a book about society without men, and immediately knowing I had to write it. The first draft of the book had many more narrators, none of whom had more than one section of the book, so it was more disjointed. Catherine—who is, in many ways, the heart of the novel—wasn't included in the first draft. I did a significant rewrite in Autumn 2019 after I signed with my UK agent and we culled many of the perspectives and brought out the key voices for the story. The structure of the book is therefore totally different from what I envisioned, but the arc of the story—how the world is affected and then recovers—is the same as my original plan.

**The End of Men is narrated from multiple viewpoints. Did you find that some character's perspectives were easier to write than others? Did you have any favorites?**

I love writing in first-person present tense so I found the writing process relatively easy as I'm comfortable with that type of narration. One of my mum's good friends (whom I've since also become friends with) is a brilliant, practical, no-nonsense Glaswegian doctor who partially inspired Amanda. I grew up in Glasgow and a lot of my friends' parents were doctors, so Amanda came to me quite easily. I found that Lisa's voice was crystal clear in my head and so she was the easiest character to write. My favorites are Catherine and Amanda. I would want to be friends with them in real life. Also, she's a small character, but I have a soft spot for Frances, whose husband is stuck aboard a ship off the coast of Iceland.

**While the notion of a "woman's world" in theory might connote female empowerment, your novel suggests that there is much more to mourn from the subordination and eradication of the male sex. What did you wish to explore about feminism in The End of Men?**

I think that feminism is so often misunderstood as being a demand for more than men have when, in reality, it is a demand for the *same* political, economic, and social rights as men. The death of so many men would, as I show in the novel, be devastating on many levels, both personally for almost everyone on the planet and for society. But, in showing what that world might look like, I think we can explore some of the areas in which women are still not equal to men.

**What's next for you?**

I'm working on my next novel—another piece of speculative fiction—and also redrafting a YA novel I've been working on since early 2020.

*Photograph of the author © Sophie Davidson*

**Christina Sweeney-Baird** was born in 1993 and grew up in London and Glasgow. She studied Law at the University of Cambridge and graduated with a First in 2015. She works as a corporate litigation lawyer in London. *The End of Men* is her first novel, and it has been translated into fourteen languages and the film rights have been sold to a major US television studio.